LAST SEEN IN SILVER CREEK

DELORES FOSSEN

DECEPTION AT DIXON PASS

CINDI MYERS

MILLS & BOON

First Published in Great Britain 2023
by Mills & Boon, an imprint of HarperCollins*Publishers* Ltd
1 London Bridge Street, London, SE1 9GF

www.harpercollins.co.uk

HarperCollins*Publishers*
Macken House, 39/40 Mayor Street Upper,
Dublin 1, D01 C9W8, Ireland

Last Seen in Silver Creek © 2023 Delores Fossen
Deception at Dixon Pass © 2023 Cynthia Myers

ISBN: 978-0-263-30736-8

0823

MIX
Paper | Supporting responsible forestry
FSC
www.fsc.org
FSC™ C007454

This book is produced from independently certified FSC™ paper to ensure responsible forest management.

For more information visit: www.harpercollins.co.uk/green

Printed and Bound in the UK using 100% Renewable Electricity at CPI Group (UK) Ltd, Croydon, CR0 4YY

LAST SEEN
IN SILVER CREEK

DELORES FOSSEN

Chapter One

Kim Ryland fought to get out of the nightmare. It came at her in pieces that were as brittle and sharp as razors.

"Hide," he told her. "Hide now."

And that's what she'd done. What she was doing in one of those brittle dream pieces that stabbed and sliced its way through her. In the dream, she clutched the stuffed dog against her and dropped down onto the floor, scuttling under the bed and clamping her teeth over her bottom lip so the killer couldn't hear any of the sounds she might make.

Like that night when the nightmare had been real, Kim didn't hear much going on in the house. Couldn't. Not with her heartbeat crashing in her ears. But she could feel. Mercy, could she. Both then and now. And what she felt was something no eight-year-old child should ever have to experience.

Terror.

On a hard gasp, Kim finally woke, struggling to get to a sitting position while she fought for breath. Fought to get her throat unclamped. She was in her bedroom. Alone and safe. She was no longer a child.

And no killer was coming for her tonight.

Kim glanced at the clock and groaned. It was barely four in the morning. Considering the late night she'd put in preparing a case she'd be prosecuting, she needed at least a couple more hours of sleep. Sleep she clearly wouldn't get, not with her body still revving from the nightmare.

Apparently, nightmares didn't have an expiration date since she'd been having this particular one for twenty-one years now. Since she'd been eight and had cowered under her best friend's pink bed during a sleepover.

Those images of what had happened back then had now gotten mixed up with her current case. Well, one of them anyway. As the assistant district attorney in her hometown of Silver Creek, Texas, she always had several cases on her proverbial plate, rarely one as serious, though, as the domestic aggravated assault trial that was coming up in four days. There'd been plenty of violence in that crime, too, which was probably why the dream had come at her so hard tonight.

Cursing her memories and the dull headache that was now throbbing nonstop, Kim threw back the covers, dragged on the silky blue robe her mom had given her for Christmas, grabbed her phone to check her emails, and made her way to the kitchen. Just walking through her house soothed her. Some.

This was home, filled with the things that reminded her that she'd come from a loving, protective family. Heirloom furniture. Framed pictures of those family members on the mantel. The patchwork quilt throw that her great-grandmother had made. All pieces that canceled out that nightmare. Well, mostly they did. The nightmare and memories were always there, lurking just beneath the surface.

Kim programmed some strong coffee, planning to drink the entire pot herself. She wasn't sure she could focus yet on her laptop screen so, after she glanced at her emails and didn't see anything pressing, she picked up the stack of mail from the kitchen counter. Obviously, one of her parents had picked it up at the post office for her, a reminder that it had been a while since she'd checked the box herself. Not her folks though. They checked often and brought over hers since they had keys to both the post office box and her house.

With the coffee maker sputtering and pumping out the much-needed caffeine, she dragged the trash can from under the sink and started going through the mail, automatically tossing the sales papers and the junk. Then she froze and stared at the letter that'd been in the middle of the pile.

And she knew exactly what it was.

Oh, God.

Kim didn't open it, didn't touch it. Instead, she pulled out her phone and, without hesitating, called Sheriff Theo Sheldon. Despite the early hour, he answered on the second ring.

"Kim?" he said, sounding plenty groggy. Not so groggy, though, since he hadn't missed seeing her name on his phone screen. "What's wrong?"

"I got another letter," she managed to say, though her hands and voice were now trembling a little.

"I'm on my way," Theo assured her, and in that instant, the grogginess had vanished.

Kim murmured a thanks and the moment she ended the call, she used her phone to snap a picture of the envelope. Something she'd done for the other eight letters she'd received over the years. She copied the image to the online storage file where she had photos of the others, and she pulled those up now to verify that this one was indeed the same. Not that she needed verification, but it gave her something to do while she waited for Theo.

Yes, this one was the same.

A plain white envelope. No return address. Kim's name and post office address had been typed on an old-fashioned typewriter. Or rather "Kimmie" had been typed.

Her childhood nickname.

Also like the other letters, the stamp was affixed sideways in the upper right-hand corner. Maybe the position was some kind of message or clue, but if that was the case, Kim and the Silver Creek Sheriff's Office hadn't been able to figure out what it meant. It was possible the sender had positioned it that way just to play mind games with her since the figures on the stamps weren't upright but rather on their sides.

Like a dead person might be.

All the other letters had been analyzed, of course, and the lab had identified plenty of smudged prints and even some trace DNA, but not enough to attempt to find a match in any of the databases. Maybe this one would be different, though she had to imagine it'd been handled by plenty of people just to have made it into her post office box.

She considered calling her uncle Grayson, who up until the past two months had been the sheriff of Silver Creek for more than three decades. This was his case, too. Always would be. But a call could wait until a more decent hour. Ditto for the one she'd need to make to her folks.

Kim knew full well that she wouldn't be able to delay either of those particular calls much more than an hour or two since it wouldn't take long for word to get out that she'd gotten another letter. And she'd need to do some soothing there. Some reassuring. Of course, any reassurance she could give her parents and her uncle would be a lie, but she didn't want any of them to know that these letters and the memories they stirred up were still eating away at her.

But they were.

They always would.

Still, her parents didn't need to add any more layers to the guilt they no doubt felt at not being able to prevent their little girl from being caught up in the events of that tragic night. A night where two people had been murdered and Kim's best friend, Faith, had disappeared. The killer had taken her, and Kim was well aware that it could have been her instead of Faith.

Kim got herself that much-needed mug of coffee and went back to her bedroom to pull on a pair of jeans, a flannel shirt and shoes. It was best for her to be fully dressed when dealing with Theo. Mentally dressed, too. There was always that stir of heat between them. A forbidden fruit kind of thing, and it just wasn't a good idea for her to test that forbiddance or the heat tonight. Not when she was already feeling a little dinged and jittery.

With her clothing "armor" in place, Kim walked to the front window to keep watch for Theo. It was still dark, but there was a fingernail moon so she could see the cold January wind battering the now bare trees around her property. And just like that, she got another whiplash of memories.

It'd been cold that other night, too, and when her father had carried her out of the house, Kim had heard the frost crunch beneath his boots. He'd cradled her against him just as Grayson had done the same to Theo. Except Grayson hadn't actually picked up Theo, who'd been twelve at the time. Instead, Grayson had put a protective arm around him, leading Theo to the waiting cruiser. That protection had continued when Grayson and his wife, Eve, had taken Theo to live with them rather than put him into the foster care system.

The people who hadn't gotten led out of the Sheldon house by the Ryland family that night were Theo's parents and his sister, Faith. No escape for them. Kim hadn't actually seen Faith being kidnapped or the bodies of Theo's parents. Only the blood smeared on the floor.

So much blood.

She'd only glimpsed it, peeking out even after her father had told her to keep her eyes shut as he'd carried her from the house. Kim wished she'd obeyed. Wished the image of all those blood smears wasn't in her head.

Yes, she was definitely feeling dinged and jittery.

Because Kim had read all the reports of the murders and the kidnapping, she knew plenty had been done to try to find the killer and what happened to Faith. There'd been an extensive search, and Faith's photo had been added in every available missing persons database. With no results. Faith had simply disappeared.

The sudden slash of headlights caused her attention to snap to the road where she saw Theo's truck pull into her driveway. She'd figured it wouldn't take him long to get there since he lived only a half mile away and was her closest neighbor. Then again, if his two-year-old son Jack, had been staying the night, Theo would have needed to let the boy's nanny know he was heading out. That could have tacked on a minute or two to his travel time.

She watched Theo park and step out of his truck, his gaze automatically going to the window to meet hers. If he was feeling any dings or signs of needing hits of caffeine, he wasn't showing them.

Just the opposite.

Even though he likely would have dressed in a hurry, nothing about him was askew. He was wearing his usual jeans, a gray work shirt and a black Stetson that she knew had once belonged to his father. It was well worn and fit as if it'd been custom made for him.

The moonlight flickered on the badge he had clipped to his belt. A shiny silver star that was only two months old and had come with his new job title of sheriff of Silver Creek. It occurred to her that even without the badge, he looked like the cowboy cop that he was. Always had. Some people were born old. Theo had been born to be a Silver Creek lawman.

He flipped up the collar of his buckskin coat and made his way across the yard and to her porch. The relentless wind whipped against the ends of his dark blond hair, and he had to press his hand to his Stetson to stop it from flying. Kim set her coffee aside so she could disengage the security system and unlock the door for him.

"Thanks for coming so fast," she greeted. "I wasn't sure if you had Jack tonight or not."

"No. He's with Nadia."

Nadia, Theo's ex and Jack's mom. Nadia also had other "labels," such as Kim's former best friend. Emphasis on the *former*. But that wasn't something Kim intended to give any more thought to right now.

Theo stepped in, bringing with him the cold and fresh scent of the frost. It blended with the leather from his coat and his body heat. Yes, even now there was heat.

"The letter's on the counter," Kim said, shutting the door. "I'll get you some coffee."

He muttered a thanks and made a beeline to the counter. The sigh he made when he saw the envelope was long and laced with weariness.

"I'm not sure when the letter arrived," Kim went on. She handed him his coffee. "According to the postmark, it was mailed from Dallas five days ago." A six-hour drive from Silver Creek. That didn't mean that's where the sender lived though. In fact, Kim was betting the person had no connection to Dallas that could be traced back to whoever had sent it.

Theo made a sound to acknowledge that he'd heard her, and

he sipped his coffee while he studied the envelope. "You're either staying up late or getting up early," he remarked.

"Getting up early. Dreams," she tacked onto that.

He turned his intense blue eyes toward her and she saw that he knew what she meant. Not *dreams* but rather the nightmare.

"Yeah," he said. Theo repeated that *yeah* under his breath. "Sometimes, I save them in the dreams. *Sometimes*," he added in a murmur that let her know that didn't happen nearly often enough.

It wouldn't do any good for her to remind him that he'd been just twelve years old. A kid. And that if he'd tried to rescue his parents from that unidentified intruder/killer, he would likely also have been murdered.

That's what had come darn close to happening, too.

When the cops and CSIs had pieced together the crime scene, they'd surmised that the killer had managed to get out of the house mere seconds before Theo had come running down the stairs with a baseball bat. Since the killer had obviously had a weapon, one that he'd used on Theo's parents, he likely wouldn't have hesitated to use it on Theo as well.

"You saved me," Kim reminded him instead. His *hide now* order had worked. Kim had hidden, and the killer hadn't found her.

The next sound Theo made definitely wasn't one of agreement. This conversation was picking at the old wounds, bringing everything back to the surface, and in Theo's mind, the *surface* didn't paint him in a good light. He'd been too late to save his parents or to stop the killer from kidnapping his sister when she'd apparently been coming out of the hall bathroom. Too late to try to stop the killer-kidnapper from fleeing the scene.

Because Kim had obeyed Theo's shouted order of *hide*

now, Kim hadn't seen the killer, and because of the thudding in her ears, she hadn't heard the chaos of that night. Hadn't heard Faith scream for help. But apparently Theo had. Kim had read the reports, and he'd heard his kid sister calling out for him.

Help me, Theo. Help me.

A therapist would probably pretty it up a little, but Kim knew something like that could mess you up for the rest of your life. It'd certainly done a number on Theo, and he was carrying a lot of guilt because of it.

Theo drank a long gulp of coffee, put aside the cup and took out a pair of gloves and an evidence bag from his coat pocket. "Dallas," he said, obviously looking at the postmark again. "The first two came from there."

Yes, and the others had been postmarked from other Texas cities. Emphasis on *cities*. Not from small towns like Silver Creek where someone might have noticed a stranger or someone suspicious mailing a letter.

Like the other envelopes, this one hadn't actually been sealed the traditional way. The flap had instead been taped down, ensuring that no one had licked it and therefore no one had left behind any DNA from saliva. There'd been no DNA, prints or fibers previously left on the tape either.

Theo carefully slid out the single folded sheet of white paper that was the textbook definition of plain and nondescript. The message, however, was anything but. Even though Kim steeled herself up, it felt like the gut punch that it was.

"'Help me. Please help me,'" Theo read aloud.

A variation of the words that Faith had shouted the night she'd been taken twenty-one years ago when both Faith and Kim had been eight. Like the other letters Kim had received, this particular plea had been typed, and there was no signature. No explanation as to why the letter had been sent to Kim and not Theo.

Kim gave a resigned sigh, knowing that even though the letters hadn't been sent to him, the gut punch was there for Theo, too. But Theo wasn't sighing. He unfolded the bottom third of the letter and leaned in to examine the right corner. Kim leaned in, as well, until her head was against Theo's, and she saw what he was looking at.

The tiny rust-colored dot.

It was about half the size of a grain of rice. So small that Kim might have missed it had it not caught Theo's attention.

"That could be blood," he murmured.

That got her heart revving because it certainly looked like dried blood to her. There'd been nothing like that on the others, but maybe this meant Faith—or whoever was doing this—had left a little piece of herself or himself behind.

"I'll get it to the lab ASAP," Theo said, refolding the letter and putting it in the evidence bag. He took out a pen, no doubt to label the bag, but a sound stopped him cold.

Somewhere, outside the house, a woman screamed.

Chapter Two

The moment Theo heard the scream, his cop instincts kicked in. He whipped his gun from his holster and automatically caught onto Kim's arm to move her behind him before they raced to the front window. Theo kept her behind him, too, when he peered out into the darkness.

Nothing.

He certainly didn't see a woman. But judging from the sound of that scream, she was nearby.

"Stay inside," Theo warned Kim as he opened the door so he could step onto the porch.

"I think the sound came from the east side of the house," Kim provided, and he heard the worry in her voice.

Theo was worried, too. Kim's property wasn't exactly on the beaten path, and it was a good mile away from town. On a cold night like this, a person would have needed a vehicle to get there. Only a person who was in a whole lot of trouble let out a scream like that.

Of course, there was another possibility. It was the tail end of Christmas break, and it was possible some bored teenagers wanted to play a prank on the town's assistant DA who lived alone out here. He was really hoping that was all there was to it. But it felt like more. It felt like something bad.

With his gun still drawn, Theo stepped back out into that bitter cold and went down the porch steps so he could have a look around the sprawling yard. There were plenty of trees, shrubs and large brick-lined flower beds that were now empty, but nothing looked out of place.

"I'm Sheriff Theo Sheldon," he yelled. "Who's out there?"

He waited, listening for anything, including the sound of running footsteps from pranking teenagers, but he heard nothing that didn't belong to the night. The wind, the creak and slap of the tree branches, the deep stuttering rhythm of a hooting owl. Some owls could sound like a human screeching. Other animals could, too. But Theo mentally replayed that scream he'd heard.

No. It hadn't come from an animal.

Theo glanced back to make sure Kim was staying put. She was, sort of. She'd come out onto the porch, and with her arms wrapped around herself and no doubt shivering from the cold, she was firing glances all around, especially on the east side of the house. There were plenty of trees and shrubs there, too, and a barn surrounded by a corral.

"Did you leave the barn doors open?" Theo asked her.

"Yes. I wanted my horses to be able to go in if it got too cold for them."

Since the barn was on the east side of the property and therefore in the direction where they'd heard the scream, that's where Theo headed. Right toward those open doors.

"Wait," Kim insisted. "Let me grab a coat and I'll go with you."

He didn't especially want her to do that, but Theo wasn't a fan of leaving her alone either. The downside to being a cop and the survivor of a home invasion was that he could imagine all sorts of worst-case scenarios.

Hell, he'd lived through worst cases.

And while having Kim with him also wasn't an ideal solution, neither was leaving her alone. After all, one of those worst-case scenarios could include an attacker, a person who could have already slipped into the back of Kim's house while Theo and she had been out front. It could turn into a repeat of what'd happened to his family.

Kim was an assistant district attorney and, just like cops, that particular job often drew trouble and made enemies. Still, it seemed a stretch that someone after her would have sent a screaming woman onto her property in some ploy to draw her out into the open so she could be harmed. In case that was exactly what had happened, though, Theo waited until Kim ran out into the yard with him.

"Have you seen or heard anything else?" she asked, shoving her arms through the sleeves of her coat. She reached into her pocket and came up with a small flashlight.

He shook his head and started walking, making a beeline toward the barn. However, he also continued to keep watch around them. If the ploy was indeed to draw Kim out, his mere presence might stop an attack. Might.

"Come out so I can see you," Theo shouted. "If you're in some kind of danger, I can help."

Still nothing, but the owl let out more of those hoots, and this time it sounded like a warning. Owls did that, Theo knew. They were like watchdogs when someone encroached on their territory, and the owl was somewhere in the vicinity of the barn as well.

"Got any threats recently that you haven't reported?" Theo whispered to her.

When she didn't immediately answer with a no, it caught his attention, and he slowed his pace a little to give her a chance to fill him in.

"Not exactly a threat," she finally said, keeping her voice

to a murmur. "Rowena Odell called me yesterday to tell me she was worried that Quill was going to do something bad before his trial. She didn't spell out what that bad thing might be and didn't have any evidence I could use to have Quill's bail revoked. I can't revoke bail on a woman's bad feeling."

Theo was very familiar with that case since Rowena and her husband, Quill, were his ex-wife's parents. Theo had also been the one who'd arrested Quill for the latest incident of domestic aggravated assault. Quill, who was a mean man and an even meaner drunk, had stabbed Rowena in the abdomen during an argument.

By sheer luck or some would say the grace of God, Rowena hadn't died from her injuries, and now that she'd recovered, she was worried that Quill might try to go after her again. Or somehow wiggle out of a trial that would likely result in a twenty-year sentence. Or more.

With Quill's hot temper, Theo wouldn't put it past the man to threaten the judge, jury and Kim during the trial, which could result in even more charges. That's what had happened during Quill's bond hearing, and it was the reason the man had spent three months in the county jail before finally being released. Now, he was awaiting trial, and unless there was some sort of delay, it would start in just four days. Both Quill and Rowena had to be getting desperate about the man's fate.

"I mentioned Rowena only because she might try to create some kind of evidence to get the bail revoked," Kim muttered.

Yes, Theo had already gone there. "I'll talk to Rowena tomorrow," he assured Kim.

But this didn't feel like something the woman would do. No, the years of abuse had left her worn down. Yeah, she would make sobbing, pleading phone calls, begging for Kim and the cops to make sure Quill didn't get another chance to try to hurt her, but she wouldn't come screaming onto Kim's property to draw her out so she could try to coerce her in some way.

On the other hand, Quill would absolutely do something like that now he was a free man.

Quill could maybe be using someone—maybe even Rowena if he'd managed to get his hands on her—as a lure with the intentions of doling out what he would see as payback to the assistant DA and the arresting officer. But Rowena had been diligent about calling 9-1-1 if anyone even approached her house since she was afraid of Quill. That didn't mean, though, that the man hadn't managed to get to her, and that's why Theo fired off a quick text to Dispatch for someone to check on Rowena.

When Theo reached the corral gate, he stopped and listened to make sure they weren't about to be ambushed. Again, he heard nothing, not even the gate when he opened it. Obviously, Kim kept it well oiled. Too bad about that since a squeaky gate would have alerted him that the screaming visitor, or someone else, had gone through the corral and into the barn.

Of course, that visitor could have just scaled the wooden fence, and that's why Theo took hold of Kim's hand to aim the flashlight on the ground. In hindsight, he should have just instructed her to do it because touching Kim was akin to playing with fire.

He fanned the light over the corral and got a motherlode of an adrenaline punch when he saw the footprints. Not from shoes. But rather from bare feet.

Hell.

That had him moving faster, and with Kim right next to

him, Theo hurried to the barn doors. Too bad Kim hadn't left a light on because the place was pitch-black.

"Hello?" Theo called out. "If you need help—"

He stopped when he heard the sound behind them. A crack as if someone had stepped on a twig, and he whirled around, moving in front of Kim. In the same motion, he brought up his gun. Not aiming at anything, just making it ready.

"Who's there?" Theo demanded, not expecting an answer.

He didn't get one either. However, he did hear some rustling around in the trees to the right. Maybe an animal, but Theo's gut told him the sound was coming from a person. It was possible the barefooted visitor had changed her mind about going in the barn and had headed for the woods.

"I can help," Theo repeated, wishing he didn't always sound like a cop.

"I can help, too," Kim added. Obviously, she'd heard his tone and had decided a terrified woman wasn't likely to take him up on his offer.

They stood there, waiting. Listening. And even over the whipping of the wind, Theo heard the moan. Not coming from the woods but rather the barn. That got him moving again, but he kept Kim behind him when he stepped inside.

One of the horses had indeed sought out the warmth of the barn, and the gray mare whickered and flicked her tail. Theo had no trouble seeing her, but there were plenty of dark shadows caused by the stalls, hay and equipment.

Keeping his gun ready, Theo reached out and switched on the overhead light. Such that it was. The dim, bare bulb flickered on, and he immediately swept his gaze from one side of the barn to the other.

And he saw her.

A woman—and yes, she was barefooted—huddled by

some bales of hay. She was sitting on the barn floor, her arms locked around her knees that she'd pulled up to her chest, and she was rocking back and forth. This definitely wasn't Rowena.

Theo didn't see any blood or other obvious injuries, but he decided to go ahead and call Dispatch to ask for an ambulance.

"Are you hurt?" Theo asked after he'd made the call and put his phone back in his pocket.

Her head snapped up, her attention zooming straight to him, but he couldn't actually see her face that well because of the strands of her dark hair covering it. Making a small, feral sound, she scrambled back, deep into the corner, and huddled there.

"I'm the sheriff," he said, going a few steps closer. "I can help."

The woman didn't answer, but her gaze fired toward Kim when she moved. "It's cold in here," Kim murmured. She took a horse blanket that'd been draped over one of the stalls and went toward her.

The woman turned her head away, obviously trying to squeeze herself even tighter into the corner. Kim eased the blanket over her and stepped back.

"Who are you?" Kim asked, using that same gentle tone. "What can we do to help you?"

Those were both good questions, and once he had answers to them, Theo could hope she'd tell them why she was there and, better yet, who was she running from? Because it was obvious she was terrified. That terror might go up significantly when she heard the ambulance, so Theo angled himself in the doorway of the barn in case she tried to bolt.

Even though he could only see the side of her face, he tried to sort through her features to see if he recognized her.

He didn't. She definitely wasn't a resident of Silver Creek. Of course, she could have been visiting someone. If she'd driven here, though, and her vehicle had broken down, that didn't explain why she wasn't wearing any shoes.

"You need to see a doctor," he said, going for the same soothing tone that Kim had used.

But it did just the opposite. The woman whirled toward him, and she frantically shook her head. "No," she said, her voice a rusty whisper. "He'll find me."

Theo latched right onto that. "*He*?" he pressed.

The woman opened her mouth but didn't answer. That's because she no doubt heard the sound outside the barn. Not the ambulance. No. This was the sound of running footsteps.

A hoarse sob tore from her throat and she went back into "hide and cower" mode. Kim sure didn't though. Theo realized it shouldn't have surprised him when Kim whipped out a snub-nosed .38 from her coat pocket. She was the daughter of a retired cop, after all, and had come face-to-face with violence. Of course, she'd grabbed her gun before coming out into the yard with him.

"Stay here with her," Theo instructed Kim even though he hated the notion of using her as backup. Still, he'd soon have real support when one of the deputies arrived with the ambulance.

Theo gave another sweeping glance around the barn to make sure this wasn't some sort of two-pronged attack with someone else already hiding inside. But he saw nothing. He didn't hear anything else either since the running footsteps had stopped.

"I'm Sheriff Sheldon," Theo called out to cover all the legal bases in case this turned into a gunfight.

Theo waited, listening, and he didn't have to listen very long before he heard the rustling sound on the side of the barn. He motioned for Kim to get down and stepped into the doorway where the wind gave him another slam.

Whoever had done that running wasn't anywhere in sight. No surprise there. With the few pieces of this puzzle that he had, it was most likely that the person out there was responsible for terrorizing the woman in the barn and wouldn't have wanted an encounter with the local sheriff.

Keeping watch around him, Theo took a few slow, cautious steps outside, and when he didn't spot anyone about to ambush him, he went to his right where he'd heard the last of those footsteps. He inched his way to the corner of the barn, raised his gun to a shooting position and took a quick look before he ducked back.

Still nothing.

In the distance, Theo heard the wail of the ambulance siren and figured it would be less than two minutes before it arrived. He had no doubts that a Silver Creek cruiser would be right behind it. Hell, maybe even some Rylands, too, if they'd gotten the word that an ambulance had been called to Kim's.

"Last chance to show yourself," Theo warned in a growl.

Whoever was out there must have heard him because there was more movement. More footsteps. Theo leaned out again from cover and caught just a glimpse of the shadowy figure running away. The person was dressed in dark clothes and was moving so fast that he or she was hardly a blur.

"Stop!" Theo yelled.

He considered firing a warning shot but dismissed it because he didn't want the bullet hitting one of Kim's horses or ricocheting off something and slamming into the barn. However, he did text for more backup because he intended to order a thorough search of the property.

He continued to wait, continued to watch, while the ambulance squealed to a stop in front of Kim's house. Two EMTs barreled out of the vehicle. Theo called out to them, motioning for them to head to the barn. As expected, the cruiser came to a stop, too, and Deputy Ava Lawson hurried out.

Theo had more than a dozen deputies, and Ava was as good as they came. He could turn this search over to her and deal with getting those much-needed answers from the woman.

"Jesse's on the way," Ava relayed, referring to Deputy Jesse Ryland, who was Kim's cousin along with being another good cop. "Is Kim hurt?"

Theo quickly shook his head, wanting to rid Ava of that particular worry because Kim and Ava were friends. "A woman showed up. A stranger," he clarified. "And I need the EMTs to check her out and then take her to the hospital."

Ava took a moment, obviously processing that. "You need a CSI team?"

"Not yet. We're looking for an unidentified person last seen there." He pointed to the dark woods. "Once Jesse arrives, arrange a search. Consider this unidentified person armed and dangerous."

Ava gave a crisp nod and, while she kept watch, she took out her phone to set up that search. Theo went back into the barn to see the EMTs trying to examine the woman.

Trying.

It was hard to do that, though, with her scrambling away from them and making a sound like a wounded animal.

"It's okay," Kim said, moving in front of the EMTs. She stooped down so she'd be at eye level with the woman. "No one's going to hurt you. We just want to help you."

That brought on another round of frantic headshaking from the woman. "No," she whimpered. "Please no."

"All right," Kim murmured, moving in a little closer. "Can you tell us your name? I'm Kim Ryland," she tacked on when the woman didn't respond.

But that got a response from her. The woman's eyes widened and her mouth dropped open as her gaze combed over Kim. "Kim Ryland," she repeated in that hoarse whisper.

Theo didn't miss the recognition in the woman's voice, and he used that as he went closer to her. "You know Kim?" he asked.

Her attention shifted to Theo and, with a fresh wave of panic on her face, she started scrambling away again.

"It's okay," he said, repeating Kim's attempt. "I'm Sheriff Theo Sheldon. Kim and I can help you. These EMTs can help you."

The woman went completely still. So still that he got a really bad feeling in the pit of his stomach.

"Theo?" the woman muttered. "Kim?"

"Yes," he confirmed, taking a step closer to her. "Do you know us?"

She nodded, and tears began to water her eyes. "I know you," the woman verified. "Help me, Theo. Please help me." A sob tore from her mouth and her eyes rolled back in her head as she was quickly losing consciousness. "It's me, Faith. I'm your sister."

Chapter Three

I'm your sister.

Those words continued to repeat in Kim's head as she paced the waiting room of the Silver Creek Hospital. They had been the woman's last words before she had passed out.

Faith's words.

Well, maybe.

Even though the EMTs had whisked the woman into the ambulance to take her to the hospital, Kim had fixed her face in her mind. Not only her features but also the sound of her voice. Along with mentally repeating the words, Kim was trying to figure out if there was anything familiar about the woman who'd spoken them. Anything to confirm that this was indeed her childhood friend who'd disappeared twenty-one years ago.

Theo was obviously trying to do the same thing. He, too, was pacing while he was on the phone. Kim didn't know specifically who he was talking to on this particular call, but he was arranging for a fingerprint kit and DNA test to be delivered ASAP.

The fingerprint kit would be especially helpful since Faith's prints had been retrieved from several of her toys and had been placed in the various databases. In the early days after she'd gone missing, the optimism had been high that she would be found, but as the years had passed and been filled with false sightings, that optimism had dimmed considerably. Kim was keeping her "this isn't Faith" mindset for now because she didn't want to get up her hopes only to have them crushed again.

Before Theo's call about the fingerprints and DNA, he'd first arranged for a deputy to stay with Nadia and Jack. Just a precaution, Theo had said, but Kim had seen the concern in his eyes. Since they didn't know who or what they were dealing with, it was best that his son and Nadia be protected.

Kim pivoted toward the ER doors when they swished open and she saw her parents, Darcy and Nate, hurry in. She hadn't called them yet, but it didn't surprise her that they'd heard the news. By now, the buzz about what had happened was probably all over Silver Creek, and this particular bombshell would pack a much bigger punch than her merely having received another of those mystery letters.

"Are you all right?" Darcy asked, going straight to her and pulling Kim into her arms.

Darcy, the woman who'd been her mom since Kim was three. Her bio mom had died when Kim had been just a baby, and when her dad had married Darcy, Kim had gained a brother, Noah, who was now a San Antonio cop. Their younger brother, Hayden, was a marshal.

"I'm okay. Not sure about Theo, though," Kim added in a murmur when she glanced over at him.

The concern on Nate's face went up another level. With reason. To her father, Theo was family now since Grayson and his wife had raised Theo at the Ryland ranch after Theo's parents had been murdered.

He also gave Kim a hug the moment Darcy eased back. "Is it really Faith?" her father asked.

"To be determined." Rather than go over everything, Kim

started with a simple question. "How much do you know about what happened tonight?"

"Theo updated Grayson, and I got the basics from him," her father explained. "You received another letter, called Theo to come over and then this woman showed up. Theo also spotted someone near the barn, but the person ran off before Theo could get a good look at him."

Kim nodded and appreciated the bottom-line approach. Her dad knew full well that she was an emotional wreck right at the moment, but he was keeping her focused on the specific elements of what was now a police investigation. Because, as he liked to say, *Sometimes the devil was in those details*. Kim might unknowingly have more details to make this picture a whole lot clearer.

"I haven't noticed anyone hanging around my place," Kim volunteered. "I've had no concerns that anyone was watching or following me. No odd phone calls. Well, none that weren't connected to Rowena and Quill Odell," she added, speaking of the troubling case she was prosecuting. A case that both her parents were well aware of.

"Grayson asked Theo if the guy he saw was Quill," her dad volunteered. "But Theo couldn't be sure."

Of course, Grayson had asked that. Everyone in her family knew that Quill was basically a bully and that he might stoop to intimidation tactics what with the aggravated assault charges looming over him. But it seemed an unlikely coincidence that Quill would have showed up the same night as the woman.

Kim turned again when she heard the footsteps behind her, and she saw Theo making his way toward them.

"Just got an update from the doctor," Theo said. He tipped his head in greeting to her parents. "The woman's injuries don't appear to be serious, but she does have some cuts on her feet and hands."

The woman. Not said with a ton of emotion but more like a cop's briefing. Kim totally got that. It was best not to jump right into the scalding memories of the past until they knew what they were dealing with.

"Sometime over the past couple of hours, she also received an injury to her head," Theo went on. He tapped the back of his own head to show them the location. "Could be blunt force trauma, or it could have happened during a fall."

Well, there would have been plenty of opportunities for a fall, what with her running across Kim's property, and heaven knew where she'd been running before that.

"She's conscious," Theo continued to explain, "and I'm about to go in and talk to her. I want you there for that," he added to Kim. "She seemed to settle down some when you talked to her. I want to keep her calm so we can figure out if she is who she's claiming to be."

Kim nodded. "You want me to question her?"

"No, but be ready to step in if she starts to get agitated. Dr. Sanchez probably won't give me much leeway with an interview if his patient is getting hysterical." Theo turned to Nate. "One of the deputies will be bringing over the fingerprint kit. Can you hang around and wait for that?"

"Will do," her father assured him.

Theo muttered a thanks and he put his hand on Kim's lower back to get her moving. A gesture that didn't last because he pulled away just as fast. They'd learned the hard way over the years that touching wasn't a good thing.

They were still a few steps away from the examination room when someone called out Theo's name. A very familiar voice belonging to Nadia Odell Sheldon, Theo's ex.

She was wearing mint-green nurse's scrubs, and she came toward them at a brisk pace.

"I didn't know you had to work tonight," Theo immediately said to her.

"Ditto." Nadia turned her cool blue eyes to Kim. "Ditto," she repeated.

That short response bundled a frigid Texas-sized smackdown. Kim didn't think she was reading into it either. Nope. Nadia had made it clear that she believed Kim had had an affair with Theo. She hadn't, but nothing had been able to convince Nadia differently, and the woman had even cited that accusation when she'd filed for divorce.

"I got called in because we had two nurses who had to go home sick, and there were some emergencies," Nadia added. "Jack's with the nanny and Deputy Norris, who you sent over." She paused. "You said there wasn't a threat to Jack, that the deputy was there only as a precaution. I hope you're right. I wouldn't have come in if I'd thought Jack was in danger."

"He's not," Theo was quick to assure her. "But I'd like to keep a deputy in place for the next few hours. At least until we interview someone."

"The mystery woman you found at Kim's," Nadia remarked. So, the gossip had already started. Of course, Nadia was probably thinking that Theo had been at her place for something other than official business.

"I'll see you tomorrow when I pick up Jack," Theo added to Nadia.

He didn't hang around to give Nadia time to respond to that, but she kept her eyes on them while they went into the examination room. Theo shut the door and turned his attention to the woman on the bed.

There was no one else in the room, yet it was obvious the

medical staff had been here. She had an IV in the back of her left hand, and some spots on her feet had been cleaned and bandaged.

Since there was plenty of light, Kim took a fresh look at the woman's face. She was indeed covered with small nicks, and there were bits of leaves and twigs in her long brown hair. Faith had had much lighter hair, like Theo's, but some people's hair did darken as they aged. Not to mention, it could be dyed.

The eyes were the right color. Blue that had lots of gray in them. But Kim couldn't get her mind to do a mental age progression to see if Faith's childhood eyes and the rest of her features matched this one.

"Theo," the woman said.

Her voice hardly had any sound, but there was plenty of wariness in her eyes when her attention landed on his badge. She didn't try to scramble back as she'd done in the barn, but it was obvious she was uncomfortable being in the room with a lawman. Or maybe that discomfort extended to anyone and everyone right now because she didn't give Kim a welcoming look either.

"I need to know who you are and how you ended up here in Silver Creek," Theo said. He didn't go any closer. He continued to stare at her from the end of the bed.

The woman flinched as if he'd slapped her. "I'm Faith. Don't you remember me?"

Theo made a sound that could have meant anything. "My sister, Faith, went missing twenty-one years ago when she was eight."

"Twenty-one years," she repeated in a whisper. "So long." Her bottom lip began to tremble. "You don't remember me."

"If you remember me, why did it take you all this time to get in touch with me?" he countered.

She looked straight at him, but her eyes still looked a little unfocused. "Because I didn't know who I was. Because I only recently found out that I wasn't the person I believed I was."

Kim thought her time as an ADA had given her a decent gauge for detecting lies, and that sounded like the truth. But she wasn't about to believe anything until she had some more facts.

"Explain that," Theo insisted. "Why did it take you twenty-one years to find out?"

The breath she dragged in was long and slow. "Because people lied to me. Because the people I thought were my parents lied to me," she amended. She closed her eyes a moment as if trying to steady herself or fight off a dizzy spell. "Their names were Vicky and Clifton Neely, and they told me my name was Ashley."

Kim was seriously tempted to take out her phone and do a search on the people she had just named, but she didn't want to do something that might break the woman's attention. Soon though, Kim had no doubts that Theo and she would know everything about them.

Including whether or not they even existed.

Over the past couple of decades, three different women had showed up, claiming to be Faith. That'd happened shortly after the media had done stories on the anniversaries of the murders and Faith's disappearance. In all three cases, the claims had turned out to be false and motivated by money. Even though Theo hadn't touched a dime of it, his folks had left behind several million dollars in assets. Assets that might have been the original motive for the murders if the killer had come to the ranch hoping to find a large stash of cash. Apparently, there were those willing to go to great lengths, including pretending to be his sister, to get their greedy hands on the money.

"An eight-year-old would have known if the Neelys were actually her parents," Theo pointed out.

The woman shook her head. "I couldn't remember anything before age eight. They told me I'd been in an accident, that I'd fallen in a creek and had been hurt when I hit my head on a rock." She pushed back the hair on her forehead to reveal the thin white barely there scar, and then she paused. Her hand was trembling. "Sometimes, I'd get flashes of memories, but they always said I'd just dreamed it and that it wasn't real."

If all of this was true, then the Neelys—or whatever their real name was—had at best concealed a kidnapped child. At worst, they'd been killers and kidnappers. It seemed beyond extreme, though, to murder a couple just to steal a child they wanted to raise, but that's exactly what could have happened.

"What kind of flashes of memories did you get?" Theo asked.

The woman groaned softly, and her fingers twisted and tightened on the bit of sheet she'd latched onto. "Just of another house. Of toys. Of a boy and a girl. I think they were you," she said, glancing first at Theo and then at Kim. "But the memories didn't make sense, and I was always terrified of them."

Theo shifted, moving closer until he was practically looming over her. "Why did they scare you?"

"Because they didn't fit with anything that was in my life, but they were so real..." The woman stopped, shuddered and blinked hard as if she was fighting to concentrate. Or fighting to block out some images going through her head. "Sometimes, in the memories, I'd see blood on a wood floor."

There had indeed been blood, and the floor had been wood. But Kim reminded herself that a detail like that was something the woman could have gotten from the news reports.

"I'll want to speak to your parents," Theo insisted.

She shook her head. "You can't. They died in a car accident two months ago." Once again, she stopped, and this time she swallowed hard. "That's when it started. That's when the memories or whatever they were started getting stronger. Memories of being carried out of a house in the dark. Of someone running with me. I was wearing pink pajamas, and I was crying and calling out for help."

Kim tried to keep her face blank, and she figured that Theo was attempting the same thing, but Faith had indeed been dressed like that when she'd disappeared. Kim was well aware of it since she'd had identical PJs and had been wearing them on that horrific night. Faith had also called out for help.

A reminder that Kim got every time someone sent her one of those letters.

Had this woman sent those letters? Maybe. But if so, it seemed a long time to stretch out a con.

"I started looking through my parents' things," the woman went on. "Through files and old photos, to see if there was anything. I found my birth certificate. Or what I thought was mine, but I started doing some searches on the internet and I learned that my parents…that the Neelys had a daughter named Ashley who'd drowned when she was seven."

Kim glanced at Theo to see if he had a take on that. He didn't. Well, not a visible one anyway, but he was probably thinking that if this woman was lying, then she'd done her homework. The details of a drowned daughter would fit right into a couple desperate for a child. A child they might have been willing to get through any means they considered necessary. Including kidnapping and murder.

"How did you come to believe that you might be Faith Sheldon?" Kim asked her.

"More internet searches," she readily answered. "I just kept digging, looking for a child who would have been adopted or gone missing about twenty-one years ago. I thought maybe my parents had found me, hurt and maybe wandering around without my memory, and they decided to keep me."

That was a possibility, too, but most people would have reported finding a child. Well, they would have unless they had believed the girl would be in danger if they turned her over to the authorities. Yes, she really did need to do some digging into the Neelys.

"I found some articles about the couple who'd been murdered and their missing daughter," the woman went on, lifting her eyes to Theo. "I saw a picture of you. You were twelve or so, and you were the boy from those flashes of memory that I'd been getting."

The silence filled the room, corner to corner, and for several long moments, the only sound was the soft beep of one of the machines.

"You don't believe me," she said, her voice cracking and then fading to no sound whatsoever when she repeated the words like a mantra.

No way was Kim immune to the raw emotion she heard, but she couldn't let herself give in to it. Theo obviously didn't either.

"So, how'd you get to Silver Creek?" he asked.

The woman closed her eyes, a single tear spilling down

her right cheek. "I'm not sure. I, uh, must have had a blackout or something."

Theo huffed, clearly frustrated with these answers. "What's the last thing you recall before the blackout?"

She certainly didn't jump to respond. She touched her fingers to her head, shook it. "I was in San Antonio. The next thing I remember is the two of you coming into the barn."

"The barn where you'd run. And where you were hiding," Theo pointed out. "Why? Who or what were you afraid of?"

She shook her head again and this time it wasn't just a single tear that slid from her eye. She made another of those hoarse sobs and began to cry.

There was a brusque knock at the door, and when it opened and Dr. Sanchez came in, Kim figured he'd heard the crying, too. The doctor scalded them both with a warning glance to let them know he wasn't pleased about their upsetting his patient, and he hitched his thumb in the direction of the waiting room.

"You've got a visitor," the doctor said to Theo. "He's insisting on talking to you right now. Says it's important, that it's about my patient."

Until he'd added that last part, Theo had made no move to leave, but that had him muttering, "I'll be right back," and he headed into the waiting room.

Kim went with him, and she spotted the lanky man with salt-and-pepper hair wearing jeans and a plain white shirt. His face was etched with concern.

"Sheriff Sheldon." The man made an immediate beeline toward them. "Is Ashley Neely in that room? Is she hurt?"

Theo put out his hand to stop the man from charging past him and into the room. "Who are you?"

"Greg Conner," he snapped, clearly not happy with being

stopped. His attention stayed pinned to the examination room door. "If Ashley's in there, I need to see her."

"And why is that?" Theo was in the "full cop" mode now.

Greg shifted his attention to Theo, and his dust-gray eyes narrowed. "Because she's my fiancée. And because she needs help."

"She's getting help," Theo assured him. "You said her name is Ashley Neely?"

It was a simple question, but apparently the answer wasn't as simple because Greg muttered some profanity under his breath. "She told you she was Faith Sheldon," he finally said. "She's not."

Kim couldn't bite back the groan. Not another hoax. Yes, she'd sworn she wouldn't get up her hopes, but that had happened anyway. Kim had started to believe that this might indeed be the childhood friend she thought she'd lost forever.

"Then why would she believe she is Faith Sheldon?" Theo countered.

Again, Greg was slow to answer, and the sigh he made was heavy and long. "Because my fiancée isn't well. In fact, she escaped in the early hours of the morning two days ago so she could come here to Silver Creek and go through with this farce of being your long-lost sister."

"Escaped?" Theo and Kim asked in unison.

Greg nodded and scrubbed his hand over his face. "Yes, for the past two months, Ashley has been confined to a psychiatric hospital."

Chapter Four

Theo had no trouble hearing what Greg had just said. That the woman claiming to be Faith had escaped from a psychiatric hospital. Maybe it was true. In fact, maybe everything Greg was saying was the truth, but there was something about the man that set Theo's teeth on edge.

Because Theo's cop instinct told him that Greg wasn't being completely honest.

Theo took out his phone and sent a text to Deputy Ava Lawson to ask her to do a quick background check on Ashley Neely. Soon, he'd know if there had indeed been an escape. But he figured there had been. Greg probably wouldn't have told a lie that could be so easily disproved.

"Why does your fiancée believe she's my missing sister?" Theo asked Greg the moment he'd finished the text.

That caused Greg to dole out a weary sigh. "Because she read about your family being murdered. A lot of papers did articles about it last year on the twentieth anniversary. Ashley became obsessed with it and started to believe she was Faith. She isn't," he quickly added.

"You're sure?" Theo argued, but he should have been asking himself a version of that since he wasn't sure one way or another who he was dealing with here.

"I'm sure enough," Greg answered. "I've known her a

long time, and there's no proof whatsoever that she's anyone other than Ashley Neely." He added a firm nod to that. "I want to take her back to the hospital in San Antonio. You don't have a right to keep me from seeing her, from taking her."

Theo tapped his badge. "Yeah, I do. Right now, the woman in question needs medical attention."

"If her injuries aren't serious, I can have her moved back to the psychiatric hospital so she'll be with medical staff she knows," Greg pressed. There was both concern and worry in his voice and expression, but, once again, Theo got a bad feeling that the emotions weren't all genuine. "I need to see her."

Since it was possible that the woman would want to see Greg, as well, Theo didn't totally nix the idea of him seeing her. However, she wouldn't be leaving the hospital or Silver Creek until Theo had answers.

"This is assistant district attorney Kim Ryland," Theo said, tipping his head to Kim. "Were you on the grounds of her property in the past couple of hours?" he asked Greg.

Greg shifted his attention to Kim as if just remembering that she was standing there. "No. Why would I have been there? I don't even know her."

"You tell me," Theo pressed.

Annoyance flickered across the man's face. "No, I don't believe I was on her property because I have no idea where her place even is."

Maybe. But Theo was pretty sure that was a lie. If the man's fiancée truly believed she was Faith Sheldon, then Greg would have likely dug enough into the murders to know the key players. Kim was absolutely a key player because she had not only been on scene when Theo's parents had been killed, she'd also been Faith's best friend.

"Then why were you in Silver Creek?" Theo asked Greg.

Greg opened his mouth, closed it and obviously rethought what he'd been about to say. He gave a heavy sigh and re-started. "When Ashley went missing from the hospital two days ago, I hired a PI right away to look for her. He's been monitoring police reports, and he called me when he heard about the woman you found. A woman matching her de-scription. I drove here right away because I was certain it was her."

Theo leveled his gaze on the man, hoping to make him uncomfortable or even pissed off. Because uncomfortable, angry people often said things they'd rather have kept to themselves. Greg, however, stayed quiet.

"I want the name of that PI," Theo insisted since it was possible the guy had broken the law in getting that info on the woman they'd found. "And you won't mind me check-ing your GPS or your phone to verify that you got the call from the PI and then drove here."

Oh, there came the anger. "I believe you'd need a war-rant for that."

Bingo. There was something to hide. And that meant the man might be lying about everything.

"Wait here," Theo told Greg, and he made sure it sounded like the cop's order that it was. "I'll have a word with the patient."

Theo didn't linger waiting for Greg to object, but he did motion for Kim to go with him. For one thing, now that she'd had some time to think about it, Kim might be able to see something in the woman's features to help confirm who she was or wasn't. Theo also didn't want to leave Kim alone with a man he wasn't sure he could trust.

"He's lying about something," Kim muttered to Theo once they had stepped back into the examination room.

Theo didn't smile, but it was nice to know they were on the same page. Then again, Kim and he usually were. That was the problem. Along with having like minds, there was the heat. Not a soft whisper of attraction either.

Nope.

This was the full-blown deal. Normally, Theo could just put it on the back burner by not being around her, but he didn't see that happening any time soon. He needed, and wanted, her on this particular investigation. Not solely because she could help, but also because he was concerned about her safety. If this was actually Faith lying in the bed, looking at them with hopeful but wary eyes, then it meant his parents' killer might also be nearby.

"I heard Greg's voice," the woman said, her words rushed together with her heavy breaths. "I don't want to see him."

That got Theo's attention. "He claims he's your fiancé. Most people would want to see the person they intend to marry."

She swallowed hard. "He wanted me to stay at the hospital in San Antonio, but I couldn't." She leaned in, as if telling a secret. "The killer was there. The person who killed our parents was there."

Everything inside Theo went still. "Who's the killer?"

The woman glanced away, shook her head. "I don't know. He stayed in the shadows, but I know it was him."

Theo took a moment to process that. "The killer kidnapped my sister the night he murdered my parents. If you are the person you're claiming to be, then you'd know who killed them and took you."

Her gaze slowly came back to him. There were tears in her eyes, and she turned them toward Kim. "You believe me, don't you? We were best friends. You were staying at my house." She sat up, her face brightening as if she'd just recalled something. "And you had a stuffed dog. A little brown and white one. We were sort of old for stuffed animals, but you'd brought it with you for the sleepover."

Kim kept the sound that she made noncommittal as she walked closer to the bed. "There was a photo of me with the dog. A picture that someone took before the cops could secure the scene. That picture made its way to the internet."

Kim was right about that. A teenage boy, Denny Travers, had been driving past the house just as Nate had carried Kim out. And she'd had the stuffed dog with her. Denny had used his phone to snap some pictures, including the one of Kim. He hadn't posted the photo right away but rather a few years later, and yes, plenty of people had no doubt seen it.

After the photo had gone public, Denny had been questioned. Or rather, grilled, and grilled hard because it'd riled the then sheriff Grayson to have his niece put back through an emotional wringer. Theo hadn't been a cop yet, so he hadn't been a part of those interrogations, but Grayson had finally concluded that Denny hadn't been part of the murders and kidnapping or that he hadn't seen anything that would help him identify the killer.

"Well?" Theo pressed when the possible imposter just stared at him with hurt in her eyes. "Did you see the picture of Kim with the stuffed dog or not?"

"No." Her voice had dropped to a whisper again. "I remembered that she had it." She looked at Kim. "You brought it with you. I swear, I'm not lying. It's an actual memory."

So, she was sticking to her story about being Faith. But if she was, why was her fiancé so sure that she wasn't? It was definitely something Theo intended to find out.

"What else do you remember?" Kim asked her. She kept her tone soft and level, and since she seemed to have a calming effect on the woman, Theo intended to let Kim keep up the questions.

On a heavy sigh, the woman dropped back against the pillow. "Not much. Only some pieces. I remember being carried out of the house, but I can't recall the person who did that. I remember Theo and you though. Not just from that night but little pieces of memories of us playing together."

"Do you remember where or what we were playing?" Kim continued.

The woman's forehead bunched up as if she was thinking hard to make the answer come. Theo knew what she could actually be doing was trying to come up with something that would sound believable.

"Once we were playing chase, or maybe hide-and-seek, in the yard," the woman finally said. "You and I were giggling when we ducked behind a tree. I think we were hiding from Theo."

The word that came to mind for Theo was "generic." Most kids had played chase or hide-and-seek, and if this woman had seen any photos of the ranch where Faith and he lived, she would know there were trees.

"You had a crush on Theo," she blurted, aiming that at Kim.

Well, that sure as heck wasn't generic. But then Theo frowned. It was possible this woman was picking up on the heat vibe between them. Equally possible, too, that she'd simply guessed.

"Is that true?" the woman asked Kim. "Did I get that right? You had a crush on Theo?"

Kim clearly wasn't comfortable with the question but she nodded. "You recall me telling you that?"

She shook her head. "It was more of a feeling I got because of the way you looked at him." She stopped and shifted her attention to Theo. "I suppose Greg told you I've been in the hospital?"

Theo was glad for the shift in topics. Not only because the crush talk was making both Kim and him uncomfortable but since this was definitely something he wanted to know about. "He did. He said you escaped from a psychiatric hospital."

The woman huffed. "I left. I wasn't confined there. I'd admitted myself voluntarily because... I was having some problems. Horrible dreams, flashbacks, and I was upset over the deaths of my adoptive parents." She paused again, and her bottom lip trembled.

"What kind of flashbacks?" Theo asked.

"Screams." The woman shivered. "I kept hearing screams and saw pools of blood. I'd hoped if I had intense therapy that I could figure out what was real and what wasn't."

Theo might be able to confirm some of what she was saying if he could get her permission to speak to her doctor. *Might.* It was likely, though, that her doctor would claim she wasn't in any mental state to give that permission.

Theo waited to see if she'd add more but when she didn't, he shifted the conversation in yet another direction. "Before they died, did you ever come out and ask your adoptive parents about your suspicions?"

Another nod, and she didn't hesitate either. "They said I was their daughter, that I wasn't Faith Sheldon, that I was having the dreams and flashbacks because I'd gotten too involved with the research I was doing about the murders."

Theo was about to press her to explain, but his phone dinged with a text from Ava.

Fingerprint kit is on the way to you. Will have more for you soon, but here's the preliminary on Ashley Neely. She's twenty-nine, a freelance data processor with an address in San Antonio. No criminal record. Her fiancé, Greg Conner, filed a missing person's report on her nearly forty-eight hours ago.

That would have been about the time Greg had said Ashley had left the hospital. If she'd committed herself, the San Antonio cops must have decided there was a valid reason to be concerned as to her whereabouts. Then again, maybe Greg had put a spin on things to make it seem like Ashley was in danger.

That, she could be.

If his parents' killer truly believed she was Faith, then that person wouldn't want her to recall the details of that fateful night. The Neelys might not have wanted that, either, had they still been alive.

Theo thanked Ava for the preliminary and turned back to the woman in the bed. "How did the Neelys feel about you trying to recover memories of anything that happened before the accident they'd claimed you had?"

"They weren't in favor of it," she readily admitted. "They thought the best thing for me to do was go ahead and marry Greg and focus on that."

"They approved of Greg?" Kim jumped right in to ask.

"Yes." Her mouth tightened. "Greg and my parents were close friends. Greg's twenty years older than me, and they'd known him all his life."

Theo took a moment to decide how to best put this. It wouldn't be wise to start with an attack on the Neelys or Greg that might make the woman go on the defensive. "Since they were friends, your parents must have been pleased when you got engaged to Greg."

"They were pleased," she admitted. "And they weren't

especially concerned that Greg was so much older than I am. They thought it was best for me to get married and have children. That it would make me feel more settled."

So, an old bond between Greg and the Neelys, and if Greg was twenty years older than Ashley, it would have made him twenty-eight at the time Theo's parents had been killed. Theo didn't want to build a theory on that just yet, but he had to at least consider that Greg had gotten Ashley for the Neelys. Maybe not by killing but by being associated with the killer.

Theo glanced at Kim to see if she was thinking the same thing. She must have been because she gave him a subtle nod. But for that theory to be true, it had to mean that Ashley was indeed Faith. It was time for him to push a little harder so he could try to find out if that was possible.

"Tell me the childhood memories you've been able to recall," Theo instructed her. "Not ones triggered from photos or what you've researched. Nothing vague, either, like hide-and-seek. Try to give me something specific."

He figured she'd have to take some time on that and might not even be able to come up with anything. Especially might not be able to do it if all of this was a fake. Or if she were delusional.

But she didn't take time. She didn't even hesitate.

"I remember Kim shrieking when you sneaked up on her and put an ice cube down her back. It was summer and very hot."

Theo didn't have to take any time either. Because he recalled such an incident. Apparently, so did Kim because she gave him a knowing glance. A memory like that wouldn't have been on social media since they'd all been too young for that sort of thing then. Kim and Faith would have only been about six years old, and he would have been ten.

Theo would have definitely pressed for more such memories had the door not inched open. He immediately pivoted, stepping in front of the bed and placing his hand on the butt of his weapon. Kim moved to his side, and while she didn't draw a gun, she appeared ready to give him backup if needed.

Greg poked his head in. "Oh," he muttered when his attention landed on the position of Theo's hand.

"I told you to wait outside," Theo snarled.

"I know, but I just needed to see Ashley for myself. I have to make sure she's okay."

Theo turned so he could get a glimpse of the woman's reaction while also keeping an eye on Greg. It wasn't happiness he saw on her face. More like dread.

"It'll help to talk to me," Greg insisted, his gaze drilling into Ashley's. "You know it will."

Ashley gave a slight nod. Definitely not a convincing one. And it gave Theo another bad feeling. A feeling that maybe she was accustomed to doling out the reactions that Greg wanted. Then again, if what she'd said was true, she had gone against Greg when she'd checked herself into that hospital.

"I'll be able to take you home as soon as the doctor gives the okay," Greg added to her. "I just checked with one of the nurses, and he'll be in here in a few minutes. I could have you home in an hour or so."

Ashley didn't shake her head, didn't refuse, but her gaze flew to Theo, and he could almost hear her pleading with him to intercede. That, he would do. No way did he intend for her to leave, especially with Greg, until he had some proof about her identity. Added to that, it might not be safe for her to go back to her house. It especially might not be safe for her to be alone with Greg.

Theo's phone rang and he saw Ava's name on the screen. Probably an update on the background check, which he wanted. But he kept his attention on Greg while he took the call.

"You're going to want to get as many people out of there as possible right now," Ava immediately said the moment he answered. "We just got a report that someone's about to detonate a bomb in the hospital."

Chapter Five

Even though Theo hadn't put the call on speaker, Kim was standing right next to him so she had no trouble hearing what his deputy had just told him.

A bomb.

The chill rippled over her skin, and Kim felt herself go on autopilot. They had to get out of there now. Because the killer could be back to finish what he'd started twenty-one years ago.

She took hold of the woman's arm, helping her from the bed, while Theo practically pushed Greg out of the room. No doubt because Greg could have been the one who'd planted an explosive before he'd even made his way toward his fiancée's room.

If there was an explosive, that was.

Since she was the daughter of a cop, she could see this as a hoax. A dangerous one. Meant to get them running outside so they could be attacked.

Still, they had no choice but to move. The killer hadn't created a hoax when he'd murdered Theo's parents, and this could also be the real deal now.

"Both of you stay close to me," Theo instructed the woman and Kim. He'd already drawn his gun, and he now pressed the speaker function on his phone so that Ava could fill him in on the details.

"An anonymous 9-1-1 call came in through Dispatch," Ava explained as they moved. Not quickly. The woman was obviously weak, and she sagged against Kim. Greg started to move in as if to help, but Theo waved him off and hooked his left hand around Ashley's waist. "I've already sent you backup, and I've contacted the bomb squad."

Backup. Thank God. Kim knew all the cops in Silver Creek, and she trusted each and every one of them with her life. Good thing because it was possible their lives were on the line right now.

"I can help," Greg snapped. "Ashley is my fiancée. I want to take her away from here. Obviously, you're not able to protect her."

Theo shot the man a glare. "Back off now, or I'll charge you with obstruction of justice and impeding a police officer."

Greg gave Theo a return glare, but he didn't reach for Ashley again and moved out of their paths as they headed for the ER doors.

They weren't the only ones evacuating. Clearly, word had gotten out that the place might be blown up, and the medical staff was already in the process of assisting any mobile patients toward the exits. No one was running or screaming, but the feeling of panic was so thick that Kim could practically see it.

Of course, the flashbacks came. *Of course.* Of that sick panic when she'd been eight. It occurred to her that all the players who'd been in on that nightmare could be here right now. Faith, Theo, her.

And the killer.

Mercy, the killer could be right here.

"You're breathing too fast," Theo murmured, and Kim realized he was talking to her.

He spared her a quick glance that was likely meant to be reassuring, but what reassured her most was that it stayed just a glance. Theo then pinned his attention to keeping watch, no doubt to make sure they weren't about to be attacked. That steadied Kim enough that she was able to do the same.

The doors swished open as they approached, the winter air slamming into them, and when they stepped outside, Theo paused for a few seconds to look around. Apparently, he didn't see anyone who could be a threat because he headed toward his cruiser.

Kim glanced around, too, including a quick look over her shoulder where she expected to see Greg trailing along behind them. But he wasn't there. In fact, he was nowhere in sight, and she had no idea if that was good or bad. She didn't believe, though, that they'd seen the last of him.

"Is the killer after me?" Ashley murmured. She was shivering from the cold, and her teeth were chattering. "Because he thinks I know who he is."

That was a possibility. A strong one. Well, it was if Ashley was actually Faith. Of course, even if she wasn't, the killer might believe she was indeed Theo's missing sister. If so, then Ashley could definitely be the reason for this bomb scare.

Kim heard the wail of sirens, the ripple of panicked chatter and shouted orders from the medical staff. Someone was sobbing.

They were still a good ten yards away from the cruiser when Kim heard another sound. One that sent her heart leaping to her throat.

A gunshot.

She was certain of it. Apparently, Theo was, as well, because, muttering some profanity, he pulled them to the ground behind a car.

"This is Sheriff Sheldon. Everyone get down," Theo shouted. "There's an active shooter."

"Someone's shooting at us?" Ashley cried out. In a panic, she would have scrambled away from them if Kim hadn't caught onto her and put her facedown on the ground.

"Don't get up," Kim insisted.

Just as there was another blast from a bullet.

This shot tore through the car windows and sent glass spewing over them. Kim protected Ashley and herself as best she could by covering their heads with her arms, but she knew that wasn't going to stop a bullet from killing them.

Crouching next to her, Theo made a quick call to Ava to let her know what was going on. What he didn't do was get down. With his gun ready, he stayed in a position so he could peer over the hood of the car.

"Is it the killer doing this?" Ashley asked. "Is it the man who took me when I was a kid?"

That definitely fell into the "to be determined" category. And later Kim would need the answers to both of those questions. For now, though, she just tried to tamp down the fear crawling through her and focus on helping Theo. She did that by containing Ashley and trying to keep watch around them.

A third shot slammed into the car and hit just above their heads. Kim hadn't needed confirmation that they were the targets, but that gave it to her anyway. Someone was trying to kill them and just might succeed. Might succeed when it came to collateral damage, too, if the bullets ricocheted and hit someone else. She hoped everyone who'd evacuated had taken cover.

"The shooter's on the roof of the hospital, and he's using a rifle," Theo muttered in between some ripe profanity. While keeping his gaze pinned there, he took out his phone and called someone. A deputy, no doubt. "Get someone on that roof now. Take plenty of backup with you and be careful."

Even over her own heavy pulse causing her head to throb, Kim knew what that meant. It could take a deputy minutes—long, crawling minutes—to get to the roof and put a stop to this. Plus, the gunman would no doubt be ready for that and would likely try to take out any cop who came up after him.

Ashley was crying now, her body shaking from the sobs. Probably from the cold, too. Kim was certainly freezing.

"The roof," Ashley muttered. "He has us in his sights."

Probably, which was a good reason to stay down. Theo kept his position, though, looking up and trying to pinpoint the exact spot of the shooter.

Kim had actually been up on the roof. There was a sitting area with an awning, and she recalled going up there when she'd been a teenager after her father was injured in the line of duty. Not a serious wound, but she had gone there to get away from her family so they wouldn't see her break down and cry.

The shooter would have had no trouble gaining access to that roof area as it wasn't hard to figure out how to get there.

A fourth shot hit the car again, but this time, Theo didn't just duck down. He took aim at the roof and fired. Considering the distance and the fact the shooter had plenty of cover, it would be hard for Theo to actually shoot him, but he was probably hoping it would cause the gunman to back off.

Kim held her breath, praying it would do just that. Of course, that meant the shooter might turn and run now that he knew he could get a taste of his own medicine, but if that happened, maybe the deputies would be able to apprehend him. It could turn into a shootout, though, with plenty of people getting hurt. But that might happen anyway if the deputies couldn't put a stop to it.

She hoped they didn't have to kill whoever was doing this. Because a dead man wouldn't be able to give them the answers they needed.

Kim counted off the seconds in her head. The *silent* seconds where there were no more shots. There were other sounds, though, of running footsteps that she hoped belonged to law enforcement. More sobs and murmurs, too. Then she heard a very familiar voice.

Her uncle, Deputy Jesse Ryland.

"The shooter's not up here," Jesse shouted. "I need all exits covered."

That caused Theo to whip out his phone again and make a call. He also shifted, keeping watch around them, and it occurred to Kim that if the shooter was no longer on the roof, then he could have bolted down the stairs and be coming for them.

Kim hadn't thought it possible, but her fear skyrocketed further. The shooter had missed them while he'd been aiming from a distance. However, if he could get close, he might be able to finish what he'd started.

The seconds crawled by, turning into minutes with Theo standing guard. Kim had her gun with her in a slide holster in her jeans, but she didn't have a target in sight. As it was, she could only cower and try to keep Ashley alive.

Kim got another slam of fear when she heard approaching footsteps, but she soon heard something that had her exhaling with relief.

"He's nowhere in sight," Jesse said, his tone the same he would have used when cursing.

Theo did curse, but he didn't ease up on his vigilant watch. Maybe because he knew the shooter could be hiding in the crowd of those who'd evacuated.

"Get the bomb squad in here so we can get the building cleared," Theo instructed. "Warn them that the shooter could be hiding inside, so they'll need a deputy with them."

"Will do," Jesse assured him, and he came around the side of the car to look down at Kim. "What about them?" he asked Theo.

"Have an ambulance sent here. I want Ashley loaded in it, and you stay with her. Once the hospital is cleared and she's back inside, I want a guard on her at all times. No one goes into her room or speaks to her unless they have permission from me." Theo paused only long enough to gather his breath. "And get someone out to Nadia's right away."

Kim's head whipped up, her gaze firing to Theo. "You think the shooter could go there?"

Theo shook his head. "I can't risk it."

No, he couldn't, not with his two-year-old son there.

Jesse gave him another assurance and took out his phone to get started on the calls he needed to make.

Theo shifted his attention to Kim. "Are you okay?" he asked.

She wasn't. Kim's nerves were firing on all cylinders, but she nodded. No need to give Theo any more worries than he already had.

And he did have worries.

Regret and guilt, too. Because he would take the blame for Ashley, her and the others being in danger. No way was this his fault, but he would see this as his fault for not being able to prevent it.

"When Ashley is secured," Theo continued a moment later, "you and I will go to my office. I need to find Greg.

Find the shooter, too, if he's not the one who was pulling the trigger. If Greg had fired those shots, he got to the roof awfully fast, but he could have maybe managed it."

Yes, finding the gunman was a must. But there was something else on their proverbial plate, and it was something Kim could help him speed along. She could find out if the woman cowering beneath her was Faith Sheldon. If so, Theo's long-lost sister had finally made her way home.

And she'd brought a killer with her.

THEO STARTED RECEIVING updates from his deputies while he got Kim settled into his office. A familiar place for her since it was where her uncle Grayson had worked when he'd been the Silver Creek sheriff. He was hoping that familiarity and keeping her busy would soon settle her nerves.

His own nerves needed some settling as well. The shooter had fired four shots into a parking lot jammed with folks who'd evacuated from the hospital. They'd been damn lucky that there'd been no serious injuries.

And that's why he had to catch the SOB who'd pulled the trigger.

So far, there was no sign of him. No sign of Greg either. But there was a security camera on the ER doors and the footage could be analyzed. Theo would work on that once he was certain Kim was okay. She'd already briefly spoken to her parents, to assure them she was all right, but that was one of those kid-necessity deals. Theo had already done the same with a quick call to Grayson and Eve, and by now the Ryland clan had no doubt sprung into action.

Those with reserve deputy status, Mason, Gage, Dade and Kade, would already be assisting in any way they could. Some would almost certainly be at the hospital, trying to sift through the crime scene while making sure everyone was safe. One or two might also be at Kim's to assist the CSI team there. Any one of them would have also offered bodyguard duty to Jack. Theo might not have been born a Ryland, but he'd never doubted for a second that he was part of their family.

To give both Kim and himself a minute, he closed his door and looked her over to make sure there were no scrapes or cuts from when she'd landed on the concrete with Ashley. He didn't see anything other than a smudge of dirt on her cheek, and he automatically rubbed his thumb over it.

She flinched a little, no doubt because she'd trained her body to resist him. Especially resist any touching. Because, in the past, being so close to him had triggered flashbacks and even a panic attack. But she didn't back away this time.

With his fingers still on her cheek, Kim stood there, their gazes connected while the heat came. Stirred. And actually helped. The heat reminded him that she was alive. Safe. *Here.*

And at the moment, that was the best he could hope for.

"Thank you," she said, not naming anything specific, and then she finally stepped back. Not far. And she fluttered her hands to his desktop computer. "Jesse should have taken and loaded Ashley's fingerprints by now. While you deal with the aftermath of the shooting and the bomb squad, I can see if the prints are a match to Faith's."

That was indeed a critical step in all of this and, either way, the news would be hard. If she wasn't Faith, then he'd have to deal with another imposter. Another gut punch over the crushed hope. But, if by some miracle, she was his sister, then he'd have to deal with that as well.

Along with the fact that someone wanted her dead.

Perhaps wanted Kim and him dead, too. Right now, there were too many unknowns, and the prints were a start.

He nodded, motioned for her to take his desk, knowing that she'd know how to work her way through the fingerprint database. She took off her coat, draping it over the back of the chair, and got to work.

Theo also took off his coat before he went to the laptop he kept on the corner of his desk. While he waited for his computer to boot up, he made his first call to Jesse, who told him the hospital had been cleared, that Ashley was secured in a room and that he'd called in a reserve deputy to guard her door. The reserve deputy was not only to make sure no one got in but that Ashley didn't try to leave. Theo doubted she would. That said, she had admitted she'd left the hospital in San Antonio, so it was possible she might try to do the same here.

With that base covered, Theo went to his next call. To Ava this time. But the deputy didn't have good news about the shooter. No sign of him. Thankfully, there had been no sign of a bomb either. Ava was going to remain at the hospital to help process the roof and the parking lot. If they could find spent shell casings, it could help them identify the type of gun used. Maybe even the shooter if he'd left prints on any of those casings. Though Theo figured that was a long shot.

After he'd made some other calls to the CSIs and to arrange for more reserve deputies to be brought in, he started the background checks on Greg and the Neelys while he glanced through the data that had come in on Ashley. He didn't see any immediate red flags, but he'd need to do a more thorough interview with her after he'd gathered as much info as possible.

He got an immediate red flag on Greg, though, when he saw the man had been taken to court over some unpaid debts. There was a current court order directing him to repay a lender ten grand.

"Greg's got money problems," he relayed to Kim.

She looked up, her gaze colliding with his. "Money problems that could be fixed if he marries Ashley?"

That's exactly where Theo's thoughts had gone. "Maybe. She's not hurting for funds. The Neelys left her an inheritance of nearly a million dollars."

Plenty enough money to fix Greg's legal problems, which might explain why he was pressing so hard to get Ashley to go with him. However, that wouldn't give him a motive for killing her. Well, it wouldn't unless she'd named Greg as her beneficiary in her will. That was something Theo needed to check.

"Jesse already loaded the fingerprints," Kim told him after a heavy sigh, "but the system is having trouble locating Faith's prints."

"'Trouble,'" he repeated, not liking what immediately came to mind. "As in maybe someone tampered with them?"

"No, it's more of a compatibility issue," she quickly answered. "Faith's prints were submitted in an older electronic format so a tech will have to go in and do a manual match. It might take a while."

"Hell," he grumbled. He was hoping he'd have an answer right away.

"I can go through reports as they come in from the deputies or the CSIs," Kim said, her forehead bunching up. She paused, muttered something he didn't catch. "Please give me something to do. I don't want to just sit here and think about how close we came to dying."

Theo mentally repeated his "hell." There was plenty he could give her to do—including checking social media for Greg, Ashley and the Neelys—but he doubted it was going to erase the worry he saw in her eyes. Nothing was going to erase it for him either. And that's why he did something reckless.

He pulled Kim to her feet and then into his arms.

They landed body to body and, mercy, every part of him was well aware of that. This hug might be for comfort, but it was impossible for him not to feel other things. Judging from the slight silky hitch of her breath, she was feeling them as well.

"I would say this was a bad idea if it didn't feel so good," she murmured.

Yep. He was in complete agreement with her. Theo didn't push things though. He definitely didn't put his mouth against her cheek even though that was what he wanted to do. However, he did draw in her scent, which, of course, gave him another hit of heat.

They stayed there, pressed against each other, with his breathing picking up the rhythm of hers. That helped, too. Because it felt like they were together on even that most basic level. Along with the heat, he could feel his nerves leveling off. Could feel some of the tightness ease up in his muscles.

It didn't last.

The door opened and they flew away from each other as if they'd just been caught in the act of doing something very wrong. And, judging from the expression of the woman who froze in the doorway, they'd committed a whole host of wrongs.

Nadia.

His ex's mouth tightened. Her eyes narrowed, and Theo steeled himself for the onslaught. Oh, and it came all right.

"This is a sheriff's office," Nadia said, her voice snapping like a bullwhip. "There has to be rules or laws against this sort of thing."

"Theo was just giving me a hug because I was so upset," Kim blurted, obviously trying to defuse Nadia's anger. "Nothing else happened."

Of course, Nadia didn't believe that. Never had. She'd always thought Kim and he had had a raging affair. In Theo's mind, they had, so that's why he didn't even try to defend himself. Nadia could no doubt see what he felt for the woman he'd spent a lifetime keeping at arm's length.

"Is something wrong with Jack?" Theo asked Nadia, not just to shift the conversation, but because it was an immediate concern for him. "There's supposed to be a deputy with Jack and you."

Nadia didn't jump to respond, probably because she wanted to hurl more accusations or hang on to her anger since she was spoiling for a fight. But Theo just kept his calm stare on her.

"Jack's fine," Nadia finally said. "He's still with Deputy Norris and the nanny. The house is all locked up, and the security system is set."

Theo was glad those security measures were in place, but he would have preferred having Nadia tucked away with Jack instead of coming into town when a gunman was still at large. Deputy Roger Norris had plenty of experience in protection detail since he'd once been a marshal. Still, Norris couldn't help keep Nadia safe if she didn't stay put.

"I'm here because I got a call from Rowena," Nadia explained. Rowena, not *my mother*. Theo wasn't surprised by that since Nadia wasn't close to either of her parents. "She was upset and crying. Quill called to tell her he was on his way to her place to talk to her."

Theo groaned. "Did that SOB threaten to hurt her again?"

Nadia shook her head. "He didn't hurt her because he didn't show up." She paused and a fresh wave of concern took over her expression. "Look, I'm just going to come out and say it. I think Quill is the one who fired those shots at Kim and you."

Chapter Six

Kim had already geared up to try to assure Nadia that nothing was going on between Theo and her. No way did she want his ex playing dirty and maybe trying to keep Jack from him. But any assurances she'd planned fell away after she heard what Nadia had just said.

"You believe Quill tried to kill us?" Kim asked.

Nadia didn't jump to confirm her accusation. "I think it's possible," the woman finally admitted. She glanced over her shoulder and then her attention turned not to Kim but to Theo. "I don't want to be here when Rowena arrives, and I know she's on her way. Listen to what she has to say and then decide for yourself if Quill might have gone off the deep end and is going after the two of you."

Kim very much wanted to hear what Rowena intended to tell them, but she wanted more from Nadia. Dealing with Rowena wasn't always an easy task, and despite Nadia's wrong assumption about Theo and her having an affair, Nadia might have some correct info that could help them see the big picture here.

"What exactly has Quill done?" Kim pressed.

That caused Nadia to give an impatient huff and she shifted her purse in such a way to indicate she was leaving. "Quill is playing some kind of mind games with Rowena and I know he's very angry at Theo and you for his arrest and upcoming trial. Just talk to Rowena and then Quill instead of getting anything second-hand from me. It's hearsay. Isn't that a term you lawyers like to bandy about when something won't be admissible for trial?" she added with more than a hint of snark. "I have to go."

Nadia turned and walked out. Kim watched her leave before she turned to Theo. But Theo was already taking out his phone, and she saw him press Quill's number. Even though he didn't put it on speaker, she heard the call go straight to voice mail.

"This is Sheriff Sheldon," Theo snarled as he left a message. "I need you to come into the sheriff's office right away. If I haven't heard from you in an hour, I'll put out an APB and have you arrested and brought in."

Maybe Quill would comply, not because of Theo's threat but because any wrongdoing at this point could land him back in jail. With his trial less than a week away, even a short jail stay could play into the outcome of the verdict.

"I'm so sorry," Kim said once he'd finished leaving the voice mail.

Theo slowly lifted his gaze and leveled his eyes on her. "Please don't tell me you're apologizing because I hugged you. That hug was intended to comfort you after someone tried to kill you."

She gave him a level look right back. "I'm apologizing because of Nadia walking in on that hug." No way could she say she hadn't needed it and that it hadn't helped. It had. "I don't want her to give you any hassles about seeing Jack."

He sighed. "The terms of custody and visitation are all spelled out. What she can't spell out is who I hug." He paused a heartbeat and his gaze dropped to her mouth. He didn't say "or kiss," but she could tell that's exactly what he wanted to do.

And, oh, Kim wanted that as well.

The spent adrenaline and nerves were clearly playing into this, but she didn't need those things to feel the heat for Theo. Nope. Didn't need them and had no idea how to cool them down. It seemed as if they'd knocked over some old barriers, and she wasn't sure she could build them back up fast enough to stop this firestorm that was happening between them.

Kim didn't have time to give that more thought, or worry, because she heard the voices in the squad room, and she looked out, expecting to see Rowena. It wasn't. It was Greg, and he wasn't alone. He was with a beefy gray-haired man wearing a suit.

"I understand you've been looking for me," Greg said, his attention skirting right past Kim to land on Theo. Every muscle in Greg's face was tight with anger. A contrast to the man next to him, who appeared calm.

"I have been," Theo assured him at the same moment the guy in the suit said, "I'm Duran Davidson, Greg's lawyer. We're here to secure the release of his fiancée."

"No," Theo said without any hesitation whatsoever. "Ashley is in protective custody. You might not have heard, but someone tried to kill her."

"Oh, I heard," Greg shot back as he came closer. "I heard, and I'm blaming you for her nearly being killed. I told you she should be with me, and you didn't listen. And now I suppose you're going to say I had something to do with the shooting."

Again, Theo didn't hesitate. "Did you? Because you disappeared mighty fast shortly before those shots started."

Greg responded to that with an "if looks could kill" glare,

and he no doubt would have launched into a venomous comeback if the lawyer hadn't stepped in front of him.

"My client is upset," Duran said, still using that calm voice. "His fiancée, the woman he loves, was nearly killed, and he hasn't been able to see her, to make sure she's all right."

Theo kept his own glare on Greg. "She's safe, and until I'm convinced you're not a threat, you won't be seeing her."

Duran gave Greg's arm a pat before the man could speak. "Rather than stand here and debate this, why don't we all sit down and talk." He turned to Kim. "I'm guessing you're Kim Ryland?"

"I am," she verified. "How did you know that?"

"Greg told me that you were Faith Sheldon's childhood friend, so I did a quick check on the drive from San Antonio. You were at the Sheldon home the night Faith was taken."

"And the night Faith and Theo's parents were murdered," she quickly tacked on.

Duran nodded. "Now, you believe the shooting might have had something to do with what happened over twenty years ago."

"Did it?" she asked, trying to keep her tone as even as his.

"I don't think so, but it's something we should discuss. May we sit?"

Theo pulled in a long breath, stepped back and motioned for them to come in. They did, and Duran shut the door behind them.

"Since what I'm about to say is speculation and might harm reputations, I'd rather this chat be kept private," Duran insisted.

"I'd rather it be legal," Theo countered. "And since you're here with him, I'll go ahead and Mirandize him."

That caused Greg to curse and toss out another glare, but

Duran simply put his hand on his client's arm again and motioned for him to sit in the chair next to Theo's desk. Obviously, Duran had a rapport with Greg and was keeping him in check, but his client clearly had a temper.

"All right," Duran said the moment Theo had finished reading Greg his rights. "My client understands what you've just told him, and he's here to cooperate by answering any questions you might have. But we'd like a show of good faith by allowing him to speak to his fiancée."

Theo shook his head. "He's not speaking to her until I'm positive he won't try to intimidate her or do anything that'll add to her already terrified state."

"Terrified because someone shot at her," Duran quickly qualified. "My client will be able to help soothe her. She needs to be returned to the hospital in San Antonio so she can get both the physical and mental medical attention she needs."

"That's to be determined if he can do any soothing whatsoever," Theo argued, and he spoke right over Greg's loud and profanity-laced objection. "I want your client to submit to a gunshot residue test. If he doesn't, I'll get a court order, and I'll hold him here so he doesn't have a chance to try to change his clothes or attempt to wash it off."

Theo knew that GSR didn't wash off easily, and Greg was indeed wearing the same clothes he'd had on earlier. But even if he was the shooter, if he'd used a rifle to fire those shots or had worn gloves, then there might not be any traceable GSR. She had no idea what Duran's legal background was, but if he'd been involved in any trials or charges that involved a shooting, he was likely well aware of it.

"My client submits," Duran said, and it seemed to Kim that he gave Greg a warning glance.

Theo didn't waste any time. He made a call to the head

of the CSI team that was still at Kim's house and asked that someone come to the sheriff's office right away to do the test.

"She'll be here in ten minutes," Theo relayed while he put his phone away.

"And when you get back the negative results, and they will be negative," Greg insisted, "then I'll be able to see Ashley."

"Again, to be determined," Theo fired back.

Kim was betting that visit wouldn't happen any time soon. Theo wouldn't want to allow Greg to have any undue influence over what Ashley might say.

"What needs to happen before my client can see his fiancée?" Duran came out and asked.

Theo didn't hesitate. "For starters, he'll need to tell me the truth about Ashley, about any part he might have had in the shooting, and if at any time he was anywhere near Kim Ryland's house."

"I've already told you I was never at her house," Greg snarled before Duran could respond. "And I didn't shoot at anyone, especially the woman I love. Ashley and I are getting married. I have no reason to want her harmed."

Maybe. But Kim could think of a couple of reasons. Perhaps Ashley was becoming aware of who she actually was. Or rather, who she thought she was. If she believed she was Faith, then she might want to go to the cops, and if so, that could get Greg arrested if he had any knowledge of the Neelys' wrongdoing. Or if he'd participated some way in kidnapping her all those years ago.

But there was another possibility that Kim had to consider. Ashley might have fallen out of love with Greg or changed her mind about marrying him. Knowing that Greg had a temper, that loss of love or potential breakup with him could have caused the man to snap.

"And the other part," Theo prompted. "What's the truth about Ashley?"

Greg didn't snarl out a response this time, and Duran paused to take in a deep breath. It was Duran who answered. "It's possible Ashley is Faith Sheldon."

The air in the room went still, but Kim saw the muscles in Theo's jaw turn to iron. "Explain why you just said that."

Duran obviously needed to take another of those long breaths. "I knew the Neelys very well and have known Greg for years. I can tell you that Vicky and Clifton were simply crushed over the death of their daughter, and they were thrilled when they managed to adopt Ashley."

"How'd they get her?" Theo quickly asked.

Duran shook his head. "I don't know. I didn't handle the adoption, and when I pressed them on it, they said it'd been a private arrangement." He sighed. "Yes, I know how that sounds, but I can't believe either Vicky or Clifton would have participated in any way in a double murder for the sake of getting a child."

They might if they were desperate and, from the sound of it, they had been. Desperate to ease the grief over losing their daughter.

"You honestly think Ashley could be Theo's sister?" Kim challenged.

"It's possible," Duran said after a long pause. Greg only shook his head. "You'll have tests done to see if she is," the lawyer added to Theo. It wasn't a question.

"Of course," Theo verified. "But if she's not a match, that still leaves me with a huge problem. Who would want to fire those shots at her?"

"Well, it sure as hell wasn't me," Greg insisted, the anger

rising up in him again. He got to his feet. "I want to see my fiancée. It's my right."

Theo huffed. "No, it's not your right. But if you're clear on the GSR test and everything both of you have just told me checks out, then I'll ask Ashley if she wants to talk to you."

Kim had no doubt that if a visit actually happened, then Ashley wouldn't be alone with the man. Theo would make sure a deputy was with her in case things turned ugly or if Greg tried to browbeat her into leaving with him.

There was a knock at the door and when Theo opened it, Kim saw Veronica Reyes, a county CSI. Behind her, there was another familiar face.

Rowena.

So, Nadia had been right about the woman coming in and, judging from her nervous expression, this would not be a pleasant visit. Then again, that was the norm for any encounters with Rowena. Unlike Greg and even Quill, she didn't have a temper. Just the opposite. With her history of abuse, the woman always seemed to be on the verge of completely falling apart, so you had to be careful with everything you said to her.

"Go ahead into the squad room with CSI Reyes," Theo instructed Greg and Duran. "Once the GSR test is completed, you can wait until I call you back in for the rest of the interview."

Greg clearly didn't like being dismissed, but Duran and he went out of the office and followed Reyes to one of the unoccupied deputies' desks. Theo then motioned for Rowena to come in.

"Look, I'm not trying to defend Quill or anything," Rowena immediately said. "Not after what he's done to me. But I think someone's trying to set Quill up."

Kim sighed. "Why do you think someone is trying to set him up?"

Rowena took out her phone, pulling up a picture. "This was left on my doorstep last night. I found it this morning."

Kim looked at the photo and saw what appeared to be a dead rat. And blood. From the looks of it, something or someone had bashed in the rodent's head. Maybe because it'd gotten caught in a trap.

"Someone left that dead thing there to scare me," Rowena continued, her words rushed together. "To make me think it was Quill."

Kim couldn't see the logic in that. "Perhaps Quill left it to try to intimidate you."

"He wouldn't do that," Rowena quickly insisted. "He doesn't use scare tactics. He prefers his fists."

Quill's style was definitely more in your face. A direct confrontation—sometimes with his fists. But Quill probably understood that anything direct could and would put him back behind bars. So, perhaps he'd taken to something like leaving a dead rat to try to coerce Rowena into not testifying against him.

It wouldn't matter though.

Yes, it would be good to have the woman's testimony, but there was more than enough physical evidence for the man to be convicted of the vicious attack.

"Anyway, it was there when I opened my door this morning," Rowena went on. "It was disgusting, and I didn't want it there, so I got out the hose and washed it away."

Theo groaned softly because by washing it away, Rowena had also destroyed any potential evidence.

"Why would you think someone is trying to set Quill up?" Theo asked.

Again, Rowena answered without hesitation. "Quill's

made some enemies over the years." She looked back at Kim again. "For instance, you could have put the rat there to make Quill look even guiltier, and you could have done that to make sure you don't lose at the trial."

Kim sighed. "Even if I was so inclined to fabricate evidence, which I'm not, I haven't had time to do anything like that." She paused, looked Rowena straight in the eyes. "Quill could be getting desperate. This could be a way he's hoping to get you to back off at the trial."

Tears sprang to the woman's eyes and her bottom lip trembled. "You must think I'm mad. And sometimes it feels as if I am. I want Quill in jail. I want him punished, but it'll twist me into a thousand knots to get on that stand and tell everyone what he did to me. What I allowed him to do to me by staying with him all these years," she added in a murmur.

And there it was in a nutshell. The effect of the damage that Quill had managed to inflict.

"Do you believe you're in danger, that Quill will try to assault you again?" Theo straight-out asked the woman.

Rowena shrugged but then shook her head. "No. Quill knows that coming after me now could send him to jail for the rest of his life. And whoever left the dead rat just wanted to do it to make me think it was Quill. Maybe to get Quill in trouble."

There was another possibility. Perhaps Quill had persuaded one of his friends to leave the dead rat. If Quill got Rowena scared enough, she might ask that the charges be dropped against him. They wouldn't be. But Quill might be willing to do anything to stay a free man.

Kim exchanged a glance with Theo, and she saw that he wasn't buying the notion that Quill wouldn't hurt Rowena again. The man likely would if he had the chance. Kim wanted to make sure that chance didn't happen, though she figured that Quill would eventually serve his sentence and get out. She doubted Quill would just forget about Rowena and let the woman get on with her life.

"If you honestly believe someone left you a dead rat to set up Quill," Theo said, keeping his voice calm, "then you should try to install a camera so you can see who's doing it."

Rowena's eyes widened a little, and her expression seemed to brighten. "Yes, that's a good idea. I can record whoever's doing it."

Yes, and if it was Quill, and Rowena managed to capture it with the camera, then that could be used against Quill at the trial.

"Also, if anything like this happens again," Theo went on, "call me immediately. Don't wash anything away."

Rowena nodded. "I'll make sure to keep my doors locked, too."

Kim had hoped the woman was already doing that, but maybe now she'd take even more precautions.

"I need you to file a report about the rat," Theo explained to Rowena, and he motioned toward the lone deputy, Nelline Rucker, in the squad room. The others were obviously still tied up with the shooting at the hospital. Nelline stood, listening to what Theo was saying to Rowena. "You'll also need to show Deputy Rucker the photo you showed us so she can get a copy of it."

Rowena muttered a thanks and headed in the direction of the deputy just as Theo's phone rang. "It's the lab," he muttered as he answered. He put the call on speaker. "Sheriff Sheldon."

"Hi, Sheriff. This is Shelby Martinez. I worked out the compatibility problem with the fingerprints you wanted examined and was able to run them."

Kim dragged in her breath. Waited. But she wasn't sure

what to hope for. She wanted answers, but she hadn't thought it would come this soon.

"They're a match," Shelby added a heartbeat later. "Ashley Neely's prints are a match to those we have on file for Faith Sheldon." She paused. "The woman is your sister."

Chapter Seven

Theo heard what the lab tech had just said, but it took a couple of long moments for it to sink in. It didn't sink in well.

Ashley was his missing sister. She was Faith.

He heard the strangled sound that Kim made, and he knew this was hitting her as hard as it was him. They'd both been there that god-awful night when Faith had been taken. The night that had changed their lives forever. But it had changed Faith's, too. She hadn't died, as Theo had feared. She had survived, and was back here in Silver Creek.

"Sheriff?" the tech asked. "Are you still there?"

Theo had to clear his throat before he could speak. "Yeah. Thanks for the info. Could you document the match and send me a copy? Also, has anyone else recently asked for a comparison of my sister's prints?"

"I'll check and get back to you." There was a hesitation in her voice as if she wanted to add something. Maybe some kind of congrats or good wishes. But the tech must have realized what a shock this was for him and only muttered a goodbye.

Theo hung up and then just stood there, trying to process everything. Apparently, Kim was doing the same because she didn't say anything for a long time.

"Are you okay?" she asked.

No, he wasn't. One look at her and he knew she wasn't either. Theo shut the door and pulled her into his arms. She didn't resist, not one little bit. Kim made a hoarse sob and dropped her head onto his shoulder.

"This changes everything," she muttered.

It did. He had his kid sister back, but this wasn't going to be a completely joyful reunion. He was beyond thankful she was alive, that her kidnapper hadn't killed her all those years ago. But it was possible someone didn't want her alive. Maybe the same someone who'd kidnapped her and murdered their parents.

"I'll have to tell her," Theo muttered. "*We'll* tell her," he amended.

Kim made a sound of agreement and held on. There was no fire-hot attraction in this embrace. Just the need to comfort each other, something they hadn't been able to do in over twenty years.

She eased back, her gaze automatically locking with his, and even though the shock was still on her face, Kim also managed a slight smile. "Faith's alive," she said in a whisper.

Yeah, and maybe it was because of that smile he lost his mind for a couple of seconds and brushed his mouth over hers. It was barely a touch, but man, it hit him hard. Just as he'd known it would. There would never be any such thing as casual kisses between them. Not with this heat.

"Sorry," he murmured. But the apology was a lie. He wasn't sorry at all and, in that moment, he knew something else.

That there would be other kisses.

The danger and Faith showing up had snapped something inside him, and he no longer wanted to keep his hands off Kim. He could use those old adages about life being short and never knowing what tomorrow would hold because they definitely applied here. Maybe she felt the same because her eyes stayed locked with his a few seconds more before she finally muttered some profanity and stepped back.

"The hospital," she said. "I'm guessing you have enough deputies there, so we won't be going with backup."

He nodded and wasn't even sure he had backup available here. Still, he'd take precautions, and they'd make the short trip in a cruiser just in case the shooter decided to fire any more bullets at them. First though, he had a call to make.

Theo pressed the number for Deputy Norris who would still be at Nadia's with Jack and the nanny. He had to make sure his son was okay.

"Everything's fine here," the deputy immediately said.

Some relief cut through the tension in his chest. "Good. Has Nadia made it back yet?" Theo had arranged for a reserve deputy to escort her home from the hospital, but he hadn't heard back on that.

"She just called and should be here within the hour," Norris verified. In the background, Theo heard his son's chatter. "I think Jack wants to say hello to you."

Despite everything else going on, Theo smiled when Jack came on the line. "Daddy, you see me soon?"

Not soon enough, and Theo silently cursed that. His time with his son was precious, and he hated that he couldn't be there.

"Sorry, but I won't be able to pick you up this morning," he told Jack. Hopefully soon though. "Daddy loves you, and I'll be over to see you as soon as I can."

"Love you, too. Bye-bye," Jack tacked onto that, and he must have handed the phone back to Norris because the deputy spoke a moment later.

"Don't worry," Norris said. "I'll keep him safe."

"Thanks." And Theo meant that, too. It was a huge relief to know his little boy was being protected. "One more thing. Make sure Quill and Rowena don't come near Jack. As of now, they're both suspects in the attack at the hospital."

"Will do," Norris assured him.

Once Theo put his phone away, Kim and he grabbed their coats and when Theo opened his office door, he saw a welcome sight. Mason Ryland was standing there waiting, as if reporting for duty. Even though Mason was in his late fifties now, Theo knew he was capable of still kicking some butt.

And he sported a scowl that proved it.

Deputy Nelline Rucker was at her desk and was still in the process of taking Rowena's statement, but she looked up at Theo and gave him nonverbal confirmation that Greg had been making a nuisance of himself.

Mason hiked his thumb to Greg, who was sporting a scowl as well. "This guy seems to think the sun revolves around him and that no one has anything more important to do than to cater to his whims. Any chance I can arrest him for something?"

Theo didn't smile, but he appreciated how Mason had a way of spelling out a situation. "No arrest...yet," he added, knowing it would earn him narrowed eyes from Greg. It did.

"I'm standing around here when I need to be talking to my fiancée," Greg groused.

"He keeps saying that," Mason supplied. "Again, it's that 'sun revolving around him' attitude. Hush," he warned Greg when the man opened his mouth again.

Maybe because it sounded like the threat that it was, Greg hushed.

"My client has submitted to the GSR test," Duran volunteered, "but Deputy Rucker said we had to wait for you. Then, this reserve deputy showed up—"

"And I told them they had to wait for you," Mason interrupted.

"They do," Theo attested. He tipped his head to Greg. "He needs to be interviewed as to his whereabouts at the time of the hospital shooting."

Greg huffed, opened his mouth again, but one sharp glance from Mason had him hushing.

"I can interview him," Mason offered. "After that, what should I do with him?"

"If he confesses to any wrongdoing, arrest him. In the meantime, Kim and I have an errand to run."

Mason shifted his attention to Kim and gave her a once-over. "Your mom's worried about you. Should she be?"

"No," Kim said, though that wasn't anywhere near the truth. "I'll call her again after...later," she amended.

Mason's gaze stayed on her a moment before he turned back to Theo. "Call me...later. After you've run this *errand*." He had to know it was an important one for Theo to take Kim out and about. "You've got backup?"

Theo shook his head. "All my deputies are tied up."

"I've finished with Rowena, so I can go with you," Nelline said, standing. "If Mason will hold down the fort here."

"Consider it done," Mason agreed. "Don't get shot," he added to Theo and Kim.

"I expect to be able to see Ashley very soon," Greg snarled to them as they headed out with Nelline.

Theo ignored him, knowing that Mason would be able to keep the man in line. And at the sheriff's office. No way did Theo want Greg showing up at the hospital while he was trying to break the news to Ashley that she was indeed his sister.

The cruiser was parked right out front so, thankfully, they didn't have to be out in the open for more than a couple of seconds while they jumped in. Theo got behind the wheel with Nelline riding shotgun and Kim in the backseat. He'd just pulled away from the station when Kim's phone dinged with a text.

"It's from Hudson," Kim relayed.

Theo knew she meant Hudson Granger, who owned the company that installed and maintained the security equipment on the Silver Creek Ranch. No small endeavor, either, since there were more than a dozen residences there along with the many outbuildings necessary for such a large ranch. Added to that, Hudson also employed private investigators that Kim sometimes used for her cases. Theo knew the man was darn good at his job and trusted him.

"I asked Hudson to take a look at Greg, Duran and the Neelys," Kim relayed. "He's going to try to find out if any of them did any big payoffs or got any big deposits around the time Faith was taken."

Good. Of course, Theo had set up those automated searches to do the same, but it wouldn't hurt to have Hudson looking as well.

"Hudson also requested the report on the car accident that killed the Neelys," Kim added. She met Theo's brief glance in the rearview mirror. "Just in case it wasn't an accident."

Yeah, Theo had already gone there, and it had occurred to him that the person who'd given Faith to the Neelys might have wanted them eliminated since there was no statute of limitations on murder. Of course, that left Theo with a big question. Why had the person waited all those years to tie off that particular loose end? That might be something Ashley could answer.

Or rather, Faith.

He did the mental correction and then silently repeated her name several more times, hoping he could quickly come to terms with her being alive. That's because Faith would no doubt need plenty of help to deal with it. Perhaps plenty of protection, too, if it turned out that someone did want her dead.

However, there was another player when it came to motives for the shooting. Quill. The man hated Kim and Theo enough to kill, and that meant Theo had to make interviewing Quill a top priority. Then again, he had a lot of priorities at the moment and first he had to find Quill and have him brought in.

There were still plenty of signs of activity when Theo pulled into the hospital parking lot. Along with two cruisers, there were vans for both CSI and the bomb squad. The wind slapped at the yellow crime scene tape that had cordoned off most of the area. Probably so the CSIs and deputies could search for those spent casings or anything else the shooter might have left behind.

"Want me to go in with you?" Nelline asked Theo when he stopped as close as he could to the entrance.

He shook his head. "Go back to the station and make sure Greg isn't giving Mason any trouble."

The deputy chuckled because she almost certainly knew that no one gave Mason trouble for long. Still, there were a ton of reports that needed to be done, and Mason's forte wasn't paperwork. Nelline was best suited for that.

"Just try to track down Quill," Theo added to the deputy as Kim and he got out of the cruiser. "And I'll text you when we need a ride back."

They hurried into the hospital, where there was more activity going on. Theo spotted a bomb squad member packing up equipment. A CSI was examining one of the stairwells, and Grayson was talking to a doctor. His stand-in dad, or "bonus dad" as Theo had always called him, ended his conversation and made a beeline toward him.

"Are you both okay?" Grayson immediately asked.

Kim and he nodded in unison. "We weren't injured," she added.

Grayson made a sound of disagreement. "Maybe not physically. Your mom's worried," he told her, causing Kim to sigh.

"So Uncle Mason said," she verified. "I'll call her as soon as I can. Noah, too." Yeah, she'd need to dole out some reassurances to her brother, who must have been on shift at SAPD or he would have been there.

"You're here to check on things or see the woman you brought in?" Grayson asked, aiming that question at Theo.

"Both. But more the second than the first. I figure you've got things under control here. Thanks for that, by the way."

Grayson waved it off while continuing to study Theo. "You found out something about the woman?" He stopped, groaned. "You have proof that she's Faith?"

"Yeah. Fingerprints," Theo answered.

Grayson dragged in a long breath. "She's in room 112, with Gage guarding her door."

Gage, Kim's uncle and Grayson's brother. He was a retired federal agent and wouldn't let anyone get past him to try to hurt Faith.

"You want me to go with you to tell her?" Grayson asked.

Theo shook his head. "Just keep an eye on things here."

His bonus dad could handle the multifaceted operations of a crime scene of this size. So could Theo. Because Grayson had been the one who'd taught him how to handle such things. But right now, Theo knew he had to focus on Faith.

Kim and he made their way through the hospital, which

wasn't huge by anyone's standards, so it only took them a couple of seconds to make it to the hall where the first floor rooms were located. He spotted Gage, who was leaning against the door. He was also wearing a shoulder holster and his reserve deputy's badge.

Gage smiled when he saw them. A real-deal smile despite the nightmare of the past couple of hours, and he brushed a kiss on Kim's cheek.

"How many people have told you that your mom's worried about you?" Gage asked.

"Enough," she answered, and she took out her phone and fired off a text. To her mom, no doubt.

"Were you the shooter's target?" Gage asked and then tipped his head to the door. "Or was she?"

"To be determined," Theo answered. "She's Faith. That's what I'm here to tell her."

Gage's usual cocky expression faded. "Hell."

That about summed up Theo's feelings. A mixture of dread, worry, relief and elation. He tried to tamp all of that down, though, and Kim and he stepped inside.

Faith was in the hospital bed, but she wasn't sleeping. Just the opposite. She was practically sitting at attention, and she had the plastic water pitcher gripped in her hand as if she might plan to use it to defend herself if that became necessary.

"Did you catch the person who tried to kill us?" she immediately asked.

Theo shook his head. "No, I'm sorry."

She lowered the pitcher and sank back against the pillows. "I've been thinking about the shooting, and I must have been the one the gunman was after."

Even though Theo had to tell her about her real identity, the comment got his attention. "Why do you say that?"

She sighed. "Because the gunman could have gotten to you other times. I mean, you both live here in Silver Creek. But no one shot at you until I was with you."

That was a good theory, but Theo immediately saw the flaw in it. "It could be the timing just worked out better for the shooter. Or maybe he wanted us to believe you were the target."

Her eyes widened. "Why would he want you to believe that?"

"To throw suspicion off himself and onto someone else," Kim readily provided. She glanced at Theo. "Because of our jobs, both Theo and I have made enemies. The shooter might be one of them."

Faith seemed to consider that a moment and then she nodded. Paused. "Could it have been Greg?"

Again, that stopped Theo from spilling the news they'd come to tell her. "Why would you think that?"

She lifted her shoulder. "I think he knows I'm having second thoughts about marrying him, and he could be angry." But then she shook her head. "He's never been violent with me, though, so he probably wouldn't try to hurt me."

"You're having second thoughts about continuing the engagement?" Kim prompted, taking the question right out of Theo's mouth.

Faith didn't exactly jump into an explanation. She took a couple of moments. "My parents wanted me to marry him. Or rather, they pressed me to marry him," she amended. "But now that they're no longer alive, I don't feel that pressure, and it's making me want to call off the engagement."

"You were planning on marrying Greg because you wanted to please your parents?" Theo asked.

Faith winced a little. "I know how that sounds, but the therapist at the hospital talked to me about this. It sometimes happens with adopted kids. The child is so grateful for the loving family that she wants to please the adoptive parents." She drew in a long breath. "But I'm seeing there's a fine line between pleasing and bending to their will."

And Greg was part of that bending. It explained how Faith could end up with a man like that, but Theo had to wonder—why had the Neelys wanted their adoptive daughter, a daughter they seemingly loved, to be with a domineering man with a temper?

Unfortunately, a reason quickly came to mind.

If Greg had been the one to kidnap Faith and commit two murders, then he might have blackmailed or "pressured" the Neelys by reminding them they could end up in jail right along with him. Of course, that would mean the Neelys had known what'd happened. Maybe their knowledge hadn't come until after the crimes had already been committed, but they still could have been charged as accessories after the fact.

Theo's phone dinged with a text and he glanced at the screen to see that the CSI has already run the GSR test on Greg.

Negative.

That didn't mean the man hadn't been the shooter, but Duran could use the results to try to pressure Theo into letting Greg see Faith. But Theo had no intentions of letting that happen.

"Is something wrong?" Faith asked, obviously noticing his reaction to the text.

He put his phone away and met her gaze. "Your fingerprints came back as a match to Faith's." Theo didn't add anything else. He just gave her some time to let that sink in.

Faith gasped, and she tried to speak, but it took her a while to get out the words. "You're sure?"

Theo settled for a nod since he thought he might have trouble getting out words as well. Even though he'd known the truth for about a half hour now, the emotions were still coursing through him.

This was his sister.

Obviously, she'd changed a lot from the eight-year-old kid she'd once been, but now that he had studied her face, he could see Faith.

"It's true," Faith muttered, and she reached out her hand to Kim. Maybe because she was closer than Theo.

"It's true," Kim confirmed, and she not only took Faith's hand, she pulled her into a hug.

That brought about tears of a happy reunion, one that only added to the storm of emotions. Theo was happy, too. Damn happy. But there was another side to this. It was possible someone was trying to kill the sister he'd just found.

Faith motioned for him to come closer, and when he did, she hooked her other arm around him, pulling him into the hug with Kim and her. Some of the tension that Theo had been carrying for years fell off him. A hefty amount of guilt replaced it. Because he should have found Faith before now. Better yet, he should have stopped her from being kidnapped.

The hug lasted a while, and Theo didn't do anything to put an end to it. Finally, though, Faith eased back and, smiling, she swiped tears from her cheeks.

"Thank you," she said to both Kim and him.

He had no idea why she was thanking them, and he would have let her know that had she not continued before he could say anything.

"But I've brought danger right to your doorstep," Faith added. Her smile vanished and the worry bunched up her forehead.

"You don't know that," Kim assured her. "In fact, Theo and I could be the ones bringing danger to you. Just know that Theo is a darn good cop, and he'll do everything in his power to protect you. So will I."

That caused a fresh round of crying, and Faith turned those tear-filled eyes toward Theo. "I honestly don't have any clear memories of the night I was taken. Just those bits that I've already told you about." Her bottom lip quivered. "You should know that I also had a breakdown after my parents…after the Neelys died. I'm not delusional," she quickly added. "But I did have a breakdown."

Not surprised by that, Theo nodded. "That's why you got help at the hospital in San Antonio?"

"Yes, and I also wanted to try to make sense of those memory fragments I was having."

"Did you ever tell Greg or anyone else about those fragments?" Theo asked.

Faith stared at him and he saw the alarm go through her eyes. "I told Greg. And my parents…the Neelys," she amended. And, judging from the way she shivered, that reminded her that their parents had been murdered.

Maybe killed by the same person who now wanted her dead.

Because a dead person wouldn't have a memory to regain. Especially a memory that could get someone convicted of a double murder and kidnapping.

"I didn't exactly keep the memories a secret," Faith admitted, shivering again. "I should have."

"No," Kim quickly disagreed. "You had no reason to distrust those people." She paused a heartbeat. "Did you?"

Faith wasn't so fast to answer, and that put a knot in his gut. Hell. What had she been through all these years?

"I trusted the Neelys," Faith finally said. "I mean, I always sensed they were keeping something from me, but trust me, I had no idea they were holding back on telling me who I really was. And they might not have known. I can't believe they would have had any part in killing our parents and kidnapping me."

No, but again, there was that after-the-fact possibility. Or maybe the Neelys had learned about it more recently than the night someone would have brought a kidnapped child to them.

"Are you sure the Neelys' car accident was actually an accident?" Theo asked. Bringing this up was a risk because Faith already seemed right on the edge of not being able to hold it together. She was emotionally fragile. Still, the more they knew, the faster they could catch whoever was responsible for the attack.

Faith stared at him a long time. "You think the person who took me killed them to keep them quiet."

"It's a theory," Theo admitted, and he was pleased that instead of another shudder or shiver, he thought she was steeling herself up and trying to grasp the big picture. "That means I have to look at Duran and Greg as persons of interest."

She nodded. "*Persons of interest*. That's a cop's way of saying suspects."

In this case, yes. They were indeed suspects.

"What I need you to do is write down the names of anyone close to the Neelys, anyone who might have had a part in what happened," Theo instructed. "Think back to anything that was said about when they adopted you. *Anything*," he emphasized.

Theo could see that was the right thing to do. It gave her a task, something that could help the investigation. There was also something else she might be able to help them with.

"By any chance, have you sent Kim letters over the past fourteen years?" he asked.

Faith immediately shook her head. "No, I haven't. I didn't know until recently who Kim was. What kinds of letters?"

"Ones connected to that night your folks were killed since they're addressed to Kimmie, the nickname everyone called me back then," Kim provided. "All of them say *Help me. Please help me.*"

Faith looked at Theo. "That's what I called out that night?"

He settled for a nod since his throat and chest had tightened again, and Kim filled in the rest for him. "But those weren't your exact words. It's more of a generic version of what you said."

Faith nodded slowly. "So, maybe the killer isn't the one sending the letters to you."

Kim made a sound of agreement. "The letters could be horrible pranks."

Theo was still holding on to that hope. As bad as pranks like that would be—and they were bad—it would be worse if the killer was sending them as some kind of unfinished business.

"I don't know of anyone who'd send letters like that," Faith insisted. "But I will make a list of the Neelys' friends and acquaintances. Their employees, too." She paused. "How long will I have to be here?"

"Unfortunately, you'll have to stay a while longer," Theo told her "but I'll arrange to have a laptop brought in for you. Pen and paper, too, if that's how you'd rather create that list."

Faith nodded, swallowed hard. "What if the killer comes after me here?"

"He won't get in," he quickly assured her. "Right now, Gage Ryland is on the door, and no one will get past him."

Theo could see the wariness in her eyes. But there was trust, too. He was her big brother. The sheriff of Silver Creek. And he was going to do something he hadn't managed when she was eight.

He was going to make sure she was safe.

"I don't want to go with Greg when it's time for me to leave," Faith said. "Can I go with you?" She glanced at both Kim and Theo.

"Yes," Theo assured her. "I don't live at our old house." Too many bad memories. "I have a small ranch."

He was about to explain he could take Faith there. Or to Kim's. But his phone rang, and when he saw Ava's number, he knew he had to take the call.

"I found something," the deputy said the moment Theo answered. "I'm sending it to you now." His phone dinged with an incoming message. "It's some still images taken from the hospital surveillance camera about five minutes before the first shot was fired."

Theo didn't put the call on speaker in case Ava had news that would upset Faith even more than she already was, but he did have a look at the trio of photos.

And Theo cursed when he saw the man's face.

Chapter Eight

Kim hurried to Theo, and she immediately saw what had caused him to curse. She wanted to curse, too.

Because it was Quill in the photos.

No mistaking that, and judging from the timestamp for when he disappeared out of camera range and into the hospital, he would have had time to go up the stairs to the roof and start shooting.

"He's not carrying a rifle," Kim pointed out. But that didn't mean Quill hadn't been the shooter. "He's got a backpack, so it could have been a firearm that he assembled on scene."

In fact, any of their suspects could have done that. Or even planted the weapon there earlier. Faith had been in the hospital for well over a half hour before the bomb scare had happened.

We'll keep checking the surveillance footage, Ava texted.

Good because Kim was certain that Theo would want to know when Quill had exited the building. Greg or Duran as well. It was possible, though, that none of them had been the gunman, that they could have hired someone to do the job.

"I need to have Quill tested for GSR," Theo muttered, and after he put away his phone, he looked at Faith. "I'll arrange for that laptop so you can get started on those names."

Faith gave a shaky nod. Shaky because their reaction to the text had no doubt alarmed her. "This man, Quill, could have been the one who tried to kill me?" she asked.

"If Quill was the shooter, then he was gunning for Kim or me, not you," Theo corrected. "Kim is the prosecuting attorney at his upcoming trial, and I was the arresting officer."

Faith's face stayed tight. "Please, both of you be careful. I don't want to lose either of you."

"We'll be careful," Kim assured her.

That wasn't just lip service either. They would both be on high alert, and that meant doing something that would break down more of those long erected barriers.

They'd have to stay together.

Yes, she could get protection from another Silver Creek lawman. Heaven knew she had enough of those in her family. But she wanted Theo safe, too, and that meant being together so they could watch each other's backs.

They said their goodbyes to Faith, both Theo and Kim hugging the woman. It wasn't exactly like old times, but Kim didn't have any doubts now that this was her childhood friend. No doubts, either, that Theo and Faith could start to rebuild their relationship once the threat of the danger had passed.

When they went out of the room and back into the hall, Theo texted Nelline so she could return to the hospital with the cruiser. Theo added a Be careful as they made their way to the exit. It wouldn't take the deputy long to get there, and Kim knew they wouldn't be going back outside until the cruiser was in sight.

"Are we going to Quill's house?" Kim asked.

"No." Theo didn't even hesitate. "I want Quill to cooperate with a GSR test, and he won't do that if you and I show up. It'd be like waving a red flag in front of a pissed-off bull."

It would indeed. Theo would have no trouble getting a warrant for a GSR test, but it would go even faster if a pair of deputies could get the man to do it voluntarily. And Quill just might do that if he thought it would prevent him from being arrested—something that would happen if he refused the test.

"Agreed," she said. "But if the CSIs clear it, I would like to drop by my house and get some things." She paused a heartbeat until his gaze met hers. "I figured it'd be better to stay at your place."

She knew the suggestion wouldn't come as a surprise to him. His ranch would be easier to secure than her house because he had hands who could keep watch. Added to that, she knew he had a topnotch security system since she'd heard her own security specialist, Hudson, mention that he'd personally done the work at Theo's.

"Or we could go to the Silver Creek Ranch and stay with either my folks or Uncle Grayson and Aunt Eve," she added.

Kim could practically see him working his way through those options. "My place," he finally said. "When Faith gets out of the hospital either later today or tomorrow, it might be overwhelming for her to stay at the Silver Creek Ranch."

No way could Kim argue with him about that. The ranch was indeed overwhelming and was larger than some small towns. Yes, it was secure, but she thought they could make Theo's equally safe while not adding more stress for Faith. Of course, the ultimate stress reliever for all of them would be to catch the person who'd fired those shots and stop him from launching another attack.

"It's nearly lunchtime," Theo noted a few seconds later. "You need to eat," he insisted when she was about to say she wasn't hungry. "After we get your things from your house, we can go back to my office, order some food and dig into the investigation. I need to go over the statements from Rowena, Greg and Duran."

Yes, because any of the three might have said something that would give them clues about the shooter. She could also go tit for tat here and make sure he ate something as well.

"I also want Quill found, tested for GSR and then brought in for questioning," Theo spelled out while he sent a text to Ava, telling her to make that happen.

Maybe Ava wouldn't have any trouble finding the man. Or bringing Quill in. But no way would Ava go to Quill's alone. She'd take backup, and if the man resisted, then the deputies would have solid grounds to arrest him.

When Nelline pulled the cruiser to a stop directly outside the ER doors, Theo flipped off the safety strap on his holster so his weapon would be ready, and he hurried them out of there. Theo sat in front with Nelline and Kim took the back.

As she drove away, and while everyone kept watch around them, the deputy began giving Theo updates on the various reports she'd been getting from the CSIs and the lab. Kim very much wanted to hear what Nelline was saying, but her phone rang. When she saw the name on the screen, she knew it was a call she had to take.

"It's Hudson," Kim relayed to Theo just as she answered it.

"I've found out a few things," Hudson immediately said to her. "Ashley didn't lie when she said she'd voluntarily committed herself to the hospital. No one can force her to go back." He paused a moment. "FYI, don't ask me how I learned this, but Ashley actually is Faith Sheldon."

It shouldn't have surprised her that he'd managed to confirm that because Hudson was the best at tracking down info. "Yes, Theo just told her about her prints being a match to his sister. Faith has finally come home," she added in a murmur.

She glanced up, meeting Theo's gaze, and she saw both the relief and the worry in his eyes. This would no doubt trigger a new round of grief for him. No way to avoid that since it would also trigger the memories. That meant both of them were in for a hard night. Faith, too.

"You want me to keep digging on Faith to see what she's been doing for the past twenty-one years?" Hudson asked.

"Yes," she answered. Even though they were going behind the woman's back, it was best for Theo and Kim to have as many pieces of this puzzle as possible. One of those pieces might lead them to the shooter.

"Will do. I also got some more on Greg and Duran," Hudson went on, and Kim went ahead and put the call on speaker since it appeared Nelline was done with her updates. "Greg's made some lousy investments over the years, and I've found two occasions where the Neelys bailed him out."

"Why?" Kim had to ask. "I mean how is it they were so close to Greg?"

"You want to know if they were paying him off to keep him quiet about who their daughter really was."

"Yes," Kim verified.

"No actual proof of that *yet*," Hudson admitted, emphasizing that last word to let her know he was still looking in that area. "I'm sure Greg would say the Neelys gave him the money because of their longtime friendship with him and his late parents. But it's a lot of money. Nearly a quarter of a million, if you tally up both times they did the bailout."

It certainly felt like hush money to her, especially since Greg didn't seem to have a winning personality to instill that closeness to the Neelys. But maybe the couple thought of Greg as the son they'd never had rather than a kidnapper and killer who'd provided them with a daughter.

"You said you found something on Duran?" she prompted as Nelline took the turn into the driveway of Kim's house. Kim glanced around but didn't see anyone, including any of the CSI team.

"Oh, yeah," Hudson declared. "Definitely not squeaky clean. He's been investigated for embezzlement and money laundering. Nothing seems to stick, though, since he's never been charged with anything. But are you ready for this? There's a rumor that Duran has brokered some black market adoptions."

Theo's head whipped up. That obviously got his attention. "This is Theo," he spoke up. "Any facts to back up those rumors?"

"Working on it," Hudson assured him. "But my researchers dug up some old social media posts where two people in Kerrville were gushing thanks to Duran for finding them a baby and arranging a private adoption. I can send you the couple's names or talk to them myself."

Theo stayed quiet a moment. "Send me the names but keep digging to see what you can find on them. And on Duran."

"Will do," Hudson assured him. "I'll get back to you as soon as I have anything."

They ended the call just as Nelline pulled to a stop in front of Kim's house. "Wait here," Theo instructed the deputy. "And make some calls. I want the adoption paperwork the Neelys filled out. My guess is Duran handled that."

Yes, and that could possibly include him finding the child for them. Even if the paperwork did lead back to Duran, though, he could always claim he had no idea that Ashley was actually Faith. No way would he admit to anything connected to the kidnapping since there'd been two murders involved.

"The CSIs are done with their search," Nelline explained when Kim glanced around the yard. "They said they locked up."

That was good because the locks would have automatically engaged the security system. Kim used the app on her phone to disengage her security system and unlock the door so that Theo and she could hurry into her house.

Even though it'd only been hours since they were last here, it felt much longer. Probably because so much had happened. This had been one of those "lives changing on a dime" mornings.

She glanced around and didn't see anything out of place, but that didn't mean the deputies and the CSIs hadn't done a thorough search. They'd just taken more care than usual because of her family's connections to law enforcement.

"According to the update I got," Theo said, doing his own glancing around, "there were no signs that the man we saw actually got inside the house."

That was good, but it had to be ruled out. "How about the barn? Did they find anything in there?"

Theo shook his head and followed her as she made her way to her bedroom to pack a few things. He didn't go in with her but instead stopped in the doorway and bracketed his hands on the frame. Then again, he didn't have to be closer for her to feel him, and she knew he was watching her. Maybe just looking for signs that the hellish morning was going to make her break. Maybe because they just had trouble keeping their eyes off each other.

That was certainly the case with her.

"What else did Nelline fill you in on?" she asked, taking her small suitcase from the closet. Best to try to stay focused on the investigation.

"It was more of filling me in on what we don't have. They found shell casings but got no prints off them. Ava and Jesse are going out to Quill's to deal with him. Your uncle Kade is doing reserve deputy duty by going through the rest of the feed from the surveillance camera at the hospital."

Kim had to hope that some or all of that would give them the answers they needed because the sooner the shooter was caught, the sooner her life could get back to normal.

But she rethought that—after she made the mistake of glancing at Theo again.

He certainly made a picture standing there in the doorway. He'd kept on his coat, but it was open, revealing his shirt. And the muscles beneath it. She'd had an up-close-and-personal encounter with those muscles earlier when they'd hugged.

Theo made a sound, a sort of throat clearing, and that's when Kim realized her hands had frozen and she was blatantly just staring at him. Theo was staring back, and the heat was zinging between them.

Kim made her own sound, a weary sigh, and after zipping the suitcase, she picked it up and went to him. "This is a mistake," she said. "But I'm having a hard time remembering why it's a mistake."

The corner of his mouth lifted in that sizzling smile that could be considered foreplay to a really hot round of sex. The timing was all wrong for her to be having a reaction like that to him. All wrong and yet somehow right. Of course, that "right" feeling was because of the urging of certain parts of her body, but Kim went with it anyway.

She leaned in and brushed her mouth over his.

Talk about a hard slam of lust. Pure, hot lust. There was

no other word for it. No words, either, for the avalanche of feelings she got when Theo let go of the doorjamb to slide his hand around the back of her neck and pull her to him. He put his mouth to hers, and it wasn't a brush. It was a full-pressure, scalding kiss she felt in every inch of her.

Oh, mercy.

He was good at this. Of course, he was. This was Theo, the man she'd fantasized about for years, so it would have been next to impossible for him to let her down with that clever mouth of his.

Kim made a sound of pleasure and heard Theo make a version of the same. There was no hesitancy in those sounds. No hesitancy in the kiss either. He went for long and deep. For a kiss that was begging her to latch onto him and do something about this fire and need he'd been building in her for years.

But she forced herself to stop and ease back.

Emphasis on "forced" because there was no way her body wanted her to quit. Theo was no doubt going through the same experience, and she had proof of that with the next sound he made. Not pleasure but frustration.

He muttered a choice curse word, his warm breath hitting against her mouth and instantly making her regret she'd been the one to put an end to it. She didn't have time to deal with that regret for long, though, because Theo's phone rang, and she saw Nelline's name on the screen.

She watched as Theo took a couple of seconds to shake off the effects of that mind-numbing kiss and fortify himself before he answered. "Is everything okay?" he asked.

"Maybe," the deputy answered. "A truck just turned into Kim's driveway, and I'm pretty sure it's Quill Odell."

Chapter Nine

Theo definitely wanted to interrogate Quill, but he darn sure didn't want it to happening here at Kim's. She'd already been through enough today without coming face-to-face with the man who was a prime suspect in the shooting that could have killed her.

He went to the window at the front of the house and confirmed that it was indeed Quill. The man parked his truck next to the cruiser and got out. At least it didn't appear that Quill was ready to go on the run. There also weren't any weapons in his hands. That didn't mean, though, that he wasn't carrying. Nelline would have known that, and that's why she'd gotten out of the cruiser and was in the process of frisking him.

Quill was a big man. Six-three with plenty of muscle even though he was now in his fifties. He wore a black stocking cap, but Theo knew that beneath it Quill had shaved his balding head.

Kim joined Theo at the window, and she glanced at him. "It appears Quill has something he wants to say," she remarked when Quill started cursing the deputy for patting him down.

"Yeah." Theo sighed. "Any chance you'll stay put and let me handle this?"

She looked him straight in the eyes and he saw she wasn't happy with that idea. "Since he's at my house, it's likely he's come to talk to me. You could be the 'red flag to the bull' scenario, and since you'll want to question him, then it'll be best if he finishes whatever business he feels he has with me."

He couldn't dispute that. Theo knew he always seemed to bring out the worst in Quill. Probably because Quill was well aware that Theo despised him.

"I'll have Quill come onto the porch, and we can both stand inside while you talk to him." Theo spelled it out for her. "Nelline can get back in the cruiser just in case Quill is innocent in the hospital shooting and the actual gunman is still out there. And if Quill tries to start any trouble, you'll get out of the doorway."

Kim nodded. "I'll get out of the way, but I do have my gun just in case things get ugly." She pointed to the back waist of her jeans where there was no doubt a slide holster.

As compromises went, it was a good one, but he still would have preferred her not having to put herself through this. It was never easy to deal with Quill, and he was bound to be in an especially bad mood since he'd likely heard he was a suspect in the shooting.

Theo opened the door about halfway, and he kept his hand on his gun. "Let him come to the porch," he called out to the deputy. "You get back in the cruiser."

The deputy immediately did as he said, but she lowered the window, no doubt so she could still provide him with some backup. But he had backup right next to him since Kim knew how to handle a firearm.

As Quill began approaching the porch steps, Theo recited the Miranda warning to him. Of course, that riled the man, but Theo didn't want anything Quill might say to be inadmissible because he hadn't been read his rights.

"All that's not necessary," Quill growled, his gaze and index finger going straight to Kim. "I hear you're trying to get my bail revoked."

"You're a person of interest in a shooting," Kim admitted. "Revocation of bail comes with the territory."

First, though, Theo and Kim would have to convince a judge that Quill was guilty. Right now they had circumstantial evidence with the surveillance footage, but that alone wouldn't be enough for revocation of bail. That's why neither Kim nor Theo had started the process. Apparently, though, Quill believed they had.

Quill cursed. "I had nothing to do with that shooting. Nothing." He spat the word out. "Somebody's trying to set me up."

"But you were at the hospital at the time of the incident," Theo quickly pointed out.

Quill's eyes widened a moment, only a moment, before he covered his surprise about Theo having known that. "I was," he admitted. "Because I heard about you bringing in the woman you found, and I wanted to see what was going on."

Either that was a really bad "wrong time, wrong place" deal, or Quill was lying. "Then, if you're innocent, you'll submit to a test to detect gunshot residue," Theo countered.

The man shook his head, muttered more profanity. "And if I don't, I guess you'll toss me in jail."

Theo nodded. "I will."

He expected that to bring on a round of vicious profanity, but Quill merely shook his head and gave a resigned sigh. "All right. When and where do I get the test?"

Theo took out his phone and requested a deputy to come to Kim's to collect the man. "About ten minutes at the sheriff's office," Theo informed him. "And then you'll be questioned about what you were doing at the hospital because I've never thought of you as a curious man. Seems farfetched that you'd just want to be up on the latest gossip."

He sighed again. "A friend texted me and said this woman might be your long-lost sister. I knew your mom and dad, even did a little work for them on their ranch, and I knew both you and your sister. I just wanted to know if it was Faith, especially since you were once married to my daughter and are my grandson's father."

Quill had indeed done some work for his folks, and it didn't surprise him that there'd been talk about the woman being his sister. The EMTs or someone on the medical staff could have known the mystery woman's prints were being taken. But what was puzzling was why that would interest Quill.

And that puzzlement gave Theo a really bad feeling in his gut.

Because, what if Quill had had something to do with Faith being kidnapped? If so, he would want to make sure she didn't incriminate him in any way.

Theo glanced at Kim to see if she was following along on this mental thread. He was pretty sure she was.

"I didn't go to the hospital to shoot anyone," Quill insisted. The silent response Theo and Kim were giving the man seemed to make him uncomfortable. Or maybe Quill just knew they were piecing together a very bad possibility.

That they were looking into the face of the man who'd murdered his parents.

"So, you were curious enough to drive to the hospital," Theo summarized, "and be in the same area where shots were fired. FYI, before you answer, know that surveillance footage from the security camera is being analyzed as we speak."

Quill opened his mouth and then seemed to rethink what he'd been about to say. "Rowena knew I was at the hospital. She drove past the parking lot as I was getting out of my truck."

Theo gave the man a flat look. "Are you saying Rowena fired those shots to set you up?"

Quill gave a firm nod. "That's exactly what I'm saying. If she didn't pull the trigger herself, she could have got somebody else to do it. I think Rowena would do anything to make sure I'm put away for good."

"Really?" Kim said, the sarcasm heavy in her voice. "The woman you battered for years would do this?"

But Quill ignored Kim's tone. "Yeah. She would. Rowena's got a mean streak, and she's playing all nice with the likes of you, but I think she's got it in for me."

The woman deserved to have it in for Quill after what he'd done to her, but Theo kept that to himself. Before the deputy arrived to take Quill in, Theo wanted more info from the man, and pointing out the obvious wasn't the way to go about getting those answers.

"I know you were questioned about my parents' murders, but thinking back, do you recall anything suspicious going on in the days or even weeks leading up to their deaths?"

Theo tried to keep anything accusatory out of the question, and it must have worked because he didn't see any of the usual anger flare up in Quill's eyes.

"No." Quill said that on a sigh. "I've gone over all of that plenty of times, and like I told Grayson way back then, I didn't see anybody who could have done that."

Theo had known that was a long shot, but he'd had to try. Sometimes, people did recall little things years after the fact, and on rare occasions, those little things provided clues to help solve the case.

"Is that woman your sister?" Quill asked. "Because she's the one who'd be the best person to give you answers about your folks' murders."

Theo took a moment to decide how he wanted to answer. It wouldn't take long for word to get out that Ashley was Faith. No way to keep that a secret. So, he'd use the info and gauge Quill's reaction to it.

"She's Faith," Theo confirmed.

Quill's face registered surprise before he quickly shut it down and tried to make his expression blank. "So, she knows who took her and did those murders."

"No." Theo needed to make this very clear so that Faith wouldn't be a target. "She doesn't have any memories of that night."

Not the truth. She did have those fragments, and with some help, she might recall more. And that was the reason she would stay in protective custody until the danger had passed.

Quill shook his head. "I guess that's expected," he murmured. "Poor kid, she had to be traumatized by what she saw and what happened to her."

Yeah, Theo had been, too, and he had to wonder if Quill was the person responsible for that nightmare. Because of Quill's association with Theo's parents, the man had been a person of interest. Quill had been questioned, and questioned hard, but he'd never admitted to any wrongdoing. Nor had there ever been any evidence uncovered to point the finger at him.

However, Theo needed to take another look at the interview notes to see if he could spot any inconsistencies.

"I'm glad you got your sister back and all," Quill went on

a moment later, "but what are you going to do about Rowena trying to set me up?" He slid glances at both Theo and Kim.

"Give me the names of someone Rowena could have talked into firing those shots to set you up," Theo simply said. "And I'll investigate."

"I don't know the names of people she considers her friends," Quill insisted. "Heck, she might not have even known the person. You can hire gunmen off the internet."

Yes, you could, but Theo couldn't see Rowena having ready knowledge of how to do that. Still, he'd check.

"Think of names," Theo instructed as he saw the cruiser turn into the driveway. Jesse was behind the wheel. "Also, did you leave a dead animal on Rowena's doorstep?" he tagged on.

Oh, that caused the ugly anger to rise again. "Hell, no. Did Rowena say I'd done that? Because if she did, she's lying through her teeth."

Theo had no intentions of informing Quill of what Rowena had said, but he needed to give the man a reminder to keep him away from his wife. "If you go near Rowena, you'll be arrested, and your bail will be revoked."

That didn't tamp down any of Quill's temper. However, he didn't spew out any threats.

Jesse pulled the cruiser to a stop and Theo held up his finger in a wait-a-second gesture so he could ask Quill one last question. "Do you know anything about letters that someone's been sending Kim?"

Judging from the stare Quill gave him, he hadn't been expecting the question. But the man didn't immediately dismiss it, either, or snarl out a denial that he'd had any part in doing that.

"Letters," Quill muttered. And it wasn't a question. Traces of the anger vanished and some smugness crept into his expression. "Yeah, I might know something about that. I think Rowena's the one who's been sending those letters to Kim."

Chapter Ten

Kim felt everything inside her go still. Then she remembered who'd just made that accusation.

Quill. A man who couldn't be trusted.

Obviously, Theo felt the same way because he huffed. "Why would Rowena want to send letters to Kim?" He didn't add especially letters that clearly meant to taunt her with the events of that horrible night.

"I told you Rowena likes to make people think she's nice and all, but she's got a mean streak," Quill insisted. "But a couple of years ago, when we were still together, I walked in on her typing something on that old typewriter she kept on the top shelf of her closet."

The letters had indeed been typewritten, but Kim still wasn't convinced. "What made you think she was writing to me? Did you see what she'd typed?"

"I didn't see. She snatched it out of the typewriter and wadded it into a ball, but right before that, she'd been complaining about you." Quill aimed his attention at Kim to let her know he'd meant her. "Like I said, that was when we were still together, still trying to make things work between us, and Rowena wasn't happy that you were pressing her to file charges against me for…a disagreement me and her had."

The "disagreement" was Quill had blackened both of Rowena's eyes and dislocated her shoulder. When Rowena had gone to the hospital, they'd reported the injuries, and Kim had indeed tried to talk the woman into filing charges after Grayson, who was then sheriff, had failed to convince her to do that.

"When did this happen?" Theo demanded. "When did you see Rowena typing the letter?"

Quill's forehead creased. "A few years back. Maybe four or five years ago."

The letters had begun arriving six years ago, around the same time Kim had started working in the district attorney's office, so the timing could fit. *Could.* But there was another possibility.

"You could have used the typewriter as well," Kim pointed out, knowing it would earn her a glare and a denial.

It did. Quill's reaction was fast and filled with instant venom. Oh, yes, he had a quick trigger on that temper.

"I'm trying to help you," Quill snapped, "and you accuse me of something I didn't do."

She shrugged. "It was merely an observation since you admitted you knew the location of the typewriter."

More anger came, and this time his nostrils actually flared, making her think of that bull about to charge the waving red flag. "This conversation is over." He turned and headed down the porch steps.

"Sorry about that," Kim muttered to Theo as they watched Quill storm his way to the waiting cruiser.

"Not to worry. It was good to see his reaction to being accused of writing those letters."

It was, but Kim wished she had a magic lie detector to know if Quill had indeed written them, if Rowena had, or if neither of them had had anything to do with it.

"When will you bring Rowena in for questioning?" Kim asked.

"Soon," Theo assured her. "But first I'll get a warrant to pick up the typewriter from her house. I don't want to alert her to what's going on in case she decides to toss it somewhere."

"Good point. But even if she did write them, it doesn't mean she actually had anything to do with the murders and Faith's kidnapping."

"No," Theo agreed. He didn't shut the door until Quill was in the cruiser with Jesse and they'd driven away. "Finish packing while I get the warrant started," he said, taking out his phone to do that. "Then let's get your things to my place, and we can work from there for a while until we have both the typewriter and Rowena in custody."

Kim got moving, but she felt her anxiety rise some more. Not solely because of the worry of going back outside where they could end up in the path of the shooter but because she was going to Theo's.

A place she'd avoided.

Then again, she could say the same for Theo. But it wasn't possible to avoid him now, not with the danger bearing down on them. Besides, they wouldn't actually be alone for long since Faith would be joining them as soon as she was released from the hospital.

By the time she'd gathered the rest of her things and gone back to the door, Theo had obviously finished his call about the warrant for the typewriter because he was now talking to his head ranch hand, Rusty Chavez. She heard him mention Rusty's name along with giving the hands instructions for the security measures he needed at the ranch.

"We're all set," Theo told her once he'd finished the call. He stopped, took a deep breath. The kind of breath a man took when he was steeling himself up. "I want to swing by Nadia's and check on Jack. I know it's risky—"

"It's something you need to do," she interrupted. She didn't have to be a parent to know how much Theo loved his son. "If you think it'll be awkward for me to be in the cruiser when you do that, I can wait at the sheriff's office or at your place."

Kim saw some of the tension ease from his face, but there was still plenty of worry and concern in his eyes. Worry no doubt because going anywhere could mean making themselves easier targets.

"It'll be awkward no matter what we do," he said, and she knew he was talking about more than just this visit. "But if you're in the cruiser, it'll save time. We can go straight from Nadia's to my place."

She nodded, well aware that he hadn't spelled out that he'd also have to tell Nadia about his houseguest, one who always spurred a mountain of jealousy for his ex. Yep. Theo had needed that steeling-up breath he'd taken.

"You can use your phone to lock up?" he asked as he picked up her suitcase.

"I can." She grabbed her purse and her laptop bag while she pulled up the app to do that. The moment they were on the porch, she secured the house, and they hurried to the cruiser.

"I'll need to go to Nadia's before heading to my place," Theo relayed to Nelline before he made a call to Ava to check for updates.

Nadia's house wasn't far—nothing was "far" in Silver Creek—but Kim decided to spend the five minutes that it would take to get there texting Hudson. She asked for a price quote on a security camera for Rowena's house. It might turn out to be unnecessary if they found out that Rowena had planted the dead rat. Still, there was a good chance that the woman was innocent of any wrongdoing and that Quill had simply wanted to stir up trouble for her with his accusations.

Kim thought back through the letters she'd gotten over the years. If the typewriter that Quill had mentioned actually existed, it could be tested, and a match would point the finger at both Quill and Rowena. However, since the letters had been postmarked from all over Texas, it might be possible to track the couple's whereabouts during those dates.

She got a quick reply from Hudson on the price just as the deputy pulled the cruiser into the driveway at Nadia's. The house was on a quiet street just on the edge of town, and Kim immediately spotted the cruiser. She recalled that Deputy Norris was doing protection detail, but since he wasn't in the cruiser, that hopefully meant he was inside.

"I won't be long," Theo muttered as he got out.

Obviously, Norris had either heard the approaching vehicle or Theo had alerted him to the visit because the deputy opened the door before Theo even reached it. The angle was right for Kim to also see Nadia. She was standing back, holding Jack, and the moment the little boy saw Theo, he shouted out a very happy, "Daddy." Theo went to him, pulling his son into his arms for a long hug.

Kim felt something she didn't want to feel. A longing. She'd always wanted a child, but she hadn't wanted to go the single parent route, and she had never met a man she loved enough to marry.

Well, she had met him, but he had been off limits.

She sighed and admitted to herself that she could have loved Theo enough if the past hadn't always come between them. If they'd both been able to get beyond the grief and loss of that night. However, that grief and loss seemed to be healing now that Faith had returned. That didn't mean they had a clear road ahead though. No. And she got proof of that when she looked at Nadia again.

The woman was staring at her, and while Kim couldn't hear what she was saying to Theo, she figured it was some unpleasant comment because Theo had just informed her that Kim would be his houseguest. Kim didn't want his ex's jealousy playing into her feelings for Theo.

But it did.

Because, in turn, the jealousy could cause more tensions between Nadia and Theo. No way did Kim want that when a precious little boy would be caught in the middle.

Theo handed Jack back to Nadia and, giving Jack a kiss on the cheek, he turned and walked out of the house. Nadia managed to shoot Kim one last glare before the deputy shut the front door.

Kim didn't say anything to Theo when he returned to the cruiser and they started the drive to his ranch. There was nothing to say. She'd apologized so many times for Nadia's feelings toward her, but another "I'm so sorry" wasn't going to fix this. Maybe nothing would.

And that riled her.

Kim didn't care much for that jab of anger, either, but it was there, and she admitted something else to herself. She resented Nadia's totally unwarranted jealousy. Or at least it had been until today. Until today, Theo and she hadn't kissed. They'd kept their hands off each other. But since Kim didn't like lying to herself, she figured there'd be more kissing. And worse, Theo and she would just end up growing closer and closer.

She forced her thoughts off Theo and kept watch out the windows as they drove. Even though this wasn't that far out of town, it was very much in the country. There were woods on each side of the road, and those woods soon turned to pastures as they approached Theo's ranch, Willow Woods—a name he'd taken from the ranch where his mom had been raised.

Nelline took the turn off the road and Theo's house soon came into view. Definitely not small like her own house. This was a two-story Victorian that had once belonged to a family with four kids. Since Theo had bought the place after Nadia and he had divorced, Kim figured he hadn't had more children in mind, not in the near future anyway, but he'd wanted plenty of room for Jack and the horses he boarded, bred, raised and trained.

Kim spotted one of the ranch hands delivering hay to the livestock in the front pasture. The guy was armed, and he immediately looked up, no doubt to make sure it wasn't a gunman trying to get onto the grounds. There was a second hand, also armed, near the front of the house.

"You can drop us off and head back to the office," Theo told the deputy. "See what you can do to hurry the search warrant I've got started for Rowena's house, and if the woman comes into the station before I get back there, call me first so I can give you some interview questions."

"Will do," the deputy assured him and, when she pulled to a stop in front of his house, Theo disengaged the locks and Kim and he hurried up the steps. The moment they were safely inside, he reset the security system.

It wasn't the first time she'd been here. She'd come years ago back in high school because she'd dated a boy who'd lived here, but Kim had avoided the place after Theo bought it.

"Wow," she muttered. "You've redecorated and removed some walls." She stopped, gave a nervous laugh. "Or someone did in the past sixteen years."

"I did," he verified, following her sweeping glance around

the now open floor plan. "I wanted to be able to keep an eye on Jack when I was getting his meals ready."

Well, he'd accomplished that. Theo had gone for a caramel-leather sectional in the living area and a massive eat-in kitchen. Since Kim counted six bins of toys, she figured this was an area where Jack played a lot.

"How much grief did Nadia give you about me staying here?" Kim came out and asked as they shrugged off their coats. They placed them on the rack next to the foyer table, and she shifted both her purse and her laptop bag to her shoulder.

The corner of his mouth lifted for just a moment before he sighed. "Some. She knows it's the smart thing to do to have you here though."

Yes, Nadia probably did know that, but it would still sting for her. That reminder gave Kim another flick of annoyance that she hoped she could tamp down before Theo saw it.

She failed.

"I'm stating the obvious, but her reaction bothers me, too," Theo volunteered. He paused a heartbeat. "It bothers me even more that I've accommodated her jealousy for years. I should have tried harder to tamp it down."

Kim nearly said that no tamping would have fixed that, but instead she focused on what Theo hadn't said. Was he wishing he'd pushed Nadia to end this jealousy stuff so he could move on with his personal life?

When their gazes connected, Kim realized she was right. And Theo wanted that moving on to include her. She wanted that as well. Mercy, did she. But the timing was as bad as it could get for them to dive into an actual relationship. Still, she felt the heat slide over her when his gaze lowered to her mouth.

"If we kiss right now, it wouldn't stay just a kiss," she pointed out.

The corner of his mouth lifted again, but this time it was a real smile. A short-lived one, though, followed by a groan of frustration. "True, and I need to go through a whole bunch of reports that have been coming in over the past hour." He tipped his head to the kitchen. "Help yourself to anything in the fridge. There's stuff to make sandwiches."

She wasn't hungry, but it occurred to her they should both eat. If she made some sandwiches, Theo might eat one as well. However, when she went into the kitchen, she spotted something on the counter that had her coming to a stop. There was a stack of file folders, and she recognized the one that was open. Because she had a copy of the same file.

"These are from your parents' murders," she muttered. Since he hadn't been back home since they'd found Faith, it meant he'd been digging into it before he'd even known his sister was alive.

Theo made a sound of agreement and walked closer, looking down at one of the crime scene photos with her. It was a shot of the blood smears on the white-tiled kitchen floor. There'd been no recoverable foot or shoe prints, but the killer had walked through that blood either shortly after committing the murders or else on his way out of the house once he'd had Faith.

"Sometimes in my dreams, I can fix it before it happens," Theo said, his voice tight, and there was regret—oh, so much regret—on his face. "Sometimes, I can stop him."

She echoed his sigh with one of her own because that was true for her as well. But those were rare dreams. Mostly, she got the nightmares.

Kim risked touching his arm with just her fingertips, and she rubbed gently, hoping it would soothe him in some small way. It did. His eyes were less troubled when he looked at her, but she immediately saw another round of the blasted heat, too. Muttering some profanity, she pulled back her hand because she hadn't lied when she had insisted a kiss wouldn't just stop at a kiss. Her body and mind were primed for Theo, and while she might get to have him down the road, it couldn't be now.

She repeated that to herself several times.

Finally, she forced her gaze off him, and Theo obviously did the same because he motioned to the stairs. "Come on, we can put your things in the guest room."

Kim followed him, trying to ignore the incredible view of his backside as they made their way up the steps. She truly did have a bad case of Theo-itis.

When they reached the top of the stairs, he opened the door of the first room on the right. The room, which was actually a suite with a sitting area and bathroom, didn't disappoint with the décor in varying shades of blue.

"My room is just across the hall," he said.

"So, if I get tempted, I won't have far to go," she blurted out before she realized what she was going to say. Kim so wished she'd just kept her mouth closed, but at least it caused Theo to smile again.

"That works both ways," he reminded her, setting down her suitcase. "Once you're settled, you really should get something to eat."

He turned, wisely so, as if ready to leave, but his phone rang. Theo told her it was Ava and answered.

"You're on speaker," he informed Ava. "And Kim is with me."

"Good, because this is something you'll both want to hear. Grayson has been doing some digging, and he found something on Greg."

"Is this about his financial troubles?" Theo asked.

"No, this is about something that happened twenty-one years ago, on the day before your parents were murdered."

That got Kim's attention. Obviously, Theo's, too, and she saw his jaw muscles stir. "I'm listening," Theo assured her.

"The day before the murders, Greg was involved in a minor car accident," the deputy explained. "The fender bender happened just two miles from your parents' ranch."

Chapter Eleven

Two miles.

Those two words had repeated through Theo's head for nearly twenty-four hours now. Ever since Ava had told him about the report Grayson had found, proving that Greg had been in the vicinity near the time of the murders and Faith's kidnapping.

That meant Greg had had the means, motive and opportunity to have carried out the crimes.

The problem was Theo hadn't been able to question Greg about it because, according to Duran, Greg had ended up in an ER in San Antonio with a stomach bug. Theo had confirmed the man's visit to the ER, had also confirmed that the ER doctor had advised Greg to isolate for twenty-four hours in case he was contagious.

Maybe Greg was faking, but with Duran fighting the demand for an interview, Theo knew he was going to have to wait a little while longer to get the answers he needed. Still, Greg and Duran couldn't indefinitely put off talking to him, and that's why they'd agreed, finally, to come into the sheriff's office today around eleven.

Two hours from now.

Greg and Duran wouldn't be the only ones in interrogation either. Pending the results of the GSR test, Quill would be as well. Rowena was also on the schedule. Theo was hoping that by the time of her interview, they'd have the results back from the typewriter confiscated from her house. Even without that, though, Theo still wanted to know if the woman had had any part in sending those letters to Kim. He was getting conflicting stories from Quill and Rowena, and it was time for one or both of them to spill the truth.

Of course, all those interviews meant he'd be going to the sheriff's office. It also meant taking Kim with him since he doubted she'd want to stay at his place while all of their suspects were being questioned. Besides, Quill's and Rowena's statements could be relevant to the trial that was now only two days away. The trial itself paled, though, in comparison to the danger that Kim, Faith and he were facing, but it was still important because Quill had to pay for what he'd done.

Theo turned toward the movement on the stairs and he got a quick jolt of adrenaline before he convinced his body that it wasn't a threat.

It was Kim.

A different kind of threat, and he got a different kind of jolt. One of the sizzling heat.

Somehow, Theo had managed to stop himself from going to her room the night before, but he wasn't sure he wanted to stop himself from kissing her. He might have done exactly that if she hadn't dropped a dollar bill on the counter next to his mug of coffee.

"I know it's normally a penny for your thoughts," she said, "but I figured you've got way more than a penny's worth."

"I do," he admitted, and he watched as she went to the coffeepot to help herself to a cup.

Maybe because of all the interviews stacked up, she'd opted not for jeans but black pants and a silver-gray sweater that was almost the same color as her eyes. She also hadn't pulled back her long dark brown hair but instead had it falling onto her shoulders.

"Well?" she asked. "Do I get my dollar's worth on you sharing those thoughts?"

He wouldn't be spilling about this heat or about the way he kept noticing everything about her body. Instead, he focused on the investigation and was sorry there hadn't been a lot of progress in that area.

"Still no ID or anything else on the shooter," Theo relayed. "The lab is working on the typewriter."

She nodded as if that's what she'd expected to hear. "I saw a cruiser pull up earlier in front of the house. Anything wrong?"

"No. I had the deputies drop off a cruiser for us to use. I'm short-staffed because of the protection details at the hospital and Nadia's, and I figured I'd get two of the ranch hands to follow us into town when we have to leave."

"Good idea. Speaking of the hospital, I called Faith this morning. She had a restless night, but she's hoping to be released from the hospital today."

Theo definitely hadn't forgotten about that, and moving Faith to his house was a biggie on his to-do list. He'd need to time her release, though, for when he was finished with the initial interviews.

"Thanks for calling her," Theo said.

Kim shrugged. "I figured it'd ease some of the awkwardness if Faith and I had talked before she gets thrown into the thick of things."

Awkwardness. Yes, that was the word for it. Even though he knew the woman in the hospital was his sister, Theo was still plenty uneasy about her.

"I didn't mention anything to Faith about Greg being in-

volved in a car accident right before your folks were killed,"
Kim went on as she drank her coffee. "But I did ask her
if she recalled Greg ever talking about Silver Creek or her
parents. Not the recent stuff over the memories she was getting back. I wanted to know if it was something he brought
up years ago. She said she didn't remember anything like
that, but that she'd give it some thought."

Good. If Faith could recall Greg mentioning anything
about that, then Theo could maybe use it in the interview.
Talking about an incident like that wasn't a crime, but coupled with Greg being in the area around the time of the murders could possibly be enough circumstantial evidence to
threaten Greg with an arrest.

"There's plenty of breakfast stuff in the fridge," he offered just as his phone rang. Theo actually smiled when he
saw Nadia's name on the screen because he knew this call
would be from Jack. His son had gotten into the habit of
phoning Theo nearly every morning.

"Daddy," Jack greeted the moment Theo answered the
call.

"Good morning, buddy." Theo held back on asking how
he was, but he'd listen for any signs of tension in the boy's
voice. "What'd you have for breakfast?"

"Marsh-a-mellos," he quickly provided. Definitely no
tension. Just happiness and excitement. But Theo was puzzled by the food choice.

"You didn't have marshmallows for breakfast," Nadia
corrected in the background. "You got one mini marshmal-
low for using the potty. You had spinach, eggs and biscuits
for breakfast."

"A pink marsh-a-mello," Jack happily added. "Yummy."

Theo smiled again. Maybe the treats would help with the
potty training process. "Are you playing with Miss Maya

today?" Maya was the nanny, and since Jack wouldn't be going anywhere for security reasons, Theo suspected the nanny would have lots of indoor activities planned.

"Yep," Jack confirmed. "Playin', readin' books, marsh-a-mellos."

"Marshmallows only if you use the potty," Nadia interjected. "And let me talk to your dad when you're done."

Apparently, Jack was done because he muttered a quick "I love you, Daddy," and Theo heard him handing off the phone to Nadia.

"Jack, go read your books over by the sofa," Nadia instructed, and Theo knew she was probably trying to get the boy out of hearing range. "Are you actually going to arrest Rowena?" she demanded a few moments later. "She called here, all upset, saying you had cops search her house and that you were going to lock her up."

Theo sighed. "I'm questioning her in a couple of hours. At this point, I have no plans for an arrest." That would change, though, if he found out that Rowena had been harassing Kim all these years with those letters.

"Did you search her house because of something Quill did?" Nadia pressed.

"Sorry, but I can't get into that with you." Theo didn't want Nadia and Rowena discussing the letters or the typewriter since it could give Rowena opportunity to construct a story that might keep her out of hot water.

Even though Nadia didn't voice her protest of being shut out of this, Theo could practically feel her disapproval coming through the phone line.

"There's a lot of talk about this," Nadia finally said. "Talk of Faith's return, too."

Again, it was what Nadia didn't say, but there was probably talk of Kim staying with him at his place as well.

There'd been rumors about Kim and him for years, rumors that they were some kind of star-crossed lovers, and this situation would no doubt bring on more of that kind of talk.

"The deputy's still there with you, right?" Theo asked, already knowing the answer, but he wanted to shift the conversation.

"Yes," Nadia responded after a long pause. Then she paused again. "I have some paperwork I need to do. Jack?" she called out. "It's time to say goodbye to your dad."

Theo heard the sound of running footsteps, and a few seconds later, his son came on the line. "'Bye, Daddy. You get marsh-a-mellos for me?"

Despite the awkward conversation with Nadia, he had to smile. "I will, and you'll get them when you use the potty. Have a good day, buddy. I'll see you soon."

Theo ended the call, looked up and saw that Kim was smiling, too. "You're a good dad."

He shrugged but was more than pleased with the compliment. "I try to be."

Theo would have added more about how easy Jack made it for him to be a good dad, but Kim moved closer, and she stunned him by brushing a kiss on his cheek. She'd no doubt meant to keep it chaste, but Kim and chaste just didn't go together.

She started to step back, but Theo moved in to return the kiss. Not on the cheek either. He'd been burning for Kim all night, so his mouth landed on hers. He felt the immediate kick of lust that was always there just beneath the surface. Felt the wash of heat go through him.

And he felt the need for a whole lot more.

The day before, Kim had warned him that a kiss between them wouldn't stay just a kiss, and she was so right.

There was too much need. Too much…everything, and Theo stepped in even closer so he could deepen the kiss.

She responded with a throaty moan and fumbled around to set her coffee on the counter. He soon learned that was to free up her hands so she could take hold of him and pull him to her. Body to body.

Oh, man. He was toast.

The touching and kissing caused the heat to skyrocket, and as Kim had predicted, things quickly got out of hand. Grappling for position, he turned Kim so that her back landed against the rim of the counter, and he pressed himself to her.

She moaned again, the sound of need and pleasure, and he felt his body pressure him to keep taking more, more, more. Mercy, he wanted more. He wanted Kim. But he had just a shred of logic and sanity left to remind him that the timing for this still sucked.

Theo might have ignored that shred, might have started getting Kim naked, but his phone rang again. His first thought was that it was Jack calling back because he'd forgotten to tell Theo something, but when he was able to focus, it was Ava's name on the screen.

He cursed, and even though Kim didn't voice any profanity, her groan was filled with disappointment—and some shreds of her own logic and sanity. Theo cleared his throat. Tried to clear his head, too, and he answered.

"Please tell me none of our suspects has tried to cancel their interviews," Theo greeted.

"No, just the opposite. Greg and Duran just showed up and asked if they could talk to you earlier than planned. Apparently, they have other business to take care of and wanted to get this out of the way."

Interesting. That shook off some of the mental haze left

over from the scalding kiss. Maybe Greg had learned that Ashley was Faith. Or the man could have realized they'd find out about the car accident he'd had in Silver Creek and thought it would make him look like less of a suspect if he got all of that out in the open.

Theo glanced at Kim, silently questioning if she was ready to go. She gave him a nod and went to the front of the house to get her purse and coat.

"Kim and I are on the way," Theo explained to Ava. "I want Kim to observe all the interviews today." No need for him to spell out that Kim had a vested interest in anything and everything that might be said.

"Of course. I'll make sure the camera feed is set up so she can view it in your office."

The camera feed, a replacement for the old two-way glass, was a recent update. It allowed multiple people to watch at once, and in addition to Kim, Theo texted Grayson to have him observe the feed from home. Since Grayson had been the primary investigator of Theo's parents' murders, he would no doubt want to hear what Greg had to say about that car accident.

Theo sent another text to the ranch hands, the ones that Theo had chosen to follow Kim and him to the station. Since the hands were already on guard duty out front, they were waiting in a truck parked behind the cruiser.

Thankfully, it wasn't nearly as cold as it had been the day before, but the wind still had a bite to it. That was yet another reason to hurry inside the cruiser. The main reason, though, was so a sniper wouldn't be given a chance to try to kill them again.

"I don't want you to apologize for that kiss," Kim insisted as they drove away from the ranch. The truck with the hands was right behind them and, despite the conversation that Kim had launched right into, Theo knew they were all keeping watch.

"I wasn't," he assured her and gave her a quick glance to let her know when the opportunity arose, he'd kiss her again. "Once I've arrested the shooter and the danger is over, I also plan on letting Nadia know that I intend to start seeing you. It's long overdue," he tacked onto that.

She made a quick sound of agreement, but Theo knew this was going to cause some conflict with Nadia. No way to avoid that, though, and he was tired of tip-toeing around his ex's feelings when it came to Kim. He wanted to be with Kim and, judging from that kiss, she wanted the same thing.

Theo had to push all such thoughts aside when he pulled to a stop in front of the sheriff's office, but the idea of actually taking Kim on a date was yet another reason for him to plow forward in this investigation and arrest the person who'd fired those shots at them.

The moment they got inside the sheriff's office, Theo spotted Greg and Duran. Even though they'd come in early for the interview, it was obvious they were impatient and maybe even riled that he hadn't been there to accommodate them. Theo didn't accommodate them now either. He spared them both warning glances and ushered Kim into his office.

As expected, Ava was there, and she was setting up the camera feed on Theo's computer. "You want me in the interview with you?" Ava asked him.

Theo shook his head. "Both Rowena and Quill are coming in, and I'd like you to be out here to make sure they don't get into one of their altercations. If Quill makes any wrong move, even a minor one, arrest him."

Ava assured him that she would be happy to do that, and while she showed Kim how to work the camera feed, Theo motioned for Greg and Duran to follow him into the interview room.

"I brought a copy of the medical report for my client's visit to the ER," Duran said as they walked. "Just in case you doubted that he'd been sick."

"I've already verified he was there." But Theo took the report anyway just in case there was anything in it to indicate Greg had faked the illness.

"I also need to tell you about an incident that happened twenty-one years ago," Greg volunteered the moment they stepped into the interview room. "It just didn't occur to me to mention it before now. It has nothing to do with your investigation, but I thought it might come up in a background check, and I didn't want you to jump to the wrong assumption."

Theo held up his hand to stop the man from continuing and read Greg his Miranda rights again just to make sure Duran couldn't squawk later about his client not understanding that he might have been incriminating himself by offering up this info. He also didn't pull back on the flat look he gave Greg because Theo figured it had indeed occurred to the man to perhaps *mention* it before now. Of course, Greg hadn't because it would make him look guilty of some kind of participation in the murders and Faith's kidnapping.

"Twenty-one years ago, my client was involved in a minor vehicular accident near Silver Creek," Duran spoke up once Greg had been Mirandized. "We understand the timing of that accident could make you—"

"Jump to the wrong assumption," Theo interrupted. "Well, I've already jumped." He leveled his stare on Greg to finish what he had to say. "You were in the vicinity of a double murder, home invasion and kidnapping. Added to that, you've admitted to being close friends with the couple who illegally adopted the kidnapped child. In fact, you were engaged to her."

"*Am* engaged," Greg corrected.

Theo didn't respond. He just stared at the man until Greg huffed.

"I still love Ashley, and as far as I know, she's my fiancée," Greg insisted. "Of course, I haven't been able to personally confirm that because you're refusing to let me see her." Duran and he exchanged glances. "Is she still claiming to be your sister?"

"She *is* my sister," Theo said, and he studied both of the men's expressions. No surprise whatsoever for Duran, but there was plenty in Greg's eyes. Surprise, though, could be faked.

"You have proof of that?" Greg wanted to know.

"I do." Theo threw it out there, and then he paused. He wanted Greg to squirm over the possibility that Faith had remembered who she was. And that she could identify him as the man who'd taken her.

Greg did some squirming all right, and Theo was pretty sure that was fear he saw go through the man's eyes. He'd have to quell that fear soon, though, because he didn't want Greg or Duran going after Faith to try to silence her. Still, he could hold off a couple of minutes before he spilled that Faith couldn't identify her kidnapper, and in those minutes maybe Greg would confess to the crimes.

"She's Faith," Greg muttered. He was examining Theo's expression, as well, and that's why Theo kept on his cop's face, which he knew would be hard for Greg to read.

"Ashley... Faith is aware of who she is?" Duran asked.

Theo nodded. Waited. He hoped either Duran or Greg would want to fill the uncomfortable silence with something Theo could use to make an arrest.

"Well," Greg finally said. His breathing was rushed now, and he scrubbed his hand over his face. "She was right after all."

Again, Theo just settled for a nod.

"This means it's even more important that I speak to her," Greg went on. "She'll need help trying to come to terms with this."

"My sister is getting help." Theo kept his voice flat. Kept his intense stare on the man.

"But she'll want to see me," Greg insisted. "I'm sure she's asked to see me."

Theo shook his head. "No, Faith doesn't want to see you."

There. It was like a gauntlet being thrown, and Theo hoped it would cause Greg to verbally explode. It might have done exactly that if Duran hadn't taken hold of his client's arm. Duran gave Greg a squeeze that was no doubt a warning for him to stay quiet.

Greg heeded the warning, but Theo could see him wrestling with the reins he had on his temper. "Faith will want to see me once she's thinking straight. She knows how much I love her." He paused now, his gaze coming back to Theo. "She remembers what happened to her that night your parents were killed?"

Apparently, those minutes of watching Greg squirm were up. "Faith doesn't remember." Theo spelled it out. "Well, she doesn't remember anything other than what she's already told you. She did tell you about the memory flashes she's been having, right?"

"Of course," Greg readily answered. He shook his head and seemed to be frustrated with himself. "I didn't believe her. I thought the flashes were simply things she'd picked up when she was reading all those articles about your parents' murders. She was obsessed with them."

And that brought Theo back to the reason Greg was in the interview room. "Explain why you were near Silver Creek less than twenty-four hours prior to those murders and Faith's kidnapping."

Greg didn't get defensive, nor did he hesitate, which meant he'd already figured out how to put the best spin on this. If there was a best spin, that is. "I was visiting a friend in Wimberly, and I got lost," he stated.

Theo was certain his look turned skeptical. "Wimberly," he repeated. "That's over twenty miles from Silver Creek."

Greg gave a quick nod. "Like I said, I got lost, and it took me a while to find a place so I could turn around."

"I know the area where you had your accident," Theo pointed out. "There have been ranch trails out there for over a hundred years. Plenty of places to turn around."

"Plenty if you're familiar with the area," Duran quickly interjected. "Greg wasn't. He was lost, and his friend's address wasn't showing up on the GPS."

There was a notepad and pen on the table, and Theo slid both toward Greg. "Write down the name and contact info for your friend."

"I don't have it. Uh, I mean I don't know how to get in touch with him." He stopped and huffed. "For Pete's sake, it was twenty-one years ago."

Theo kept staring at him. "Then, write down his name, and I'll contact him to verify you were indeed supposed to visit him that day at that time."

"He didn't know about the visit," Greg insisted. "And after I got lost and went home, I didn't tell him I'd tried to go see him."

"Convenient," Theo muttered. "Write down his name anyway. I'll talk to him and ask if you two had the kind of friendship where you would have just showed up unannounced at his place."

Something went through Greg's eyes. Panic, maybe. Perhaps even fear. And that's when Theo knew the guy was lying about why he'd been on that road near Silver Creek.

It was possible Greg just wanted to say something, anything, that would take him off the suspect list for a double murder. People lied for all sorts of reasons. However, the circumstantial evidence was starting to stack up. It still wasn't enough for a warrant, but after chatting with the friend whose name Greg finally wrote down, Theo might be able to build a case against him.

When Greg passed the notepad with the name back to him, Theo looked up at the surveillance camera. "Deputy Lawson, contact a man named Jason Pennington who lived in Wimberly twenty-one years ago. I need to speak to him right away."

"Even if Mr. Pennington doesn't remember Greg's account of things," Duran spoke up, "it doesn't mean Greg is lying. He didn't know your parents and had no reason to want them dead."

Yeah, he would have had a reason if Faith had been the target that night. "You were twenty-eight when you had that car accident," Theo continued, not verbally addressing what Duran had said, "and shortly thereafter the Neelys adopted Faith." He left it at that and waited to see Greg's reaction.

Greg shoved back the chair, the metal scraping against the tile floor, and he got to his feet. Apparently, he'd lost the wrestling match with his temper. "I had nothing to do with that. Nothing," he repeated. He looked at Duran as if he expected the lawyer to magically produce some kind of evidence that would make him innocent.

Duran cleared his throat and pinned his attention to Theo.

"I'm assuming you have no evidence to indicate Greg's participation in the crimes of twenty-one years ago, or you would have already charged him."

Theo shrugged. "Evidence could come to light. As we speak, I have deputies going over the adoption papers, and they're talking to the Neelys' neighbors and friends. We'll keep digging until we find out who kidnapped my sister and took her to the Neelys." He leaned in, meeting Greg eye to eye. "Because whoever helped with that is also connected to two murders."

Some of the color drained from Greg's face and he eased back down into the chair. "Has Faith said something about the adoption? Has she accused me?" But he didn't wait for Theo to deny it. "Because she could be lying. Faith lies about things, and you can't trust her."

Theo felt the gut punch of emotions that went along with the need to defend and protect his kid sister, even though she was no longer a kid. "Explain what you mean by that," Theo insisted.

Greg opened his mouth, closed it. "Uh, I need to speak privately with my lawyer for a moment. Privately," he emphasized, pointing to the camera.

"I'll turn it off," Theo assured him before he got up and walked out, shutting the door behind him.

Kim was waiting for him in the doorway of his office. "Greg had better not try to put any of the blame on Faith for her own kidnapping," Kim insisted. Obviously, she was feeling a boatload of emotions about Faith, too.

"I won't let him," Theo assured her. He would have added more, but he spotted Rowena walking in.

As usual, the woman looked ready to jump at her own shadow, but Theo had to consider part of that might be an act. Even though Quill wasn't exactly a trustworthy source,

Theo had to at least question Rowena about any part she might have had in taunting Kim.

Rowena's gaze zoomed right in on Theo, and she started toward him. "I haven't used that typewriter in years," she insisted. "You can't arrest me for something I didn't do."

"I'm not arresting you," Theo said, and he motioned for her to come into his office.

Rowena, however, stayed put, and she frantically shook her head. "Quill said you were going to arrest me for writing some letters. I haven't. I swear I haven't."

Theo didn't come out and say he was leaning toward believing her. But he was. "Come into my office, and we can talk. For a couple of minutes anyway. I have someone else in Interview, but once I've finished with him, I can take your statement."

"I need you to clear my name," Rowena demanded. Well, it was a demand for her anyway. She didn't raise her voice, but her tone was more adamant than usual. "I saw Quill using that typewriter. I don't know what he typed on it, but it could have been letters."

Yeah, it could have been, and Quill would absolutely do something like that. Theo would need to check the timing, but it was possible the first letter did indeed coincide with when Kim had started working at the DA's office. With as many run-ins with the law as Quill had had, he would have crossed legal paths with Kim and might have wanted to get back at her for doing her job.

"Sheriff," Theo heard Duran call out. The lawyer rounded the corner and froze.

Rowena froze, too, and her gaze seemed to lock with Duran's. The woman suddenly darted behind Theo.

"Do you two know each other?" Theo asked.

Duran's mouth tightened and he sighed. However, it was Rowena who spoke first.

"Yes, we know each other," the woman muttered, her voice a tangle of nerves and fear. "And I think he might be here to kill me."

Chapter Twelve

Of all the things that Kim had thought Rowena might say, that wasn't one of them. But since the woman was trembling all over, it was obvious she was terrified of the lawyer.

"I have no reason whatsoever to kill you," Duran insisted after he huffed. He definitely wasn't trembling, but he was shooting eye daggers at Rowena.

"But you know each other," Kim pointed out.

"Oh, I know Rowena all right," Duran admitted.

Rowena supplied even more. "Quill worked for him a while back."

Even though *a while back* was plenty vague, Kim's thoughts immediately went to twenty-one years ago. With the rumors of Duran's connections to black market adoptions, Quill would have been a good local source for Duran to find a child for the Neelys.

"When exactly did Quill work for you?" Theo pressed, taking the question right out of Kim's mouth.

Duran muttered a single word of profanity under his breath. "We need to talk."

Kim wanted to curse, as well, and she studied Duran's body language. He didn't appear to be getting ready to flee the scene. Or to confess that he was a cold-blooded killer. But a need to talk probably meant he had some information or at least some speculation about Theo's parents and Faith's abduction.

"You want to talk with or without your client?" Theo asked.

Duran didn't jump to answer and, after several really long moments, he finally said, "With."

Theo nodded and motioned for them all to follow him to the interview room. Kim didn't stay put. She went with them while she heard Ava call out that she'd start the recording again.

Kim expected Duran to object to that, but he didn't. However, he did go into the interview room ahead of them, and he went straight to Greg and whispered something in his ear. Whatever he said caused Greg's eyes to widen, and he shot Rowena a wary glance.

Or Kim thought it might be wariness. There was something she couldn't quite put her finger on, and whatever it was, Rowena must have been feeling some of it, too, because she dropped back a step.

"Best to get this all out in the open," Duran insisted. "Quill did some part-time work about twenty-plus years ago. Just routine things like tracking down witnesses who might be needed to clear a client's name."

"Hired muscle," Kim quickly provided, earning her a glare from Duran. "Quill's size and attitude make him very intimidating."

"I never used intimidation on a witness," Duran countered. "And I never instructed Quill to do that either." He paused, and it looked as if he was trying to rein in his anger. Or come up with an excuse for hiring a known thug. "I hadn't been practicing law for long then, and I couldn't afford anyone better."

"How'd you know about Quill?" Theo asked. "He's never lived in San Antonio."

"I heard about him through a friend, and he only worked for me a couple of months because I was getting too many complaints about him."

No surprise there. Quill's temper wasn't a recent development.

"You said he worked for you twenty-plus years ago," Theo stated. "Specifically, was that twenty-one years ago?"

Now, Duran dragged in a lengthy breath. "Yes." And that was all he said for a long time. "You want to know if Quill could have had some part in your parents' murders and your sister's disappearance, and I have to say it's possible."

"Quill wouldn't have done that," Rowena spoke up. She frantically shook her head. "He wouldn't have killed your parents."

Since the woman didn't address the second part of that, Kim did. "But he might have taken Faith so she could be adopted."

Rowena went sheet-white. "No," she muttered. "No." But everyone in the room had to have heard the doubt in her voice.

"I did the adoption paperwork for the Neelys," Duran went on, "but I didn't get the child for them. There'd be no need for me to do that. I had connections to adoption agencies, and I could have found them a child without having to kidnap one."

"Maybe," Kim agreed. "But you might not have been able to find them a child who looked so much like their late daughter."

That turned Duran's jaw to iron. "I didn't have anything to do with getting them that girl."

"Neither did I," Greg interjected.

Kim was certain Theo's skeptical look matched hers. "Then why were you so close to Silver Creek when Faith was taken?" Theo fired back.

"I've already told you…" Greg stopped, groaned. "I was seeing someone in Silver Creek. A married woman, and I was going to her house."

"So, you lied earlier when you said you were visiting a friend and got lost," Kim pointed out.

"Yes, I lied." There was no remorse in the man's tone, only defiance. "She's still married, still lives here, and I don't want to make things hard for her by bringing up something that happened a lifetime ago. We broke off things shortly after the car accident," Greg added.

Theo opened his mouth and Kim knew he was about to demand the name of the woman, but he stopped. Turned. And his attention landed on Rowena. One look at her, and Kim saw the guilt.

Oh, mercy.

"You had an affair with Greg?" Theo came out and asked.

Rowena shook her head as tears sprang to her eyes, and it didn't take long for the tears to turn to a full sob. "It was a mistake, and I don't want Quill to ever find out about it."

"Quill would kill both of us," Greg added to that. "Even after all this time, he'd kill both of us."

If Quill got the chance, yes, he would. And that's why Kim wanted to sigh. Because all of these statements had to become part of the investigative reports. *Had to*. Rowena and Greg would have to be questioned, would be asked to provide proof they'd been together so it could either corroborate or disprove Greg's claim of innocence in the murders and kidnapping.

And word of that could get back to Quill.

"Deputy Lawson," Theo said looking at the camera, "have Quill brought in right away."

"He'll kill us," Rowena echoed with the tears streaming down her cheeks. "The affair with Greg was a mistake, but Quill won't ever be able to forgive me for it."

"I want you in protective custody," Theo told the woman.

That was a wise move, especially considering that Quill would get some fuel for his temper once he found out he was now connected to the murder of Theo's parents. Even though it was a much lesser charge, Quill would soon find out that he was the most likely suspect for sending those taunting letters. That in itself wouldn't be a serious charge, but all of this was adding up, and it wasn't adding up in Quill's favor.

"You mean like go to a safe house?" Rowena asked just as Greg said, "I need that, too."

Theo ignored Greg and focused on Rowena. "Yes, a safe house, or I can ask the marshals to provide security if you want to stay at your own place."

"I don't want to be at my place where Quill can find me," Rowena answered in a whisper.

"I need a safe house," Greg demanded, his voice a lot louder this time.

"Hush," Theo warned him. "You're not going anywhere until you've made a full and correct statement as to your whereabouts at the time of the murders and kidnapping. Lie again," Theo said, his voice hardening even more, "and I'll toss you in a cell."

"My client will give you an honest account of that time," Duran spoke up.

There was some hardness in his voice, too. Maybe because he was trying to save Greg from being charged with murder. Maybe because the lawyer was just trying to put a quick end to this so he could get out of there without having to answer too many more questions about Faith's adoption.

But there would be questions.

Hard ones. And every word of the adoption Duran had done for the Neelys would be examined.

Kim turned when she heard the footsteps in the hall. Theo did, too, and he was obviously primed for a threat or attack because he moved his hand to his gun. No threat though. It was Ava. She motioned for Kim and Theo to step out into the hall with her.

"Gage just called from the hospital," Ava said, keeping her voice at a whisper. "Faith is ready to be released, and she's asking for the two of you to pick her up right away. She says she's scared and doesn't want to be there any longer."

Theo groaned softly and dragged his hand over his face. The timing wasn't exactly ideal, and both of them knew that.

"Jesse and Nelline are in the squad room, so let us mop up here for you," Ava volunteered. "Jesse can help with the interviews, and Nelline can go with you to the hospital."

"But Quill needs to be brought in," Theo reminded her.

Ava nodded. "I just tried to call him, and he's not answering his phone, but I'll arrange for another deputy to go out to his place, and if he's there, he'll be brought in. After I call the marshals for a safe house, or two—" she gave Greg a quick glance "—I can take the statements of these three while you go deal with your sister."

"I'll call the marshals." Theo compromised after glancing at his watch. "One safe house for now for Rowena. They'll move fast on that because of Quill's history with her. Did Quill get his car from Kim's?"

Ava nodded. Then, she sighed, and Kim knew why.

That meant Quill could be anywhere right now since he had a vehicle.

"We got back the results from Quill's GSR," Ava added. "Negative."

Theo huffed. A positive would have been grounds for an arrest, but a negative meant pretty much nothing. Quill could have still fired those shots and managed not to get an GSR on him if he'd worn gloves or used a rifle.

"After you've given your statement to Deputy Lawson," Theo said, turning toward Greg, "she'll decide if charges will be filed against you. If not," Theo continued over Greg's howl of protest, "then I'll see about a safe house for you, too."

Duran put his hand on Greg's arm, but he aimed his glare at Theo. "Since it'd be a travesty if my client were to be charged with anything, I believe he'll soon be leaving Silver Creek. I have a place where he can stay and be safe in case Quill decides to, well, be Quill."

Since Theo stayed put, Kim figured he was having a debate with himself about all of these arrangements. But there was also the fact that his sister was waiting for him to come and get her. A sister who was terrified but might also be able to provide them answers as to what had happened the night of her abduction. It was possible that, with some questioning, Faith would be able to clue them into the identity of the person who'd taken her. That, in turn, could help them arrest the person who was trying to kill them now.

Because Kim was convinced it was the same person.

Or someone connected to the same person.

That didn't rule out any of their suspects. Quill, Greg or Duran. Heck, it didn't rule out Rowena assisting, either, especially if she'd been romantically involved with Greg at the time. If Greg had asked his lover to help, she might have done it even though Kim couldn't see the waif-like Rowena hauling an eight-year-old child down a flight of stairs and out of the house.

Theo finally got moving after telling Ava to call him immediately if Quill showed up or if Duran and Greg gave her any trouble with the rest of the interviews. Considering that Duran and Greg both wanted to get the heck out of there, they might cooperate. Of course, there were no guarantees they'd tell the truth either.

"I wish I had enough to hold Greg and Duran," Theo muttered as they made their way to the front of the police station.

So did she, but Kim couldn't imagine getting an arrest warrant with what they had. They needed physical evidence or a confession to add to the circumstantial.

As Ava had said, Jesse was in the squad room, and he was on the phone. "Trying to track down Quill," he informed them.

Theo gave him a nod of approval and went to the door where Nelline was waiting to drive with them to the hospital. Since Theo likely wouldn't want to bring Faith back to the sheriff's office, that meant they'd be going straight to his place where he might get a chance to listen to the interviews if they were still going on by then.

"How many lies do you think Greg has told us?" Theo muttered after they'd all gotten in the cruiser.

"Well, he lied about why he was so near Silver Creek, but I think that's just the tip of the iceberg," Kim said. "At minimum, I believe he also knew the Neelys had illegally adopted Faith. His association with Quill and Duran likely means he was involved with what happened, even if it was some level of accessory after the fact."

Theo made a quick sound of agreement. "They could all

be in on it, and if so, all of them will pay. I'll make sure of it."

Even after all these years, his need for justice hadn't waned one bit. Neither had hers, and Kim was hoping that if they finally found the person or persons responsible, she might be able to get through a week without having nightmares.

As with their other trip to the hospital, Nelline parked right by the ER doors. According to one of the updates Theo had gotten yesterday, the crime scene tape had been removed shortly after the bomb squad had cleared the building, and with it gone, there were no signs of the shooting that'd happened nearly twenty-four hours earlier. But Theo and Kim were well aware of it and that's why they didn't waste any time being outside.

They went straight to Faith's room, where a reserve deputy, Mike Gonzales, was standing guard. When they went in, they found Faith not in the bed but pacing the small room. She wasn't near the windows but rather using the very narrow space between the bed and the bathroom.

"You came," she blurted out. The relief eased some of the tight muscles in her face. "I was worried you wouldn't."

"Of course, we came." Theo went to her and pulled her into a hug. Not exactly a natural one since both of them looked a little stiff. Still, it was a hug, and Kim was hoping it would soothe them some.

"I'm going to your house, right?" Faith asked. "And you'll be there?" she added to Kim.

Kim made a quick sound of agreement and gave Faith her own hug once Theo had stepped back. "I'll stay as long as Theo and you want me there." That, Kim was hoping, would be until they'd caught the killer.

Faith let out a quick breath of relief. "Good. And Greg won't be able to see me, right?"

"Right," Theo confirmed. "Greg and Duran are at the sheriff's office right now." He paused, no doubt trying to decide how much to tell her. Faith didn't look exactly steady, and none of the recent revelations was going to help with that unsteadiness. "Greg admitted to being near Silver Creek at the time of your kidnapping. Is there any chance he was the one who carried you out of the house that night?"

Faith made a strangled sound and pressed her hand to her heart as if to steady it. "Greg wouldn't have done that." She paused, her breath shuddering. "Would he?" She repeated that while catching on to Theo's arm.

He looked his sister straight in the eyes. "I'm not sure, but it's possible."

Faith began to frantically shake her head. "If it'd been him, I would have known. I would have felt…something." She stopped again, and this time pressed her fingertips to her trembling mouth. "Oh, God."

Kim figured that Faith's thoughts were whirling right now. Whirling with possibilities she didn't want to accept. After all, she had gotten engaged to Greg, so that meant she had at least some feelings for him. Had maybe even loved him. If he'd been the one who'd kidnapped her, then this was the worst kind of betrayal. Added to that, it also meant Greg might have had some part in her parents' murders.

"All this time I trusted him," Faith muttered, and she sank down on the foot of the bed. The tears pooled in her eyes. Eyes that she turned up to Theo. "I have to tell you something. Something you aren't going to like. God, Theo. I'm so sorry."

Kim felt the whirl of her own emotions and she definitely

didn't like the sound of what Faith had just said. Judging from the glance Theo gave her, neither did he.

"What are you sorry about?" Theo asked.

Faith didn't give them a quick answer. She continued to shake her head and then buried her face in her hands. Kim moved toward her, to try to settle her enough so she could explain that apology.

But the sound stopped her.

One second the room was quiet and the next second there was a deafening blast. The window shattered and glass spewed through the room. Kim had just a split-second awareness of what was happening.

Someone had just fired a shot at them.

She moved fast, but Theo was faster. He caught onto both Faith and her and dragged them to the floor just as the next shot came. It slammed into the wall near the door.

"What the hell?" she heard Deputy Gonzales shout.

"Stay down," Theo warned the deputy when he opened the door.

The deputy did, but he dropped to the floor and crawled toward them while Theo shoved Faith and Kim under the bed. No way would the bedding and frame stop bullets, but for the gunman to get to them, he'd have to change the angle of the shots.

"Is Greg doing this?" Faith blurted.

Kim seriously doubted it. If Duran and he had already left the sheriff's office, Ava would have no doubt alerted Theo, and he hadn't gotten any calls or texts since they'd arrived in Faith's room.

More shots came. Not a single bullet this time. But a barrage of gunfire that Kim could hear blasting through what was left of the window. Maybe, just maybe, none of the shots would go through the wall and hit any of the staff or patients.

Kim heard the deputy call for backup and inform Dispatch there was an active shooter. That meant responding officers wouldn't be able to just charge in and get this snake who was trying to kill them. It could be a slow process with them at the mercy of someone who wanted them dead.

Dead.

And this time, he just might succeed.

She cursed the wave of flashbacks. Cursed her too-fast breathing and heartbeat. The panic was crawling its way through her. Through Faith, too. Faith latched onto her, burying her face against Kim's shoulder, and Kim thought the woman might be on the verge of a full-fledged panic attack.

"It'll be okay," Kim murmured to her. Maybe a lie, but if she couldn't get Faith at least somewhat level, the woman might try to run.

"Put out an alert for everyone to get inside and stay away from the windows," Theo instructed Mike. "I want the entire block cordoned off."

The deputy rattled off those instructions to whoever was on the other end of the phone line. "Done," he told Theo. "Do you see the guy?"

That's when Kim realized that Theo had moved. He was no longer by the bed but had levered himself up to peer out the window. She nearly shouted for him to get back, but a bullet accomplished that. There was another barrage of gunfire, and Theo dropped back down to the floor.

"The shots are coming from the west," Theo explained to the deputy. "My guess is the rooftop of one of the buildings up the street."

Mike relayed that to the responder he had on the line,

but he had to repeat it several times because of the gunfire drowning him out. "Nelline's driving the cruiser back there now. She won't get out, but she's hoping the approaching siren will spook him and cause him to run."

Good. That might be enough to put an end to this nightmare, but Kim prayed it wouldn't cause the guy to turn the shots on Nelline. The cruiser was bullet resistant. That didn't mean those shots couldn't get through.

More glass came flying through the room and crashed onto the floor when the gunman managed to fire through another portion of the window. And that caused Kim's heart to sink. Because it likely meant the guy was on the move. Looking for the right angle to take the kill shots.

In the hallway, Kim could hear the shouts and the sounds of panic, but even with that and the gunfire, she heard the welcome sound of sirens. Maybe the shooter heard them, too, or maybe Nelline had managed to get close enough to him that he knew he had to get the heck out of there. Either way, the shots stopped.

Kim held her breath, waiting and praying, but as the seconds passed, there was no more gunfire.

Theo peered under the bed at them. "Are you both okay?"

Not trusting her voice yet, Kim went with a nod. Neither Faith nor she had been physically hurt and, considering the sheer number of shots that had been fired, that was somewhat of a miracle.

"Are you all right?" Kim asked him though, thankfully, she couldn't see any injuries.

Theo nodded as well. "I need you both to stay put while I make sure there are no injuries in the hall."

Injuries, yes. Perhaps even deaths if bystanders had been hit. It twisted at her to think someone else could have paid the ultimate price because a gunman had been reckless enough to fire into a building crammed with people.

"I need to know if Greg did this," Faith muttered, and Kim hadn't thought it possible, but the woman began to tremble even more.

"I'll find out who's responsible," Theo said like a promise. He started to move away when Faith took hold of his arm.

"I…" Faith stopped, a broken sob tearing from her throat. "I might be responsible. This might all be because of me."

Kim was about to assure her that it wasn't her fault, but she heard something in Faith's voice. Something more than the panic and the fear.

Regret, maybe.

"Theo, I'm so sorry," Faith blurted out. "I've been lying to you about so many things."

Chapter Thirteen

Even with the adrenaline slamming through him and the urgent need to go after the shooter, Theo had no trouble hearing what Faith had just said.

I've been lying to you about so many things.

Hell. That was not what he wanted this woman to say, and he immediately recalled Greg telling him that Faith was a liar.

If this was actually Faith, that is.

"Did you somehow fake the fingerprint match so it would look like you're my sister?" he snarled.

Faith flinched, maybe at his harsh tone or maybe because she was so stunned by his accusation. "No," she said, and she repeated it several times. "I really am Faith. I didn't lie about that."

That didn't do much to soothe his anger. Heck, he wasn't even sure he could believe her. It sickened him to think this woman was playing some kind of mind games with them.

"Theo," Kim murmured, her voice soft and soothing. It was a serious contrast to his own tone. "We should go to another room. It's not safe for us to be in here with the windows."

He certainly hadn't forgotten about the shot-out windows. Or the cold winter air slamming through them. Or the fact there was a shooter out there somewhere who would kill them if he got the chance.

"Nelline's in pursuit of the shooter," Mike relayed to Theo. "Not alone. She's got backup."

Good. Maybe they'd be able to catch the SOB. While Theo was hoping, he added a hope that there wouldn't be any injuries. To get started on checking that, and to move Faith and Kim, he motioned toward the door. It was riddled with bullet holes but was still closed and in the frame.

"We'll need to crawl out of here so we can stay out of the line of fire from the windows," he explained. "Be careful of the glass."

There was so much of it spewed across the floor, it was hard to avoid it, but Kim started inching out from under the bed. When Faith didn't budge, Kim caught onto the woman and pulled her along with her.

"I'm so sorry," Faith kept muttering.

Theo shut her out. Shut out what exactly she'd lied about. He was the sheriff, and right now, he had a job to do.

"Come with us," Theo told Mike. "Secure the hall and start checking for casualties and injuries. I also want updates on Nelline. Make sure she has all the backup we can give her."

Mike followed orders as they all made their way across the room. Once Theo reached the door, he opened it a couple of inches and looked out to see a welcome sight.

Gage was there.

"I was coming to relieve Mike," Gage said, sparing them a glance. He had his weapon drawn, his back pressed against the wall, and he was volleying his attention to both ends of the hall. No doubt looking for the shooter in case he'd managed to make his way into the hospital. "Are all of you okay?"

"We're not hurt," Theo settled for saying. Thankfully, Gage didn't appear to be hurt either, and Theo didn't see any other wounded.

Theo led the others out of the room while he, too, had his gun drawn. When he didn't see any signs of a threat, he took Kim and Faith to a small alcove where there were vending machines. There were no windows there, but he had to make sure the gunman didn't try to get at them some other way.

"No reports of injuries," Mike called out to him. "Since Gage is here, I'll start securing the entrances and exits while I get a status report on Nelline."

Theo thanked him and turned first to Kim. Just to see for himself that she hadn't been hurt. There was a tear on the sleeve of her coat and he realized it'd been made by either flying glass or a bullet. That definitely didn't ease the hard knot in his stomach. He'd come damn close to losing her.

"I'm okay," Kim assured him. Probably because she could see the worry and regret on his face.

Both emotions were there. Regret that he hadn't been able to stop this attack and worry that there might be another one if the gunman wasn't captured. Even then, that might not put an end to it because it was entirely possible the shooter had been a hired gun. No way could Greg or Duran have gotten in place so quickly to do this.

And that left Quill.

Yes, he definitely could have been in place, and that's why questioning the man was a high priority. For now, though, the priority was catching the gunman and keeping everyone safe. However, he also wanted answers, and while this wasn't an ideal time to get them, they also couldn't go anywhere.

"Start talking," Theo demanded, staring directly into Faith's eyes.

She was crying, not quietly, either, but with a steady stream of tears and quick jerks of breath. "I really am your sister. I swear, I didn't lie about that." She stopped and clearly tried to calm herself down so she could continue. It didn't work. "I told you I found the birth certificate for the Neelys' daughter, Ashley, and that's when I got suspicious about my adoption. But I found it before then." Another pause, followed by a sob. "About a year ago."

Theo latched right onto the timing of that. "The Neelys were alive then. You would have been able to ask them about the details of the adoption and how it was you ended up with them."

She nodded. "I did. I asked them a lot of questions, and I could tell this wasn't something they wanted to talk about. They got upset when I pressed, so I spoke to Greg since he would have been around when I was adopted."

"Greg got you for the Neelys?" Theo asked bluntly.

Faith's head whipped up and she shook it. "No." But she stopped. "Maybe. If he did, though, he's never admitted anything about it to me. In fact, after doing some research on our parents' murders, Greg said that he believed you had been the one to kill them."

Theo felt as if she'd punched him, hard, and the breath seemed to swoosh out of his body. Not the anger though. Definitely not that. It riled him to the bone that someone would believe he'd had any part in the killings.

"Why did Greg think that?" Kim asked. Good thing, too, because Theo definitely wanted to know the answer but wasn't sure he could speak just yet.

"Like I said, he'd done a lot of research, and he claimed he'd spoken to some people in Silver Creek who thought Theo might have argued with our parents and things escalated from there."

"That didn't happen," Theo managed to snarl.

"It didn't," Kim confirmed. "Theo was twelve years old. A kid, just like us. And he loved your parents. Added to that, there's no way he kidnapped you. Did Greg have an explanation as to how Theo would have managed that?"

Faith groaned and squeezed her eyes shut a moment. "Greg said it was probably one of Theo's friends who carried me away."

Again, Theo had to tamp down the anger. Hard to do since it had gone bone-deep. "Again, why would I have done that?"

Faith wasn't so quick to answer, and she shook her head. "I was gullible, and Greg convinced me that you wanted me out of the way so you could inherit our family's ranch."

"Greg must have been very persuasive," Theo said, his voice both an accusation and a warning. A warning because Greg was going to pay for filling Faith's head with these awful lies.

"He was," Faith confirmed. "He had what looked like police reports where the cops said they thought you might have been involved but couldn't prove it."

"I've gone over all the reports many times," Kim interjected. "So have plenty of other people, and there's absolutely nothing in them about Theo participating in the crimes in any way."

And that meant Theo could charge Greg with creating a false police report. Probably obstruction of justice, too. It might not lead to any real jail time, but it was a start.

"So, what motive did Greg have for telling you these lies?" Kim asked, but she didn't wait for Faith to answer. "I'm guessing he wanted you to come back to Silver Creek, confront Theo and get your share of the inheritance?"

Bingo. Theo could tell from the shame passing through

Faith's eyes that it had gone down that way. And Greg's motive would have been to get his hands on her money to pay off his debts.

"Greg said I had a right to the money," Faith continued a moment later. "A right, too, to put away the person who murdered my parents. He just kept pressing, just kept saying I could right an old wrong." She stopped, groaned, and pressed her hands to both sides of her head. "And that all got mixed up with the grief I was feeling because of the Neelys' dying. I loved them, they'd been good to me, and they were dead."

Theo was definitely listening to her, but he was also keeping an ear to what was going on around them. No sounds of gunfire, but the chatter told him there was a lot of movement to make sure everyone was secure.

"If Greg wanted you to return to Silver Creek to get the money, then why would he insist to us that you weren't Faith?" Kim asked.

Faith shook her head. "I'm not sure. Maybe because he thought you'd arrest him if you found out that he'd put me up to this."

It probably wasn't smart for Theo to believe her, but heaven help him, he did. Well, he believed the parts about Greg pushing Faith to return so she could get the money. That said, the woman might know more than she was saying about her return to Silver Creek.

"You said you had a breakdown after the Neelys were killed," Theo reminded her. "Is it possible Greg pushed you to that breakdown? Maybe even gave you some kind of medication to make you believe you were losing your mind?"

Faith opened her mouth, and Theo was certain she was about to say, *No, that wasn't possible*. But he watched as she worked through the facts. And the fact was he hadn't killed their parents, he hadn't kidnapped her.

But Greg could have done both of those things.

"Oh, God," Faith murmured, and she buried her face against Kim's shoulder while she began to sob again.

Theo wasn't immune to those tears, and he could see his sister was hurting, but he wasn't done yet with getting those answers he so desperately needed. "Who took you from the house the night our parents were killed?"

"I don't know." Faith lifted her head so she could look him straight in the eyes. "That's the truth. And yes, it could have been Greg."

"Or his lawyer, Duran?" Kim pushed.

Faith stayed quiet a moment, obviously processing that, and she nodded. "He could have done it."

"How about a man named Quill Odell?" Theo asked. "Did you ever hear Greg, Duran or the Neelys mention him?"

Her forehead bunched up while she gave that some thought. "No. Is he a suspect?"

Oh yeah. Not just for the murders and kidnapping but also for the two shootings. If Quill had been the one to kidnap Faith, no way would he want her to stay alive to be able to ID him.

Theo's phone buzzed, and even though he wanted to continue this line of questioning, he knew it was a call he had to take.

"First of all, there have been no reported injuries. But Nelline saw a man with a rifle running in the alley behind the hardware store, and she called out for him to stop," Ava immediately said. "She identified herself, ordered him to stop, and when he turned and took aim at her, she fired."

Hell. All of that had gone on while he'd been here tucked

away in the hospital. "What happened?" Theo couldn't ask fast enough.

"Nelline is fine. He shot at her but missed. She believes she hit him, but he still managed to run away. Should I call in the Rangers to assist?"

It would take too long, maybe an hour or more, for the Rangers to send someone out. "No, I'll call Silver Creek Ranch and get us some help."

There were enough lawmen, retired lawmen and ranch hands who could be temporarily deputized, and Grayson could have a team in place in a fraction of the time it would take the Rangers to respond.

"Are Greg and Duran still at the sheriff's office?" Theo asked the deputy.

"They are. They're in the interview room, and when I got reports of a shooting, I warned them to stay put. So far, they have. Rowena, too."

"Good. Make sure word gets out for everyone to stay inside," Theo instructed Ava. "And keep me posted," he added.

He ended the call with the deputy so he could phone Grayson. As expected, Grayson assured him that he and others would be right there to start the search for the gunman.

"Is Nelline okay?" Kim asked Theo the moment he put his phone away.

"She is. Ava said there have been no reported injuries." Theo took a breath of relief over that. Of course, someone could still be hurt, someone who hadn't been able to let anyone know they'd been injured, but for now, the gunman hadn't managed to claim another target. "Nelline believes she shot the guy as he was running away."

Kim seemed to take a breath of relief, too, and she gave a satisfied nod. "I hope there's a trail of blood to follow."

Theo hoped the same, but he very much wanted the guy alive. Dead men couldn't give him those answers he needed.

"You really believe Greg or Duran could have hired this gunman," Faith said, drawing his attention back to her.

He settled for a nod, as well, because unless it'd been Quill firing those shots, then the most likely scenario was that Greg, Duran or both had paid someone to do their dirty work.

His nod caused Faith's mouth to tremble again, and more tears came. "Greg could have done this if he thought I was going to tell you the truth about why I came here."

Maybe, but if Greg was responsible for these attacks, then he had a lot more at stake than Theo learning why his sister had returned. Greg could want her dead so he wouldn't be facing murder charges.

"I'll leave Silver Creek," Faith said, her words as shaky as the rest of her. "You won't want me near you now that you know the truth."

He wasn't especially happy with a sister who'd not only thought he was a killer but had returned to try to make him pay for that. Still, he couldn't let her go while someone out there wanted her dead.

"You can still stay at my place," he said.

Faith started shaking her head. "No. I can't do that to you. Not when you're obviously disgusted with me."

Theo hadn't known the disgust was showing, but apparently he hadn't been able to hide it. Except it was more disappointment than disgust. And he'd have to get over it. Yeah, Faith had screwed up by believing and trusting Greg, but it was also possible the man had manipulated her in some way. Kim could have been right about Greg having used some kind of drugs on Faith.

"Is there a hotel or inn?" Faith asked him. "Or maybe I

can stay at the police station? Just please don't make me stay here at the hospital. Not after what just happened."

Theo groaned then he sighed. "I'll take Kim and you to my place as planned."

Faith looked at Kim, no doubt to take note of her expression, to see if there was disgust or disappointment.

But Kim gave her a reassuring nod. "You'll be safe at Theo's," she said.

Theo certainly hoped that was true because, hell's bells, there'd been enough shooting and danger. He needed to have both Kim and Faith protected so he could dive into this investigation and find the person or persons responsible.

His phone rang again, and he answered it right away when he saw it was from Ava. "Please tell me you have good news," Theo greeted.

Ava made a sound that could have meant anything. "We have several witnesses who reported seeing Quill in the area at the time of the shooting."

Hell. "And I don't suppose he's answering his phone."

"Nope," Ava verified. "But as soon as someone is available, I'll dispatch them to his house." She paused a moment. "We'll be able to arrest Quill since the lab results just came in and the typewriter is a match to the letters that Kim's been receiving."

Good. They wouldn't necessarily be able to charge Quill with the two shootings or anything to do with what happened twenty-one years ago, but holding him on the letters would get him off the streets. It should be enough to have his bail revoked.

"I'll have to get back to you," Theo told Ava when his phone dinged. "Nelline's calling."

He very much wanted to hear what the deputy had to say

so he immediately switched calls. "Are you okay?" Theo asked her.

"I am. Not our gunman though." Nelline muttered some profanity. "We just found him one block up from the hardware store. I'm sorry, Theo, but he's dead."

Chapter Fourteen

Kim felt both exhausted and on pins and needles. That was often the case with an adrenaline crash, and she was indeed dealing with the aftereffects of that slam of adrenaline she'd gotten during the shooting.

Theo was dealing with it, as well, but unlike her, he couldn't go on autopilot. He was running a full-scale investigation, one that might finally catch his parents' killer. Of course, that *finally* couldn't come soon enough since whoever had hired the shooter might come after them again.

As they'd done on their other trips since the attacks had started, they hurried from the cruiser and into Theo's house. What was different this time was that Faith was with them, and instead of Nelline, Mike had driven them. Along with Theo's three ranch hands doing guard duty, Mike would have the next four-hour shift in the cruiser before being relieved by another deputy.

The moment the door was closed, Theo engaged the security system and then continued his call. Over the past seven hours since the shooting, there'd been a lot of calls. So many updates.

And some disappointing news.

For starters, the dead gunman—a thug who'd been immediately identified as Donnie Barker, a man with a mile-long criminal record along with a drug problem. Not a good combination, but Kim suspected the man's need for drugs had helped in him not being able to put bullets in Theo, Faith or her.

Of course, the question now was who'd hired Donnie, but judging from the updates Theo had been getting while they'd been holed up at the hospital and then the sheriff's office, there was no immediate money trail that led from Donnie to any of their suspects. There was enough circumstantial evidence to get a warrant to look at the financials of all three—Quill, Greg and Duran—but that kind of search took time. Added to that, Duran didn't seem careless enough not to cover his tracks.

"I want the tails to continue on Duran and Greg," she heard Theo tell Ava. The deputy had to be worn out, as they were, but Kim figured Ava wouldn't stop until her boss was out of danger. "Also, set the Rangers on Quill. He's on bail and can't just disappear like this."

There was plenty of frustration in Theo's voice, and Kim was right there with him. The fact that Quill hadn't surfaced made him look guilty.

Then again, he could be dead.

If Greg or Duran had used the man to do their bidding, they could have eliminated him. Yes, even with tails watching them, they could have managed it with a phone call to another hired thug.

Since Theo was still on the phone and Faith was looking very much like a fish out of water and ready to drop where she stood, Kim took hold of her hand and led her to the guest room that she'd used the night before. There were probably other guest rooms in the huge house, but this one was convenient, and she wanted Faith away from the constant barrage of updates that were no doubt reminders of how close they'd come to dying. Again.

"Theo doesn't want me here," Faith muttered. She paused in the doorway of the guest room and glanced around. "Not after I lied to him." She turned to Kim. "I'm so sorry I did that. So sorry for all the pain I've caused."

Kim decided to cut the woman a break. "Hey, you've been through a lot, and Theo might be uncomfortable with the way you went about coming here, but he wants what's best for you."

Since Faith wasn't budging from the doorway and they had some time while Theo was on the phone, Kim went with trying to get some facts about Faith's arrival in Silver Creek.

"Now that you've had some time to rethink things—did you tell us the truth about what happened at the hospital in San Antonio?" Kim asked.

Faith practically snapped toward her. "Yes. I had a breakdown, and I've been mulling over what you said about maybe being drugged. The hospital did a tox screen on me when I checked in, and there were some sleeping pills in my blood. I don't remember taking anything like that, but I blew it off. I just figured I was so out of it that I forgot what I'd done."

Sleeping pills. Depending on the type of medication and the dosage, it could have made Faith groggy enough to forget things she might now be remembering. But if Greg had given her those pills, there's no way he would have wanted her to check into a hospital where she could get help in reclaiming her childhood memories.

"You also told us the truth about why you left the hospital?" Kim pressed. "Because you thought you saw the killer?"

"I did," Faith insisted. She stopped, though, and shook her

head. "Things are still fuzzy, but I remember Greg came to see me to take me home. He didn't want me to stay there at the hospital. I refused to leave with him, but after he left, I saw the shadow. Or something. I thought someone was trying to kill me, so I ran away and came to Silver Creek."

Kim thought about that for a moment. "Did you eat or drink anything while Greg was there?"

"Yes," Faith told her. "Greg brought me a BLT from my favorite deli." Her eyes widened. "Do you think he drugged it?"

"Possibly. Something caused the fuzziness." No way to prove it though, but there were other things that might link back to Greg. "How'd you get to Silver Creek?"

Her face brightened a little, the way a student's would when they knew the right answer. "I remembered that last night. I used an Uber. I didn't go to Theo, though, because of what Greg had said about him being a killer."

That made sense. Well, it made sense if you'd been drugged and lied to. "Why go to my house? How did you even know where I lived?"

"I found it when I was researching. It's not hard to access tax records, and you were listed as the owner of the property." Faith paused and tapped the center of her forehead. She was obviously trying to recall something. "On the drive, my head started hurting, and I got really dizzy. And confused. I had the driver let me out just up the road from your place so I could try to decide if I should go see you or not."

"You ended up in my barn," Kim reminded her. "And someone had followed you. Greg, maybe." But it could have been Duran or Quill as well. If either of them had been worried about what Faith might remember, they could have been keeping tabs on her and known when she'd left the hospital in San Antonio.

"Yes, Greg maybe," Faith muttered, her words a little slurred now. Not from drugs this time but from sheer exhaustion.

"Why don't you lie down and get some rest?" Kim motioned toward the bed. "Theo will be tied up for a while, and you should try to take a nap."

Kim thought maybe Faith would protest doing that, but as testament to just how exhausted she was, she made her way to the bed and dropped down on it. She kicked off her shoes and pulled the cover over her.

And that's how Theo found her when he finally joined Kim in the hall.

One look at his face and Kim knew he was bone-tired. That's why she reached out and pulled him into a hug. She'd intended for it to be short and sweet. A gesture of what she hoped would be comfort, but it lingered on. And on. With the heat from his body seeping into her.

"You look like you needed that," she said when she finally eased back and faced him.

"I do. Especially from you." He brushed his mouth over hers. "I needed that, too."

Kim managed a smile. And felt the slam of heat from what was barely a kiss. Then again, any kiss from Theo packed a punch. A punch that she needed to put aside and focus on what he'd learned.

"Faith and I talked. I have a lot to fill you in on. Nothing that will help us find a killer," she quickly added. "Any updates that will help us find who's doing this?"

He shook his head. "More like stonewalls and roadblocks. Duran is fighting the warrant to go through his financials. Quill is nowhere to be found, and Greg is either holed up in his house in San Antonio or else he's managed to sneak out."

That shot some alarm through her. She nearly asked—

could he do that?—but she knew the answer was yes. Suspects slipped surveillance all the time.

Theo must have seen the alarm because he touched her cheek, brushing aside a strand of hair that'd landed there. "If Greg is the killer, he didn't do his dirty work this time. He hired the thug. That means he likely won't come after us himself but will look for someone else to hire."

True. But if Greg got desperate enough to silence Faith and stop her from remembering that awful night, then he might try to kill them himself.

"I have good security," Theo said, no doubt trying to soothe her.

The second kiss he gave her did some soothing as well. It also gave her another kick of that heat, and she might have leaned in to take a whole lot more from him if his phone hadn't dinged with another call.

He dropped back a step, looked at the screen and said, "Quill." Theo spoke the man's name in the same tone as a really bad curse word.

Kim glanced at Faith and saw that the woman had her eyes closed, so she shut the door so the conversation wouldn't disturb her.

Theo took the call, putting it on speaker.

"Where the hell are you?" Theo demanded.

"Well, I'm not trying to kill you if that's what you're asking," Quill fired back.

"I'm asking where are you. It's a simple question."

"No, it's not, because you want to arrest me for something I didn't do. It's all over town that you think I'm the one who fired those shots at you and your women, and hey, I didn't."

"Prove it," Theo snapped. "Go straight to the sheriff's office and submit to another GSR test."

Quill did some actual cursing. "I can do that, but you've

got to swear you won't arrest me. I don't want to be locked up while I'm awaiting trial."

"I'm not promising you anything. You've got a lot of questions to answer, and you need to quit dodging my deputies."

"I'll quit dodging them when they quit trying to arrest me. Hell, Theo, you know I'm not the one trying to kill you."

Kim knew that Theo didn't know that at all. Quill was just as prime of a suspect as Greg and Duran.

"Look, I told you that Rowena's trying to set me up," Quill went on a moment later. "She wants me behind bars, and she'll do anything to make sure that happens."

Again, Kim held her tongue, but she wanted to say the woman didn't have to do anything to put him away for a long time. Well, nothing other than show up in court and testify against him.

"If I didn't know better, I'd think somebody's persuading Rowena to set me up," Quill continued.

And that made Kim think of Greg. Rowena and he had been lovers years ago, but maybe they still had a connection. A connection that would cause Rowena to allow Greg to use her, especially since setting up Quill would benefit the woman by ensuring that he'd end up in jail for a long time.

"You can put all of this in your statement," Theo told the man. "Your suspicions about Rowena, how you feel you've been set up. All of it. Just go to the station now, and I'll arrange for a deputy to start the interview."

Quill certainly didn't jump on that offer. In fact, he cursed again. "I'd think you'd cut me some slack since I'm Jack's grandfather."

"You're a grandparent in name only," Theo was quick to say. "You've never even asked to see Jack."

"Because I knew you'd object." Quill tacked on some profanity to that.

"Yeah, I would have. But a grandparent who cared about his grandson would have at least asked to see him. You didn't. And your shared DNA with my son won't keep you out of a jail cell if you're responsible for what's going on. Trust me on that."

Quill cursed again and ended the call. Theo tried to phone the man right back, but Quill didn't answer. Not a surprise. The man obviously intended to dodge them as long as he could. Kim was hoping, though, that wouldn't be long.

"I'll let Ava know about the call," Theo said as he texted the deputy. "Nothing she can do about it though."

No. But Theo was going after those long shots to locate Quill because he then called the CSIs to see if they could get Quill's location through the phone records. There was little chance Quill would still be there—a definite long shot—but it was worth a try in case he was hunkered down somewhere.

When he finished with the CSIs, he looked up, his gaze connecting with Kim's. He opened his mouth but then closed it and shook his head. "I was about to suggest that you try to grab a nap, like Faith, but I know you won't do that."

Kim made a sound of agreement. She was certainly tired enough to nap, but there was no chance she could turn off her mind. Neither could Theo though he had to be as exhausted as she was.

It was a mistake, of course, but she went to him and pulled him into another hug. She knew what she was doing. Knew that with this supercharged energy between them, it wouldn't stay just a hug.

And she was right.

Almost immediately, Theo's mouth came to hers, and this was no light peck. It was a hard and hungry kiss that was filled with not only the heat but also the emotions of what they'd just been through. It was long, deep and extremely effective at making her want a whole lot more.

Theo clearly wanted more, too, because he backed her against the wall, pressing his body to hers while he took her mouth as if she were the cure for, well, everything. He certainly tasted like the cure to her, too, and she didn't even try to slow him down. Didn't try to tamp down the intensity. She just rode the wave of heat, letting the pleasure crash into her.

Of course, the kissing only led to more need. More fire. And Theo ran his hand between them, cupping her right breast and swiping his thumb over her erect nipple. Kim moaned, trying not to allow any thoughts in her mind that would put a stop to this. She didn't want to stop. She wanted Theo, and she wanted him now.

Theo was on the same page because he fumbled around and opened the door to his bedroom. They didn't stop the kiss or the touching and nearly tumbled into his room when they finally managed to move. Theo got them inside and shut the door.

Kim had just enough common sense left to lock it, as well, in case Faith got up from her nap and walked in on them.

Because she wanted—no, she needed—her hands on him, Kim went after his shirt. It wasn't easy to unbutton it since he obviously wanted her out of her clothes as well. She won that particular battle first and had the victory of being able to run her hands over his bare chest. The man was built. So many muscles, and she got another slam of heat at feeling them respond to her touch.

She responded, too, when Theo shucked off her top, shoved down her bra and lowered his head to kiss her breasts. This time the slam of pleasure made her legs go limp. Theo took care of that though. He just scooped her up and, without stopping the sweet torture of the tongue kisses on her breast, carried her to his bed.

He eased her down on the mattress, following on top of her, and Kim got another pleasure slam by feeling his weight on her. Especially the weight where his sex pressed against hers. That really upped the urgency.

"You'd better have a condom," she managed to say.

Theo didn't answer, not with words anyway. Nor did he stop kissing and touching her. He maneuvered them to the side of the bed and he thankfully took out a condom from his nightstand. She expected him to start shedding the rest of his clothes so he could put it on. But obviously he had other plans.

Really good plans.

Tossing the condom on the mattress beside them, Theo began to trail some slow, wet kisses down her throat. Over her breasts. And to her stomach. He didn't stop there either. Ridding her of her clothes as he went, he kissed each inch of skin that he bared. Kissed and used his clever tongue to skyrocket the heat and pleasure until Kim was ready to beg him to give her release.

Theo didn't release her though. Sliding off her panties, he continued the kissing torture. Continued until Kim was certain she wasn't even capable of begging. She could only lie there and let the wash of pleasure take over. He didn't finish her off that way though. Theo took her right to the brink and then reversed the kisses, sliding his tongue back up her body. By the time he reached her neck, Kim could take no more.

"I want your clothes off now," she demanded.

Theo certainly didn't cooperate with that. He kept kissing, kept touching, kept driving her up, up, up, only to pull back before she could climax.

Cursing him and the hungry gnawing heat, Kim managed to remove his holster and belt. No easy feat. It was an even bigger feat when she shoved down his jeans and boxers.

Oh, yes. The man was built.

Later, she'd take the time to savor his body and return some of the kissing torture he was doling out. For now, though, she just reached for the condom. Theo did help with that, maybe because she began kissing his neck, and that was clearly a hot sexual button for him. He finally hurried. Then slowed again to lock gazes with her when he slipped inside her.

More pleasure came. Man, did it. So much pleasure that she had to fight to stave off the release. Yes, she wanted that. Desperately wanted it, but she wanted to savor this night as much as she could.

His thrusts convinced Kim to quit fighting it. Theo must have realized she was close and that this time he wasn't going to pull back. He simply kissed her, long and deep, and gave her exactly what she needed to fly right over the edge.

Chapter Fifteen

While Theo dried off from his shower, and shower sex, he watched Kim as she dressed. He wanted to see if she was showing any signs of regret for having had sex with him not once but twice.

She wasn't.

Then again, maybe there hadn't been time for regrets to surface. They'd taken a very short reprieve and less than five minutes after they'd both gotten some release from the intense heat, his phone had rung. And it'd continued to ring with reports from Ava to let him know that Quill hadn't been found and that Greg still hadn't showed his face. Maybe that was because he was hiding in fear from Quill, but it was giving Theo a bad feeling.

The bad feeling continued because Duran was doing the opposite of Greg and Quill. He was making himself seen. Maybe too much so by going to his office only to leave ten minutes later to go to a coffee shop for another short stay. Duran could be trying to make himself look innocent by being so visible, but that didn't wash with Theo because he knew the man could have already hired someone else to make another attempt to kill Kim, Faith and him.

"Well, what's the verdict?" Kim asked, drawing his attention back to her. Not that it had strayed far. Kim had a way of occupying his thoughts even when his thoughts should be firmly on the investigation.

He wasn't sure exactly what verdict she meant, so Theo went with the obvious. "Sex with you was great."

That made her smile. For a couple of seconds anyway. "Ditto. I knew it would be and that's why I've avoided you."

Theo understood what she meant. Now that they'd given in to the intense attraction, there was no going back. And that meant they had complications to face. One of those complications surfaced almost immediately when his phone dinged again, and he heaved a sigh.

"Nadia," he relayed to Kim and, like him, she began bracing herself. She also finished dressing.

"Is everything okay?" Theo asked Nadia the moment he answered.

"Yes. I mean there's no sign of a gunman or anything like that, but I wanted you to know that Quill called me."

"Where is he?" Theo couldn't say fast enough.

"He wouldn't tell me. He just went on about how Rowena was setting him up. We both know he's a liar, but he keeps pressing this so much that I have to wonder if it's true. Have you gotten any sense from Rowena that she might be doing something other than what she usually does?"

Theo considered that a moment. Normally, after Quill battered her, Rowena would file charges against him and then try to pull those charges when she either got too afraid of reprisal or if she simply didn't know how to have a life without her abuser. But nothing was "normal" about what had been happening.

"It's possible she is trying to set up Quill," Theo finally admitted. "I'll call her and have another chat."

But there was something about this conversation with Nadia that puzzled him. She sometimes let him know if she had any encounters with her parents, but this felt like, well, more.

"Is there something else you wanted to tell me?" Theo asked.

Nadia certainly didn't jump to assure him there wasn't. She paused a long time and then he heard her sigh. "Look, I know Kim is staying there with you, and I understand why."

Theo silently groaned. He figured Nadia was about to launch into her usual gripes about Kim. But he was wrong.

"I understand why," Nadia repeated. "What I don't understand is why it bothers me so much that you two might get together." She paused again. "It's true, isn't it? You might get together?"

Theo had a nice flash of memories of the great sex with Kim. "Yes," he verified. "Kim and I might get together."

He locked gazes with Kim to see if she would silently dispute that. Nope. But, like him, she did look concerned as to how Nadia would deal with that. Because anything that affected Nadia ultimately affected Jack.

And that's why he wanted to tell Nadia that it wouldn't be just a fling with Kim. Nadia wouldn't have to worry that Jack would get used to having Kim around only to have her not be around at all. But he didn't have time to say any of that because he got an incoming call from Ava.

"Sorry, but I have to go," Theo told Nadia. "It's a work call."

"All right." A moment later, she repeated that, and he had the feeling that she was trying to apologize for how she'd always reacted to hearing Kim's name. That feeling was enough for now. A start that maybe things could be different in the future.

Of course, nothing could be different until he'd made sure none of them was in danger.

I'll check on Faith, Kim mouthed when he ended the call with Nadia and switched to Ava.

Theo nodded and listened to what Ava had to say. "Rowena stopped by the station. She wants to talk to you."

"Good, because I was about to call her. Put her on," Theo instructed. He heard Ava do that, but he didn't wait for Rowena to say anything. He just went with his gut. "I know you're trying to set Quill up, and I want you to spill everything you've done."

Silence. For a long time. But the woman didn't deny it, which meant his gut was right. "I put the dead rat on my doorstep," Rowena finally admitted. "And I sent him texts to tell him to meet me at places where I knew Kim and you would be, like the hospital. I wanted him to start something with you that would get him tossed back in jail."

He nearly asked how she knew where Kim and he would be, but Theo doubted that was much of a secret. Still, he didn't appreciate the woman giving Quill a sort of road map to their whereabouts.

"You told Quill where we were, and he might have tried to kill us," Theo pointed out to Rowena.

"No." She didn't hesitate that time. "I wouldn't have told him if I'd known there'd be attacks. Do you really believe he could have been the one to shoot at you?"

"Oh, yes. I believe it's possible, and with his history, you should believe it, too."

"No," Rowena insisted. "Quill uses his fists or a knife, not guns."

"And you thought he'd try to use his fists or a knife on Kim or me?" Theo snapped, not bothering to pull back on the anger.

He heard Rowena's sharp sob. "I just thought he'd lose his temper and try to hit you, and then you could arrest him.

He shouldn't be out and about. Especially if he gets word about what happened with…well, with me and you know who twenty-one years ago."

Apparently, Rowena was still trying to keep Greg's name under wraps, and Theo couldn't blame her for that. No need to give Quill a reason to go after his battered wife's former lover. But that did give Theo an idea.

"Did Greg ask you to do the things you've done to set Quill up?" Theo prodded.

"Of course not. I haven't talked to him in years, not since we ended things."

Maybe, but Theo would like some proof of that. "Give Deputy Lawson access to your phone records so we can verify you sent those texts to Quill to give him Kim's and my location. It'll also prove you haven't called Greg."

Theo wished he could see the woman's face because he could practically feel the fierce debate she was having with herself. If she refused, he'd just get a warrant and access the phone records, but if she agreed to let Ava have them right away, she might be caught in a lie.

"All right," Rowena finally said. "But I did call Greg earlier. He gave me his number when he was here at the sheriff's office for his interview."

"Mind telling me what you two discussed?" Theo asked.

Again, she hesitated. "I told him to watch out for Quill, that he was a dangerous man."

That was likely the truth, but Theo was betting that wasn't all they'd talked about. "Give Deputy Lawson an account of that conversation. If nothing you two said pertains to the investigation, she'll keep Greg's name to herself."

"Good," Rowena muttered.

When Rowena handed the phone back to Ava, Theo instructed Ava to take a statement about any and all of Rowena's text and phone conversations with Greg and an account of the texts she'd sent Quill in the past forty-eight hours.

He ended the call and made his way into the hall. The guest room door was open, but Kim and Faith weren't there. He heard them in the kitchen and followed the sound of their voices, but what his sister said had him stopping in his tracks for a moment.

"I have to go," Faith said, her voice much stronger than it had been earlier. "I have to see it for myself."

Theo definitely didn't like the sound of that, and it had him moving again. "See what for yourself?" he asked when he walked into the kitchen. Judging from their expressions, Kim and Faith had been involved in a serious debate.

Faith whirled toward him, not with surprise, but she went to him as if searching for an ally. "The house."

No need for him to ask which house. She meant their family home, and Theo looked at Kim to hear her take on this.

Kim dragged in a long breath before she spoke. "When Faith woke up from her nap, she said she remembered something. Not the killer's face," Kim quickly added. "But—"

"But I remember the coat he was wearing," Faith interrupted, her words rushing together. "I remember him carrying me down the stairs and out of the house."

Theo nodded. "All of this is a good start, and I think we should arrange for you to speak with a therapist who might be able to help you recall even more."

Faith shook her head and took hold of his arm. "No. I have to go to the house. I have to see it myself." She stopped, her mouth trembling now. "Because if I see it, I know I'll be able to tell you who killed our parents."

Chapter Sixteen

Kim knew that what Faith had just said had to be a tempting offer for Theo.

I'll be able to tell you who killed our parents.

That had been the question that'd haunted them for twenty-one years. But it just wasn't a safe idea going to the house where that nightmare had happened.

"No," Theo said, looking Faith straight in the eyes. "It's too dangerous for us to go to our old place."

Faith started shaking her head before he'd even finished. "You can make it safe by bringing along a deputy. And I might not even have to get out of the cruiser. I think if I can just see the house, then I'll remember the rest of what I've blocked out."

Judging from Theo's skeptical expression, he wasn't buying that. Neither was Kim. "There are pictures of the place you can look at."

Though that wouldn't be an especially pleasant sight. However, Faith didn't have the same nightmarish memories that Theo and Kim did. They hadn't been able to block out much of anything.

Still shaking her head, Faith turned to her. "No, a picture won't do. I need to be there, to take it all in."

Theo's sigh was long and weary. "Even if we risk a trip

like that, there are no guarantees you'll remember any more than you already do."

Faith tapped her finger to her chest. "I can guarantee it. And don't ask me how I know, I just do. Seeing the house will be the trigger that will bring it all back."

Kim couldn't totally dismiss that, but there was still the risk of a killer finding them there.

"Please," Faith added, volleying pleading looks at both of them. Apparently, she didn't get the "let's do it" reaction she wanted because she huffed. "All right, let me borrow one of your deputies, and I'll go without you." She moved closer to Theo to stare at him. "Because one way or another, I am going. We'll finally learn who killed our family and made all of our lives a living hell."

Kim couldn't dispute the "living hell" part either. Yes, Theo and she had healed, some, but it would never be a total healing until they had the answers as to who had set things in motion that night.

"I'll go without you," Faith stated.

Theo just stared at his sister. Or rather, he glared, and maybe he saw the determination or something in Faith's eyes because he cursed. Then he shifted his attention to Kim.

"I don't suppose I could talk you into staying here with a deputy while I go with Faith to the house?" he asked.

Kim didn't even have to think of her response. "No chance whatsoever of me staying behind. If the two of you go, I go. The three survivors of that night," she tacked on.

Though there was likely one other survivor.

The killer.

Was he monitoring the house to see if they'd go there? Maybe. But it might be the last place he thought they'd ever return. Because of the memories. The flashbacks. The hell it would bring to all of them.

The muscles stirred in Theo's jaw and he took out his phone. Kim wasn't sure who he was calling until she heard him say, "Mike, you've relieved Nelline and are in the cruiser in front of my house?"

Deputy Mike Gonzales. Since Theo put the call on speaker, she heard the deputy answer, "Yes. Something you need, boss?"

"Yeah, I need my head examined," Theo muttered.

"Excuse me?" Mike asked.

Theo didn't repeat that, but he sighed again. "My sister believes she'll recover some of her memories if we go to the house where my parents were murdered."

Mike's silence probably meant he was processing that. "What do you want me to do to make that happen?"

"The four of us will go there in the cruiser," Theo explained. "I'll call the Silver Creek Ranch and see who's available to meet us there. One of my ranch hands will follow up to give us even more backup."

Theo stepped aside to make those calls, but Faith didn't wait. She went to the rack near the door and got the loaner coat that Gage had brought to the hospital with him when he'd done guard duty. Faith peered out the window, a combination of both nerves and anticipation on her face.

"I know this is a risk," she told Kim. "I know I'm putting both of you in danger, but I need the truth."

All parts of that were true, but Kim sighed and pulled her into a hug. "We're already all in danger," she reminded Faith, and a part of her wanted to face that danger head-on. To have a final showdown with the killer who'd taken so much from all of them.

But Theo could be hurt or killed.

That reminder robbed her of her breath and caused her heart to race. That could happen. Heck, it could happen to all of them, but the same might be true if they stayed put. They couldn't stay inside Theo's house forever, and the killer had to know that eventually he'd get another shot at them.

Kim pulled back from the hug and met Faith eye to eye. "No unnecessary risks. By that I mean, don't try to bolt from the cruiser. If we get out, Theo has to agree to it."

She waited for Faith to nod, waited a second longer to make sure the nod was the truth, and then Kim gave her own nod before she went to her purse that she'd put on the highest hook of the rack. She took out her gun that she'd brought with her and slipped it into the slide holster in the back of her jeans.

Faith didn't react to the gun as Kim had hoped she would. She'd thought that Faith might see the weapon and have it sink in that there could be danger, but judging from her expression, she remained determined to go to the house.

"Don't do anything to make me regret this," Theo muttered to his sister as he put on his coat.

He, too, waited for Faith to nod. Waited again until Kim gave him the okay. She was really hoping nothing happened for him to regret this either.

"This isn't like when we were kids," she reminded him. "We know how to defend ourselves."

Still, she got a flashback of hiding under the bed with her stuffed bear clutched to her. Maybe Theo saw the effects of that flashback in her eyes because he gave her hand a gentle squeeze before they headed out.

Mike was right there waiting for them with the cruiser already running and warm. Good thing, too, because the temp had dropped, and the wind was whipping across the ranch. It rarely snowed in this part of Texas, but the air felt heavy, cold and wet. Not exactly a good vibe to take with them to the scene of the crime that had changed their lives.

As Mike started the short drive, Theo got another text, and after he responded, he relayed, "Still no sign of Quill." After he said that, he turned and looked at Faith. "Do you remember him?"

She nodded. "Only a little. He worked for Mom and Dad for a while." She paused a moment. "And you were married to his daughter for a couple of years."

"I was. I have a two-year-old son named Jack."

That caused Faith to smile a little. "Maybe when this is over, I can meet him."

Theo made a sound of agreement and looked at her again. "Is it possible Quill was the one who took you that night?"

Faith's smile vanished, and she stayed quiet a moment, obviously considering that. "Maybe." She stopped, repeated it. "He would have known the layout of the house. Would have known where to find me."

Her voice broke on the last word, and Kim figured she was thinking some horrible thoughts right now. That if it hadn't been for her, her parents wouldn't have been killed; that they'd died because someone had wanted to get to her. It wasn't much, but Kim repeated what Theo had done to her earlier by giving Faith's hand a gentle squeeze. Kim didn't even attempt to voice any reassurances that all would be well because she couldn't be certain it would be.

Nothing would be well until they'd caught the killer and made him pay for what he'd done.

With that dismal thought flashing in her head, Kim tried to keep her breath steady when Mike took the turn toward the Sheldon ranch.

Kim hadn't been back to the Sheldon ranch since the night of the murders. In fact, she often went out of her way just so she didn't have to drive by the place. But she actually welcomed seeing it now because, like Faith, she wanted to see if it triggered anything other than the nightmarish memories.

After all, she could have seen the killer, too, and blocked it from her mind. It made her wish that she'd done this trip before. Before there'd been two attempts to kill the three of them.

No one had lived at the place since the murders, and even though she knew Theo often sent in workers to do repairs, the ranch still had that abandoned feeling. No livestock in the pastures, and the barn doors were nailed shut with boards. Maybe to keep out any trespassers.

"When I was reading articles on the Internet, some people called it the murder ranch," Faith muttered.

They did. Kim had seen that on social media. It had also become a place where some teenagers dared each other to go since some believed it to be haunted with the ghosts of the dead.

When Mike drove over a small hill, the house came into view. Even though the sun would set in about a half hour, there was still plenty of light, so Kim could clearly see the place. Once, she'd been thrilled to come here because it meant spending time with her best friend. She certainly wasn't getting any happy feelings now.

She spotted one of the Silver Creek Ranch trucks and saw her uncle Dade behind the wheel. Good. He was a retired deputy and could give them backup if needed.

Dade tipped his head in greeting, but he stayed in the truck. So did the ranch hand who'd followed them there.

"You've been back here since it happened?" Faith asked, aiming the question at Theo.

"When I was eighteen. I thought I was coming to say goodbye to the place because I intended to sell it. Grayson had been managing the upkeep on it, and I figured it was time to let go of it." He paused, his gaze fixed on the two-story white house with what had once been a welcoming porch. "I couldn't sell it. Couldn't burn it to the ground," he added a moment later after he cursed.

Mike pulled to a stop in the curved driveway, positioning the cruiser so it was directly in front of the house. All of them stayed quiet, studying it.

Letting the memories slam into them like sharp knives.

Kim tried not to make any sounds since she knew anything that came out of her mouth right now would be doused in nightmare, but she did meet Theo's eyes for a moment and saw he was feeling the same thing.

Faith moved closer to the window, peering out through the glass. Her gaze swept around the house, the porch, the grounds.

"Yes," Faith muttered. "I remember something."

EVEN THOUGH FAITH had spoken so softly that her words hardly had any sound, Theo still heard her. He snapped toward her and saw that she had her attention pinned to the house.

"What do you remember?" Kim and he asked in unison.

"A silver watch that was blue behind the numbers." Faith kept staring at the house, her eyes fixed as if she were in a trance. "He was wearing one on his left wrist. I was trying to get away from him, but he had me clamped against him as he ran from the house. I saw the watch when he shoved me into a car."

Theo latched onto every one of those details. Not exactly earth-shattering info, not yet anyway, but anything at this point was fresh info that could be used to find the killer.

"Did you see his face?" Kim pressed.

Faith shook her head. "He was wearing a ski mask." She stopped, swallowed hard. "He smelled like blood."

Theo didn't ask her how she recognized that particular smell. Like him, Faith had been raised on a working ranch, and she would have been a witness to some injuries and even some procedures done on the livestock.

"'Blood,'" Kim repeated, and Theo knew what she was thinking. One person working alone could have committed the crimes if he'd done the murders first. Then, he could have easily taken Faith.

And Theo hadn't stopped any of that.

He had to stomp down that thought. That guilt. It would only eat away at him as it'd done for the past twenty-one years, and it sure as heck wouldn't help him keep a clear head. Right now, he needed that and as many little details as Faith could recall so they could try to piece this together.

"What about the car?" Theo asked. "Do you remember anything about it?"

Faith stayed quiet a moment. "It had four doors because he opened the back and tossed me on the seat. Then he jammed a needle in my leg. It hurt, and I yelled. Maybe I yelled," she amended. She shook her head. "He shoved something in my mouth. A wad of gauze, I think."

It twisted at him to hear what Faith had been put through that night. Dragged from her home, drugged and kidnapped. So many things could have gone wrong, and she could have ended up dead.

"I woke up in a bed," Faith continued. "But I was woozy, and the man in the ski mask kept giving me shots." She paused again, probably because she had to. Her breathing was so fast that talking had to be hard. Especially talking about all of this. "I don't know how long that went on."

And when the drugging had finally ended, the Neelys had

lied and told her she'd been in an accident. They'd brainwashed her into believing she was their daughter.

"Other than the blood, ski mask, watch, and the car, do you remember anything else about the man?" Kim asked. "His scent? His size?" she prompted when Faith didn't respond.

After several long moments, Faith shook her head and made a sound of frustration. "Let me keep thinking."

Theo gave her that time, but he sent a quick text to Ava.

If Rowena's still with you, ask her if Quill ever owned a silver watch with a blue face.

It didn't take Ava long to answer.

Rowena says he's owned a lot of watches, that he buys a new one every year or so, and that one of them might have been silver and blue.

Hell. A *might* wasn't going to cut it. He needed proof.

Get a search warrant for Quill's house, Theo instructed. Go through all his watches and see if there's a silver and blue one.

Of course, the odds were slim that Quill had kept it all this time, but if he had, there could still be traces of blood on it. That was exactly the kind of link that Theo had been searching for.

"I need to go inside," Faith insisted. "I need to see where I was taken from."

Theo didn't even have to consider this. "No. You're not getting out of the cruiser."

Faith whirled around to face him, no doubt ready to argue, when the ground around them exploded into a fireball.

Chapter Seventeen

Kim heard the blast a split second before the cruiser went flying. Her brain didn't register what was happening at first, not until the vehicle landed with a hard thud. Around them, there were other deafening blasts, and that's when she realized that someone was trying to kill them.

"Explosives," Theo shouted, and Kim could see him trying to assess their situation.

Their situation definitely wasn't good.

There was a massive hole to the right of the cruiser and another in front between it and Dade's truck. Both the truck and Dade seemed to be fine, but the front end of the cruiser was a tangled mess. The blast had torn it apart and there was steam spewing from the busted radiator.

Kim looked behind her at Theo's ranch hand. The front of his truck had been blown to smithereens, as well, and the windshield was cracked and webbed, but she could see some movement behind the glass and prayed that he hadn't been hurt.

"Someone set bombs?" Faith blurted.

Faith was fighting to get out of her seat belt, no doubt so she could go into a panicked run, but Kim held on to her even though she wasn't sure how long they could stay put. She especially wasn't sure of that when there was another blast that jolted through the cruiser, tossing them around like ragdolls. Kim was certain if they all hadn't still been wearing their seat belts, they would have been seriously injured.

Or worse.

Theo cursed, and Kim followed his gaze as it slashed to the front of the cruiser. Except there wasn't much left for them to see. And then Kim caught a scent she didn't want to smell.

Gasoline.

Both Mike and Theo cursed again. "We have to get out now," Theo insisted. "There's enough of the engine left that the gas could cause it to blow."

That could burn them alive, and this time when Faith started to release her belt, Kim didn't stop her. Kim undid her own seat belt and drew her weapon, getting ready for what could be an attempt to gun them down. The killer could have set the explosives, hoping that would kill them, but since they hadn't, he could be out there waiting for them.

Theo threw open his door and looked back at his ranch hand. "Carver, are you okay?"

Carver Daniels, a man who'd worked for Theo for years. "I'm not hurt," he answered right away. "I think we need to get out of here though."

"Agreed," Theo barked and then called out, "Dade, we're heading to your truck." He'd probably chosen that one because it had the least amount of damage and was already parked facing the road for a faster exit. "Faith and Kim will go inside with you. The rest of us will get in the truck bed. The second we're in, take off."

Kim didn't like that plan one bit. She knew they wouldn't all fit inside the cab of the truck, but she didn't care for the fact that Theo would be in the bed where he'd be an easy target for a sniper. Still, there wasn't time to argue. She could only hope and pray that all of them would make it out of there alive.

"Move now," Theo told them.

They did, but Kim had barely made it a step when there was another explosion, and her heart dropped to her stomach when she saw the front of Dade's truck go up in flames. Dade had to bolt from his vehicle.

"Take cover," Theo yelled.

Dade hurried back to them, taking hold of Faith's arm to get her moving to a thick cluster of pecan trees. The rest of them followed, all dropping down so they wouldn't be easy targets.

"We could go inside the house," Faith muttered, her voice shaking like the rest of her.

"It could be rigged with explosives, too," Theo fired back.

Yes, it could be. In fact, maybe that's what the killer wanted, all of them inside the house so he could finish what he'd started twenty-one years ago.

The flashbacks came like fists, slamming into Kim, robbing her of her breath and causing the panic to rise in her throat. She heard the strangled sound she made and hated it. Because it alerted Theo, and he scurried toward her. He put his left arm around her, pulling her to him. Not good. She needed him to focus on their surroundings and not her.

"I'm all right," she said. At the moment, it was a huge lie. She wasn't all right by any means, but she soon would be. Kim had no intention of letting the fear and the flashbacks get them killed.

"The killer wouldn't want us in the house," Kim murmured more to herself than Theo. "That could trigger us remembering something about him. Something that would tell us who he is."

Theo made a quick sound of agreement just as there was

another explosion. Not in or near the house but rather by the vehicles again. The blast shook the ground beneath them and ripped apart even more of the cruiser.

Obviously, someone had set explosives there in the driveway, figuring that, eventually, they would return. Or rather, Faith would. Whoever had put the explosives in place had to be watching them.

Waiting for them.

Kim got confirmation of that a split second later when the first shot came bashing into one of the trees.

HELL. THEO DEFINITELY hadn't wanted to deal with a gunman when there were explosives tearing up the vehicles. Worse, there could be explosives waiting to rip apart the ground beneath them.

But he rethought that.

If there were bombs in the trees, the killer would have set them off when they'd run for cover. So the shots were likely meant to draw them out, to get them running so they could be picked off. Or rather, so Kim, Faith and he could be killed. Theo was pretty sure that the killer would consider Dade and Carver collateral damage.

A bullet slammed into the pecan tree right next to Faith. Way too close. Theo took hold of her arm and pulled her deeper into the grove. Thankfully, there were a lot of trees, nearly two dozen, that were already tall and mature when his parents were still alive. There was now enough thick undergrowth beneath them that, hopefully, would give them some good places to hole up until...

Well, until he could put a stop to this.

And he would have to stop the shooter. No way did he want any more of his deputies or the Rylands running into this danger. He needed to pinpoint the shooter and try to get to him. First, though, he had to make sure Kim and Faith were safe.

"This way," Theo instructed Kim and Carver in a whisper as he continued to lead Faith toward the center of the grove.

Moving them there was somewhat of a risk since the killer could have hired someone to lay in wait for them. However, staying near the line of fire wouldn't be smart either.

Once he reached some thick shrubs, he motioned for Faith and Kim to get down. "Wait here," he added.

But Kim took hold of his left hand. "You're not going out there," she insisted. Even in the thick part of the grove, there was still plenty of light for him to see the fear in her eyes. Not fear for herself, he knew, but for him.

Theo considered trying to reassure her that he would be all right, but this was Kim, and she would know he had no way of guaranteeing that. He wished he could. Not just so he could erase that look in her eyes but because he truly wanted to put an end to the danger so he could tell her how much she meant to him. How much he wanted her in his life.

"Don't you dare get hurt or killed," Kim said before he could figure out what to say.

For some reason, that made him smile. It was very short-lived thanks to another round of gunfire, but Theo still took a second to brush a kiss on her mouth.

"No getting hurt or killed," he murmured, and then he looked at Faith. "Stay down and stay put," he added in a warning.

He could see his sister's eyes, too, and she was worried as well. She also looked fed up with being the target of someone who'd already ruined her life by kidnapping her. Faith looked ready to do something foolish, like make herself a target to draw out this SOB, and that's why Theo repeated his warning. Whether or not she'd obey, he didn't know, and that's why he had to hurry.

"Make sure the killer doesn't get to them," Theo told Carver.

He knew he could trust his ranch hand to do whatever was needed to keep Kim and his sister safe, but it was still hard leaving them there and walking away.

Theo went back toward the front of the grove where Dade was positioned behind one of the larger trees. Since Dade was a retired deputy, he had plenty of experience in dangerous situations, and, like Carver, Theo knew he could trust Dade to help in any way he could. Right now, Theo needed him to make sure a gunman didn't come charging in to get to Faith and Kim.

"The shots are coming from that direction," Dade pointed out, tipping his head to the west. Specifically, to the area by the barn.

Dade had taken aim there but hadn't fired, maybe because he wasn't sure if Theo had workers on the grounds. He didn't. And that's why Theo lifted his gun and looked around. He didn't see anyone, and the barn doors were boarded up, but it was possible the gunman had knocked a hole in the wood and was firing from there. It was also possible, though, that the guy was either on the roof or in the hayloft.

"Let me see if I can get him to show himself," Theo muttered, and he sent two bullets into the wall to the right of the barn door.

The gunman responded and responded fast. Not by showing himself but by sending two rounds of fire in Theo's direction. Like Dade, Theo had already taken cover, had been expecting the retaliation, but the angle of the shots gave him some critical info.

"He's on the roof," Theo relayed to Dade.

Theo hadn't left any ladders around to tempt trespassers into using it to gain access to the second floor of the house where the windows weren't boarded up, but the shooter could have brought a ladder with him. If so, he would have needed a vehicle and had probably parked either behind the house or along one of the ranch trails.

"I've got plenty of ammo," Dade told him. "You want us to double team and just start shooting at the roof? We might get lucky."

Yeah, they might, but since there was no telling how long the guy had been there waiting for them, he'd likely set up in the position where he was least likely to be shot. After all, the SOB would have known that Theo would return fire. Besides, it could be the shooter who got lucky and managed to hit and kill one of them. Maybe even Faith or Kim. Depending on the weapon the guy was using, none of them was out of range of the shots.

And that meant Theo had to stop and catch this snake.

It wouldn't do for the gunman to keep firing until he ran out of ammo because then he would just flee. No doubt using that ladder he'd brought with him. Then he could regroup and come after them again.

Theo wanted to end this right here, right now.

Twenty-one years was too damn long to wait for justice. Added to that, neither Kim nor Faith would be safe as long as this killer was still out there.

"I'm going to circle around," Theo told Dade, "and come up from behind him."

Dade immediately glanced around, assessing if that was even possible. It was. Even though this place was no longer home for him, Theo knew it like the back of his hand.

"I can cut through these pecan trees to that row of mountain laurels," Theo explained just as more shots came their way.

The mountain laurels wouldn't provide as much protection as the trees, but they might give him enough cover so he wouldn't be seen. He could follow them all the way to the back of the house and use the shrubs on the other side to get to the barn.

"You keep him busy by firing shots at him," Theo told Dade. "I'll text you when I'm close to the barn so you won't hit me with friendly fire."

Dade made a quick sound of agreement. "You should go ahead and let Carver know you'll be moving around. Don't want him to mistake you for the gunman."

"Good point," Theo muttered, and he took care of that right away.

The moment Theo started moving, Dade fired a shot at the barn roof. Theo knew that Dade wouldn't make the diversion obvious. Instead, Dade paced his fire and, judging from the sound of the shots, wasn't aiming at the same spot each time. He was spreading the bullets around, and Theo could hope Dade would get lucky and hit the guy.

Threading his way around the pecan trees, Theo moved fast and tried not to think about Kim and his sister. Tried and failed. He was worried for their safety. Worried that he'd fail again as he had the night his parents had been killed. It ate away at him to think of losing Faith.

Of losing Kim.

Mercy, he wouldn't lose her. Not when they'd finally managed to break down some old barriers so they actually stood a chance of being together.

Because of where he'd positioned Kim, Faith and Carver, Theo couldn't see them, and he forced his mind off them so he wouldn't miss anything that might end up getting them all killed. After all, the shooter on the roof might be just another hired gun, and the killer could be waiting for his chance to go after them.

Theo had just made it to the mountain laurels when he heard something he didn't want to hear. Faith.

"I remember who you are," his sister shouted.

Hell. What was she doing? The gunman could use the sound of her voice to identify her position.

"It won't do you any good to kill us because I just sent off a text to everyone I know, telling them who you are," Faith shouted. "I remember the watch, your boots, the car you used. I remember the smell of blood on your clothes, but most of all, I know who you are."

It was a bluff.

Well, probably.

If Faith had truly recalled the name of the person who'd killed their parents and kidnapped her, she would have used the name. His sister was obviously trying to save them by taking away the killer's motive to murder them.

"I know who you are," Faith repeated, and Theo could hear some kind of struggle going on. Probably because Carver and Kim were trying to hush Faith and keep her down so she wouldn't be shot. After all, if Theo figured it was a bluff, then the killer would as well.

Cursing, Theo knew he had to change his plans. He sent quick texts to Carver and Dade to let them know he'd be approaching the area where he'd left Kim and his sister, but Theo hadn't had time to head that direction when he heard another sound.

Someone screamed.

Chapter Eighteen

Kim wasn't sure how things had turned so ugly so fast, but they had. And if she didn't do something right away, they could get even worse.

One second, Faith had been muttering to herself that she had to do something to save them, and the next the woman had jumped up from the ground and started shouting. She might as well have put a big neon sign on herself to advertise to the killer where he could shoot her.

"Get down and stay quiet," Kim whispered to Faith, and she tried to wrestle her back to the ground.

Faith didn't cooperate with that one bit. She continued to yell and, as Kim had suspected, the gunman started sending bullets their way. Thankfully, there were enough trees between them and the shooter that the shots were slamming into the thick trunks. But that might not last. If the killer could chip away enough of the wood, then he might be able to put them in his sights.

Carver joined in the wrestling match to pull Faith down, and they'd just managed to get her back to the ground when Kim heard Carver's phone ding.

"It's Theo," the hand relayed once he'd had a chance to see the text. "He's heading our way."

Kim wanted to curse because, if Theo was moving, it

meant he wasn't taking cover, something they all needed to be doing right now.

"Don't put your brother in danger by trying to get back up," Kim warned Faith.

That warning finally seemed to get through. Faith wasn't saving them by taunting the killer. Instead, she was leading the guy straight to them.

Kim's head came up when she heard a rustling sound to her right. Someone was moving through the trees, trampling down the thick underbrush. She was certain it was Theo.

But she was wrong.

Both Carver and she whipped their guns in the direction of those footsteps when the man bolted through the trees and into a small clearing in front of them. Definitely not Theo.

Greg.

"Put your hands in the air," Kim demanded, and she moved away from Faith so she could shoot Greg if necessary.

However, Greg wasn't armed. Or rather, he didn't have a gun in either of his hands. Kim could see that when he lifted them in the air as she'd ordered. But he was wearing a bulky coat with plenty enough room to hide a small arsenal.

"Faith," Greg said, the single word rushing out with his gusting breath. "Are you all right?"

Kim wasn't sure what to make of the man calling her Faith instead of Ashley. Or what to make of Greg's concern. Probably an act. If so, he could be playing the worried ex-boyfriend so he could get close enough to kill them.

But she had to rethink that, too.

Rethink it because the gunman continued to fire and one of the bullets slammed into a tree a fraction from Greg's head. The man automatically dropped to the ground and cursed.

"We have to get Faith out of here," Greg insisted.

Kim wanted to roll her eyes. "Someone's trying to kill us. We're pinned down. How did you know we were here?"

"I followed you," Greg readily admitted. "I needed to see Faith, to tell her I want her back."

Despite the deafening shots continuing to tear into the trees, Faith made a sound of raw outrage. "Are you the one who kidnapped me?" she snarled.

Even though he was on his belly now, Greg lifted his head enough to look at her. "No." With his eyes wide, he repeated it. "You know it wasn't me. I heard you. You said you remembered who it was, and if you remembered, you know I didn't do that. I'm certainly not the one firing the shots since I'm right here in front of you."

"Then who is shooting?" Kim snapped before Faith could say anything.

Still looking confused, or maybe pretending to be, Greg shook his head. "I don't know."

Kim was about to demand more, but the sound of footsteps stopped her. "Keep your gun on Greg," she instructed Carver, and Kim turned her weapon in the direction of the sound.

This time, though, it was Theo.

Kim felt the slam of both relief and fear. Relief because he appeared to be unharmed, but he was also on his feet and an easy target. His gaze swept around, taking in the situation, and while turning his gun toward Greg, Theo scrambled to Faith and her.

Of course, Theo didn't pull Kim into his arms, but he moved close enough to her so they were shoulder to shoulder, and that helped steady her nerves some. Then again, just having him there had already started the steadying.

"Why is he here?" Theo asked, tipping his head to Greg.

"I needed to make sure Faith was all right." Greg spoke up. "I know you don't believe me, you think that I only want to be with her because of her money, but I really do love her."

Theo huffed. "Cover me while I frisk him," he told Kim and Carver.

He stayed low, crouching, while he made his way to Greg. And with all the efficiency of a veteran cop, he had Greg patted down within seconds. Theo yanked a small handgun from the back waist of the man's jeans and shoved it in his own coat pocket.

Since the shots were continuing nonstop, Theo latched onto the back of Greg's coat and dragged him closer to one of the trees. Not near Faith and Kim though. Theo obviously wanted to keep some space between them.

"Who's shooting at us?" Theo demanded. "Someone you hired? Or is it Duran?"

Again, Greg acted surprised. "I have no idea who's shooting. Faith said she knew."

Faith opened her mouth and Kim was certain the woman was about to own up to her lie about knowing the identity of the killer. Kim didn't want her to do that, and she figured Theo didn't either. Best to let Greg believe they knew so he could maybe spill something that would tell them who the killer was. Then again, it could indeed be Greg. That's why Kim kept her gun aimed at him.

Even over the gunfire, Kim heard more rustling, and her gaze slashed to Theo's. "Is that Uncle Dade?" she asked.

He immediately shook his head. "Dade would have texted me to let me know he was approaching."

Oh, mercy. Then it could be the killer. He could be using a hired gun to keep them pinned down so he could get closer.

If so, he wasn't exactly being silent about his approach. He was trampling through the dead leaves and twigs.

Theo put his index finger to his mouth in a stay-quiet gesture, and he pivoted in the direction of the noise. Since Carver kept his gun trained on Greg, Kim adjusted enough so she, too, would be able to shoot whoever was coming at them now.

But the person stopped.

So did the other gunfire.

And for several heart-stopping moments, there was just the silence. The only sounds were their gusting breaths and the winter wind in the trees.

Then all hell broke loose.

Someone, a woman, made a feral shout and came bursting through the underbrush.

Rowena.

She had a gun, and she started firing.

OF ALL THE people Theo had considered might start shooting at them, Rowena hadn't been on his list. In fact, he'd never seen the woman show any signs of aggression. Just the opposite. She'd kowtowed to Quill for decades.

But she sure as hell wasn't kowtowing now.

Theo dived away from her, tossing himself in front of Kim and Faith so they wouldn't be hit. However, Rowena wasn't even trying to shoot at them. No. She appeared to be trying to kill Greg, though the woman's shots were going wild and missing everything but some trees.

"Stop," Theo shouted to her.

He stayed down, but he could now hear the woman sobbing. Maybe it was because of the crying that she hadn't been able to aim well. It was also possible, though, that she simply didn't know how to hit a target.

"Rowena," Greg yelled and, with his hands covering his head, tried to scramble away from her. "Why are you doing this?"

Theo wanted to know the same damn thing, but first he needed to stop Rowena from firing again. Since she didn't seem to be listening to demands for her to cease fire, Theo launched himself at her and tackled her. It was a risk, anything he did at this point would be, but he had to take that gun from her.

Rowena didn't make the disarming easy. She fought to get away from Theo, all the while trying to take aim at Greg.

"He has to pay for what he did," Rowena rasped. "Greg has to pay."

"I agree, if he's done something wrong," Theo told her while they struggled. He finally managed to knock the gun from her hand, and Carver moved in to scoop it up from the ground before she could try to grab it again.

Rowena made another of those feral sounds of protest, but the fight finally seemed to go out of her. Her body went limp beneath Theo, and she began to sob even louder.

"She's lost her mind," Greg insisted. His voice was shaking. He probably was, too, but Theo didn't look in his direction yet. He focused on Rowena.

Theo whispered the woman's name, hoping that if he stayed calm—well, as calm as he could be considering what had just happened—that she'd stop crying long enough for him to find out what the heck was going on. First, though, he needed to alert Carver to a possible problem.

"Since the gunman stopped firing, it means the guy could be on the move," Theo explained. "Everyone needs to keep watch. Kim send a text to Dade to let him know what's going on."

With that taken care of, Theo maneuvered himself off Rowena, and rolled the woman onto her back so he could face her. "Now, tell me what it is that you believe Greg's done."

She shook her head from side to side and pressed her hand to her mouth for a moment. "He used me so he could get to Faith. He's the one who took her."

"I did not," Greg practically shouted.

"He did," Rowena insisted. "I put it all together, and I went back through the conversations we had. He asked me about Faith."

Well now, that was interesting, especially considering Greg shouldn't have even known Ashley and his sister were the same person. Faith must have thought so, as well, because she gasped. This had to be a shock for her, too, especially considering she had once intended to marry the man.

"What specifically did Greg ask about Faith?" Theo asked Rowena.

"I just wanted to know who she was," Greg blurted out before Rowena could speak. "I saw her in town, and she looked so much like the daughter the Neelys had lost. I thought maybe she was a relative."

Theo fired one short glare at Greg. "And you asked Rowena about her because you were planning on kidnapping Faith to give her to your good friends."

"No," Greg snapped just as Rowena said, "Yes. He asked me a lot of questions about her, including where she lived."

That put some ice in Theo's blood, and his glare got a whole lot worse. "I'll ask this once, and you'd sure as hell better not lie. Did you kill my parents and kidnap Faith?"

"No." Greg's answer was fast and adamant. Theo still wasn't convinced, and he wished he had Greg in an interview room so he could grill him. This wasn't the time or the place to do a thorough interrogation. "I've told you I had nothing to do with any of that." He paused and made a sob that sounded similar to the ones Rowena was making. "But I think I know who did."

Slowly, and while he tried to rein in the fury slamming through him, Theo turned to Greg.

"Then, tell me now." Theo spoke each word through clenched teeth and a boatload of fury. If this SOB had known all this time who'd committed those god-awful crimes, then Greg was going to pay for keeping his silence.

"You did this to me?" Faith yelled, interrupting whatever Greg had been about to say. Or what he'd been about to lie about anyway.

Faith didn't wait, though, for Greg to respond, and his sister must have believed he was indeed the man who'd taken her that night because she launched herself at him. She tackled Greg much as Theo had done to Rowena, but Faith didn't stop there. She began to punch and kick the man.

Theo had to move away from Rowena to get to Faith. He doubted she could actually kill Greg with her bare hands, but Theo didn't want Greg to be able to file any charges for not protecting him.

It wasn't easy, not with Faith fighting as if her life depended on it, but Theo finally managed to grab a handful of her coat and haul her off the guy. Greg was whimpering now like a wounded animal, but Theo couldn't see anything on his face beyond a few scrapes and red marks.

"He needs to die," Faith yelled, still fighting Theo. "He killed our parents, and he needs to die."

"If Greg did that, he'll be punished," Theo assured her. He took hold of Faith's shoulder to force eye contact and repeated what he'd just said.

"If?" Faith howled. "You heard what Rowena told you."

"And Rowena might be wrong," Theo said, keeping his

voice low and with just a tinge of a warning in case Faith was thinking about trying to have another go at Greg.

"I'm not wrong," Rowena said through her sobs, but she quickly amended that. "I don't think I'm wrong."

There it was. That shadow of doubt that would get Greg a not-guilty verdict if this ever went to trial. They were a long way from anything like a trial though. First, they had to get the heck out of there.

Theo glanced around to assess the best route for them to use, but a sound stopped him. Not gunfire or a scream this time. It was more of a muffled gasp, followed by the sounds of frantic movement. He turned.

And his heart dropped to the ground.

Because he saw a man in a ski mask dragging Kim away.

KIM HEARD THE footsteps behind her.

A millisecond too late.

Before she could even turn around to see who it was, someone knocked her gun from her hand and grabbed her by the hair, yanking it so hard that she could have sworn she saw stars. The person—a man—dragged her to a standing position with her back against his chest, and he started moving.

Fast.

So fast that Kim barely got a glimpse of Theo when he realized what was happening. And what was happening was that someone was trying to kidnap her. She had no doubts—none—that the someone was the killer.

The fear slammed through her, but Kim tried not to let it immobilize her. She had to fight. To think. She had to figure out a way to stop herself from being murdered.

At the moment, her abductor obviously didn't want her dead or he could have just killed her when he was sneaking up on her. That meant he probably needed her as a shield so he could escape, or else he wanted her as a bargaining tool. Maybe to draw out Theo and Faith so he could kill all three of them.

But who was doing this?

Who had her in a chokehold and was dragging her through the trees and underbrush?

It wasn't Greg. Kim had been keeping an eye on the man since he'd showed up. She'd watched Rowena, as well, and the woman hadn't moved after Faith had gone after Greg. So was this Quill or Duran?

Maybe.

But it could be just another hired gun, a thug, who was dragging her toward the real killer.

Kim got another slam of fear when she heard Theo call out for her. The sound of running footsteps followed, and she had no doubts that Theo was coming after her. And that would make him an easy target. It didn't take long for that to happen. Her captor stopped right by the last pecan tree in the cluster and, with her in front of him, ducked behind the tree for cover.

He fired a shot at Theo.

"Get down," Kim yelled. But she knew her warning had come too late.

She was almost too afraid to look, but when she did, she finally saw that Theo had dived to the ground, hopefully out of the line of fire.

"There are nearly a dozen lawmen and retired cops heading this way," Theo called out. "And there's no way in hell I'm letting you escape with Kim."

There was so much anger and determination in Theo's voice. Kim wanted to hold on to it, to let it assure her that they'd all get out of this alive, but there were no guarantees. Maybe no second chances, and it crushed her heart to know she might die without ever telling Theo how she felt about him.

That she was in love with him.

It was something she should have told him after they'd had sex. She'd certainly known her feelings then. But now it could be too late for him to ever know.

Her captor fired another shot and Kim prayed it had missed Theo. She had no way of knowing, though, because the guy started moving again. This time, he darted across the small clearing toward the road. It was possible he had a vehicle there waiting, and if so, he could be taking her somewhere to use her as bait.

Bait that would work.

Because Theo would come after her. She had no doubt about that, and Kim was betting the killer knew that as well. In fact, he'd be counting on it.

Kim felt herself falling and then she landed hard in the deep ditch by the road. The fall didn't loosen the man's grip on her, though, and she didn't have enough of a footing yet to try to kick him. So she tried something else. A ploy that might distract him enough that he wouldn't be able to get a clean shot when Theo came barreling after them.

"Faith remembered who you are," Kim said.

She didn't whisper it, didn't make it sound like a ploy or question. She wanted him to believe that he'd just been outed. It was a long shot. But it worked. She heard the man curse and instantly recognized his voice.

Quill.

There was no mistaking it since she'd heard one of his profanity-laden tirades often enough.

"Then everybody who heard Faith will have to die," Quill concluded.

Kim's mind was reeling with the slam of adrenaline and

the fear for Theo, but she forced herself to think of something, anything, that might make Quill back off. "Rowena was there. She heard. Are you going to try to kill her, too?"

That brought on more profanity. "Damn right, I will. She should have died a long time ago."

"Twenty-one years ago." Kim threw it out there. She purposely raised her voice so that Theo could hear her. Not only because he could pinpoint their location in the ditch but also because she wanted him to hear if Quill was about to confess. "Did Rowena help you kill Theo's parents and kidnap Faith?"

"No. Hell, no," Quill snapped. "She's not smart enough for that, and she has no spine."

"Rowena couldn't have killed two people," Kim added, and she had to fight another slam. Not adrenaline this time but pure raw anger. This SOB had murdered two wonderful people and made life a living hell for Theo, Faith and her.

"No, she couldn't have," Quill agreed, as if that were a weakness.

"But you did," Kim continued.

"Yeah, because I had to. They were supposed to be asleep, and they caught me sneaking in. I didn't have a choice."

Oh, yes. He'd had plenty of choices that night, but Quill had made the worst one. "Did Duran pay you to kidnap Faith or was it Greg?"

"Neither. It was the Neelys. Greg told him about this girl he'd seen in Silver Creek. A girl the spitting image of their dead kid. Greg put them in touch with me, and they paid me a hundred thousand to get the kid."

Kim hoped the Neelys had been gut-punched when they'd heard Quill had killed two people to get Faith. But maybe not. Maybe they'd just been so pleased about getting a daughter that they hadn't cared. It was too bad they were both dead or they could have been arrested for the part they had played in this nightmare.

Even though Quill still had his arm anchored around her neck, Kim managed to move her feet, and she found solid ground. Good thing, too, since she heard the movement to her right and she knew that couldn't be good. It was either Theo, who could be gunned down, or a thug Quill had hired.

"The Neelys paid you a hundred grand," Kim repeated. "And when Faith started to remember, you hired a gunman to try to kill her. Or maybe you were the shooter at the hospital."

"I was," Quill answered almost absently, but his body tensed. He was bracing for a fight. "Now shut up so I can hear if your boyfriend's trying to sneak up on us. I've got to finish this."

Finish this. By adding yet more killings to his list of crimes.

"You must have gotten awfully nervous when Nadia hooked up with Theo," Kim went on, hoping that her voice would cover the sound if Theo was indeed sneaking up on them.

"Yeah, you could say that." Quill gave a dry laugh. "I knew Theo was still poking around in the investigation, but then I figured it was a good thing he was with Nadia, that if he said something she'd mention it to Rowena, and Rowena would whine about it to me."

Too bad that hadn't happened, but the investigation hadn't pointed to Quill until after these latest attacks.

"You sent me those letters," Kim insisted. "Why? Why not just stay quiet and let your crimes stay buried?"

"The letters," he repeated like profanity. "Those were a mistake. But I figured if you thought Faith was alive and that her kidnapper, or she, was taunting you, that you wouldn't be looking close to home for the person responsible. I figured you definitely wouldn't be looking right under your own nose."

So, the letters had been an attempt to throw Theo and her off his scent. And in a way, they had worked because it had muddied the waters of the investigation.

"I kept tabs on Faith," Quill went on. "And after the Neelys died, I heard she was snooping around, looking into the Sheldons' missing kid and their deaths. I knew that couldn't be good, and I had to do something to stop her."

Quill's solution to stopping Faith had obviously been to kill them all. New murders to cover up old murders and a kidnapping.

"Sheriff, if you want to keep your woman alive, you'll need to do as I say," Quill called out.

"I'm listening," Theo assured him a moment later.

"Good. Call off your deputies and all those badge-carrying Rylands. This is between you and me. I'll trade Kim for you. All you have to do is surrender."

Oh, mercy. No. Kim didn't want Theo to even consider that. But Theo had to know that Quill intended to murder them all, so he wouldn't just go in without a way to save himself and her.

"All right," Theo agreed. "First, though, tell me if you're the one who set the explosives and if there are any more."

"Of course, I set them," Quill readily admitted. "I've got a militia buddy who taught me how, and I reckoned that sooner or later, you'd be bringing your sister back here. If not, then I would have figured out another way to get to her."

"And what about hired guns?" Theo pressed. "We've got the dead one, but is there another?"

Kim could tell Theo had moved his position and was closer now. It was possible he'd already arranged for Dade or Carver to circle around and come up on Quill from behind. They wouldn't have clean shots because she would be in the way, which meant Kim had to do something.

She adjusted her feet again, intending to drop her weight so that someone would have a head shot for Quill. However, before Kim could do that, she heard someone she didn't want to hear.

"Quill," someone yelled.

Faith.

And Kim just knew the running footsteps she heard was Faith charging toward them. She'd probably heard Quill confess to murdering her parents and kidnapping her, and judging from the sound of her voice, Faith was in a state of pure rage. Rage that could get her killed.

Kim went ahead and dropped down, but she also rammed her elbow into Quill's gut. The man grunted and cursed her. What he didn't do was loosen his grip. He managed to hang on to her.

"Faith, no!" Theo shouted.

From the corner of her eye, Kim saw Faith launch herself at Quill, and she rammed into them, sending all three of them to the ground. Kim didn't try to move away. Instead, she located Quill's right hand and latched onto it, clawing her fingernails into his wrist.

Quill howled in pain and backhanded her, the impact hitting her right in the jaw. This time, she had no choice but to stagger back, but she didn't break the hold she had on his shooting hand.

Even though she couldn't see Theo, Kim knew when he'd reached them. He dropped down into the ditch, maneuvering his body so that he was between Quill and her. Theo made Quill pay by bashing his head with his gun. Quill staggered back just a fraction, and Theo punched Quill in the gut.

Theo probably hadn't wanted to risk firing a shot, not with Faith and her right there, but the punch was effective enough. Quill finally released his grip on the gun, no doubt so he could shove his fist into Theo's face. The man was still going to try to fight his way out of this.

But the gunshot stopped him.

The sound tore through Kim's ears and sent a stab of pain across her entire head. For a moment, she thought she'd been shot, but it was just the reverberation of the bullet being fired.

A shot that could have hit Theo.

That gave Kim a jolt of terror and she got images even worse than the ones she'd been battling for twenty-one years. Her heart stopped, her breath stalled in her chest, everything inside pinpointed to Theo. He had to be all right. He just had to be. She couldn't lose him now.

Theo looked at her, and he seemed to be experiencing his own moment of terror. There were spatters of blood on his face, but Kim couldn't see an actual wound.

Not until she looked at Quill.

He had no color in his face, not a drop. But, mercy, there was plenty of blood. It was on his chin and chest, and he clamped his hands over the gaping, bleeding wound in his chest. His dull, dying eyes went not to Theo or her.

But to Faith.

Faith was holding a gun that Kim recognized because it belonged to her. Quill had knocked it from her hand when he'd dragged her out from that pecan grove.

"I picked it up," Faith said, glancing down at the gun that she kept pointed at Quill. She wasn't shaking, didn't appear to be in shock. In fact, Faith looked steady and resolved that she'd finally gotten justice for her parents and herself.

Still clutching his chest, Quill dropped to his knees. "You killed me," he gurgled out, his gaze fixed on Faith.

"Yes," Faith admitted. "Payback's a bitch, isn't it?"

Quill managed a sneer before the last breath he'd ever take rattled in his throat. He collapsed onto the frozen ground.

Theo waited a moment and then pressed his fingers to Quill's throat. "Dead," he relayed.

There was no relief in his eyes though. No hint of satisfaction that the man who'd murdered his parents was dead. "Get down in the ditch," Theo told them. "I'm not sure if Quill was the one firing shots at us from the barn. There could be a gunman about to carry out Quill's orders to kill us."

Chapter Nineteen

Theo hated the stark fear that shot through Kim's and his sister's eyes. With Quill dead, they'd no doubt thought the danger was over.

But there could be another round.

Theo wasn't even sure there was a gunman out there, but according to the text he'd just gotten, Dade was looking for the guy. So were Grayson, Gage, Kade, Nate and Mason, who'd arrived at the ranch shortly after Quill had managed to grab Kim. If there was a hired gun, the Ryland lawmen brothers would find him, but Theo needed that to happen before the SOB managed to fire more shots at Kim and Faith. They'd been through enough.

Not just today but for the past twenty-one years.

Kim and Faith probably didn't care much for sharing a ditch with a dead man, especially a dead man who'd caused so much hell for them. Added to that, Faith was possibly in shock. Even after Theo had pulled her into a sitting position in the ditch, she'd kept her glassy eyes pinned to the man.

"I remembered it was Quill who took me," Faith muttered. "Too late, but I remembered."

"It wasn't too late," Kim assured her, and she pulled Faith into a hug. Something that Theo wanted to do to both of them, but he needed to keep watch. Carver was helping with that, but there were a lot of trees and shrubs that an attacker could use to sneak up on them.

"If I'd remembered sooner, Theo could have arrested him," Faith argued. But then she stopped and looked at both Kim and him. "And if that had happened, Quill would still be alive. I'm glad he's dead. I'm glad he'll never be able to come after us again."

Yeah, Theo wasn't shedding any tears over a killer getting a taste of his own medicine. And that caused him to think of Rowena, Nadia and Jack. Jack didn't even know Quill so he wouldn't be affected, and Nadia and her dad hadn't been close. Still, Nadia had lost her father, and she would have to deal with that. Theo would help her with it if she wanted.

Rowena would get his help, too. But Theo had to wonder if the woman would grieve for her dead husband, or would this be a relief for her, too? He thought that maybe, eventually, Rowena would be able to move on with her life and find her new normal.

He'd need to find a new normal as well. Heck, so would Kim and Faith. No way did he want to go back to the way things had been before. No. He needed both Kim and his sister in his life.

"Will you have to arrest me for killing Quill?" Faith asked.

Theo silently cursed and shook his head. "No. Quill had a gun and had taken Kim hostage. He would have killed all of us had he gotten the chance. You stopped him before he could do that."

Of course, Faith would have to live with the memory of doing that. Even though taking his life was justified, it would stay with her, and she'd never be the same. Of course, Quill had made sure she'd never be the same when he'd kidnapped her and handed her over to people who'd paid him to steal her from her family.

Faith blew out a long breath, maybe a little relieved that she wouldn't be arrested, and she leaned her head against the wall of the ditch. She was clearly exhausted, and once the adrenaline had run its course, she was going to crash. Maybe he'd have her safely out of there by then.

Kim, too.

Though she didn't look nearly as exhausted as his sister. In fact, she still seemed revved, but it might take a while for it to sink in just how close she'd come to dying tonight.

"I'm all right," Kim muttered, inching toward him. She didn't pull him into her arms, probably because she knew he was keeping watch, but she pressed her head against his shoulder. "Are you?"

"I'm getting there," he assured her, and having her this close to him was definitely helping.

She made a sound of agreement. "I know the timing for this sucks, but I need to tell you something. There was this thought that kept going through my head when Quill had me. I didn't want to die without letting you know how I feel about you. And how I feel about you is that I'm in love with you."

Her words hit him hard. Not in a punch-to-the-gut kind of way when he'd seen Quill dragging her away. No. This was a warmth that spread through him and immediately eased some of the dark places.

He didn't smile, or kiss her, though that's exactly what he wanted to do. Heck, he wanted to whoop for joy, but the dinging sound of his phone meant such things had to be put on hold.

We've got the shooter, Dade texted. Just one. We found him at the back of the barn trying to get away. Grayson and Kade are dealing with him and will get him in a cell ASAP. By the way, he's a chatterbox and will confirm that Quill was the one who hired him.

Now, the relief came, and rather than risk his voice, he showed Faith and Kim the message. Kim did whoop for joy, and she threw herself into his arms. Not a punch of warmth this time. It felt as if everything in his life moved into just the right place. Theo would have liked to have lingered there for, well, forever, but he had to send a reply to Dade to let him know their situation and location.

"It's over," Faith muttered. She was clearly relieved, too, and Kim reached out, pulling in both Theo and his sister to make it a group hug.

While he needed this—man, did he—Theo wanted to hear Kim repeat that part about being in love with him. Just so there was no doubt that she actually meant it. But he got another text before he could say anything.

It was Dade again.

We're on our way to you now. Mason's dealing with Greg and Rowena and will take them to the sheriff's office.

Good. That was one less thing for Theo to deal with. Mason could easily handle the pair and get them in for interviews. Both Rowena and Greg would need to be questioned to make sure they hadn't had a part in the murders and kidnappings. And even if Greg hadn't directly participated in those particular crimes, he was still guilty of not reporting that Ashley was Faith, something he'd admitted knowing if Quill was telling the truth about that.

Ava would be able to deal with that, along with giving Duran one final round in the interview room to be certain he hadn't done anything unlawful with his part in what was definitely an illegal adoption.

Since Quill had confessed and named the Neelys as the people who'd hired him, Rowena wouldn't be charged with those crimes. However, she could face charges for reckless endangerment for firing those shots at Greg.

Theo would also have to make it clear to Greg that even if he didn't end up in jail, he was to keep away from Faith. Well, keep away from her unless his sister changed her mind about that, but he was thinking that Greg was now a thing of the past for her.

Hopefully, a lot of things fell into that category for all of them.

Dade finally came out of the trees and started toward the ditch. He wasn't alone. Kim's father was with him, and Nate hurried to the ditch, no doubt to make sure his daughter was unharmed. Nate pulled up, though, right at the edge when he saw that Kim had her arm around Theo and she'd dropped her head on his shoulder. Nate lifted an eyebrow and shifted his attention to Theo. Maybe Kim and he were sending off some kind of vibe, one not connected to what had just happened, because the corner of Nate's mouth lifted in a smile.

"About damn time," Nate muttered.

The knot in Theo's stomach loosened a bit. Not that he'd thought Kim's family wouldn't approve of them being together. He'd known they would. Still, it was good to have confirmation.

Dade helped Faith out of the ditch and then he dropped down next to Quill's body. "I can call for the medical examiner and the CSIs," he offered.

"And I can wait here with him," Nate added while he took hold of Kim's hand. He pulled her from the ditch and into his arms for a long hug. "Are you all right?" he murmured to his daughter.

"I'm better now," she settled for saying. "I don't think I have a scratch on me."

"Yeah, you do." Nate brushed his fingers over her chin. "I want to beat Quill to a pulp for doing that, but I think I'd have to stand in line. Theo would probably get first dibs."

Theo would take first dibs if Quill were still alive. He had a lot of anger for what the man had done to them and his family. But some of the anger melted away when Theo climbed out of the ditch and Kim moved away from her father to pull him into her arms. She didn't stop there. Nope.

She kissed him.

It wasn't tame. It was long, deep, and filled with relief, need. And love. Oh, yes. He felt all of that.

"I'm in love with Theo," Kim announced when she finally took her mouth from his. "Anyone have a problem with that?"

There were some grumbled replies of approval. No objections, though, and Theo would have given those three words right back to her if his phone hadn't rung. Not one of the Rylands or deputies this time. It was Nadia.

Hell.

He certainly hadn't forgotten about his ex, but he hadn't wanted to talk to her until he'd had a chance to clear his head. Still, she'd maybe heard about the trouble at the ranch, and he didn't want her to be kept in the dark.

"Give me a minute," Theo said to no one in particular. He gave Kim a quick kiss and took the call.

"I heard there'd been a shooting at the old place," Nadia blurted out. "Are you all right?"

"I'm fine." Theo took hold of Kim's hand and moved her away from the others while Nate and Dade started checking

Faith to make sure she hadn't been injured. "So is Faith." He paused, gathered his breath. "But Quill isn't. He's dead, Nadia. He's the one who killed my folks and kidnapped Faith."

He heard her gasp and was about to offer to go over there.

"He's responsible for the attacks?"

"Yes, and he tried to kidnap Kim just minutes ago." Theo would give her a more detailed account of events. If she wanted it, that is. "Rowena is all right, too, but she showed up as all of this was going down. She's being taken to the sheriff's office, if you want to see her."

"Is it safe for me to go out?" Nadia asked.

"It is. The Rylands captured the gunman Quill hired. But if you can hold off an hour or so, I can come over and take you to see your mother."

"Yes, please do that." She paused again. "Is Kim okay?"

"She is," Theo verified. "She's right here with me." Now it was his turn to pause. "I'd like to bring her with me to see Jack, if that's all right?"

Nadia took her time answering. "Yes, that'll be fine. I mean, Jack should get used to seeing you two together. You're in love with her?" Nadia tacked on.

Theo didn't want for Kim to hear those words from him while he was responding to his ex's question, so he went with a simple, "Yes."

He heard Nadia drag in a long breath. "All right. I'll see both of you when you come over."

Theo couldn't help it. He smiled. Nadia wasn't exactly jumping for joy over his feelings for Kim, but she wasn't hostile about them either. That was a good start. In fact, there'd been a lot of good starts today.

And that's why he ended the call, turned to Kim and kissed her.

He poured a lot of emotion into that kiss. A lot of hope, too. Because he had no doubts about his feelings for her, no doubts that he wanted her in his life.

The kiss lingered a lot longer than it should, especially considering this was a crime scene—with her father and uncles watching. Still, Theo had needed it. Judging from Kim's sound of pleasure, she had needed it as well.

He finally pulled back and looked her in the eyes. Amazing eyes that he'd hopefully get to see every morning, every night.

Forever.

"I'm in love with you, Kim," Theo said. Not mere words but a promise.

She smiled, and though there were tears in her eyes, he knew these were happy ones. "Then, we're the luckiest people on earth because I'm in love with you. And you're going to need to say those words over and over to me again because I want to hear them a whole lot of times."

"No problem," Theo assured her. He could tell her he loved her, well, forever.

* * * * *

DECEPTION
AT DIXON PASS

CINDI MYERS

For Dawn

Chapter One

Snowflakes danced in the snowmobile's headlight, swirling and corkscrewing in an elaborate ballet before adding to the already knee-high drifts on either side of the narrow path leading up to the cabin. Grace swept one gloved hand across the face shield of her helmet to clear the snow and leaned forward, squinting to try to get her bearings in this shaken–snow globe landscape.

A dark shape lurched onto the path ahead of her, and she squeezed the brakes, the back of the snow machine fishtailing right, then left. She gasped as the headlight's blue-white glare spotlighted the muscular image of a man, his face contorted in pain, fresh blood smeared across the side of his face, more blood on his naked chest.

All of him was naked, his skin a ghostly blue-white in the headlight's glare. Heart pounding, she braked to a stop, the snowmobile wallowing a little in the mounting drifts. "Hello!" she shouted.

The man took a step toward her, then swayed. She stood in her seat, then vaulted to the ground as he sank to his knees and toppled sideways, like a great tree felled.

He was conscious, but barely. She bent over his still form, then touched his shoulder. His skin was icy to the touch, his breathing shallow.

"Get up," she ordered, then louder, "You have to get up!" She slapped his face, and he turned away from her and moaned.

Grace shoved at his shoulders and managed to get him into a sitting position, then prodded him to his feet once more. He was a big man—over six feet tall and muscular. Snow swirled around them as she tucked her shoulder under his arm and staggered against the weight of him leaning into her.

"Come on!" she shouted over the howling wind. "We have to go."

They took one step forward, then another. Despite the exertion, her teeth chattered violently as she maneuvered him alongside her snowmobile. He didn't resist as she coaxed him onto the seat. She shrugged out of her heavy parka and draped it over him, a pitiful covering barely hanging on his broad shoulders. Then she stood behind him on the sideboard and managed to get the machine going again and headed up the path to her cabin, the single light she had left burning a beacon to guide them.

Bear, her shepherd mix, met them at the door, barking, but she quieted him. He stood back, wary, gaze flitting from her to the newcomer as she led the man to the sofa, sat him down and draped an afghan over him. He stared at her with empty, frightened eyes.

"I'm going to start a fire," she said, speaking louder than necessary, as if he was hard of hearing. She lowered her voice to a more normal tone. "We need to get you warm, then I'll help you clean up and we'll see how badly you're hurt." All that blood worried her.

She built a fire in the woodstove, and when it was blazing, she set water to heat on the gas stove in the kitchen. She grabbed the plastic basins she used for washing dishes and filled them with cool water from her storage tank and carried them to the man. "Put your hands and feet in here," she said.

When he made no move to comply, she knelt in front of him and lifted one bare foot and then the other and plunged them into one of the basins, splashing water onto the knees of her snow pants. When he tried to take them out, she pressed down. "No. Leave them in there. You'll be lucky if you don't lose toes to frostbite." His feet—large, masculine feet with fine dark hair on the toes—were so pale they were almost blue.

She looked up into his eyes, to see if he understood. He met her scrutiny, and for a moment she was caught by that gold-flecked gaze. He no longer looked so dazed.

He nodded. "Thank you," he said, his voice raspy and deep, sending a shiver along her spine.

"The second basin is for your hands." She set it on the sofa beside him.

He nodded and immersed his hands to the wrist, wincing as he did so, but he left them there.

The kettle began to sing, so Grace returned to the kitchen and made hot cocoa—a large mug with two packets of mix. She was about to add a healthy slug of brandy, then remembered the head wound and thought better of it. Instead, she poured the rest of the water from the kettle into a bowl and dug a packet of gauze and some antibiotic ointment from the first aid kit over the sink.

He was sitting where she had left him, hands and feet in the basins of water, head back and eyes closed. Bear had stationed himself by the woodstove but kept his gaze fixed on the man. Grace paused in the doorway to assess her visitor more calmly. He was probably six foot three and healthy, with well-defined muscles and good skin, a faint shadow of dark beard showing against his pale skin, well-cut dark brown hair falling across his forehead. He wore no jewelry and had no tattoos. The afghan lay across his lap, but she had a good memory of what he had looked like unclothed. Like a sleek wild animal. A little scary. A lot fascinating.

He opened his eyes and looked right at her, and heat spread up her face, as if he had known what she was thinking. "What happened?" he asked.

"I was going to ask you the same thing." She moved to his side and wet a square of gauze in the basin. The water had cooled enough now that it wouldn't burn him. She dabbed at what looked to be the source of the blood—a gash just behind his temple, jagged and already bruising at the tender edges. "I was on my way home, and you stepped out of the woods, naked and bleeding. I thought at first you were some kind of hallucination."

He grunted as she touched what must've been a tender spot. "Sorry," she said. "But this is pretty nasty. Who hit you?"

He didn't answer right away. She stopped her ministrations and tilted her head to check his expression. "I don't know," he said, his voice still ragged. "I can't remember."

The hurt in his voice touched a corresponding tender place inside of her. She had to work to catch her next breath. "It's okay," she said. "It's going to be okay." She turned her attention back to his head wound. "You might need stitches," she said. "But there's no way to get you to the medical center from here. Not in this storm."

"Where am I?" he asked.

"Officially, you're at the San Juan annex of the Rocky Mountain Biological Laboratory," she said. "Otherwise known as my house." Which, of course, made zero sense to him. Even some people who lived in Eagle Mountain didn't know about this place. That was part of its charm, both for research and personal purposes. "I collect data about weather, snowfall, rainfall, migration patterns of various species, plant growth—all kinds of things that show patterns across the years. My grandfather started the research back in 1960. It's one of the best databases of the effects of changing climate in the United States."

"You're a scientist," he said.

"Yes." So much better than other things she had been called, from *hermit* to *weirdo*. Not by her friends, of course, but some people were quick to judge. This man wasn't one of them.

"My name is Grace," she said. "Grace Wilcox."

He winced as if in pain, but not physical, she didn't think. "I can't remember my name," he said, and panic tinged the last word.

She put a gentling hand on his shoulder. "It's okay," she said. "This is a nasty head wound. You might have a concussion. Your memory will probably come back to you."

Except hers never had. She had lived most of her life with a five-month gap in her recollection. Five months that had changed everything about her, yet she couldn't remember anything. She hoped this man didn't suffer that fate.

She finished cleaning the wound, dabbed on some ointment and applied a dressing. "Let me check your eyes," she said.

That direct gaze hit her again. Assessing. As if he could see all her secrets. She looked away. "Your pupils are the same size, so that's good. Any nausea?"

"A little."

"Pain?"

"Head hurts. Most of the rest of me, too."

Not a surprise, considering how far he must have walked

over rough terrain. She had some ideas about that. "Do you remember anything about a car?" she asked. "A woman?" Her stomach clenched at the memory of that woman. So cold and still.

"I'm sorry," he said. "No."

She patted his shoulder again. "Let's see your hands."

The fingers were swollen now, red and painful. But she didn't think he would lose any. She dried them off, then moved to his feet. A couple of toes still showed signs of waxiness, but maybe he would be okay. If her suspicions were correct, he had been out in the weather for about an hour. Plenty of time to do damage, but not as bad as it could be.

She picked up the mug of cocoa. "Drink this," she said. "It will warm you up, and the sugar will help, too."

He couldn't really hold the mug with his swollen hands, so she held it for him while he sipped, his eyes watching her over the rim of the cup in a way she felt to the pit of her stomach. It wasn't an unpleasant feeling, but surprisingly intimate, considering she didn't even know his name.

When the mug was empty, she stood once more. "I'm going to find you some clothes." She assessed him. "They won't fit well, but they'll keep you decent."

Grace had to climb into the loft to reach the trunk with her grandfather's things. While she dug through it, she pondered her guest's possible origins. When she had found him, she had been returning from a search and rescue call up on Dixon Pass. A car had been abandoned on the side of the highway, and law enforcement had discovered a dead woman in the back seat, and a man's bloody footprints leading away from the vehicle, into the canyon. Search and Rescue had combed the area for the man responsible for those footprints but had to abandon the search after only half an hour because of the growing blizzard.

Was the man on her sofa the one who had wandered from that car? Had he killed the woman? Given his head wound, it seemed more likely to her that he had been a second intended victim and had fled for his life. It was an interesting puzzle, but one she didn't think she would know the answer to any time soon.

Near the bottom of the trunk, she found an oversized sweatshirt, a flannel shirt and a pair of sweatpants. The pants would be too short, but she added long wool socks. That would have to do. No underwear—because even she wasn't sentimental enough to have saved Granddad's Jockey shorts.

Her visitor had dozed off by the time she got back to him, but she woke him and told him sternly to dress, then left the room before he could throw off the blanket and get her heart racing again.

HE WOKE TO a crackling, popping sound and the aromas of coffee and pinion smoke. He opened his eyes and looked into the face of a woman. A beautiful woman, with dark hair falling in soft waves to her shoulders, big dark eyes framed by lacy black lashes, full pink lips and skin he ached to touch. It looked so soft.

"How are you feeling?" she asked in a gentle contralto voice.

He shook his head, not knowing how to answer. His body ached, but worse was the confusion in his mind.

She moved away and he took in the room behind her— log walls lined with bookcases, fire crackling in the woodstove and a large gray-and-black dog with a wolfish face watching him from in front of the stove.

"Your hands look better this morning," she said. "Do you think you could hold this cup of coffee?"

He looked down at his hands. They were slightly swollen and ached. He curled them into fists, then reached for the cup, even as his stomach growled.

"I'll have breakfast in a little bit," she said. "There's cream and sugar there on the table if you want them." She pointed to a small table beside him and started to turn away, but he reached out and put a hand on her arm.

"What was your name again?" He felt he should know.

"It's Grace. Grace Wilcox."

"Hello, Grace. I'm Declan Owen." Relief flooded him as he said the words. He remembered his name. That was a start.

She smiled, and he felt the warmth of her expression deep in his gut. "Do you remember what happened, Declan?"

He looked around the cabin again, then down at himself. He was dressed in too-short, too-tight sweatpants, drooping wool socks, a gray sweatshirt and a faded green-and-black flannel shirt. "I don't know how I got here," he said.

She squatted down until she was eye level with him. "What do you remember?"

He thought a moment. "I remember driving," he said. "I was following someone, I think. Or looking for someone."

"Were you alone?" she asked.

"Yes." He was certain of that. Certain that he was almost always alone.

"Were you searching for a man or a woman?" she asked.

"A man." The answer came readily.

"Anything else?" she asked.

Declan shook his head.

Grace stood. "All right. I'll make breakfast. The bathroom is right through there if you need it." She indicated a door on the far wall.

She left the room and he finished the coffee, then went to the bathroom, which was outfitted with a composting toilet, an old-fashioned pedestal sink and a small shower. A glance out the window showed two-foot drifts with new snow falling and deep woods as far as he could see.

"The cabin is off-grid," she said when he returned to the living area. "If the snow keeps up, I'll have to go out and start the generator to recharge the batteries, but we'll be fine for a while. Breakfast is almost ready. Come into the kitchen and we'll eat there."

The kitchen was no more than an eight-foot square, with a half-size stove, refrigerator and sink and a single four-foot stretch of tiled countertop. "My grandfather built this cabin," she said. "He wasn't much of a cook and preferred to have more room for bookcases. You can sit there."

"This looks good," he said, pulling out the chair she indicated at the small table, which also looked handmade. The small space made him feel outsized, though she seemed to fit in it perfectly. "How far are we from the road?" he asked.

"There's a Forest Service road one mile down the mountain that the county plows for me, though it's not a priority." She filled a mug with fresh coffee next to a glass of orange juice, then passed a plate of bacon. "I park my Jeep at the end in winter and travel the rest of the way on a snowmobile. That's how I got you home last night."

He had brief shards of memory, like images illuminated by flashes of lightning: a woman supporting him as he tried to walk, the same woman wrapping him in a blanket. The sting of antiseptic at his temple.

He touched the bandage on the side of his head. "What happened to me?"

"It looks like someone bashed you in the head. Hard enough to knock you out, I guess." She stopped eating and laid aside her knife and fork. "I volunteer with Search and Rescue," she said. "We had a call yesterday about a car abandoned on the side of the highway up on Dixon Pass. There were a man's bloody footprints leading away from the car, and we were searching for that person. But we had to cut the search short because of the snow."

"You think the man was me?"

"Does any of that sound familiar?"

"No." He focused on his plate once more. He was famished, so much so that his hands almost shook as he spooned eggs onto his plate. They ate in silence for a while, then a new thought occurred to him. "What happened to my clothes?" he asked.

"You weren't wearing any."

He let that sink in. "Not any?"

"Not a stitch." Dimples tugged at the corners of her mouth. Was she trying not to laugh? Not exactly a thing to laugh about. "It was why I was frantic to get you inside, before you froze to death," she said.

"You made me stick my feet and hands in cold water." Why had he suddenly remembered that?

"It's supposed to allow any frozen digits to thaw, but slowly."

He looked down at his hands again. "It must have worked."

"You really should have that head looked at by a doctor," she said. "It will have to wait until the snow lets up and the plow clears the road. But I think you'll be all right until then."

"Do you have a phone?" he asked.

"I have a cell phone. And a booster so it works here. Is there someone you need to call?"

He wracked his brain but could think of no one. He shook his head. They finished eating, then he helped her clear the dishes. The kitchen was too small for them to work together, so she sent him out to the porch to retrieve more firewood. The dog, Bear, went with him and patrolled around the cabin. Declan stood for a long moment, staring at the snow falling on the silent expanse of woods. He spotted the solar panels on the roof of a nearby shed and the snowmobile parked under a lean-to beside the shed. This place was so isolated. And she lived here all alone?

Bear came up onto the porch and barked at him. "I'm not going to hurt her," Declan said softly. He knew that about himself, the way he knew his name. And then another fact popped into his head.

He went back inside and dumped his armload of wood into the old copper boiler beside the woodstove, then went to stand in the doorway to the kitchen.

Grace looked over her shoulder at him, her hands wrist-deep in soapy water. "Is something wrong?" she asked.

"I remembered something," he said. "Something important."

"Oh?"

"I'm a United States marshal. Deputy US Marshal Declan Owen."

Chapter Two

"The car is registered to Declan Owen." Sergeant Gage Walker looked up at his brother, Travis Walker, sheriff of Rayford County. Travis stood in the doorway of Gage's small office at the sheriff's department, a cup of coffee in one hand, the other braced on the door frame. Two years older than Gage, Travis was the more serious of the two, well suited to the responsibilities of sheriff. But Gage was his right-hand man, the person he counted on most to handle the toughest jobs.

"What else?" Travis took a sip of coffee and waited.

"Declan Owen is a deputy United States marshal. I tracked down his supervisor in the Denver office." He checked his notes. "Oscar Penrod. He said Owen is on vacation at the moment."

"And the woman?"

"Agnes Cockrell. She lives over in Rocky Ridge. Her husband, Ronald, said she was driving back from visiting a friend in Purgatory."

"Driving?"

"Yeah. Her car is missing. A white Honda Element." Gage checked his notes again. "She was shot once in the back of the head with a .40-caliber bullet. We're still waiting for the ballistics tests to come back, but my guess is the bullet came from the Glock 22 found on the back floorboard near her. A gun registered to Deputy Marshal Declan Owen."

Travis let out a low whistle. "So he flags down Ms. Cockrell, shoots her and steals her car?"

"And leaves his gun behind?" Gage shook his head. "And what about those bloody footprints leading away from the car?"

"So maybe Owen was with Ms. Cockrell for some reason and a third party killed her, wounded him and he escaped."

"We might could get a frozen sample of the blood from the snow to test for blood type and DNA," Gage said.

Travis made a face. "Probably pretty diluted by snow by now, but we could try, if we have to. It would be easier to find this Declan Owen and ask him. Before tomorrow, if possible. I'd like to know what happened before I leave."

"You don't think I can handle it?" Gage asked.

Travis's look grew more pained. "I'm sure you can, but now is a terrible time for me to leave, with us being short-handed."

"I'm not going to let you talk yourself out of taking this vacation," Gage said. "Lacy would never speak to me again. She'd probably never speak to you." Travis's wife, Lacy, had finally convinced him to take a long-delayed honeymoon to Aruba. True, the departure of Deputy Ronin Doyle, who had decided to pursue photography full time, had left them short an officer, but Gage was sure he could handle things.

"As soon as the snow lets up, we're going to ask Search and Rescue to go back out," he said. "Owen couldn't have gotten that far in that weather, bleeding the way he was."

"The blood might have belonged to Agnes," Travis said.

"I guess so."

"Anything else?" Travis prompted.

Gage consulted his notes again. "Owen spent the night at

the Creekside Motel in Purgatory. His belongings are still in his room—luggage and a laptop—so it sounds like he planned to return."

"You put a BOLO out for him?"

"I did. Let's hope he turns up. Preferably alive and not dead in the snow." Alive, they could talk to him and try to get at the truth of the situation. Dead, and they would only have more unanswered questions.

DECLAN FOUND A pair of boots by the back door that he was able to shove his feet into. He took a wedge and a splitting maul from a shelf at the end of the woodshed. He had split the first log when Grace came onto the end of the porch, a man's plaid wool shirt pulled on over her sweater and leggings. "You probably shouldn't be doing that with your head injury," she said.

"I need to do something." He brought the maul down on the wedge, and the log split with a satisfying *crack!*

She watched him a moment longer, then returned inside. He spent the rest of the morning splitting wood, until one corner of the small living area was filled with logs and his shoulders and back—and his head—ached. "Thank you," Grace said and went back to whatever she was working on at a desk in the corner of the living room.

"The snow has pretty much stopped," he said. He fed a log to the woodstove, then stood with his back to it, watching her as she studied a notebook filled with small handwriting, then typed something into a laptop. "How long before the plow makes it up this way?"

"It could be hours," she said. "Or days."

The thought of days trapped here in forced idleness grated. The idea that he needed to be somewhere, pursuing someone, gnawed at him. "Who do these clothes belong to?" Declan asked, bracing himself that the owner—her husband/boyfriend/jealous lover—would arrive shortly.

"They were my grandfather's." She held up the notebook. "This was his, too. Part of my job is to enter the data he collected for over sixty years into the lab's database. There is a lot of it, so it's taking a while." She indicated a wall of shelves behind her, which he now realized were filled with row upon row of spiral-bound notebooks.

"I'm still fuzzy on the details from last night," he said. "You're some kind of scientist?"

"That's right." She turned to face him more fully. "I spent most of my summers growing up with my grandfather, here in this cabin. I helped him collect data, which meant we spent days hiking and measuring things like how much water was in a creek and how thick the bark was on the pines and how much grass the pika were collecting for winter. I was never happier than I was when I was with him, so when it came time to go to college, I studied environmental biology. When he died two years ago, he left this cabin and all his records to me, and he also left a letter to his bosses at the lab that essentially said if they wanted the historical data he collected before he went to work for them, they needed to hire me to fill his former position."

"How did they react to that kind of demand?"

Grace laughed. "They knew my grandfather was an eccentric when they originally hired him, and old age hadn't mellowed him. I was able to show them all the proper credentials, and they were happy to hire me. It's not as if everyone wants to live up here on the side of a mountain."

"Your family doesn't worry about you up here by yourself?" he asked.

Some of the light went out of her eyes. "My grandfather was my family. And I have Bear." She ruffled the dog's head. "And I'm not a complete hermit. I volunteer with Search and Rescue and with the Colorado Avalanche Information Center, which means in winter I go out and assess avalanche conditions at various locations around Eagle Mountain and report to the center."

"You have a lot of useful skills," he said.

"And you're a marshal," she said. "What do you do, exactly?"

"The US Marshals Service is responsible for protecting federal judges and judicial witnesses," he said. "We also transport and manage prisoners, serve warrants and handle assets seized in federal cases. But I worked primarily in fugitive apprehension." The words rolled easily off his tongue, as if he had said them many times before.

"You said you were looking for someone," she said. "A fugitive?"

"I think so. I have a picture in my head, and I sense the name is almost there. More things are starting to come back to me. I hope I remember everything soon."

"Hmm." She looked as if she was going to say something, but her phone interrupted them. She picked it up from the desk beside her and checked it. "It's from Search and Rescue." She swept her thumb across the screen and read the message. "They're asking for volunteers to report to Dixon Pass to resume our search for a missing person. Oh, and they have a name now." She looked up at him. "Marshal Declan Owen."

GRACE TEXTED THAT Declan was with her, then telephoned the sheriff's department to tell them the same. The sheriff himself came on the line. "How did Deputy Marshal Owen end up with you?" Travis asked.

"I found him wandering near my cabin, disoriented and

bleeding from a head injury." No need to mention his state of undress at the moment.

"How is he now?"

"Better, but he doesn't remember what happened to him. He took a pretty bad blow to the side of the head. I can bring him into town as soon as the plow clears the road up here."

"We'll come and get him," the sheriff said. "Sit tight."

The sheriff ended the call, and she laid aside the phone. "I heard most of that," Declan said. "They're coming to get me."

"I guess a fellow law enforcement officer gets first-class service," she said.

"Thanks again for everything," he said.

She looked away, pretending to tidy papers. They had only spent a few hours together, but she could admit she would miss him. It was probably the novelty of the situation. It wasn't every day that a sexy stranger ended up on her doorstep.

An hour later she heard the growl of a snowmobile climbing the hill to her house. She and Declan and Bear were on the front porch waiting when a quartet of snow machines pulled in front of the house. Sheriff Travis Walker and his brother, Sergeant Gage Walker, climbed off the first two machines, pushed up the visors of their helmets and approached.

"Deputy Marshal Owen?" Travis addressed Declan.

"Yes, sir," Owen snapped off the words with military crispness.

Travis turned to Grace. "How are you, Ms. Wilcox?"

"I'm well, Sheriff." She turned to Declan. "Marshal Owen has been a model guest."

"That's good to hear."

Gage came to stand beside Declan. "We need you to come to the station and answer some questions."

"Of course," Declan said. "Maybe you can fill me in on what happened."

Travis frowned. "What do you mean?"

"I don't remember anything from when I was driving down the highway until I woke up on Grace's sofa," he said.

"Head injuries can cause memory loss," she said.

The sheriff was still frowning. "Come with us to the station and we'll talk," he said. He turned to Grace. "We'd like you to come, too, and give us a statement."

"Of course," she said. "If you'll drop me off at my car, I'll follow you to the station. Let me get my coat."

She made sure the fire was dying down and that Bear had plenty of water, then fetched her heavy snowmobile jacket from the hook by the door. She also brought an old fleece-lined parka that had belonged to her grandfather and handed it to Declan. "You'll need this for the ride down," she said, then followed Gage to his snowmobile. The sheriff and his brother were making her uneasy, and she felt protective of Declan. Which was ridiculous. He was clearly capable of defending himself, although that hadn't been the case with whoever had attacked him.

DECLAN KNEW HE was in trouble when he saw the sheriff had brought three extra men with him. This was no courtesy ride to town. The fact that they wanted to question both him and Grace pointed to some crime having been committed—a crime beyond someone bashing him in the head and stealing his clothes.

And his gun. He was sure he'd had a gun. The thought of it missing landed a rock of dread in his stomach. He had a sense of having been in this situation before. Why couldn't he remember? Or why could he remember some things—his name, his job—and not remember why he was here or how he had ended up wandering around naked in a snowstorm?

The ride to the road was too noisy and cold in spite of his borrowed coat to make conversation possible. When they reached the forest road, Grace went to her car while Declan was ushered to a sheriff's department SUV while the two deputies were left to load the snowmobiles onto a waiting truck and trailer. Declan had plenty of questions he wanted to ask but decided to save them until he was at the sheriff's department. Instead, he looked out the window, hoping to see something familiar that would spark his memory.

Eagle Mountain proved to be a postcard-pretty community full of snowcapped Victorian buildings, tourist shops, restaurants, homes and a town park. The sheriff's department was located off the main street. Grace and Declan were led to separate interview rooms. Sergeant Walker and Sheriff Walker, apparently brothers, sat across the table from Declan and read him the Miranda notice.

"Am I being charged with a crime?" Declan asked, struggling to keep his temper in check.

"We have questions for you about the murder of Agnes Cockrell," the sheriff said.

The words landed between them like a ball of mud. Cold and ugly and feeling out of place. "Who?" Declan asked.

"Ms. Cockrell's body was found in the back seat of your car on the side of Dixon Pass," the sheriff said. "She had been shot in the back of the head with a gun registered to you. The gun was also found in the car and yours are the only fingerprints on it."

Declan closed his eyes and groaned.

"Deputy Marshal Owen, did you shoot Ms. Agnes Cockrell?" the sheriff asked.

I don't remember, Declan thought. Could he have shot this woman whose name he didn't know?

Then a thought filled his head, icy and bracing and absolutely certain. He had been in this situation before. He knew how this worked. He sat up straighter. "No, I did not shoot Agnes Cockrell," he said. "But I think I know who did."

Chapter Three

Deputy Jake Gwynn, whom Grace knew from Search and Rescue, took down her account of how she had found Declan wandering in the snowstorm and taken him in.

"How did he get from Dixon Pass to your place?" Jake asked.

"I assume he walked," she said. "There's the hiking trail toward the falls, then an old logging road he could have followed."

"He wouldn't have been able to see the trail or the road in all that snow."

"Yes, but human instinct is to take the path of least resistance. He would have tried to steer clear of brush and trees. I think he was running for his life."

"Why do you say that?" Jake asked.

"Someone hit him in the head. And they took his clothes and shoes."

Jake frowned. "How do you know this?"

"Because he was naked when I found him. He would have frozen to death if he hadn't come to my cabin. Maybe that was what whoever hurt him intended."

"I've heard people suffering from hypothermia will sometimes strip off all their clothes," Jake said. "Their body tricks them into thinking they're overheating."

"I've heard that, too, but I don't think that's what happened here," she said.

"What did he tell you about what happened to him?" Jake asked.

"He doesn't remember. He said he knows he was driving here, and he thinks he was looking for someone, a man. But he can't remember a name or anything that happened until he woke up on my sofa this morning."

"Do you think he's telling the truth?"

"Yes!" The word came out more insistent than she had intended. She needed to calm down. But the memory of all the people who hadn't believed her when she couldn't remember was like a hand squeezing her heart. She fought against that panicked feeling. "He's been remembering some things," she said. "He didn't know his name at first, but that's come back. And he remembered he's a US marshal."

Jake made notes on a pad. "Anything else?"

She leaned toward him. "I don't think he killed that woman. I think whoever killed her tried to kill him, too."

"Her name is Agnes Cockrell," Jake said. "She lived over in Rocky Ridge."

"What was she doing up there in Declan's car?"

"Did you ask him?"

She shook her head. "No."

"Why not?"

Because she had been afraid to let him know about the dead woman. Just in case he was the killer. She shook her head. "It just didn't come up," she said.

"You gave him the clothes he's wearing now?" Jake asked.

"Yes. They belonged to my grandfather. They don't fit him very well, but he had to have something."

"Did he have anything else with him when you found him?" Jake asked. "Did he say anything, mention any names?"

"No. He was practically in a stupor when I found him, and very disoriented. He needs to see a doctor."

"We'll take care of that as soon as we've had a chance to talk to him."

"You can't think he did anything wrong," she said. "You should be looking for the person who attacked him and left him to die out there."

Jake gave her a curious look. "You seem pretty upset on behalf of a man you just met."

Heat burned her cheeks. He was probably thinking this was the most emotion he had ever seen her display. She knew she had a reputation of being a little standoffish. She wasn't one to get close to people. "If you had seen him out there, bleeding and half-frozen, you would feel the same," she said. Though she doubted it. The deputy looked at Declan as a murder suspect. She could only see him as someone damaged in the way she had been damaged. She had never known anyone else she shared that experience with. It felt like a gift, though one Declan probably wouldn't have wanted.

"Who do you think shot Agnes Cockrell?" Travis asked.

"His name is Terrence Barclay," Declan said. "He's a fugitive, convicted of the murder of three women in Utah, Idaho and Colorado. I was part of a detail transporting him last April for his sentencing on a fourth charge when he escaped. I think he's responsible for other murders, too."

"How did he escape?" Gage asked.

"He managed to get my gun, and he shot one of my fellow marshals and ran." Declan swallowed down the aching knot in his throat as the memories flooded back. "Later he shot another woman. With my gun."

"And you were pursuing him?" Gage asked.

Declan fisted his hands, struggling to hold his composure against a flood of anger and shame. "I was removed from the case. But then I had a tip that Barclay was headed this way. I took a vacation and decided to follow the lead."

"You were disobeying orders," Travis said.

"I was not." Not precisely. He shifted, trying to get more comfortable on the hard chair, but that was impossible. "My plan was to follow him to wherever he went to ground, then report his location to the marshals and step back and let them do their job."

"So what happened up there on the pass?" Travis asked.

"I don't know." Declan shut his eyes, but all he saw was blackness. He opened his eyes again. "There's a blank spot in my memory. I can recall before and after, but nothing up there on the pass."

Travis nodded. "Grace says you had quite a blow to the head. We'll get you to a doctor soon."

"I'm okay," Declan said. "I want to get this over with."

"You've been following this guy, Barclay," Gage said. "I assume you've studied his habits and methods. If you had to guess, what would you say happened?"

Declan took a deep breath and considered the question. This was more familiar territory, trying to guess a fugitive's next move. "He planned his kills, but he was also opportunistic. All his victims were women. Even the marshal he killed. I think maybe he came upon this woman up there. Maybe she was a hitchhiker or she had car trouble. He killed her, and maybe I interrupted him?" His head hurt. "I wish I could remember."

A knock on the door interrupted them. Gage stood and

spoke to someone at the door, then sat down again. "Grace says when she found you, you were bleeding and naked. Somehow you had walked all the way from Dixon Pass."

"That's about two miles," Travis said.

"In thigh-high snowdrifts, in a storm," Gage said.

"If Grace hadn't found me, I would have died out there," Declan said. She deserved all the credit.

"Grace thinks the person who hit you took your clothes and left you to freeze to death," Gage said.

He nodded. "That sounds like something Barclay would do. He kidnapped a couple of campers once. He killed the woman, but he left the man tied to a tree in the middle of a flooded river. The water was up to the man's neck by the time someone found him."

"Why do you think Barclay was coming to Eagle Mountain?" Travis asked.

"I've got a source who said Barclay was in this area before and liked it. Then I found him registered at a motel in Purgatory under a version of one of the aliases he had used before. A man fitting his general description was using the name. By the time I checked into the same motel, Barclay had checked out, but he told the desk clerk he planned to drive to Junction."

"We should alert law enforcement in Junction," Gage said. "He could have headed there after he shot Agnes Cockrell."

"Or he's still here," Declan said.

"Why would he stay here?" Travis asked.

"I told you he likes to plan his killings. Every time before, when there's been an opportunistic murder, he's stayed in the area until he could plan and carry out a more methodical crime. He may not do that this time, but it's a pattern he's followed twice before."

"Eagle Mountain is a small community," Gage said. "Once we have his description, we should be able to spot him."

"Maybe not," Declan said. "He's very good at blending in and at establishing a false identity. He's very average-looking to begin with, and he changes his appearance. He usually takes some kind of service job and becomes part of the community. People don't recognize him for the monster he is. We haven't been able to recognize him, either." The knowledge weighed on him.

"We'll contact the Marshals Service to get the information they can give us," Travis said.

"I should speak to my supervisor," Declan said. Penrod was not going to be pleased. After Barclay's escape, Declan had gone from one of the unit's top officers to the head of Penrod's crap list.

"I contacted him when we found your car and weapon," Gage said. "I let him know you were missing and the circumstances."

Declan nodded, though inwardly he was cringing. One more black mark against him. He could almost hear Penrod now. *How could you let this happen again?*

"That's all the questions we have for now." Travis rose. "I'll ask you to stay in town until we complete our investigation into Ms. Cockrell's shooting."

"I'd like to return to the motel in Purgatory to retrieve my belongings," Declan said. He needed his own clothes and his laptop with all the information he had amassed about Barclay.

"Of course," Travis said. "And let us know if you need help finding a place to stay."

"But first, we need to get you to the doctor," Gage said. "I'm not sure you're in good shape to drive anywhere."

He wanted to object, but he knew Gage was right. His head pounded now. And maybe a doctor knew some trick to getting his memory back.

GRACE INSISTED ON waiting for Declan. She sat on a padded chair in the small, chilly lobby, and office manager Adelaide Kinkaid brought her tea in a cardboard cup. "I guess you feel responsible for that young man, now that you saved his life," Adelaide said. Sixtysomething with a swirl of white hair and red-framed bifocals, Adelaide had a gaze sharp enough to drill through steel. She had a reputation around town as knowing everything about everybody, a powerful force for every good cause and the scourge of anyone who got out of line.

Grace blew on the tea, though it wasn't really that hot, and thought about how to answer that question. "I want to make sure he's all right," she said.

"It doesn't hurt that he's very easy on the eyes, does it?" Adelaide said and laughed.

Grace couldn't keep back a smile. There was no denying that Declan—all of him—was as close to perfect as she had had the pleasure to see. Looks weren't everything, but his were certainly nice.

The door on the left of the lobby opened, and Declan and Gage Walker emerged. Grace set aside the tea and stood. Declan seemed surprised to see her. "Is everything all right?" he asked.

"I'm fine," she said. "But I thought you might need a ride to the medical clinic."

"I can take him," Gage said. "And he'll need to get his belongings from his motel."

"I could drive you," she said.

"I thought I'd rent a car," Declan said.

"But you don't have your wallet."

He looked stumped. He turned to Gage. "Did you find my wallet in my car?"

Gage shook his head. "We didn't find your clothes, either. We combed the scene pretty thoroughly, too. And we've got your car in our lot. We're still going over it."

Declan turned back to Grace. "Thank you. I'd appreciate it if you could drive me to Purgatory to get my things."

"Doctor first," she said and took out her keys.

He followed her to her car. When they were both safely buckled in, he turned to her. "Are you okay?" he asked. "I'm guessing you've never been questioned by the police before."

"No." Not exactly. "It was okay. I know the deputy who talked to me. He's with Search and Rescue also." She put the key in the ignition but didn't start it. "I was afraid they were going to arrest you."

"Why didn't you tell me about the dead woman in my car?"

"I didn't want to upset you."

"You seem like a smart woman. You probably thought I killed her."

"I thought whoever killed her had tried to kill you." She started the engine and put the Jeep into gear.

"I think it was a man named Terrence Barclay," he said. "I've been following him. He's an escaped murderer."

The words, said in such a matter-of-fact way, still sent a chill down her spine. "You're remembering," she said.

"I remember Barclay, but I still don't remember what happened up there on the pass. I think Barclay killed Agnes Cockrell, though. I'm sorry if she was a friend of yours."

"I didn't know her," Grace said. "But it's still awful."

"It is."

They waited an hour at the clinic before he could be seen.

Declan fidgeted and paced, but Grace remained calm. She'd had years to learn to sit still. It was useful for observing nature. For blending in and observing other people, too.

She'd assumed he would go back to be examined by himself, but he wasn't gone a minute before Grace was called back, to vouch for his identity and the reason for his lack of paperwork. Declan gave the number for his employer, who could provide his insurance information. He looked grim throughout the exchange, the picture of a proud man reduced to helplessness and furious about it. Grace ended up staying with him through the exam and an X-ray.

Finally, a doctor delivered a verdict. "You have a mild concussion. The amnesia you're experiencing is normal, as is the headache. You may have difficulty concentrating for the next few weeks and should limit screen time if this exacerbates your symptoms. The best treatment is rest. Don't do anything too strenuous, and try to avoid anything that could lead to another blow to the head. Your symptoms should resolve in about a month. If you're still having problems after six weeks or so, you should consult a neurologist, preferably someone with a specialty in traumatic brain injury."

Grace thought guiltily of all the firewood he had split for her that morning. That definitely qualified as strenuous activity.

"Will my memory return?" Declan asked.

"Maybe." The doctor shrugged. "Maybe not. That space of time may be a blank for the rest of your life, but you shouldn't have any permanent problems remembering other things. It may be that the cells in your brain responsible for that memory are too damaged to recover. It doesn't have any bearing on your long-term prognosis. Try not to stress over it. Stress can slow your recovery."

They dealt with the last of the paperwork and walked to

Grace's car. She checked the time. It was after one. "What do you want to do now?" she asked.

"You probably have work to do," he said. "I don't want to take up more of your time."

"I set my own schedule," she said. "And I already collected the data I needed this morning." Every day she recorded the amount of snowfall on a table set up on her property for that purpose, as well as high and low temperatures, barometric pressure and other readings. It was a pattern established by her grandfather sixty-three years before. The consistency and volume of his information was one of the things that made it so valuable. "Let's drive to Purgatory and get your belongings," she said. "I'm sure you'd like to have your own clothes."

"Yes!"

She laughed at the emphatic way he spoke.

"It's not that I'm not grateful to you. And your grandfather." He looked down at his patched-together outfit. "I'm just feeling a little…exposed." It was true that the tight sweatpants clung to his backside and thighs in a distracting way. Distracting for her, at least.

"Then let's get you something more comfortable."

Grace hadn't even realized she had slowed the Jeep as they neared the top of Dixon Pass until he asked, "Is this where they found my car?"

"Yes." She pressed down on the accelerator, thinking she would speed past.

"Stop," he said. "Please. Maybe something here will trigger my memory."

She did as he asked, pulling over on the patch of packed-down snow where emergency vehicles must have parked. They both got out, and she led the way to the edge where his car had been. Fresh snow had dressed the scene in white, theirs the only footsteps on the surface, though she could see the ruts and ridges where others had walked and parked the morning before.

Declan stood, hands in the deep pockets of her grandfather's old jacket, and stared into the valley below. "I was down there?" he asked.

She moved to stand beside him. "There's a trail down from here." She pointed to a path along a narrow ledge that followed a series of switchbacks down. "It's the only way you could have traveled from here. There were bloody footprints leading down there. We followed them as far as that clump of trees." She pointed to a stop a quarter mile down the trail. "Then the snow got too heavy. It wasn't safe to keep looking."

"How did I manage to stay on the trail in a snowstorm?" he asked. "I couldn't have known where I was going."

"You have good survival instincts," she said. She had heard plenty of stories from fellow rescue volunteers about impossible situations where people shouldn't have lived but had.

Declan stared for a long while, then turned away. "I'm not remembering anything."

They returned to the Jeep and set out again. "What happens if I never remember?" he asked.

"You'll get on with your life," she said. "It might not be easy, but you'll do it, because you can't do anything else."

"You sound so sure." He shifted to turn toward her. "How do you know?"

She swallowed. She didn't talk about this with anyone. But he needed to hear. To know he wasn't alone. She would have given anything to have that comfort. "When I was nine years old, I was injured in a car accident. I don't remember anything for two months before the accident or three months after. Five months of my life are a total blank. They probably always will be."

"You don't remember anything?" he asked.

She shook her head. "Only what people have told me." What her mother had told her, the words full of so much anger and pain. Anger and pain Grace carried inside her.

"I'm sorry," he said. "I guess I'm lucky to have only lost a day."

"It's still a loss."

He didn't say anything for a long moment. She stared out the windshield, mechanically guiding the car through a landscape of towering cliffs and icy waterfalls that most times left her in awe. All she felt now was the familiar numbness that she pulled around her like a shield.

Then Declan reached over and took her hand. She felt the strength of him in spite of his gentleness, and a warmth that seeped into her, thawing places that had been frozen for as long as she could remember.

Chapter Four

"What do you think?" Gage settled into the chair in the sheriff's department and studied his brother. Travis would have an opinion about Declan Owen, though he rarely volunteered anything, even to Gage.

"We'll have to see how much of his story checks out." Travis drummed his fingers on his desk. "Ask Ronald Cockrell if he or his wife knew Owen or Grace Wilcox."

"Grace?" Gage felt the tension in the back of his neck. "You think she's tied up in this?"

"Do you think Owen made it all the way from Dixon Pass to her place, naked and bleeding, in a blizzard?" Travis asked.

"I don't know," Gage said. "People do all kinds of seemingly impossible things. Last year there was a guy who climbed Everest, by himself, with no supplemental oxygen. In winter."

Travis shook his head. "Maybe. What do you know about Grace Wilcox?"

Gage thought for a moment, gathering what he knew about the quiet brunette. "She's one of the new trainees with Search and Rescue. I've seen her on a few calls. She's some kind of researcher or something—lives in that cabin up past Forest Service Road 617." He shrugged. "That's about it."

"She works for the Rocky Mountain Biological Lab," Travis said. "She took over the position from her grandfather. That's his cabin she's living in. I guess she inherited it along with the job. She moved here from Iowa after he died last year."

Gage didn't ask how Travis knew this. Big brother prided himself on knowing about every one of his constituents in this small county. "I don't see the connection to Owen," he said. "He's from Denver."

"They struck me as pretty close for two people who just met," Travis said.

"If she really found him the way she said she did, she saved his life, taking him into her cabin," Gage said. "Maybe she feels responsible."

"Maybe."

"Do you think Owen is telling the truth when he says he can't remember what happened to him?" Gage asked.

"I've heard head trauma can cause temporary amnesia," Travis said. "But there's no way to prove that. There's one thing that bothers me about his story, though."

"If he was following Barclay, where's Barclay's car?" Gage asked. "And where's Agnes Cockrell's car?"

Travis nodded. "Let's say Barclay did kill Cockrell, put her in Owen's car and hit Owen in the head, stole his clothes and abandoned him to freeze to death. He leaves Owen's car and drives away in either his own or Cockrell's car. That still leaves one vehicle unaccounted for."

"What do you think happened?" Gage asked.

"I don't know. Maybe Barclay and Owen were together. Maybe Owen stopped to help Cockrell and Barclay took advantage of the situation."

"Owen is supposed to be on vacation," Gage pointed out.

"He's already admitted he was using that time to track Barclay."

"I guess if a felon had taken my weapon and used it to kill a fellow officer, I'd want to track him down, too," Gage said.

Travis sent Gage a sour look. Of course big brother would never step out of line that way, but Gage had sympathy for Owen—if what he had told them was true.

Gage pulled out his phone. "I'll get the official records from the Marshals Service, but in the meantime..." He pulled up a browser and typed in *Terrence Barclay*. He scanned the search results, then sat up straighter. "Here we go." He read from the news story he had found. "Convicted murderer Terrence Barclay escaped custody today. Barclay was being transported to Larimer County Courthouse to stand trial for the murder of Alice Faye Cumberland when he overpowered one of the federal marshals escorting him, then used that marshal's gun to kill a female marshal." He looked up from the screen. "So that part of Owen's story checks out."

"See if you can get more details from the Marshals Service," Travis said. "And I'd be interested in knowing where they think Barclay is headed."

Gage tucked the phone away and stood. "I'll get on it."

Adelaide leaned into the office. "We just had a call from dispatch. Some climbers found a wrecked car over in Carson Canyon."

"That's not far from Dixon Pass." Travis shoved back his chair and stood.

"Maybe it's one of the missing vehicles we're looking for," Gage said.

Adelaide consulted the slip of paper in her hand. "The climbers who called it in didn't see any sign of a driver, but they did note the license plate number. It's registered to an Angela Jimenez in Purgatory."

"And?" Gage prompted. The knowing look in Adelaide's eye told him there was more.

"And Ms. Jimenez reported the car stolen yesterday morning."

"We'll need to send Search and Rescue down there to check for anyone in the vehicle or someone who might have been ejected when the car went over," Travis said.

"I'm betting we don't find anyone," Gage said.

"Does this have anything to do with that US marshal you were questioning earlier?" Adelaide said. "Or Grace Wilcox?"

"What do you know about Ms. Wilcox?" Travis asked.

Gage wished he had thought to ask the question first. Adelaide made it her business to find out everything she could about everyone in town. It was one of her finer qualities—and a source of irritation, since no one kept secrets for long from Addie.

"She used to come here every summer as a child to stay with her grandfather, Hugh Wilcox, up in that cabin near Wilson Peak," Adelaide said. "I would have said that old hermit had about as much business taking care of a little girl as a bear, but she seemed to take to running half-wild in the woods all summer. I hadn't seen her around for a few years when she came back to settle his affairs, and then she ended up staying on. She moved into the cabin and took up his old position with the research lab. I was half-afraid she would turn into a hermit like him—a pure waste—but she seems to be making an effort lately to get involved. She volunteered with the Avalanche Information Center, adopted a dog from the animal shelter and joined up with Search and Rescue."

"You sound like you like her, Addie," Gage teased.

She fixed him with a gaze that automatically made him want to stand up straighter and apologize for whatever he had done wrong. "I admire people who do good work and don't complain. Grace is like that. I worried about her being lonely up there in that remote cabin with just a dog for company, but now she's turned up with just about the handsomest man to show up around here in a long time. So I guess I admire that, too."

Gage worked to suppress his laugh. Men of all ages and stripes had been left speechless by Addie's not-so-subtle flirting, though he suspected she enjoyed the game more for her ability to unsettle the opposite sex, since she remained steadfast to the memory of her late husband.

"Thanks, Addie," Travis said.

"Grace isn't in any trouble, is she?" Adelaide asked.

"Not sure." Travis moved past her. "But if she is, I expect you'll find out before we do."

DECLAN'S HEAD THROBBED, and the bright sun streaming through the windshield of Grace's Jeep made his vision blur. He closed his eyes and leaned his head against the passenger window for the rest of the drive to the motel. Why could he remember some things—like the number and location of his motel room—but not what had happened up there on the pass? Not knowing what Barclay might have done—and what he himself had failed to do—clawed at him like briars under his skin. After Barclay had taken his gun the first time, Declan had sworn that would never happen again. He would never let his guard down that way. That failure in his duty still haunted him.

And yet he had ended up stripped of everything, including his weapon, and Barclay must have been responsible. If only he could remember.

"Is this the place?"

Grace's question brought him back to the present. Declan opened his eyes and looked at the sign for the Miner's Rest Inn. "This is it," he said. "My room is around back."

"We'll need to get the key from the front desk," she said.

Right. Because he had nothing. Not even his room key.

The clerk on duty was the same young woman who had checked him in two mornings ago—Kimberley, her name tag identified her. She smiled as he stepped in the door. "Mr. Owen! I was getting a little worried about you. Housekeeping said they didn't think you'd been back to your room since yesterday morning."

"I got delayed." He looked down at his mismatched clothing. "Actually, I was in an accident."

"Oh no!" She put a hand to her mouth, then her gaze shifted up to the bandage at his temple. "What happened?"

He opened his mouth to make up some story, but his brain refused to come up with anything. Grace stepped forward to rescue him. "He was in a car wreck," she said. "He ended up losing everything, including his wallet and his room key. But I'm sure you have his information on file from when he checked in?"

"Oh, sure," Kimberley said. "And we can get you a new key."

"Thanks," he said, including both women in the sentiment. "I just need to change clothes, then I'll be checking out."

"No problem." Kimberley programmed a new key card and handed it over. "I'm so sorry about your accident. I hope everything is okay."

"It will be," he said, hoping that statement was true.

They returned to Grace's Jeep, and she drove him around back to his room. Relief flooded him when he saw nothing in the room had been disturbed. His laptop was still locked in the case in the closet, his clothes hanging on the rod above.

"Is everything okay?" she asked.

He nodded. "I'll change in the bathroom, and then we can go."

"Don't rush on my account." She sat in a chair by the window and pulled out her phone.

One look in the bathroom mirror made him groan. His right eye was swollen, the white bandage at his temple was stained with a little dried blood, as was his hair, which needed a trim and combing. His beard was coming in heavy along his jaw. He wanted a shower but settled for wetting down his hair and combing out as much of the blood as possible, and shaving. Then he changed into jeans and a fleece pullover, put on the running shoes he found in the closet next to his suitcase, then folded the borrowed clothing and tucked it in the plastic bag meant for laundry.

"I can't thank you enough," he said when he handed the bag to Grace.

"I'm happy to do it," she said.

"You even sound like you mean it."

Her lips curved into a smile, and the heat behind the look hit him in the gut. "My normal life is pretty boring. It's nice to have something to shake things up."

That was one way to put it. "No daring rescues in the mountains?" he teased.

She shook her head. "I've only been with the group a few months." She stood. "Are you ready to go?"

He picked up his suitcase and computer bag. "I need a

phone," he said. "And I need my credit cards and a driver's license before I can get the phone."

"You can borrow mine to call the credit card companies." She pulled the phone from her pocket. "Do you remember what cards you had?"

"I have a file on my computer with that information."

"That's very organized of you."

"My dad was a general in the Army. He drilled organization and being prepared for anything into me and my sister."

She nodded and opened the door. He followed her to the Jeep and stowed his luggage in the back. When he joined her in the front again, she was staring at her phone. "I just got a text from Search and Rescue," she said. "They need people to search for survivors of a wreck in Carson Canyon. Apparently a car went off the road." She started typing. "I'm letting them know I'm in Purgatory and won't be able to make it."

"I'm sorry," he said. "I'm keeping you from things you need to do."

"It's all right." She tucked the phone away again. "Not everyone can make every call. And I'm still a rookie. I'm not going to be the person they send into a canyon. I'm still training on climbing and canyon descents and things like that."

"I'm impressed," he said. "I'm not sure I'd want to do that."

"I'm sure as a marshal you're used to doing dangerous things." She pulled out of the motel lot, back onto the highway.

"I doubt I can get my credit cards reissued before a couple of days," he said. "In the meantime I'm going to need somewhere to stay." He glanced at her. "I'm not asking you to take me in. You've done enough." And it would be easier for him to keep tabs on the sheriff's department's investigation if he was staying somewhere less remote.

"I have a friend in Search and Rescue," she said. "Her parents own an inn in town. I think they'll put you up. I'm sure the sheriff will vouch for you."

He wasn't so sure of that. To Sheriff Walker, he was still a murder suspect. Nothing personal—that was just where the evidence pointed. And Declan hadn't been able to say much to defend himself. *I can't remember* could sound like a convenient excuse to someone who wasn't sitting where he was sitting.

"The canyon where that vehicle is isn't very far from Dixon Pass," Grace said. "Do you think the car they found might belong to the man you're looking for?"

The hair on the back of his neck stood up. He shifted toward her. "Why do you say that?"

"I was just wondering. If he was there and the woman who was killed was there and they both had vehicles, he could have driven away in one car, but what happened to the other one?"

"Can I borrow your phone?" he asked her.

"Of course." She pulled the phone from her pocket and handed it over again. He searched and found the number for the Rayford County Sheriff's Department and asked to speak to Travis Walker. "I'm with Grace in Purgatory," he said. "We just picked up my things from the motel, and Grace got a text from Search and Rescue about a vehicle in a canyon."

"The car belongs to Angela Jimenez," Walker said. "Do you know her?"

"No. But Barclay has stolen cars before."

"You said you were following him yesterday," Travis said. "If he stole a car, why not report that?"

"I don't know," he admitted. A stolen car would have been the perfect excuse to stop Barclay and hold him. "Unless I didn't know the car was stolen." Had he missed that, too? Or had Barclay obscured the plate or been far enough ahead of Declan that he hadn't been able to read the license? What had really happened? "You should check the vehicle for Barclay's prints."

"You don't have to tell us how to do our job," Walker said.

"Of course not."

"Do you know yet where you're going to be staying in Eagle Mountain?" Walker asked. "How we can get in touch with you?"

"Grace is taking me to a place owned by friends of hers."

"The Alpiner," she interjected.

"The Alpiner," he repeated. "I'm going to contact my credit card company and get them to reissue my cards and cancel my old ones, then purchase a new phone. I'll give you the number when I have it."

"Do that," Walker said.

"Will you let me know what you find out?" he asked, trying not to sound like he was begging. "With this car and with Agnes Cockrell's murder?"

"You're supposed to be on vacation," Walker said.

The call ended before he could think of a suitable answer. He stared at the phone. "The call dropped," he said.

"It's hard to keep a signal here in the mountains," she said. "You can try again when we get back to Eagle Mountain."

He didn't bother telling her he wasn't going to waste any more time with the sheriff. Like his bosses, Travis Walker would tell him this was none of his concern.

But their reputations weren't on the line like his was.

And right now, Terrence Barclay was at the top of the US Marshals' priority list. If Declan could track him down, he had a chance at redeeming himself.

Chapter Five

Declan wore his frustration in the hunch of his shoulders and the furrow of his brow. Grace wanted to reach out and smooth those lines of pain away, to erase the fear she suspected was at the base of his barely contained anger. *What happens if I never remember?* The plaintive note in his voice when he had asked the question still burned her.

You'll live, she wanted to tell him. *But part of you will always be missing.* He wouldn't want to hear that. A man like him wouldn't want to accept that there was something—especially something about himself—that he couldn't fix.

"Maybe this Barclay you've been hunting died when his car went into that canyon," she said. Not that she wished anyone's death, but would knowing his quarry was no longer on the loose give him any peace?

"That car is in the canyon because Barclay put it there," he said.

"Why?"

"To buy time. He's left a string of stolen vehicles behind over the years. Barclay used a stolen vehicle in connection with every murder he committed. He'll end up ditching Agnes Cockrell's car, too, as soon as he thinks it's a liability."

"Have you been following him for a long time?" she asked.

"Five years," he said. "I was part of the team that tracked him down after his fourth murder. Larimer County was getting ready to try him for that one when he escaped."

"Where do you think he is now?"

He blew out a breath. "My best guess is that he's in Eagle Mountain." He glanced at her. "I'm not trying to frighten you, but it's what he's done before. After every spontaneous killing, like the murder of Agnes Cockrell, he's picked out another victim and stalked her. It's as if he has a need to carry out a meticulously planned crime, one where he thinks he can control all the variables. It may sound strange, but he doesn't really like risk, for all the risky things he's done."

"He could have killed you," Grace said, her mouth dry at the knowledge.

"I don't know why, but he doesn't kill men."

"I don't think I could do what you do," she said.

"I imagine there's less violence in nature," he said. "At least, malicious violence."

"Yes." There was sadness and death in nature, and the story the data she collected told about the changing climate could be frightening. But there was no hatred behind the facts and figures, and no personal threat to herself, at least not in the short term.

She drove to the Alpiner and led the way inside. Brit Richards looked up from behind the front desk. "Hello, Grace." She glanced past her to Declan, her expressive face not hiding her curiosity. "What can I do for you?"

"This is Marshal Declan Owen," she said. "Declan, this is Brit Richards. Her daughter, Hannah, is a local paramedic and one of the search and rescue volunteers I work with."

"Deputy Marshal Owen," he corrected and offered his hand. "It's nice to meet you, Ms. Richards."

"Call me Brit. Everyone does. How can I help?"

"I need a place to stay for a few days," he said. "But I was in an accident and lost my wallet with all my credit cards. I'm going to contact my bank today about reissuing them, and I'll get the information to you as soon as I can."

"The sheriff can confirm his identity if you need him to," Grace said.

"Oh, that won't be necessary." Brit turned to her computer terminal. "We've got a single on the second floor available, if that's all right," she said. "It includes breakfast."

"That would be great," he said. "I really appreciate it."

While he was completing the registration, the front door opened and Hannah entered, accompanied by her fiancé, Deputy Jake Gwynn. "Hey, Grace," Hannah said. "We missed you on the accident call. Sheri said you were in Purgatory." She cast a curious glance at Declan.

"Hello, Grace," Jake said. "Marshal Owen."

"Did you find anyone at the accident site?" Declan asked.

Hannah sent another questioning look to Grace, but before she could explain, Jake said, "Nobody was there. We think whoever was driving the car may have sent it into that canyon on purpose."

"Why would someone do something like that?" Brit asked.

"For the insurance money," Jake said. "To hide evidence. There are all kinds of reasons."

The muscles bunched along Declan's jaw, as if he was clenching his teeth to keep from saying something.

"I hear you think you know who was driving that car," Jake said.

Declan nodded. "His name is Terrence Barclay. He has a habit of stealing vehicles, then ditching them."

Jake nodded. "It's going to take a couple of days to get the vehicle out of the canyon. When we do, we'll go over it."

"You won't find anything," Declan said. "Barclay doesn't leave much behind."

"Nothing turned up on your car," Jake said. He opened his mouth as if to add more, then glanced at Brit and shut it again.

"How long will you be staying with us, Marshal?" Hannah asked. She moved behind the counter to join her mother.

"I'm not sure," he said. "Is that a problem?"

"Not at all," Brit said. "It's not our busy time of year."

"I may want to talk to you later," Jake said. "I'd like to know more about Barclay." He sounded friendly enough that some of the tension went out of Declan's shoulders.

"Sure," he said. "I'm happy to tell you what I know."

"Jake and I are meeting with Lena Griffith in a bit," Hannah told her mom. "She has some new properties to show us." She turned to Grace. "Jake and I are trying to find a house, but the market isn't very friendly right now."

"If you keep looking, something will turn up," Brit said. She handed Declan a key card. "The stairs are behind you, or head left at the end of the corridor and there's an elevator."

"The stairs are fine." Hannah and Jake said goodbye and left, and Brit disappeared into an office behind the front desk.

Declan turned to Grace. "Thank you again for everything," he said.

She plucked a business card from a holder on the counter and wrote down her name and number, then pressed it into his hand. "Call me if you need anything," she said. "A ride or a loan or…anything."

"You've done enough already," he said and tucked the card into the pocket of his jeans.

"I want to help," she said. *I don't want to lose track of you yet.*

"I'd better go." She left before she said or did something foolish. Of course, he would leave. He would go back to his job and his home, and she would never know what happened to him. That was how things worked. She ought to be used to that by now.

DECLAN SAT ON the side of the bed in his room at the Alpiner Inn and stared at the phone on the table beside him. He needed to call his bank and his cell phone provider, credit card issuers. But first he had to contact his boss. Oscar Penrod would have heard from the Rayford County Sheriff's Department by now and had probably been lighting up Declan's cell phone—wherever it happened to be.

He squared his shoulders and picked up the handset.

"Marshal Penrod's office."

"Hello, Carlos. This is Declan. I need to speak to Marshal Penrod."

Silence. The kind that held weight. "The marshal has been expecting your call. For some time."

Carlos wasn't the only one who knew how to use a pause to his advantage. Declan said nothing.

"One moment," Carlos finally said, an extra crispness to his voice. Seconds later, Declan's supervisor was on the line.

"Deputy Marshal Owen, would you care to explain to me why a county sheriff from a place I've never heard of called to tell me first that you were missing altogether, then to tell me you had been found but were a suspect in a murder investigation?"

Declan winced and rubbed his uninjured temple. "I didn't kill anyone," he said. At least, he was pretty sure he hadn't.

"This Sheriff Walker tells me a woman was shot with

your gun, her body found in the back seat of your car and yours were the only prints on the gun."

"Did he also mention someone—probably the killer—knocked me unconscious and left me for dead in the middle of a blizzard? I didn't shoot that woman—who I don't know—and then do that to myself."

Penrod grunted. "Walker also wanted to know about Terrence Barclay. He told me you claim to have been tracking Barclay, and the next thing you knew, you woke up in a strange cabin miles from your vehicle. I thought it was one of the wildest stories I'd ever heard. What is he leaving out?"

"I don't remember what happened," Declan said. "Not yet. The doctor said the head injury messed with my memory."

"But you admit you were tracking Barclay? That's not your case. And you're supposed to be on vacation."

"I had a credible tip that Barclay was in the area. I decided to follow him—discreetly—to see where he was going and report his location to you."

"Oh, you did? You obviously didn't follow discreetly enough, if he's the one who coldcocked you and used your weapon to murder a woman. I have never in my history with the US Marshals Service had an officer who was overcome by fugitives twice. Guarding your sidearm is policing 101."

"Yes, sir." Even though he was alone, Declan's face burned. "I don't know how it happened. I wasn't careless."

"You lost your weapon and your man. If that isn't careless, I don't know what is."

"Yes, sir." He held his breath, counting to ten before he trusted himself to say more. What he had to say next was really going to send Penrod over the top. "Barclay took my badge and credentials, too. I'll need replacements."

Silence. The kind of silence that drilled a hole in Declan's stomach. "Sir?" Declan said when he could stand it no longer.

"You don't need your credentials," Penrod said. "As of this moment you are on indefinite leave."

His heart plummeted. Were they sacking him? Just like that? "Sir?"

"You've had a head injury. You're on medical leave until a physician clears you to return to work. You're also on administrative leave pending the resolution of this murder investigation and our own internal investigation as to what happened. Expect to hear from our investigators."

"Yes, sir." The reply was automatic, drilled into him by his father long before the Marshals Service had reinforced the response.

"Goodbye," Penrod said and hung up.

Declan lay back on the bed and closed his eyes. He was in up to his neck this time. He'd be lucky to keep his job after this, let alone any self-respect.

He shifted and felt something in his pocket. He pulled out the card Grace had given him and studied the precise printing—like an architect's handwriting. Or a scientist used to recording accurate data in logbooks in the field to be transcribed at a later date.

He would have bet that nine out of ten women would have run screaming when he'd come staggering out of that blizzard toward her. Why hadn't she? She was the only one here who didn't look at him skeptically when he said he couldn't remember what had happened to him up on Dixon Pass. Was it because of her own experience with memory loss or an extra measure of compassion or some other quality he couldn't identify?

He propped the card on the bedside table and lay back

again. He had given Grace enough trouble already, so he should do her a favor and throw that card away.

But he wouldn't do so. He was really out on his own this time, and he wasn't going to be foolish enough to turn away from a friend if he got desperate.

Chapter Six

Saturday morning, Gage stood in the mud and gravel of the wrecker service storage yard in Delta and stared at the white Honda Element with a faded Coexist sticker on the left side of the bumper. A car registered to Agnes Cockrell. "We hauled it out of a no-parking zone in the alley behind a bakery, over off Sixth Avenue," the wrecking yard owner—a compact, wiry man with a bushy black beard—told him. "Yesterday. No plates, but when we ran the VIN, we saw it had been reported stolen, then saw the note to contact the Rayford County Sheriff's Department."

"Thanks," Gage said. "I'll get someone over this afternoon to take it to our impound lot." An evidence team would go over the car thoroughly. If they were lucky, they might get a print or some fibers, but he wasn't holding his breath. The car stolen from Angela Jimenez hadn't turned up any evidence. Apparently, Terrence Barclay was very careful. And very lucky.

"Somebody commit a crime in that car?" the bearded guy asked.

"Something like that." Gage moved closer and peered into the vehicle. A woman's purse lay on its side in the passenger well—tissues, a wallet and various pieces of paper spilling out of it. Next to that, pieces of broken plastic and glass. Gage squinted to bring the items into sharper focus and realized he was looking at a smashed cell phone. Agnes Cockrell's or Declan Owen's?

Owen had a new phone now. Gage had seen him talking on it, standing in front of the Alpiner Inn when Gage had driven past on his way to Delta. Gage had kept track of Owen the last couple of days, without appearing to do so, in between his extra duties now that Travis was on vacation. The marshal had kept a low profile. He had rented a vehicle, so he must've gotten his credit card situation figured out, though Gage had to wonder if he had been cleared to drive.

Gage hadn't seen any sign of Grace Wilcox these past two days. Had Owen persuaded her that he didn't need her anymore? Gage had been struck by how attached Grace had been to Owen, despite her reputation of being almost as reclusive as her grandfather had been.

Maybe later he would head up to Grace's cabin and ask her again about the rescue call and her first encounter with the injured Declan Owen. He wanted to see if anything about her story had changed or if she remembered anything Owen had said that might clear up the mystery of what, exactly, had happened up on Dixon Pass that day.

Gage drove back to Eagle Mountain, his mind turning over the bits of information he had collected so far, trying to make them fit together into a clear picture. But he didn't have enough yet to come to any conclusions. Owen might've had the answers he needed, but the marshal either wasn't able or wasn't willing to tell what he knew.

Gage pulled into his parking spot behind the sheriff's department and started toward the back door but stopped short when a figure stepped from the shadows to the left of the door.

"It's just me, Sergeant."

Owen looked better today, in clothes that fit, freshly shaved and his hair trimmed. The bandage on his temple was gone, the bruise still swollen and mottled purple and yellow. "What can I do for you, Marshal?" Gage asked.

Owen met his gaze firmly, almost angrily. "I need to talk to you and the sheriff about Terrence Barclay," he said.

"What about him?" Gage asked.

"There are things you need to know about him. Things I know because I've been following him for so long."

"I've read the reports the Marshals Service sent over," Gage said.

"Not everything is in those reports."

Why not? Gage wondered. But he thought he knew. Reports were full of facts. Numbers, dates and other things that could be easily measured. But part of police work was based on instinct and gut feelings and educated guesses. These were the sort of things that had no place in official reports or in courts of law. You didn't base an arrest on those nontangibles, but you didn't ignore them, either. Sometimes they made the difference between finding the person responsible for a crime and having a case grow ice-cold.

"Let's go inside and talk," he said and unlocked the door. He would listen to what Owen had to say, then decide if he believed him.

SATURDAY MORNING, Grace attended a training class at Search and Rescue headquarters. All of the new recruits were required to attend, with veterans there to assist. She took her turn practicing the knots SAR Captain Sheri Stevens demonstrated—knots they would use to secure lines to equipment to be lowered down a steep slope or into a canyon, knots to fasten a litter to an overhead line, knots they might use when climbing themselves. Grace wouldn't win any prizes for speed, but she had a good memory and was able to complete each knot perfectly.

"That's great, Grace," Sheri said. "I want you to practice those every day until you're able to tie each one in under thirty seconds, preferably in pitch dark."

"Even better if you stand in a freezer while you do them," Hannah Richards, who was helping Sheri with the class, said. "And aim a fan, turned up on high, so that it blows ice pellets sideways at you while you do it."

"You make it sound like so much fun," Grace said but smiled so they knew she was teasing. She didn't have the easy banter these two did, but she was trying.

"Don't let us scare you off," Sheri said. "You're doing great. Much better than Hannah did when she first started."

"Me!" Hannah pretended outrage. "What about you?"

"I was already a competitive climber when I joined SAR," Sheri said. "One thing I knew how to do was tie knots."

"But you couldn't place a splint correctly for the longest time." Hannah nudged Grace. "Everyone has their strengths and weaknesses," she said. "It's one of the great things about SAR. Everyone brings something to the team."

Grace didn't point out that she wasn't a climber or a paramedic, but she understood what Hannah was trying to say. "I'm glad to be a part of the organization," she said. "I'm looking forward to having the skills to be able to contribute more."

"You contribute a lot already," Sheri said. "You're calm under pressure, you have a good memory and you follow directions well. And you aren't afraid of tough situations. Those are all the perfect qualities for working search and rescue."

"I hear you already saved at least one life," Hannah said.

At Grace's blank look, she laughed. "Don't tell me you've already forgotten a certain good-looking US marshal."

Heat flooded Grace's cheeks, and she stared at the knotted ropes in front of her.

"Is it true he was naked when you found him?" Sheri asked.

Grace nodded. "I'm amazed he hadn't already frozen to death out there in that storm."

"He seems plenty healthy now," Hannah said. "Yesterday morning, I bumped into him coming out of the little gym we have at the inn. I know I'm an engaged woman, but *Mama*! He is one very nicely put-together man."

"Yes. He is," Grace agreed and couldn't keep back a smile.

"How long is he going to be in town?" Sheri asked. She began coiling up the ropes. Around them, others were doing the same.

"He's not sure." Sheri seemed to assume that she and Declan were in touch. Grace didn't want to admit she hadn't seen or even talked to him in two days. She told herself he was probably busy, but she couldn't deny her hurt. Of course Declan didn't owe her anything, but she had thought they'd had a connection. Guess he hadn't felt it.

Class ended and she said goodbye to the others and headed into Eagle Mountain to run some errands. The trek from her cabin was difficult enough that she tried to get as much done as possible when she ventured out. She collected mail from her box at the post office, returned a library book and checked out another, picked up dog food at the pet store, then decided to get a few groceries.

The strap of sleigh bells on the door of the natural foods store jangled loudly as she entered, and a young man in a green apron, brown hair cut short in back and long on top, looked up. "Hey," he said and grinned. He had an open, friendly face with ruddy cheeks and freckles across his nose.

"Oh, hello." She looked around. "Where's Arnie?" The older man who owned the store was usually behind the counter.

"He ran into Junction to pick up a new order," the man said. "I'm Mike. I just started. What can I do for you?"

"I just need a few things. I'll help myself." She headed for the bulk bins along the side wall, aware of him watching her.

"Do you like tea?" he asked after a moment.

She paused in the act of scooping steel-cut oats into a paper bag. "I do," she said.

"We have some great chai Arnie's getting from a new supplier." He came out from behind the counter and moved to her side, tea tin in hand. "It's really spicy. Lots of flavor." He took the lid from the tin and held it out to her. The aromas of cinnamon and cardamom filled the air.

"I'll try some," she said. "A small bag."

"I'll measure that out for you." He stepped back, and she relaxed a little. He had a nice smile and a friendly manner. There was no reason for her to be nervous.

She completed her shopping and carried her items to the counter. Mike handed her the bag of tea. "Let me know what you think," he said.

"Uh, sure."

He chuckled. "Not that Arnie trusts me to tell him what to stock, but it would give me an excuse to talk to you again."

She returned the smile. "I guess if you're new in town, you don't know many people yet."

"You would be right. But as you can see, I'm trying. You can be one of my first friends, Miss…?"

"Wilcox. Grace Wilcox."

"It's good to meet you, Grace." He took her hand. "I hope I'll be seeing a lot more of you."

Grace marveled at the exchange as she stowed her groceries in her Jeep, then drove to the gas station. She had never been the type to make friends easily and had to work to put herself out there, even in a place as friendly as Eagle Mountain. Joining Search and Rescue was helping her get to know more people, but she was still skilled at melting into the background. People—men—just didn't notice her. Maybe Mike was simply the type to go out of his way to make friends with everyone. It wasn't as if he'd been flirting with her. Had he?

She passed the Alpiner on the way to the gas station and hit the brakes momentarily. She should go in and see if Declan was there. She could say she wanted to check on him. Or invite him to dinner?

She removed her foot from the brake and accelerated forward. If Declan wanted to see her, he had her number and he knew where she lived.

At the gas station, she pulled up to the pump and got out of the car. Next to her, a big red van idled. The driver, a young man with an orange knit hat pulled down over his ears, came around to the pump. "Hey," he said and nodded to her.

She nodded in return and slid her credit card into the reader at the pump.

"Do you live around here?" the man in the hat asked.

"Near here," she hedged.

"Sorry. I didn't mean to make you nervous." He offered a shy smile. "I just got into town, and I wondered if you knew of any campgrounds around here. Or free places to park my van and stay a few days."

She shook her head. "Sorry. I don't know. Maybe…the visitor's center? Or the library?"

"That's a great idea. They can probably help me out." He took the nozzle from the pump. "Maybe I'll see you around again." He turned to fill his van.

Grace completed her own transaction and drove away in a daze. She could count on the fingers of one hand the number of times two good-looking young men had sought out a conversation with her in one day. She had made a lifetime habit of keeping herself apart from other people, and most of them picked up on her *leave me alone* vibe and never bothered to approach. By opening herself up to Declan, was she suddenly sending out vibes that told people she wasn't as untouchable as she had previously worked hard to appear?

"HE'S STILL HERE." Declan sat across from Gage in the sergeant's office, a space as familiar as his own cubicle back in Denver with its stacks of files, bulletins pinned to the wall and framed commendations mixed with family photos on the credenza. Gage had explained that the sheriff was away for two weeks and Gage was in charge of the case.

"Barclay's here. In Eagle Mountain." Gage didn't try to hide his skepticism.

"Or close," Declan said. "He's found a place to stay and he probably has a job. Bartender. Waiter. Janitor. Store clerk. Some position that businesses always need to fill. He'll be a model employee. Everyone will like him. If you ask them to describe him, they'll say ordinary or average. Sometimes women say he's good-looking. They'll talk about his nice smile or his nice eyes. But his eyes won't be their real color. He'll wear contact lenses. He'll have cut his hair, maybe dyed it. Or he'll wear a wig. He'll grow sideburns or a goatee. Once, he plucked his eyebrows and used makeup to sharpen his jawline and cheekbones. I don't know where he learned to do that—he doesn't show any history of having acted or been involved behind the scenes in theater, but he's good."

"Why do you think he's in Eagle Mountain?" Gage asked. "Or nearby?"

Declan clenched and unclenched his fists, trying to control his frustration. Gage didn't know the whole story. And he didn't know Declan. He had a right to be skeptical. "Because it's what he does—what he's done every time he's killed on the spur of the moment," he said. "He stays in the area, finds a target and plans his next murder. I don't know if it's a compulsion or a game he likes to play with the cops, but it's what he's done at least twice. I think it's three times, but he was never connected to a first victim who started the pattern."

"Eagle Mountain is a small town," Gage said. "New people stand out."

"But you have new people all the time. It's a popular area. A tourist spot. You must have people drift in and out."

Gage nodded. "You're right. But we try to notice, especially if we think they might be trouble."

"Barclay won't be like that. He never makes trouble, and he's not one to stand out."

"He just kills people." Gage's voice was flat.

"He kills women," Declan said. "And it will be just one. Then he'll move on. That's what he's always done before."

"One is one too many."

"It is. I want to stop him."

The sergeant didn't answer right away. Instead, he fixed Declan with a steady, brown-eyed gaze, as if daring him to defend himself. Declan waited. "You're officially on leave," Gage finally said. "Your boss made a point of telling me that."

"Yes, and before that, I was on vacation." So that was established—he and Gage both knew he had no business looking for Terrence Barclay.

"Why isn't the town swarming with federal marshals, here because Barclay is here?" Gage asked.

He had wondered how long before they got to that question. "Because they don't believe in the pattern." He sat back and sighed. "I told you I never found a first, spontaneous victim before Barbara Racine, the first woman he was convicted of killing, in Helper, Utah. Prosecutors were able to show that he stalked her for weeks before he strangled her. His next conviction was for the murder of Selena Ferguson, in Boise, Idaho. He worked in her office for three months before he killed her. Signs pointed to his having planned that murder as well."

"What about the spontaneous killing you say set him off?" Gage asked.

"Darlene Castleburg. She was shot in Boise when someone stole her car. I think it was Barclay, but he didn't leave any evidence behind. Authorities in Idaho arrested a known car thief and charged him with the crime. I think they got the wrong man."

Gage shifted in his chair and leaned forward. "All right. You say there was one other?"

"He murdered Deputy Marshal Glenda Zanett when he escaped my custody," he said. "That happened near Wellington, Colorado. A week later he murdered Elizabeth Porterfield. That was the crime where he left her boyfriend to drown in the middle of a flooded river. Barclay stalked the couple on a camping trip and attacked in the middle of the night. He had been stalking her ever since he'd shot Glenda."

"How could a man who must have had every law enforcement officer in the state after him have remained so near where his last crime took place?" Gage asked.

"I told you. He knows how to hide in plain sight. And no one ever expects him to be brazen enough to stay put."

"You told your superiors all of this?"

"Yes. But they think I'm wrong. They don't want to admit they missed him before. Because Elizabeth was killed at a campground two hundred miles from Wellington, they believe that's where Barclay was hiding. But I went to Wellington. I talked to the people there. They remembered a cleaner at a local motel who sounded like Barclay to me—he had shaved his head and wore tinted glasses. A polite, quiet guy who never gave anyone trouble. But the motel—where he also stayed in a room set aside to house employees—was only one block from Elizabeth's apartment."

"It's circumstantial," Gage said.

"A lot of it is. But that doesn't mean it isn't true. And why take a chance? The feds are looking for Barclay everywhere but here. He probably thinks he's safe."

"How are we going to find him?" Gage asked.

"I'd start by making a list of all the people who have shown up in town in the past week," Declan said. "Anybody who has decided to stay. Check new employees of businesses. You can rule out women, but he's good at portraying different ages."

"I don't have the time or the manpower to do that," Gage said. "We're short one deputy. Soon to be two, when Jamie Douglas goes on maternity leave."

"One thing I have a lot of right now is time."

"Barclay knows you," Gage said.

"He does. But law enforcement presence doesn't seem

to scare him off. In Boise, he was a waiter at a restaurant where the local sheriff had coffee every morning."

"But the two of you have a history," Gage said.

A history Declan would dearly love to put an end to. "Maybe that will work in my favor." *This time.*

"If he thought you weren't a threat, maybe because you were a murder suspect yourself, he might let his guard down," Gage said.

There was a question in Gage's voice. Declan answered it. "You mean because the locals were naive enough to fall for his setup of shooting that poor woman with my weapon?"

Gage nodded. "You're not at the top of our list for that crime, but Barclay doesn't have to know it. But that would mean the rest of the public wouldn't know, either. For this to work, everyone would have to believe you were still under suspicion. Would you be willing to accept that?"

"Yes. If it means getting Barclay, I don't care what people here think of me." Except one person. He hated to think of Grace believing he was a murderer.

Would she believe that? He didn't think so, but he would probably never know for sure. Barclay was searching for his next victim. And he was probably watching Declan. No need to bring Grace to his attention.

Chapter Seven

Temperature at 7 a.m. 12F. Wind <5 mph from northeast. Sunrise: 6:24 a.m. No new snow accumulation.
Short-tailed weasel in woodshed. Still in full winter white, except for the black tip on its tail. It was carrying a dead vole; probably unearthed from the burrow behind the woodshed. Goldfinches showing first signs of gold. Mule deer haven't shed antlers yet. Bobcat with two grown kittens from last year's litter passed through shortly before dawn.

Grace turned the page in one of her grandfather's notebooks—this one from January 1972. She pictured him, sitting in this same chair at this desk by the window, recording his observations in his neat handwriting. Every day included descriptions of the wildlife he had seen, of trees and flowers, the water levels of streams and the daily weather. He painted a picture of a rich, colorful world, but his notebooks almost never mentioned people. Occasionally, he would note that she had spotted a particular bird or animal near the cabin—the only indication that she was staying with him at the time. He never mentioned friends or other family members or later, when he became an employee of the research lab, his coworkers.

Yet Grandfather had never seemed unhappy. He had liked his solitary life. Sometimes she envied that. As much as she enjoyed the beauty and autonomy of her position here, she did get lonely. She wasn't one to need a lot of other people around her. One other person would be enough, she thought.

Loud barking from Bear jarred her from her reverie. She hurried to the front window and was surprised to see a snowmobile headed up the drive. Her heart raced as the man driving parked and climbed off the machine, but when he removed his helmet, she stepped back in surprise to see Sergeant Gage Walker.

By the time Gage reached her door, she had quieted Bear and composed herself enough to answer his knock. "Hello, Sergeant," she said.

"Hello, Grace. I need to ask you a few more questions related to Declan Owen."

She had plenty of questions she wanted to ask him: How was Declan doing? How much longer did he plan to stay in town? Had they found Terrence Barclay? But she stepped back and held the door open wider. "Of course. Come in."

Gage shed his snowmobile suit and left it on a chair on the porch, then followed Grace inside. She sat at her desk chair, while he settled onto the sofa.

"I know you already gave a statement about what happened last Wednesday, but I'd like to go over everything again." He took out a notebook and pen. "Sometimes people remember new details after the initial shock has worn off."

She clasped her hands in her lap, ignoring how clammy they had become. "All right. What do you want to know?"

"Start with your arrival at Dixon Pass and go from there until we showed up Thursday morning."

Once again, she went over the events of those two days. While she had participated in the search for the person who had left the bloody footprints leading away from the car, she hadn't done more than glance into the car. Hannah and one of the volunteers who was a nurse, Danny Irwin, had examined Agnes's body, along with Jake Gwynn, who had been the first law enforcement officer on the scene. "We only searched for about thirty minutes before the storm got too intense for it to be safe on that steep, narrow trail," she said. "I was anxious to get home before the weather deteriorated further."

"Tell me everything that happened when you got home," Gage prompted.

She told him again about the naked, bleeding man stumbling in front of her, how she helped him inside, tended to his wounds and gave him clothing.

"You weren't afraid of this stranger appearing out of nowhere?" Gage asked.

"No." She had wondered about that herself, considering an encounter with a man she didn't know at the natural foods store could make her nervous. "I think I was so focused on taking care of him that I didn't have time to be afraid," she said. "And he never said or did anything threatening. He was injured and confused."

"What did he say about what happened to him?" Gage asked.

"He didn't remember."

"And you believed him?"

His words made her feel sick. "Yes, I believed him," she said. "Trauma can cause memory loss, particularly head injuries. And I really didn't think anyone would voluntarily wander around in a blizzard with no clothes on. Obviously, someone had injured him and left him to die."

"You don't think he could have hit himself in the head and faked his memory loss?"

"That's ridiculous!" She started to stand, then forced herself to sit, to try to calm down. "I'm not a doctor, but that wasn't a tap on the head," she said. "And I've known people who lost their memories after a head injury, so I don't think Declan was faking his amnesia. It would make things a lot easier for him if he could remember what happened, wouldn't it?"

"I guess that depends on what happened," Gage said. "If he killed Agnes Cockrell, saying he doesn't remember and trying to put the blame on someone else would be convenient."

"You can't think he killed her." She rose to her feet, unable to contain her emotions any longer. "He didn't even know her. And he told you who probably killed her—Terrence Barclay. Declan was following him."

"We only have Marshal Owen's word that that's what he was doing," Gage said. "His supervisor says he was on vacation. No one else has seen Barclay."

"He had no reason to kill Agnes," she said. "And no reason to injure himself or to hike two miles from his car, in the mountains, in a blizzard, and show up at my cabin—which he couldn't have even known existed. If I had decided to wait out the storm in town, he would have died before anyone found him."

Gage nodded and closed the notebook. "Thank you for talking to me. I'll let you get back to work now." He rose and she followed him to the door.

"You can't seriously think Declan had anything to do with Agnes's murder," she said. "You should be looking for Barclay."

"I promise you, we intend to conduct a thorough investigation of this crime," Gage said. "In the meantime, we've asked Marshal Owen to remain in town, in case we have more questions for him." He nodded goodbye, stepped outside and a few moments later, he was roaring away.

Grace paced the living room, stomach churning. Declan hadn't killed anyone. How could Gage believe he had? There was a real killer out there, and he might get away with the crime. Worse, he might come back and try to harm Declan. Did Declan have any idea how much trouble he was in?

She went into the mudroom and retrieved her snowmobile suit, then collected her wallet and keys. "I won't be gone long," she told Bear, then headed out to retrieve her snowmobile. Declan needed to know what was going on. And he needed to know he had at least one friend in town who was on his side.

DECLAN STARTED HIS search for Terrence Barclay at the Alpiner Inn. "Have you had anyone come in looking for work in the past week?" he asked Brit when he found her alone at the front desk on Monday afternoon.

"One of the high school girls, Sarah Jane Utley, asked if we were hiring anyone to work the front desk after school and on weekends," she said. "I had to tell her my husband and I and Hannah take care of that."

"No men looking for work?" Declan asked.

"No. Are you looking for a job while you're here, Marshal?" Her eyes twinkled in a way that had probably charmed many a man in her day.

"No, um, I'm just curious about the employment picture in Eagle Mountain. Do you have a lot of seasonal or transient workers?"

"Oh, some. Especially in summer. A lot of young people come to climb, and they find jobs in restaurants, mostly. Maybe clerking in stores that cater to tourists. Is that what you're talking about?"

"That's it exactly." He leaned on the counter and spoke in a more confiding tone. "If I were looking for someone who might have recently taken a job in one of those places, where do you suggest I look?"

"Are you looking for someone in particular?" she asked.

"Yes, but I can't tell you details."

Her eyes widened. "Oh, I understand. Police business."

He nodded. "But I'm looking for a man, if that helps."

"You could try Mo's Pub or Kate's Kitchen. I think they pretty much always need waitstaff or kitchen help. The Nugget Hotel probably hires a lot of people, too."

"Thanks. I'll see what I can find out."

"I'm happy to help." She smiled, then looked past him and the smile widened. "Hello, Grace," she said. "It's good to see you."

Grace stopped halfway across the lobby. She stared at Declan, then looked away. "Hello," she said, her voice soft and low. He felt the impact of that single word deep in his chest.

He straightened and moved toward her without thinking. "Grace, it's great to see you." Though he had vowed to stay away from her, seeing her now made him feel twenty pounds lighter.

She met his gaze, and he cringed at the hurt in her eyes. What had he been thinking? The woman had saved his life and he had said goodbye and hadn't looked back. "I'm sorry I haven't been in touch," he said, keeping his voice soft, aware Brit was probably listening to every word. "I've had a lot going on."

Grace nodded. "I know." She glanced past him, toward the front desk. "Is there somewhere we can talk?"

He started to invite her for coffee, then thought better of it. As much as he wanted to talk to her, he didn't want to risk Barclay seeing them together. "There's a sunroom in the back," he said. "We can talk there."

He led her to the glassed-in room off the back of the inn. No one else was there, and they settled at either end of a sofa upholstered in nubby blue-and-gray tweed.

"You look much better," she said, studying the bruising at his temple. "How do you feel?"

"I still don't remember anything about what happened at Dixon Pass," he said. That reality was a constant knot in his stomach.

She nodded. "It can be especially frustrating when other people don't believe you can't remember."

She understood that, didn't she? Was that why she looked so sad—remembering her own trauma? "Are you okay?" he asked. "You look upset."

"Sergeant Walker came to see me a little while ago," she said.

"Gage Walker came to see you?"

"He asked me to tell him again everything that happened the day you came here." She leaned toward him, hands knotted at her sides. "He still thinks you killed Agnes Cockrell—that you shot her, then hit yourself in the head and stumbled off into the snow. He thinks you made up the story about Terrence Barclay to divert attention. Even though I pointed out to him how ridiculous that is."

"That was really foolish." Declan hadn't meant to say the words out loud, but really, what was Gage thinking? Sure, they wanted locals—primarily Barclay—to think he was the focus of the sheriff's investigation into Agnes's murder. But why upset Grace this way?

"I'm not under arrest," he said. "The locals are just trying to cover all their bases. They'll realize soon enough I couldn't have killed Agnes. I didn't even know her. Why would I shoot her?"

"I told him that! And there's something else. Something I thought of on the way over here."

"What's that?"

"Agnes's car! It wasn't there when Search and Rescue responded to the scene. There's no way you could have driven it somewhere else and had time to show up outside my cabin that afternoon. The real killer must have stolen her car. I need to tell Gage that."

"He already knows." Declan took her hands. They were ice-cold, so he wrapped both his hands around them. "The sheriff's department found Agnes's car in Delta a few days ago," he said. "Someone had left it in an alley. Gage knows it couldn't have been me."

She sat back but didn't try to pull free of his grasp. He massaged her hands gently, trying to bring some warmth back into them. "Then why did he act as if he was sure you were the murderer?" she asked.

"Maybe he was hoping to throw you off guard, to see if you revealed anything he didn't know."

She slid one hand free and covered her eyes. "I feel foolish, rushing down here like this," she said.

"It's good to see you."

She lowered her hand and met his gaze once more. "Why haven't I heard from you?"

He released her hand and looked away. "My life is such a mess right now. I didn't think it was fair to involve you."

Her laughter startled him. He looked around and she was smiling. "I'm already pretty involved, don't you think?" she said.

He forced himself not to return the smile. As much as he welcomed her presence, he wouldn't be doing her any favors letting her get closer. "If Gage is telling you those things about me, he's probably told other people, too," he said. "I'm only going to be in Eagle Mountain a little while, but you live here. You don't need your friends and neighbors believing you're friends with a suspected murderer."

"You're not a murderer, and anyone with any sense will realize that." She put her hand on his thigh, and he felt the heat and weight behind the gesture. "I want to help you."

He needed help, but was she really the person to give it? "How are you going to do that?" he asked.

She sat back, the moment of intimacy broken. "I thought maybe we could snowshoe the route you probably took to get to my cabin from Dixon Pass. It's a fun hike in clear weather, and it's possible we'll find something, or you'll see something, that will trigger your memory."

He hesitated but couldn't make himself say no. "That's a great idea," he said. There didn't seem much chance of Barclay seeing them together in the middle of nowhere, and the prospect of anything that might help him remember what had happened, coupled with the chance to spend the day with someone who didn't view him with suspicion, was too much to pass up.

Chapter Eight

Grace had arranged to pick up Declan from the end of the Forest Service road near her cabin on Tuesday morning. She had been surprised to learn he had rented a car. "Should you be driving so soon after a head injury?" she asked.

"I'm doing great," he said, and she didn't press. She had so many other things she wanted to know: What had the sheriff's department told him? What did the Marshals Service have to say? Did he still think Terrance Barclay was in Eagle Mountain?

But she had spent a lifetime keeping questions to herself. It was far easier to let people reveal themselves in their own time. Not always satisfying, but with less potential for rejection.

She was waiting on her snowmobile when the roar of an engine shook the still air. Moments later, a battered green pickup, lifted on oversized tires, growled toward her. It jerked to a halt, engine protesting, then died in a cloud of acrid smoke from the tailpipe. The door shoved open and Declan jumped to the ground.

"This is your rental car?" she asked.

"It was the only thing available at the local garage." He regarded the hulking vehicle. "You don't think it will help me blend in with the locals?"

"I don't know about blending in, but they'll have plenty of warning to get out of your way." She handed him her extra snowmobile helmet. "Are you ready? I figure we'll ride back up to my cabin and start snowshoeing from there."

"Sounds good." He put on the helmet, then collected a day pack from the truck and slipped it on.

She climbed onto the snowmobile and he straddled the seat behind her, then she started the engine and took off.

The steepness of the trail up to her cabin made it impossible to keep any distance between their bodies on the narrow seat. They ended up pressed together, his hands on her waist, his chest against her back. She let herself lean back against him, aware of the muscles of his thighs clenching and unclenching as he leaned into a curve or tried to steady himself. His gloved hands gripped her waist, and she wished there weren't so many layers of clothing between his fingertips and her bare skin.

She was almost sorry when she pulled up to the cabin. Bear stood on the porch, barking and wagging his tail. "Do you remember me?" Declan asked after he had removed his helmet. He held out a hand to the dog, who sniffed it, then accepted a scratch behind the ears.

"I have some snowshoes for you over here," she said and led the way to the end of the porch. She handed him the shoes and poles.

"Did these belong to your grandfather?" he asked.

"Yes. He left me the cabin and everything in it. He wasn't the kind of person to have a lot of excess possessions, so I kept everything. I enjoy reading his books and eating off the same dishes we shared when I was a child." She flushed, wondering if she had said too much. She wasn't usually so talkative. "Does that seem odd to you?"

"It sounds as if this was always a special place for you."

He stepped into the snowshoes and bent to buckle the straps. "Why did you come here in the summers?"

"My parents divorced before my first birthday, and my father died not long after that. It was easier for Mom to send me here when school let out than to try to find childcare." Her mother would have been happy to let her live with Grandfather full time, and Grace would have preferred that, too. But he had pointed out there was no way for her to get an education in such a remote setting, in those days before satellite internet and cell phones.

"Where was home when you weren't here?" he asked.

"Little towns all over Iowa. I was always happiest here," she added.

He didn't ask why a child would be happier away from her mother, though he must have wondered. People who had happy childhoods couldn't imagine how unhappy some children could be.

"How are those snowshoes for you?" she asked, anxious to steer the conversation in a safer direction.

He took a few experimental steps. "They should work fine." He looked around them. "Where exactly did you find me?"

"About halfway back down the snowmobile trail to the road." She indicated the direction with her pole. "There's a hiking trail that parallels my property line until it intersects with the road. I think that's probably the path you were following. When you heard my snowmobile, your instincts sent you moving toward the sound—and help."

"I feel like I haven't thanked you enough for what you did for me that day," he said. "It still hasn't sunk in, how close I came to dying."

"You're obviously a survivor," she said. "I don't know how many people would have made it as far as you did."

He had a strong body, of course, but in her short time with Search and Rescue, she had already learned that in dire situations, a strong mind could count for more than physical conditioning.

"I'm curious to see the route you think I took," he said.

"We can start here and intersect the trail." She started out, pausing every ten yards or so to get her bearings. Sun streamed through the bare white branches of aspen trees, making the crystals in the snow sparkle like glitter. Their snowshoes sank half a foot in the fluffy powder before providing steady footing. After a few minutes, she found a rhythm, alternating planting poles and snowshoes, until she was moving with an easy, rocking gait.

"How do you know where you're going in all this snow?" he asked.

"Right now I'm following animal trails and headed in the general direction we need to go," she said. "When we get to the actual trail, it will be easier—you'll see."

"If you say so."

They continued in silence for another ten minutes, Bear romping alongside with regular side trips into the trees, where he would paw at a fallen log or plunge his whole head into the drifts, emerging with a crown of white fluff and whiskers full of snow.

She stopped and pointed with her pole to a blue metal diamond fastened to the trunk of an aspen to their right. "That's a marker for the trail," she said. "We can follow this all the way to the pass."

Declan frowned at the five-inch-tall marker. "I don't think I would have known to even look for a marker like that," he said. "Much less follow it for miles in a snowstorm."

"You probably didn't." She turned left and resumed their journey up the trail. "But look at how, even with the snow obscuring the trail itself, there's this cleared area between the trees. It's the easiest route to take. Animals know that." She stopped to indicate the imprint of deer hooves in the snow. "Your body would have taken the easiest route."

He studied the landscape around them, while she watched him. The distress on his face clearly telegraphed what he was thinking. "It's okay if nothing looks familiar," she said.

He nodded, put his head down and moved past her.

She let him take the lead, trusting him not to get lost with the markers to guide him. "You know where I'm from," she said. "Where did you grow up?"

"All over." He glanced back at her. "My dad was an Army general. We moved every few years—Texas, Virginia, Hawaii, Georgia, Germany. I lost count after a while."

"Where are your parents now?" she asked.

"They retired to Arizona."

"They must be so proud of you."

"Mmmm." He stopped and studied the snow at his feet. "I keep expecting to see something to show I was here," he said. "Blood or clothing or something."

"The snow would have covered any blood," she said. "And if whoever hit you took your clothing, you wouldn't be likely to find it out here."

"You're right, but I was hoping for something." He stepped to the side of the trail. "You'd better lead the way again."

They were the first ones—besides local wildlife—to use the trail since the snowstorm, and she tried to focus on the beauty of the silent landscape and the pristine snow. A gray squirrel fussed from a branch overhead, setting Bear to barking, dancing on his hind legs in a futile attempt to reach the furry little varmint. Farther up the trail, a snowshoe hare startled from beneath a currant bush, big feet flashing behind him as he bounded away. After about an hour, they left the cover of the trees. The trail seemed to stop altogether at the edge of a cliff.

Grace stopped and looked down on the rushing waters of Grizzly Creek ten feet below, a noisy cascade pouring between blocks of ice.

"What now?" Declan asked, joining her at the cliff edge.

"The trail heads up this way." She indicated a ledge alongside the water that climbed steeply upward.

"I came down that? In a snowstorm?" he asked.

"It's pretty amazing, but it's the only way down here," she said.

He shook his head but followed her toward the ledge. "You can't see them now, but in the summer there are steps here," she said, and sidestepped up the steep slope.

"How did I not fall into the creek and drown?" he asked.

"Like I said—you're a survivor. You have good instincts."

"Or maybe it was just a case of ignorance being bliss. I had no idea of the danger, so I just kept going."

"I guess that's a survival instinct, too," she said.

They didn't talk much after that, as the trail became even steeper and they needed all their breath to make it up the slope. Before much longer, they could see the road above them and hear the occasional passing car.

They emerged onto the roadway less than twenty yards from where his car had been parked. Declan kicked off his snowshoes and walked to the pullout, the ruts made by the wrecker that had towed his car still visible.

Grace turned to look out across the valley, leaving him to his thoughts. She had a spectacular view of snowcapped peaks rising above the sparkling creek, against a sky as blue and clear as a sapphire.

Declan moved up alongside her. "You would think I would remember a view like this," he said.

"I don't think anyone knows how the brain really works," she said.

He turned his back on the view, and she turned with him. "I can imagine how it all happened," he said. "The woman, Agnes Cockrell, must have stopped here for some reason. Maybe to look at the view, or maybe something was wrong with her car. Barclay saw her and stopped. Maybe he offered to help her or was just a friendly guy, also admiring the view. But then he grabbed her. He would have waited until I was approaching, so that I would see and stop to help. I'm not sure how he overpowered me and got my gun, but he did. He shot Agnes and hit me in the head—probably with the gun. While I was out, he stripped me and pushed me over the edge. I landed on the trail. He put Agnes's body in my car. He drove his car back down the road to Carson Canyon, then walked back up and took her car and drove it until he ditched it in Delta."

"He took a really big chance of being seen," she said.

"Not so much. He had stolen the car he was driving, so it wasn't linked to his name. If someone saw Agnes's car parked near mine and stopped to investigate, they would have found her body. They might or might not have found me. Barclay could have seen what was happening and headed another direction. Eventually, someone would have picked him up. No one would know he had just assaulted a US marshal and killed a woman."

"Have you told the sheriff's department all this?" she asked.

"Yes, but it doesn't matter what I think happened if I can't remember what actually happened." He gripped his head with both hands and groaned. "Why can't I remember?"

She hated seeing him so distraught. "I know it's hard," she said. "But please don't beat yourself up over this. It really isn't your fault." Even as she said the words, she knew how difficult they were to believe.

"How do you live with the not knowing?" he asked. "How do you accept there's this blank in your life you can never fill in?"

"I don't know that you ever accept it," she said. "You just…learn to live with it. Maybe it helps that it happened to me when I was so young." Though sometimes she wondered if that hadn't made the experience even worse.

"What happened? Can you tell me?"

She could say no. It wasn't something she talked about. But she felt his pain—and the fear behind it. If anyone understood what she had experienced, it would be him.

"I was nine years old," she said. "My mother was driving me to a swimming lesson. My little sister was in a car seat beside me in the back. Hope was three. The car left the road and hit a utility pole. Hope was killed and I was seriously injured. I was in a coma for five days, and even after I woke up, I didn't really remember anything for weeks after." She looked into his eyes, letting him see the bewilderment that still lingered after all this time. "All I know from two months before the accident until three months after is what my mother and the doctors and therapists told me. My therapists said my brain was protecting me from the trauma, but how could what really happened be worse than my doubts and imaginings?"

He opened his arms and she moved into his embrace, her head resting against his shoulder. He held her so tightly, so securely. She closed her eyes and surrendered to this feeling of being so protected. So treasured.

A blaring horn from a passing truck on the highway made them jerk apart. "We'd better head back," she said and turned to collect her poles from where she had rested them against a mile marker.

The trip back went more quickly, the downhill grade and packed trail giving them momentum. Bear walked between them, tongue hanging out, too tired now to follow the scents of wildlife.

They emerged on the snowmobile trail and made their way back up to her cabin, where they kicked off their snowshoes.

She was about to invite him in for coffee, but he spoke first. "Thank you for telling me your story," he said.

"I don't talk about it much," she said. "But I knew you would understand."

He put his arms around her, and it seemed the most natural thing in the world to move closer. And even more right to tilt her head up for his kiss. He kissed like he knew this was what she had been waiting for—and what he had been waiting for, too. His mouth teased awake nerve endings she hadn't known existed, and she leaned into him, greedy to feel more, take more, be more. She gripped his arms, to hold herself up and to keep him near. She was greedy and didn't care if he knew it. But then, he was greedy, too, angling his mouth more firmly against her and shaping his hands to the curve of her hips to bring her even closer.

She was smiling when he broke the kiss, but the burning look he sent her could have melted her right there in the snow. "I'd better go," he said.

"I can take you." She turned toward the snowmobile.

"That's okay. I think the walk would do me good." He

touched her chin and studied her lips as if he might kiss her again. Then he turned abruptly and stalked away.

She hugged herself and watched him go, her blood still fizzing like champagne.

Chapter Nine

On Wednesday, Declan began his search for Terrence Barclay at the Nugget Hotel, clearly the largest lodging establishment in town. About half the building appeared to be under construction, with workmen moving in and out, the sounds of power tools filling the air. He stopped to study the scene. Almost any of the workers within his sight might have been Barclay—young, white, of average height and build. He studied the face of each man who passed. He had spent enough time with Barclay that he thought he could recognize him, but none of the men here looked familiar. Others before him had thought they could recognize Barclay, too, and the murderer had managed to slip past them.

"Can I help you with something?" A thin-faced man in a blue suit addressed Declan. A pin on his lapel identified him as *R. Guidry, Manager.*

"I'm a US marshal, tracking a fugitive," Declan said. "Maybe you can help me." At this point, he would normally pull out his credentials, but since that wasn't an option, he was going to have to bluff his way through this.

"Do you have some identification?" Guidry asked.

"I'm working undercover," Declan said. "But you can telephone the Rayford County Sheriff's Department and they'll confirm I'm with the Marshals Service." At least, he hoped they would.

Guidry studied him for a long moment, then pulled out a cell phone. He scrolled through it, hit a button to dial and waited while the call went through. Declan pretended to study a brochure on the county and tried not to fidget. Guidry identified himself, then said, "I've got a guy here, says his name is Declan Owen. He says you can confirm he's with the US Marshals office." Pause. "Uh-huh." Another pause. "Yeah, that's him. Okay. Thanks." He ended the call and looked back up at Declan. "Let's go into my office, Marshal."

He followed the manager into a small office to the left of the front desk and took a seat in the only chair other than the one behind the desk where Guidry settled. "Who is a US marshal looking for in Eagle Mountain?" Guidry asked.

"His name is Terrence Barclay," Declan said. "But he won't be using that name. Caucasian, fair-skinned, twenty-seven, five feet nine inches tall, about one hundred fifty pounds. He's been known to change his hair and eye color. Do you have any new employees, hired within the last week, who fit that general description?"

"What's this man done?" Guidry asked.

"He's murdered three women and is suspected in the murders of several others."

Guidry's mouth tightened. "We don't have any new employees who fit that description," he said. "Though as descriptions go, it's pretty vague."

"What about the construction crews? Anyone new there?"

"You would have to check with them. Why are you asking these questions instead of the sheriff's department?"

"Barclay escaped from federal custody," Declan said.

"I don't think I can help you. Sorry."

"Do you mind if I talk to some of the staff? Maybe they know someone I should take a closer look at."

"You're free to talk to anyone you want on their own time, but I don't need you to disrupt their workday."

Declan wanted to point out that as a federal officer he was entitled to disrupt anyone's workday but decided not to push it. Technically, he was on leave and wasn't working any case, much less the one involving Barclay. But it annoyed him that this man seemed to put the operation of his business ahead of tracking down a killer.

He stood. "I'm sorry to have disturbed you."

He left the hotel and headed back out into the kind of brisk day that winter vacationers dreamed of—blue skies, pristine snow glistening like sugar, distant mountains making every photograph look like a postcard. But all Declan could think of was how difficult it was going to be to find Barclay before he killed again. Especially if everyone he talked to gave him a reception like R. Guidry.

He spotted the sign for Mo's Pub and went inside. He sat at the bar and an older woman with curly blonde hair approached. "What can I get you?"

He studied the menu on the chalkboard behind the bar. "I'll have a bowl of the Irish stew. Water to drink."

"Coming right up." While he waited for his food, he studied the waitstaff: a young woman and an African American man. There would be other workers, of course, working other shifts or out-of-sight in the kitchen. He could find the manager and go through the same spiel he had given Guidry, but he was liable to get the same reception. Maybe he was going about this all wrong, playing the cop card. He needed a better story.

The bartender returned and slid a large bowl of stew, several packets of crackers and a glass of water in front of him. "Thanks," Declan said. She started to turn away, but he said, "I wonder if you can help me. I'm trying to help a friend back in Ohio find his brother. Last time they were in touch, the brother said he was headed to Eagle Mountain."

"What's the brother's name?"

"His real name is Joe, but he might be using a different name." He leaned forward and lowered his voice. "He was in a little trouble back home and said he wanted to make a fresh start. My friend just wants to make sure he's okay."

The bartender gave him a skeptical look. "What does your 'friend's' brother look like?" she asked.

He described Terrence Barclay. "He might have taken a job in a restaurant—he's done that before."

She shook her head. "Nobody around here like that. Everybody who works here has been around for a while now. Years, even." She looked up as another man approached. "Hey, Mike," she said. "How are you?"

"I'm doing well, Cherise. How are you?"

"I'm good. You want some lunch?"

"Yeah. Can I get a chicken sandwich and fries to go?"

"Sure thing."

Mike—twentysomething, about five-nine, with dark hair shaved at the back and long on top—came to stand beside Declan. Declan's heart beat faster. This could be Barclay—different hair style, a bit thinner than he remembered. His nose looked different, but that could be faked, too, couldn't it?

"Are you okay?" Mike asked.

"You look like someone I know," Declan said.

Mike grinned. "No kidding? Is your friend from Michigan?"

"He might be."

An odd answer, but Mike didn't blink. "That's where I'm from," he said. "I haven't been in town long, actually."

Declan sipped water, forcing himself to remain calm. "How did you end up in Eagle Mountain?" he asked.

"I thought I was just passing through, but I liked the looks of the place. My dad's college buddy owns the natural foods store, so he gave me a job and a place to stay. Who's this guy I look like?"

Declan met Mike's gaze and held it, but the young man didn't flinch. Could this be Barclay, so guileless and forthcoming?

"Hello, Declan."

Declan broke off his staring contest with Mike and turned to see Gage Walker striding toward him. "I'm glad I found you," Gage said. He slid onto the stool on the other side of Declan as Mike turned away. "I've been looking for you."

"Why is that?" Declan asked.

"I got a call from the manager of the Nugget Hotel. He said you were over there asking questions."

"I asked if he had anyone working for him who met Barclay's description." Declan kept his voice low, though Mike had moved away, to the end of the bar.

"Hey, Gage." The bartender was back. "What can I get for you?"

"Cheeseburger and fries," Gage said. "Medium rare, extra-sharp cheddar." When she was gone, Gage turned to Declan once more. "This isn't going to work if you go around upsetting people."

Declan shook his head and glanced down the bar, where Mike was accepting a bag from the bartender. "What do you know about him?" he asked and nodded to Mike.

Gage leaned around Declan to study Mike. "New clerk at the natural foods store," he said. "And I already checked him out. His dad and Arnie, the guy who owns the store, went to college together."

"You know that for sure?"

"Arnie said so. Why would he lie?"

Declan turned his attention back to the stew. It was cooler but still delicious. Mike left with his lunch. Declan stared after him. Why did he have to be hunting a man who was so ordinary he was practically invisible? He turned back to Gage. "Speaking of upsetting people, why did you question Grace and let her think I was your chief suspect in a murder?" he asked.

"Because you are."

Declan glared at him.

Gage shrugged. "I figured she would tell all her search and rescue friends and that would help establish your reason for staying in town."

"You didn't have to upset her that way."

Gage grinned. "So you two are still seeing each other?"

"She came to the Alpiner to find me after you talked to her. You really shook her up." *And then we spent the day hiking and ended up getting way closer than is good for either of us.*

Gage sobered. "I didn't mean to do that. For what it's worth, she defended you. She's certain you're innocent."

The bartender slid a plate in front of him. "Can I get you anything else?" she asked.

"No, thanks, Cherise. This looks great."

They ate in silence for a few minutes. "What have you found out?" Gage asked after a while. "Any likely candidates for Barclay?"

"No. What about you?"

"No. We did find out a couple of things about Agnes Cockrell."

"Such as?"

Gage dragged a french fry through ketchup. "Her husband has never heard of you."

"What did you tell Agnes's husband about me?" Declan asked.

"I didn't tell him anything about you, just asked if he knew you or if his wife knew you."

"So when he hears some gossip that I'm your chief suspect for her murder, is he going to come after me?"

"He's not that kind of guy."

"Does she have any friends or relatives who are that kind of guy?"

"Are you having second thoughts? Are you thinking of leaving town?"

"I can't leave. Not until we find Barclay."

Gage popped the fry into his mouth and chewed. He waited until he swallowed, then said, "He told us Agnes fell on skis last week and banged up her shoulder."

"How is that significant?"

"When we got a chance to go over her car, we found a flat tire in the trunk. The spare was on the right passenger side. The jack was muddy."

"Like it had been used to jack up a car on a snowy roadside," Declan said. "She had a flat. She couldn't change it herself because of her injured shoulder. She flagged down Barclay for help, and he killed her."

"That area is a dead spot for cell coverage," Gage said. "But if Barclay did stop, where do you come in?"

"I would have stopped to help if I had seen a woman with a flat tire," Declan said.

"But you said Barclay was ahead of you—you were following him."

"Yes."

"Are you sure? Do you remember?"

"I remember following him." He had a clear memory of driving down a mountain road, his gaze fixed on the vehicle ahead, knowing that Terrence Barclay was the driver.

"Did he know you were following him?"

He hesitated. "Maybe?"

It was Gage's turn to remain silent. Waiting.

"He may have spotted me at the motel in Purgatory," Declan admitted. "I thought I ducked out of his way in time— but he may have seen me."

"But you kept following him?"

"I wasn't going to approach him. I was going to see where he ended up and report his location to the Marshals Service."

"Why didn't you do that in Purgatory, if you knew he was at the motel?"

"As soon as I knew it was him, I called a marshal I'm friends with who was on the case. He said they would have someone check it out, but Barclay left before they could send anyone. I followed him."

"And he may have known you were behind him."

"I didn't think so, but maybe."

Gage ate the last of his burger, then pushed the ketchup-smeared plate away. "Do you think he would use Agnes as a decoy—maybe keep a gun on her and have her flag you down?"

"He would absolutely do something like that."

"Do you remember anything like that?"

He wanted to remember. He could picture how the scene would look, but he knew the difference between imagining and remembering. "I don't know for sure," he said. "I can't say for certain that's what happened."

Gage grimace. "So, bottom line, we don't know if Barclay really is in town or in the next state."

"If he's following his usual pattern, he's here," Declan said.

"A pattern you are apparently the only person to see."

"So, what are you suggesting?" Declan asked. "We do nothing and wait for another murder?"

"I'm not saying that. But it would be helpful if you could remember what happened up there on the pass."

"Except I can't."

The two glared at each other. Declan seethed, but all his anger wasn't directed at Gage. He was furious with himself, too, for his mind's inability to reveal what they needed to stop Terrence Barclay.

"You don't think you've gotten into enough trouble, going after Barclay after you were removed from his case?" Gage asked.

Was that what this was about? Gage didn't like that Declan disobeyed orders from a superior. Declan didn't like that, either, but what choice did he have? "Let me ask you something. If you believed you knew what a killer was likely to do next, even if no one believed you, wouldn't you do everything you could to try to prevent him from murdering again?"

"I guess my first question would be to ask myself if my obsession with this killer had skewed my vision. Had I let my desire to regain my reputation or get revenge for the way he had made a fool out of me before cloud my judgment?"

"The best way to regain my reputation would have been to walk away, keep my nose to the grindstone and work hard to get back in the good graces of my superiors at the Marshals Service," Declan said. He could tell himself otherwise, but he knew in his gut this was the truth. "What I'm doing now is pretty much professional suicide."

"Then why do it?"

"Because I don't want another woman to die. Wouldn't that be a good enough reason for you?"

Gage nodded. "Yeah. Yeah, it would."

"Then what are we going to do?" Declan asked.

Gage sighed. "You're free to spend your time as you like," he said. "Keep digging into this, but I don't want any more complaints from locals about your snooping around."

"So digging, but no snooping."

"You can snoop, just be more subtle."

Declan didn't bother pointing out that he didn't do subtle very well. He preferred a straightforward approach to protecting the public, but being shuffled aside on this case had eliminated his ability to do that. "I'll be careful," he said. "But I won't stop looking."

"Neither will we." The hard edge to Gage's voice lifted Declan's spirits. Maybe he wasn't in this alone. But would the two of them be enough to defeat Barclay?

Chapter Ten

The message from Search and Rescue had asked anyone available to report to SAR headquarters at 10:00 a.m. Thursday for a "nonemergency rescue call."

"You know what that means, don't you?" Hannah asked as she and Grace stood together on one side of the concrete-floored central room of the headquarters building.

Grace shook her head. "No. How can a rescue call be a nonemergency?"

Hannah leaned in closer. "It usually means a body retrieval." At Grace's stricken look, she nodded. "I know. Not anyone's favorite call. But it's still important to the person's family. Try to remember that."

"Yesterday morning, the sheriff's department got a call from some skiers near backcountry hut number three about a body in the canyon visible from the top of the ridge," Sheri said as she stood at the front of the room and indicated a spot on the map of the county behind her. "They said the person was half-buried in snow and not moving. Sheriff's deputies checked things out with binoculars and reported that, from the condition of the body, it's been there awhile."

"What do you mean, 'condition of the body'?" someone on the other side of the room asked.

Sheri frowned. "The deputy told me the skin was white

and frozen-looking and a couple of fingers that were visible were broken off."

Groans went up around the room. "Who is it?" Eldon Ramsey asked.

"We don't know," Sheri said. "The sheriff doesn't have any record of anyone reported missing. Hopefully, whoever it is will have some identification. Our job is to get down there and bring the body out." She paused and surveyed the room. "It's a technical climbing area. If you aren't certified for that work, you can opt out, but we need support people up top, and while these aren't pleasant calls, we are called upon to do them from time to time. It wouldn't hurt to get one under your belt."

Grace nodded. The idea of handling dead bodies wasn't pleasant, but she could see how retrieving someone from an isolated grave in the middle of nowhere could bring comfort to family members. "I'll go and do what I can," she said. The other rookies all agreed.

"Great," Sheri said. She turned back to the map. "We can park here." She indicated an area set aside for backcountry skier parking. "From there we'll hike to this saddle, then down-climb from there into the valley. We'll have to carry the body up on a litter. Ryan, I want you with me on the descent. Eldon and Tony, you handle the ropes up top. Danny, you're incident commander. Now, let's head out. The sheriff's department will meet us there."

Grace helped haul ropes and other equipment to the modified Jeep, known as the Beast, used for rescue work. This second incarnation of a rescue vehicle featured a heavy-duty engine, large treaded tires and extra low gears to allow it to climb steep terrain. It also had a winch, a telescoping boom and other equipment to make it useful for rescue work.

While Sheri and several others loaded into the Beast,

Grace, Hannah and two other rookies—Nancy and Todd—
followed in Grace's Jeep. Navigating the often unmaintained
Forest Service road up toward her cabin had given her plenty
of experience driving in the mountains, and she had no difficulty piloting them to the remote location from which they
would start their mission.

A sheriff's department SUV awaited them at the parking area. Sergeant Gage Walker and a deputy got out of the
vehicle and walked toward them. Grace felt a little nervous
around Gage after their last encounter, but he nodded at her
affably before turning to Sheri. "You can see the body two-
thirds of the way down the slope, in deep snow," he said and
handed her a pair of binoculars.

Grace followed the others to the edge of the dirt road,
where the landscape fell away into a steep valley. She
squinted and thought she could make out a patch of bright
red, like a hat or scarf, though it was too far below to make
out clearly. "How are they ever going to get down there?"
she asked Nancy.

"They will," Hannah said from behind them. "But I'm
just as glad it's not me making the climb."

Sheri looked up at the sky. "We don't have too many
hours of good light in this valley," she said. "We'd better
get started."

Grace joined the others in unloading gear, then watched
as Ryan demonstrated how to set anchors for the climbing
ropes and reviewed the procedure for rigging lines. Even
in the middle of an operation, the veterans took the time to
teach the rookies.

"Hello, Grace."

Sergeant Walker had approached her from behind. "Hello,
Sergeant," she said.

"Declan tells me I upset you the other day," Gage said. "I didn't mean to do that."

The apology left her speechless. "I'm fine," she managed.

"We have to gather as much evidence as we can whenever there's been a crime," Gage said. "Especially one of this magnitude. That means asking hard questions."

She nodded. "I understand."

"Declan has worked in law enforcement long enough to understand how things are," Gage said. "You don't need to worry about him."

Worry wasn't the first word she thought of when it came to her feelings for Declan Owen. Concern, maybe. Attraction, certainly. Along with a little fear—not of the man himself, but of how vulnerable she felt when she was with him.

"We've asked Declan to remain in town while we complete our investigation," Gage said.

"How long will that be?" How much longer would she get to see him?

"It could be several weeks. Has he told you he's on leave with the Marshals Service until then?"

She shook her head. They hadn't discussed his work outside of his search for Terrence Barclay.

"Grace, come give me a hand with this!" Sheri called.

"I have to go," she said and hurried away from Gage. She couldn't imagine why he had told her those things about Declan. Was it because Declan had asked him to?

For the next several hours, she and the other volunteers were absorbed in the retrieval of the body in the valley far below. Though the sun had been high overhead when they began the operation, the surrounding mountains soon cast long shadows and the temperature dropped until Grace was shivering in spite of her layers of winter clothing. She stood with half a dozen other volunteers and watched Sheri and

Ryan make the long, slow descent. The snow came to their knees in places, and they had to maneuver carefully around hidden rocks. Once the two climbers were in place, a litter would be sent down to them, then they would reverse the process, bringing the litter up behind them.

Grace tried not to think about what they would have to deal with when they reached the body. Loading a frozen corpse into the litter didn't sound like a pleasant, or an easy, task. She said as much to Hannah.

"At least they don't have to worry about hurting the poor person any more on the way up," Hannah said.

After two hours, Sheri was within a few feet of the body, Ryan not far behind. The radio Danny was using to communicate with the two of them crackled and popped. "You are not going to believe this!" Sheri said.

Ryan's comment was more succinct—a single swear word, loud and clear over the radio.

"What's going on?" Danny asked.

"We didn't go to all this trouble for a body," Sheri said. "It's a mannequin."

"Repeat that," Danny said. "I don't think I heard correctly."

"Somebody put a mannequin down here," Sheri said. "All dressed up in winter gear."

"Somebody's idea of a sick joke," Danny said.

"It gets sicker," Ryan said. "I took a look and this dummy is seriously messed up. Like—mutilated."

Danny looked around and motioned Gage to come over. "You need to hear this," he said and handed the radio to Gage.

"This is Sergeant Walker," Gage said. "What have you found down there?"

Ryan explained about the mannequin, then Sheri cut in.

"Someone did this on purpose. They cost us a lot of time and expense, not to mention endangering volunteer lives."

"If we can find out who did this, we'll be sure to charge them," Gage said. "What are you going to do about the mannequin?"

"We're going to bring it back up with us," Sheri said. "We can't leave it down here, littering up the place."

"Besides, if we leave it, we're bound to get more calls," Ryan said. "From a distance, it really did look like a person."

"When you get it up here, I want to take a closer look," Gage said.

It took over an hour to make the climb back up with the mannequin on the litter in tow. When Sheri and Ryan hauled the litter over the edge, the others gathered around to look. Someone had carefully dressed the female dummy, complete with long blonde hair, in snow pants and parka and a bright red knit cap. But then they had carved deep slashes into the torso and across the face.

"That's horrible!" Hannah cried and turned away.

"We'll take this into headquarters," Gage said. "Maybe we'll find some evidence linking this to whoever did it."

"When you do, I'd like to give them a piece of my mind," Sheri said.

"I'd like to do more than that," Ryan muttered.

Gage and his deputy took charge of the mannequin while the volunteers gathered their gear and loaded it back into the vehicles.

Grace and Nancy were walking back to her Jeep when a man skied toward them. "What's going on?" he asked. "Is someone hurt?"

Grace recognized the young man in the orange cap she had met at the gas station. "No one is hurt," she said.

"So, what are you all doing up here?" he asked.

"It's just a training exercise," Nancy said. "Who are you?"

"I'm Tommy," he said. "I came up to see. It's a gorgeous day, isn't it?" He grinned at Grace. "You're the girl from the gas station the other day, right? The one who told me to ask at the library about a place to stay?"

She nodded. "Did you find a place?"

"I sure did. Thanks again for your help."

Awkward silence while Tommy continued to grin at her and she looked everywhere but at him. "I'd better go," she said finally. "Enjoy your day." She turned and headed toward the Jeep.

Nancy caught up. "He was cute," she said. "And he seemed really into you."

"I met him at the gas station—once," Grace said.

"You made an impression on him."

"Yeah, well, he's just visiting for a little while." She wasn't interested in someone just passing through.

Liar. Her conscience pinched her as she thought of Declan. He was in town for a few more days or weeks while the sheriff's department completed their investigation—whatever that meant. But he wasn't going to stick around. Why would he want to, anyway?

DECLAN STARED DOWN at the disfigured mannequin with the sense of having been in this position before. The female figure on the table before him clearly wasn't a real person and there was no blood or bruising, but somehow that made the scene even more macabre. "You say Search and Rescue found this?" Had Grace been there to see the grisly discovery?

"Some skiers saw it, thought it was a body and called it in. It looked real from that far away."

Declan nodded. It looked real enough, even from here. "It's Barbara Racine," he said.

"Barclay's first victim," Gage said.

"The first victim we know about. She's the only one he cut up this way, which led some to believe he wasn't the one who killed her."

"So you think Barclay did this and put the mannequin in that ravine? Why?"

"I don't know. A rehearsal of sorts? Because he wants to wind us up? Or he needed a release of tension. A profiler might be able to tell you."

"No profilers here," Gage said. "He was taking a chance someone would even spot her."

"I heard it's a pretty popular backcountry ski area," Declan said. He had talked to locals enough to know that. "Remote enough that he could get the mannequin there and toss it over without being seen but count on someone discovering it eventually. And if they didn't, it wouldn't make that much difference to him."

"You don't think so?"

"I don't. I think he's just amusing himself right now, until he strikes for real."

"I spoke to your office about this," Gage said.

Declan tore his gaze away from the mannequin. "What did they say?"

"They said they doubted this had anything to do with Terrence Barclay. They suggested it sounded like high school students."

"I suppose they told you not to listen to me," Declan said.

"Something like that." Gage regarded the mannequin. "It does sound like something high school students might do, though if I knew who, I would seriously suggest counseling. The mannequin—sure, they might think throwing it into that valley was funny. But the slashing?" He shook his head. "Maybe, but…"

"But this looks like Terrence Barclay to me," Declan said. "I know you've only got my word against the rest of the Marshals Service."

Gage turned with his back to the table. "I can't see any reason for you to lie to me," he said. "Which doesn't mean I think you're right, but I'm not ready to dismiss everything you say outright."

"I appreciate that."

"You're not winning any friends back at the Marshals Service."

"We've already established that."

A tap on the door interrupted them. "Yes?" Gage called.

Adelaide opened the door. "There's a woman to see you, Sergeant," she said. She glanced at the mannequin and looked away. "It's about Agnes Cockrell."

"I'll see her in my office," Gage said. He offered a hand to Declan. "I'll be in touch."

Declan took Gage's hand with a firm grip of his own, then left. He was halfway across the street when Adelaide hurried after him. "The sergeant wants you to come back," she said.

He followed the office manager back into the sheriff's department and down the hall to Gage's office, where a plump, pretty blonde sat with a pink-cheeked baby on her lap.

"I thought you might want to hear what Mrs. Waring has to say," Gage said.

Declan nodded. He noticed Gage hadn't bothered to introduce him, which was probably just as well, in case Mrs. Waring had heard any rumors about his involvement in Agnes's death.

"Go ahead, ma'am," Gage said. "Repeat what you told me."

"I saw a notice online that the sheriff's department was looking for anyone who saw Agnes up on Dixon Pass the day she died." She jostled the baby in her arms. "I did."

"You saw Agnes Cockrell on Dixon Pass the day she was killed?" Declan clarified.

Mrs. Waring nodded. "I was driving back from a doctor's appointment, and I passed her. She was on the side of the road with a flat tire. I was looking for a place to turn around and go back to Agnes when Jess here started screaming at the top of her lungs. She was still screaming when I got turned around and drove back, but I saw that a man had stopped. He was standing with her and they were looking at the tire, so I figured I didn't need to get involved. It wasn't as if I was going to be that much help with a screaming baby."

This woman had seen Terrence Barclay, Declan thought. It was possible someone else had stopped to change Agnes's flat tire, but he knew in his gut it was Barclay. "What did this man look like?" he asked. "Would you recognize him again?"

Mrs. Waring shook her head. "I just got a glimpse of his back. I was distracted by the baby. He was wearing a dark coat and a cap and jeans, I think."

This fit the clothing Barclay had been wearing the last time Declan had seen him.

"What was he driving?" Gage asked.

"I'm sorry, I didn't notice." She shrugged. "I don't really notice things like that, and I didn't think it would be important. I was going to call Agnes later and find out how she was doing, but then I heard she had been killed." She bit her lower lip. "Do you think the man I saw killed her? Maybe if I had stopped—"

"It's all right," Gage said. "You didn't do anything wrong,

and I appreciate you stopping by. You're helping us to get a better picture of what happened that day."

"I should have stopped," she said. "But I was worried about the baby, and I thought Agnes would be okay." She was working herself up to real tears, Declan thought.

Gage picked up his phone. "Addie, could you help Mrs. Waring to her car?"

Seconds later, Adelaide swooped in and took the distraught woman by the arm. "Come with me and I'll fix you a cup of tea," she said, one arm around the woman's shoulders.

When they were alone again, Gage looked at Declan. "You may think you don't remember what happened," he said. "But I don't think your mind made up that scenario about Barclay using Agnes as a decoy to lure you in. Some part of you knows what happened, even if you can't access it."

"Maybe," Declan said. At least Gage was beginning to believe him.

"Do you think hypnosis would help?" Gage asked.

"I'm willing to try anything."

"I'll do some nosing around, see what I can find out. In the meantime, we're getting a better picture. Now if we could just find Barclay."

Declan returned to the Alpiner Inn, where he changed clothes and sat down to review his case notes again. Maybe there was something in there he had missed.

What he really missed was his office in Denver and access to the databases and support staff he relied on in investigations. Capturing Barclay was going to require more than what he could do alone. He pulled out his phone and called Oscar Penrod.

"Hello, Declan," Penrod said. "Are you back in Denver?"

"No, I'm still in Eagle Mountain," Declan said.

"I assume this means you're still under investigation."

"I didn't murder anyone," he said. "In the meantime, are you sending anyone here to look for Terrence Barclay?"

"Terrence Barclay is none of your concern," Penrod said.

"Is the FBI sending anyone to investigate?" Declan asked. "I'm not part of the search for Barclay, but I do have good reason to believe he's here. Someone who is authorized to do so should investigate."

"You're not part of the search, and how it is conducted is not your concern. That's all I have to say on the matter." *Click!* Followed by silence. Penrod had hung up on him.

Declan threw the phone onto the bed, then began to pace. He'd been right—no one was looking for Barclay in the place where he was most likely to be. No one except Declan, and he had no authority and few resources. Gage had promised to help, but Declan wasn't sure the sergeant even believed his theory that Barclay was in Eagle Mountain and planning to kill again.

What if Declan was wrong? What if the marshals and everyone else was right and Barclay was far away from Eagle Mountain? He stopped pacing. Knowing he had wasted so much time and energy here while Barclay was getting farther and farther away was like a kick in the gut. But he reminded himself that his situation wouldn't be any different if he had realized Barclay was far away. He wouldn't have had the authority to go after him, and after what had happened on Dixon Pass, he would have been foolish to try. He was stuck here in Eagle Mountain until the sheriff's department cleared its murder investigation.

That meant he had nothing to lose by continuing to search for Barclay. If the killer was here, Declan might be the only person standing between him and his next murder.

Chapter Eleven

Declan had every intention of spending the rest of the day combing Eagle Mountain for anyone who might be Terrence Barclay. He couldn't shake the image of that grisly mannequin, fixed up to resemble a real murder victim, and that was enough to motivate his search. But as he drove away from the sheriff's department, he turned away from town, toward the road leading up to Grace's cabin. Had seeing that mannequin shaken her as much as it had shaken him?

The truck he had rented, loud and ugly as it was, negotiated the slush-filled ruts and icy inclines of the Forest Service road with plenty of power, if not a lot of finesse. Declan parked at the end of the road, next to Grace's Jeep. At least he hadn't driven all the way up here only to find her gone. He pulled out his phone, intending to let her know he was here, but of course he had no signal. So he set out walking, following the packed tracks of her snowmobile and the lingering impression of his own boot prints from his visit the day before.

He had left after kissing her because he knew if he didn't walk away, he would end up staying, would end up making promises to her he couldn't keep. He had had plenty of casual relationships in his life and he knew how to handle those, but nothing in his feelings for Grace, confusing as they were, was casual. If he said half of the things that came into his head when he was with her, she would end up thinking he wanted to stay with her forever.

Part of him did want that, but that wasn't possible. His job and general logistics were minor obstacles compared to his fierce inability to make that kind of commitment. He had changed universities twice before he earned his degree, changed jobs four times, moved half a dozen times or more, dated so many women he couldn't remember them all. Every place and every person left him wanting more, though he knew enough to see the biggest lack wasn't in his choice of location and companions, but in himself. All he had to do was give himself a moment of silence and he would hear his father's voice, reminding him how inadequate he was. What woman would want that?

He heard Grace before he saw her. "Come here, boy! Bring me the ball!"

He rounded a curve in the trail and stopped. She stood on the bottom step leading up to her cabin, dressed in a bright red sweater and black leggings, her hair falling loosely around her shoulders. She raised her arm, arced it back, then sent a yellow tennis ball soaring. The dog barked excitedly and bounded after the toy, snow flying up with each leap. He caught the ball and turned to race back toward Grace, who laughed and wrestled it from him to throw again.

She was so beautiful. Strong, capable and clearly smart. Was he the only one who saw her vulnerability? He had seen her wounds and wished he knew who had hurt her.

Bear barked again but this time whirled and bounded toward Declan. He braced himself to meet the dog, but Bear turned again when Grace called him back. "Declan!" She waved and started toward him. "What a nice surprise."

Her smile was enough to rock him back on his heels. "I

should have called," he said. "I didn't think about it until I was out of phone range."

"That's okay." She stopped a few feet from him. "Is everything all right?"

"I just wanted to see you." He started toward her cabin and she fell into step beside him, the dog bounding through the snow ahead.

"Is there something in particular you need to see me about?" she asked.

"I heard about the search and rescue call with the mannequin," he said. "Were you part of that?"

Her smile vanished. "Yes. It was creepy. Someone said it must have been a prank, but who would do something like that? Climbing down to retrieve what we all thought was a body was dangerous."

"Did you make that climb?" he asked, trying to hide his alarm.

"No. Sheri and Ryan did it. They're our best climbers. But they could have been seriously injured." They stopped in front of the cabin. "How did you hear about it?"

"Gage told me." At her puzzled look, he added, "We're wondering if Terrence Barclay did it."

Deep lines formed between her brows. "Why would he do something like that?"

"I don't pretend to understand it, but serial killers do strange things." How much should he tell her? He didn't want to alarm her, but he didn't want to leave her in the dark, either. He touched her shoulder and she angled toward him, searching his face. "I told you I think Barkley is here because he intends to kill again," he said.

"Yes."

"His pattern before has been to choose a victim and stalk her. It's always a woman. This thing with the mannequin—it could be a rehearsal or a warning or just a way to relieve tension."

Some of the color left her face, but she nodded. "Are you any closer to finding him?"

"I wish I could tell you yes, but we're not getting anywhere. In the meantime, you need to be careful."

"What? You think he would come after me?" Her voice rose on the last word.

"He picks young, attractive women. Like you. Or like your friends. You should all be careful. You haven't noticed anyone behaving oddly around you, have you? Maybe paying more attention to you than usual?"

She shook her head. "No. Not really." She rubbed her shoulders. "It's getting cold out here. Do you want to come inside?"

"Sure." He couldn't tell if she believed him when he said she might be in danger. Maybe he could persuade her. Or maybe they would find another, more pleasant topic of conversation. Anything to keep her from linking him forever with grisly murders and stalking killers.

Inside, she added wood to the fire, then went into the kitchen and lit the burner on the stove under a teakettle. "Has Gage said anything more to you about Agnes Cockrell's murder?" she asked when she returned to the living room and settled near him on the sofa.

"I think he's beginning to believe that I didn't kill her," he said. "A woman came into the sheriff's department and said she saw Agnes with a flat tire on the side of the road up at Dixon Pass. By the time she turned her car around and went back to help, a man had stopped and was talking to Agnes. The woman had a crying baby with her, so she went on, sure Agnes would be okay."

"Was the man Terrence Barclay, or was it you?" she asked.

The question caught him off guard. He had been so focused on Barclay he hadn't considered that Mrs. Waring might have seen him standing with Agnes. "I'm sure it was Barclay," he said. "Someone drove Agnes's car to Delta, and we know that wasn't me."

"Of course." She hugged her arms across her stomach. "What do you think happened?"

"I think Barclay stopped on the pretext of helping Agnes, then used her as a decoy to get me to stop." He shook his head. "Or maybe I stopped, anyway. I was following Barclay. If I had seen him with anyone, especially a woman, I would have stopped." He put a hand to his head. "If only I could remember." He lowered his hand and studied her. She wasn't exactly serene, but she looked much calmer than he felt. "You really never remembered anything from the accident you were involved in as a child?"

"Nothing." She uncrossed her arms and smoothed her palms down her thighs. "My mother told me over and over what happened on the day of the wreck, but I never remembered. Sometimes I think I do, but I know it's only because I was told the story so often. It's not the same as a real memory."

The teakettle began whistling, and she stood and returned to the kitchen. He watched her go, focused on the lithe body outlined by the clinging knit of her sweater and leggings. He wanted to hold her, not to comfort her so much as to comfort himself, or at least to lose himself for a while in the feel of her body against his.

When she returned moments later with two mugs of tea, he had moved to stand in front of the woodstove and study her desk, stacks of papers neatly arranged on either side of a computer monitor. "How is work going?" he asked.

"It's going well." She handed him a mug, then stood beside him with the other. "Some people might find transcribing all those notebooks boring, but I find it fascinating to read my grandfather's writing."

"You mentioned that he kept weather records. Is there more than that?"

"Much more. He was a true naturalist, interested in everything in the natural world. For more than sixty years he made note every day of what he observed, from weather and temperature to the behavior of local wildlife. It's an extraordinary record that's a remarkable resource for science, from climate researchers to wildlife biologists to meteorologists. It's important work, and I'm so lucky to be a part of it."

"I imagine your grandfather would be proud of you."

"I think he would." She regarded him as she sipped tea. "But the work you do is important, too. Just very different from mine."

"It is important, though I don't know how much longer I'll be doing it."

"What do you mean?"

"My supervisor isn't happy with me. I suppose in his shoes I might feel the same. After Barclay escaped my custody, I was removed from the case. I had no business continuing trying to track him."

"But you found out where he was headed," she said. "Even if you weren't still on the case, that would help the people who were supposed to be looking for him."

"It would have, if they had believed me. But I'm afraid I've lost all credibility with the marshals office."

"I don't understand."

He blew out a long breath. "I'm an embarrassment. I did something foolish—let a felon get away from me. He got hold of my weapon and used it to kill someone. It's a wonder I wasn't relieved of duty immediately."

"Maybe they didn't want to get rid of a good officer because of a single mistake."

He shook his head. "It wasn't just a mistake. It was a gross failure in my duty."

"How did it happen?" she asked.

He closed his eyes. He had been over the moments so many times in his head, both awake and in his dreams. "He attacked the other marshal I was with, Glenda Zanett. He was shackled, his hands in cuffs, but he turned suddenly and slammed his fists into her face. She went down on her knees. I pulled my gun on him and he headbutted me. I didn't let go of the gun—I'm sure I didn't. But Glenda was still on the floor, screaming, blood running from her face. I turned my head for a fraction of a second to check on her, and Barclay hit me again. I fired, but the shot went into the floor, and then he had the gun."

He fell silent, the scene playing out again in slow motion.

"It's amazing you weren't killed," she said softly.

"He shot Glenda. She had the keys to the shackles, and he stripped them off her belt and managed to undo his own shackles. That's not supposed to be possible, but he must have practiced. I moved toward him, but he shoved the barrel of the gun into my stomach and said he'd kill me if I laid a hand on him. Before I had time to react, he hit me in the head with the gun and I went down. I woke up in a pool of blood, but it wasn't my blood. It was Glenda's."

Grace set aside the tea and put both arms around him. He hadn't realized he was shaking until then. She held him tightly, her head resting on his shoulder, until the tremors subsided. "You couldn't have done anything differently," she said.

"They said I failed in my duty. I failed to safeguard my weapon. I failed to protect a fellow officer." He had heard the words often enough, repeated them often enough that he could say them without emotion. They were just words now, stings that no longer hurt. Or that hurt so deeply he was past acknowledging the pain.

"What did your parents say?" she asked.

He grimaced. "The general said he was ashamed of me."

She gasped and drew back. "Your father said that?"

"It wasn't the first time," he said. "I've been failing to live up to his expectations most of my life."

"What about your mother?"

"She always takes his side."

Her eyes clouded, but not with tears—with anger. "They don't deserve a son like you."

"I think they would probably agree with you."

"I didn't mean—"

"It's all right." He put his fingers to her lips to silence her, and she softened against him once more.

She took his hand and kissed his palm, a feather touch that sent a current of electricity through him. She kissed his wrist above the fabric of his fleece top, then lifted her face and met his lips as he lowered his mouth to hers.

There was nothing timid or withheld in that kiss. She surged to him, pulling him into her with the force of a tide. She gripped the fleece of his top, her nails digging into his shoulders, arching hard against him. He slid both hands around to cup her bottom, then up beneath the soft red sweater, along the curve of her waist to the weight of her breasts in his palms.

She pulled her mouth from his long enough to stare into his eyes, her pupils dark. "Stay," she said.

"I'm not going anywhere," he said, his voice ragged, and kissed her again.

She tugged off his top somewhere between the woodstove and the door to her bedroom, and by the time they actually reached the bed, they were both naked, their skin hot against the cool sheets. She jerked open the drawer of the bedside table and began rummaging through it.

"What are you looking for?" he asked, only slightly alarmed. He knew a lot of people who kept a weapon in that drawer.

She pulled the drawer out altogether and dumped its contents onto the floor. The sight of her bare bottom up as she clawed through the scattered items sent a fresh jolt of wanting through him, and he moved toward her, but just then she rose up and waved a small packet triumphantly.

"This," she said and thrust the condom at him.

He couldn't help it—he laughed. She glared at him. "I don't see what's so funny about a condom," she said.

"No, but if you could have seen yourself, searching for it…" He chuckled and reached for her, gently this time. "You're beautiful," he said. "Everything about you is beautiful."

She let her gaze slide over him, and a smile erased her look of annoyance. "You're certainly in better shape than the last time I saw you naked." She rested a hand on his hip. "Though even then, I liked what I saw."

"Even blue and shriveled?" he joked.

"Only a little blue. And not shriveled." She slid her hand over to wrap around his erection, and he caught his breath, then gathered her close once more.

They took their time after that, touching and tasting, letting the intensity build again. When she became impatient, he settled her with murmured endearments and touches that teased at what was to come. By the time he unwrapped the condom and rolled it on, his hands were shaking a little, and when she lay back and beckoned him to her, he knew he wouldn't be able to hold back long.

But she knew how to prolong the moment. Maybe all that time sitting quietly, observing nature, had taught her the value of taking her time. She wrapped herself around him and moved with deliberate grace, leading him in a sensual dance. He watched her, mesmerized, as her face transformed and her body tensed. He held her tightly as her climax overtook her, and then he could hold back no more and lost himself to his own satisfaction.

Afterward, they clung together, neither wanting to pull away. "You're pretty wonderful for an abominable snow-man," she said.

"So you think maybe I was worth saving?" He slid down to rest his head between her breasts.

"Definitely." She brushed a lock of hair out of his eyes. "Though we could talk about who was saving who."

He wanted to ask what she meant by the words, but it had been a long hike up to her place and more than one sleepless night since he came here. Her bed was warm and she was warmer, and before he could find the right words, his eyes drifted closed and he surrendered to blackness.

Chapter Twelve

Grace woke with the last gray light of dusk filtering through the gap in the bedroom curtains. Declan lay on his back beside her, face slack, jaw dark with beard-shadow, powerful torso pressed against the mattress and outlined beneath the sheet and blanket. He smelled of man and sex, and she wanted to bury her face against his warm skin and breathe in that scent until she was dizzy with it. She was obsessed with him, which felt awkward and silly, but also powerful and amazing.

She eased out of bed and dressed, then went into the kitchen. Bear got up from his bed by the woodstove and followed her, a reproachful look in his brown eyes. "Don't be jealous," she told him and rubbed his ears. "I still love you."

She fed him, then opened the refrigerator and searched for something to make for supper, but her mind refused to consider the practicalities of omelets or soup while Declan lay sleeping in her bed. She marveled at her own boldness, inviting him to stay with her. Everything about him should have threatened her peace of mind—the fact that he was a lawman, if a disgraced one. His amnesia, which only reminded her of the big gap in her own memory. He was too aware and perceptive, the kind of man who was bound to discover all her failings. The kind of person she had always avoided.

Yet she felt safe with him, though *safe* was too passive a term. She felt needed and cherished and giddy with passion.

She was cracking eggs into a bowl when she heard him approaching. She pretended not to notice until he came up behind her and pulled her close. He kissed the back of her neck, sending a shiver through her.

"Are you hungry?" she asked.

"Mmm."

He sent her a wolfish look, and she laughed. "I meant for food."

"That, too." He kissed her again, then drew away, his expression serious. "After we eat, I should head back to town. Not that I wouldn't like to stay, but…"

She nodded. "You have work to do." And maybe they both needed some space to process this hurricane of emotion that had overtaken them. At least, she was pretty sure she did.

"I got a tip about a new waiter at a restaurant between here and Junction," he said. "I want to check him out. You could come with me."

"I don't think so. I have work to do, too." She was supposed to have finished the 1972 notebook by now, but being with Declan had her behind. "Do you want cheese in your omelet?"

"Yes, please."

"The toaster is over there." She nodded across the room. "You can toast some bread while I cook the eggs."

They ate at the little kitchen table, chatting about mundane things. It was nice. Ordinary.

Afterward, she gave him a ride down to his truck. Before he left, she took his arm and gave him a hard look. "Be careful," she said. "This man has attacked you twice. Next time he might kill you." Her voice shook a little at those words.

"I'm not going to let that happen." He kissed her—a deep, thorough kiss she felt all the way to her toes. "I'll call you tomorrow," he said when he finally lifted his head.

"What's going to happen, with us?" She regretted the words as soon as she blurted them out. He would think she was too needy. Moving too fast.

But he didn't look upset. "We'll figure it out," he said.

She waved as he drove away. She wasn't very adept at figuring things out, but she did know a thing or two about watching and waiting. Her work was all about seeing how things resolved on their own without interference. Whether that was a good approach for relationships, she couldn't say, but it was the only approach she knew.

THE WAITER DECLAN had heard about was not Terrence Barclay. He was too short, with eyes that were too close together to be faked by makeup. Declan spent a discouraging half hour nursing a beer and attempting to make conversation with the bartender about new employees of the restaurant before he gave up and headed back toward Eagle Mountain.

He debated driving up to spend the night with Grace. He wanted to be smart about her, to let his feelings cool a little so he could think sensibly. But she had imprinted herself on his body and all he could think of was getting back into her bed.

A flash of light to his right made him pump the brakes on the truck. He squinted to bring the light source into sharper focus and realized it was the glare off a strip of reflective tape on the back of the parka of a man walking along the side of the road. Declan slowed the truck further and rolled to a stop beside the walker, who was struggling through thick drifts along the side of the county road. "Do you need a ride somewhere?" he asked.

The man, only his eyes visible between a white fleece gaiter and an orange knit hat, took two stumbling steps toward the truck. "That would be great," he said. "I'm supposed to work the overnight shift at the Ranch Motel, and my van wouldn't start."

"Get in," Declan said.

The man climbed into the truck and fastened his seat belt. He hugged himself, then clapped his mittened hands together. Declan realized he was young, but telling anything about his appearance in the darkness was difficult. "What's your name?" he asked.

"Tommy Llewellyn." The man, his hat still hiding his hair and the sides of his face, swiveled toward him. He had lowered the gaiter, revealing a thin mustache above pale, chapped lips.

"Have you been in Eagle Mountain long?" Declan asked, trying to focus on the road, though he kept glancing at his passenger.

"About a week. I've been camping in my van back there." He jerked his thumb in the direction they had come. "I got a job as night clerk at the Ranch, and I'd hate to screw that up my first week."

The hair on the back of Declan's neck rose up and he tightened his grip on the steering wheel. The timing was right. The easygoing, open manner was typical of the various personas Barclay had assumed. This man had a slight Southern drawl. Oklahoma or Texas? "Where were you before?" he asked.

Tommy sat back again. "I was in Denver for a few weeks before this, but I didn't care for it much. I'm thinking of heading out to Utah soon. I've spent the last year seeing the

United States. I live in my van, take a job for a while when I need money. It's a great life."

And a good cover for a fugitive, Declan thought.

"Man, it's cold out there." Tommy settled against the side of the truck cab. "Thanks again for picking me up. I'm about half-frozen." He huddled further into his coat.

He probably was cold if he had been out in the night chill very long, Declan thought. But this was also a good excuse for remaining bundled up. He glanced over at his passenger and thought his eyes were closed. He forced his gaze onto the road again.

He had spent less than two hours with Terrence Barclay previously, and his attention had been directed as much on searching for potential danger from outside as on Barclay himself. As he was described in every bit of court evidence Declan had read since Barclay had escaped his custody, the man he had been assigned to guard and transport was polite, quiet and cooperative. Inoffensive. Which had probably made him and Glenda let down their guards more than usual and had added to the shock of Barclay's sudden, furious attack upon them.

"Do you like working at the motel?" Declan asked, not because he was interested, but as a way to keep his passenger talking.

Tommy shifted, rousing himself. "It's all right. They have me filing stuff and cleaning the lobby when I don't have customers to wait on, but that doesn't take all night, so I usually watch videos on my phone and stuff like that. It will do until I'm ready to move on."

"Have you met any women since you moved to town?"

Tommy shifted, feet scraping on the floor mat. "It's only been a week. Though there is this one woman I met. Really pretty. Hard to tell what she thinks of me, but if I get a chance, I might ask her out. Why do you ask? Do you have somebody you want me to meet?" No mistaking the teasing note in his voice.

Declan shook his head. "No, I'm just new in town myself. I noticed there are a lot more single men than women."

"That's a lot of places out west, you know?" Tommy said.

A lighted sign up ahead announced the Ranch Motel, and Declan slowed the truck. "You can let me out right up front," Tommy said.

Declan turned into the drive and parked under the portico. "Thanks for the ride," Tommy said, already pushing open the door.

Declan stared at his passenger as Tommy stepped into the harsh glow of the outdoor lighting at the motel entrance. He was pale, acne scarring standing out on his right cheek, bruised half-moons beneath his eyes.

"Is something wrong?" Tommy put a hand to his cheek. "Why are you staring at me?"

Declan looked away. "Sorry. I thought for a minute there you looked like someone I know." Except he didn't. Tommy didn't look familiar to Declan at all.

"I guess we all have a doppelgänger somewhere, right? Thanks for the ride. Maybe I'll see you around."

Then he was hurrying into the motel. Declan put the truck in gear and drove away. He was in no mood to see Grace now. He would spend another evening with the files he had compiled about Terrence Barclay. Was the fact that Declan couldn't remember exactly what he looked like a testament to Barclay's chameleon abilities? Or was it a sign that more than Declan's ability to remember a few hours up on Dixon Pass had been damaged with a blow to his head?

FRIDAY MORNING, Grace walked around the cabin, checking snow depth and moisture content, recording the tempera-

ture and observing the progress of bud formation on aspens
and the pattern of snow on the mountain peaks visible from
her yard. Then she went back inside, poured a second cup
of coffee and sat down to fire up her computer and record
her observations and submit a report that was due that day.

But the computer informed her there was no internet con-
nectivity. A quick check of her modem showed it to be in
working order. Annoyed, she took another slug of coffee,
then shrugged back into her coat and boots and went outside to check the small satellite dish attached to the side of
her cabin. This was the dish that picked up the signal that
provided phone and internet service to her cabin. The dish
looked fine, which meant something was wrong with the
cell tower or transformer. Though the service was usually
reliable, half a dozen times a year she would be without a
signal for a few hours or a few days. Last year, the problem had been thieves stealing the batteries that powered the
transmitter. Once, an ice storm had broken some equipment.
Whatever was going on today would be fixed, and while
inconvenient, it wasn't the end of the world. Her grandfather had lived here for six decades with no way to communicate with the outside world, and he had survived just fine.

She returned to the cabin, shed coat and boots, and re-
heated her coffee and made toast. She ate breakfast while
reviewing the final draft of her report, then copied the draft
onto a flash drive. She cleaned the kitchen, combed her hair
and added a touch of makeup, then donned her snowmobile
suit and helmet and slipped the flash drive and her wallet
into a pocket. "I'll be back in a couple of hours," she told
Bear, who had observed all these actions with the expression of a dog who knew he was going to be left behind. "I'll
bring you a treat."

At the library, she signed into one of their computers

and sent the report to her supervisor, then answered several emails. She was reading an amusing account of a colleague's encounter with a marmot who stole his lunch when the chair beside her made a loud, scraping noise as it slid back. She glanced over and was startled to see Tommy.

"Hey," he said. "It's good to see you again. How have you been?"

"I've been fine," she answered automatically. Politeness compelled her to add, "How are you?"

"I'm good. I'm working over at the Ranch Motel, and I've got a sweet camp set up down by the river."

She nodded and turned back to the computer, hoping he would get the message that she wanted to be left alone.

"I was wondering if maybe you wanted to go out some time," he said. "We could have dinner or something."

"Oh, um, thank you, but I don't think so."

His smile faltered, then he fixed it back in place. "You're not married or something, are you?" He glanced at her hand. "Except I don't see a ring. But I guess not everyone wears a wedding ring."

"No, I'm not married."

"You've probably got a boyfriend, right? I mean, of course you do."

She thought of Declan. He wasn't her boyfriend. He was a man she had spent one night with. A man she felt a connection to, but that didn't mean she had a claim on him. "I just don't feel like dating anyone," she said. A flash of anger immediately followed these words. Why should she have to explain herself to this man?

"I'm a fun guy, I promise."

She shook her head and focused on the monitor once more. She could feel his eyes on her but didn't dare look his way. She had been in this position before—turning down men who didn't seem able to believe that she didn't want to date them. Friends had accused her of being too picky, but most of them admitted that dating could be uncomfortable and awkward. Grace didn't feel like putting herself through all that.

She waited until Tommy moved away before she shut down her computer and stood. She thanked the librarian on her way out, then, remembering her promise to Bear, she headed to the natural foods store.

Mike was behind the counter. He greeted her with a wide smile. "It's my favorite customer," he said. "How was that chai?"

"It was good," she said.

"Didn't I tell you? What can we get for you today?"

"I just stopped to get some treats for my dog." She headed for the bulk bins in the pet section.

Mike followed her. "What kind of dog do you have?" he asked.

"He's a shepherd mix."

"I love shepherds. Actually, I love all dogs. I wonder if Arnie would let me adopt one."

"Why would he care if you adopt a dog?"

"Well, I'm living upstairs right now. Just until I can find a place of my own."

The door to the storeroom opened and Arnie emerged. A short, round man with a tonsure of brown curls, he reminded Grace of a genial monk. The loose brown sweater he wore only added to this image. "Hello, Grace," he called. "Are you finding everything you need?"

"Yes, I am. Thank you."

Mike moved back behind the counter and began straightening a display of canned olives. Grace bagged up a selection of dog biscuits and walked to the register.

"I was telling Grace here I should get a dog," Mike said to Arnie. "What would you think of that?"

"I think you should be able to support yourself before you add a dog." Arnie moved the bag of dog biscuits onto a scale. "Animals are a big responsibility. You shouldn't adopt one until you're certain you can care for it in the long term."

"You sound just like my dad." Mike laughed. "No wonder the two of you are friends."

"Mike's dad and I met in college and we both worked at an Antarctic research station," Arnie said to Grace. "We were about Mike's age at the time."

"How wonderful that you've kept in touch all these years," she said.

"Dad is in Peru," Mike said. He handed Grace the bag of biscuits. "He's a research scientist, like you."

She stilled. "How did you know I'm a research scientist?"

"Arnie told me." Mike glanced at the older man. "Or somebody did."

"No secrets in a small town," Arnie said.

She nodded, said goodbye and returned to her car. Should she text Declan and see if he wanted to get some lunch? But maybe he was busy? She didn't want him to think she had come into town just to see him.

Besides, she had her own work to do. She headed out of town. A glance in the rearview mirror showed a battered green compact car following closely. She didn't think much of it until she turned onto the Forest Service road and the green car followed.

Of course, snowshoers and cross-country skiers used this road to access some of the high-country trails. But she couldn't remember the last time she had seen another car on the road in the middle of a weekday. She looked again in the rearview mirror to see if she recognized the driver, but it was impossible, given tinted windows and the snow that had collected on her rear window.

She focused on negotiating the rough and icy road. No doubt the driver of the green car would turn around before too long, since his vehicle wasn't really made for this kind of driving. Or else he would stop at the parking area for one of the trails.

But they passed the parking area and the green car stayed behind her. Her stomach clenched, but she told herself she was being silly. It was broad daylight, and this was a public roadway. Anyone was allowed to drive it.

She slowed as she approached the sign that announced Road Ends, 100 Feet. Should she stop, or should she turn around? And head back toward the person who followed? Should she wait in her locked vehicle to see what the other driver did?

She decided on the latter. She parked in her usual spot, made sure her doors were locked and waited.

The green car slid to a stop beside her. She still couldn't see the driver clearly, but when the car door opened and he got out, she gasped.

Chapter Thirteen

Tommy, orange knit cap pulled down low over his ears, grinned and waved at her. He stomped through the snow, around her vehicle and up to her driver's side window. "I heard you lived all the way up here, but this is wild!" he said, loud enough to be heard clearly through her closed window.

She hesitated, then lowered the window a few inches. "What are you doing following me?" she asked.

He shoved his hands into the pockets of his parka and looked down. He didn't scuff his feet in a posture of school-boy humility, but he did look sheepish. "Somebody told me you lived way up in the mountains in an off-grid cabin, and I wanted to see it." He raised his head and met her gaze. "I didn't mean to freak you out. I just think what you're doing is so cool. I'd like to do that, too, one day."

"What happened to your van?" she asked. When she had seen him at the gas station, he had been driving a van.

He made a face. "It broke down. A friend is letting me use his car until mine is fixed." He looked around. "So where is your cabin? Is it just through there?" He nodded toward the snowmobile trail. "Is that your snowmobile?"

"You need to leave," she said, struggling to keep her voice shaking from a combination of anger and fear. "You had no right to follow me."

"Hey, don't be angry." He took a step back. "I told you I thought it was cool. I know you said you didn't want to go out with me, but I don't see why we can't be friends."

"I don't need any more friends," she said. "Now you really do need to leave."

His smile vanished and his shoulders sagged. "Okay, I'll leave," he said. "Sorry I upset you."

She waited until he turned his car around and had driven out of sight before she made herself get out of her Jeep. Dog treats tucked into one of the pockets of her snowmobile suit, she climbed onto the machine and headed back to the cabin.

Bear's loud barking was a welcome sound. He would let her know if Tommy came back. She loved the dog for many reasons, but one was that he was a good guard dog and his size and bark were intimidating to people who didn't know him.

Inside, she stoked the fire in the woodstove, then paced the floor, heart still racing from her encounter with Tommy. What did he think he was doing, following her to her home? The trouble he had gone to to do so, driving that little car all the way up the rough road, seemed extreme to her.

Fifteen minutes passed before she thought to check her internet and cell service. Everything was back in working order. Before she could talk herself out of it, she punched in Declan's number. When he answered, she almost burst into tears with relief but pulled herself together. "Can you come up to my cabin, please?" she asked. "A man followed me home from town today, and it was really upsetting."

"Who was it?" Declan's voice was sharp with alarm. "Is he there now?"

"He's not here anymore. I told him he had to leave. He's just a guy I met at the gas station. I ran into him again at the library and he asked me out and I turned him down. He wasn't angry or anything. It was just…weird."

"I'll be right there. Don't open the door to anyone or go outside until I get there."

"Don't worry, I won't."

She ended the call, then sat on the sofa, arms wrapped around herself. She hated this feeling, of being afraid of things that might not even happen.

DECLAN GRIPPED THE steering wheel so hard his knuckles ached, and forced himself to keep his speed down to a safe level to navigate the narrow, snow-packed road. He couldn't help Grace if he ended up stuck in a ditch. He passed no other cars as he climbed, engine growling, toward the trail leading to Grace's cabin, and saw no vehicles parked in the trailhead parking area halfway up the road.

The real fear in her voice when she had called razored through him. *A guy I met at the gas station*, she had said. Was it Barclay? And what about him had made her so afraid?

At last, muscles aching from the tension of holding back, he reached the end of the road. Grace's Jeep sat by itself nearest the snowmobile track to her house. Declan contemplated the long, freezing trek to her cabin and wished he had told her to pick him up on her snowmobile. But that would have meant waiting in the open for him to arrive, vulnerable to Barclay—if her harasser had indeed been Barclay. So Declan zipped his parka up to his chin, put his head down against the wind and began walking.

Her snowmobile sat in front of the cabin. Yellow light glowed in the windows and smoke puffed from the chimney. It looked like something out of a storybook, safe and warm. But as soon as he set his foot on the bottom step leading up to the front porch, furious barking erupted from inside.

The curtain at one window fluttered, then the door jerked open and Grace stood there, arms wrapped around herself, looking uncertain.

"Thank you for coming," she said. "I probably overreacted."

"I doubt it." He touched her shoulder briefly, then moved past her, into the warmth of the cabin and Bear's sniffing inspection.

"You must be freezing," Grace said. She took his coat. "Sit down. I've got fresh coffee."

He sat at the end of the sofa closest to the fire and accepted the steaming mug but set it aside to reach for her. "Tell me what happened," he said.

"I was just freaked out that he followed me all the way up here," she said. "He wasn't threatening or anything. It was just so odd. And you told me to be careful of anyone who paid special attention to me."

She was talking too fast, agitated, words tumbling on top of each other as she tried to get all the facts and all the feelings out. "What is his name?" Declan asked, trying to focus on essentials. "Do you know?"

"He said his name is Tommy. He said he's camping in his van somewhere near the river and working at a motel. The Ranch Motel, I think."

Declan felt a cold the fire couldn't touch. "Young guy, thin, little mustache, acne scars," he said.

Grace stared at him. "Yes. How did you know?"

"I gave him a lift to the motel last night. He was walking to town in the cold. He said his van broke down."

"He told me the same thing. He said a friend loaned him a vehicle, a little green compact car."

It was an odd coincidence, both of them interacting with

the young man, but not necessarily sinister, not in a community as small as Eagle Mountain.

"What happened, exactly?" he asked.

"My internet was down and I needed to upload a report for work, so I drove to the library to use their computers," she said. "I was almost finished when he sat down at the terminal next to me. We had run into each other a couple of times before around town."

"Where and when?" Declan asked.

"At the gas station, last Saturday," she said. "And the day Search and Rescue retrieved that mannequin someone put down in the valley, he was there."

"What was he doing there?" Declan asked. Maybe a little too sharply—Grace drew back.

"He was on skis," she said. "It's a public area. Some other skiers who had been there earlier reported seeing a body down in the valley, which turned out to be a mannequin."

"He was by himself?"

She nodded. "I think so. I don't remember anyone else around."

"What did he say then?"

"He said hello and asked what was going on. One of the other rookies, Nancy, told him it was a training exercise. He didn't ask any more questions, and we left."

"Okay. What did he say today, at the library?"

"He asked if I wanted to go out with him for dinner or a drink. I told him no, and he asked if I was married. I said no, I just didn't want to go out. Then he told me he was a fun guy. I was annoyed that he wouldn't drop the idea, so I pretended to be focused on the computer. After a little bit, he got up and wandered off."

"And he followed you home?"

"I didn't drive straight home," she said. "I went to the

natural foods store first. I bought some dog biscuits, then I started home. I didn't really notice him until I turned onto the forest road. I noticed this little green car right behind me. I almost never see other cars on this road in winter, so it made me curious. I figured the driver would turn around soon—that little car wasn't really made for these roads. But he kept following, and that made me a little uneasy."

"You should have called me while you still had a signal," he said.

"To tell you another car was behind me on a public road?" She shook her head. "He could have been a sightseer taking a drive or someone planning to snowshoe or ski on a trail."

"But he wasn't either of those things."

"No." She picked up a pillow and hugged it to her stomach. "When I got to the end of the road, he pulled in beside me, so I stayed in my Jeep, with the doors locked. When Tommy got out, I couldn't believe it."

"What did he say that frightened you?"

"I wasn't frightened right away—I was angry. I had told him I didn't want to date him, and he wouldn't take no for an answer. But he didn't get that I was angry. He asked about my cabin and said he had always wanted to live off-grid. I finally told him to leave."

"How did he respond?" Declan asked.

"He acted hurt. But he left. I waited until he was out of sight before I got out of the Jeep and headed out on the snowmobile. When I got here, I found out my phone and cell service were working again, so I called you."

"I'm glad you did," he said. "But if something like this happens again, call the sheriff, too."

"He didn't do anything illegal. He was annoying and clueless, but being awkward isn't a crime."

He hated to admit she was right. Tommy—or Terrence,

or whoever he was—hadn't threatened her or even touched her. He left when she asked him to.

Declan took out his phone. "Take a look at this photo and see if the man in it is familiar." He pulled up Terrence Barclay's most recent mug shot and showed it to her.

She frowned at the image. "Is that the man you're looking for?" she asked.

"Just tell me if he looks familiar," Declan said.

"No."

"Look closer. Is there any similarity between him and Tommy?"

She leaned in until her nose was only inches from the phone screen. She studied the photo for a full minute, then shook her head. "They're not the same man, I don't think."

He tucked the phone back into his pocket. He hadn't thought so, either.

"You believe me, don't you?"

The question—and the pain behind it—shocked him. "Of course I believe you," he said. "Why wouldn't I?"

She looked away. "It's nothing."

He touched her cheek and coaxed her to face him again. "It is something, if you're asking."

She curled her hands into fists, then pressed the fists to her cheeks and shook her head. "It's silly," she whispered. A single tear spilled from her right eye and slipped down, over her knuckle and onto the back of her hand.

He pulled her close, wanting to comfort her and wanting to lash out at whatever was causing so much pain. Did she think he wouldn't believe her because he was a cop or because other people didn't believe her? "It's not silly," he said softly. "You're not being silly. Tell me. Who doesn't believe you?"

She pressed her forehead, hard, into his shoulder and

shook with silent sobs. Bewildered, he stroked her hair and rubbed her back and waited for the flood to subside. Bear came and rested his chin on her knee, brown eyes full of accusation as he regarded Declan, as if the man was responsible for all this sadness.

Long minutes passed with only the crackle of the fire and the muffled sound of her weeping. Then she fell silent, and he wondered if she was asleep. Her head was heavy and one of his arms was cramping, pinched between her and the back of the sofa, but he wasn't going to move away from her.

Finally, she raised her head and shifted away from him. "Sorry about that," she said. "I haven't broken down like that in a long time."

Which meant she had broken down like that before. The idea made him feel sick. He shifted enough to pull a tissue from his pocket and passed it to her. "Thanks." She blew her nose. "I must look a mess."

"You look beautiful."

She smiled—a brief curve of her lips that made him feel ten feet tall. He clenched his jaw to keep from asking her again to tell him what was wrong. Was this what it felt like to be one of those naturalists who sat for hours outside some wild animal's den, waiting for the timid creature to emerge?

She sat back on the sofa and blew out a breath. "I told you about the accident when I was nine," she said. "The one where I lost my memory."

"Yes."

"I told you my sister died."

"Yes."

She bit her bottom lip, then continued. "I didn't tell you that I was the one who caused the accident. I was the reason she died. The reason my mom and I were hurt, the reason the car was destroyed."

"No," he said. "You were nine. And how do you know it was your fault? You can't remember."

"I know because my mom told me." Her eyes met his, and his anger rose in the face of her misery. "She told me all the time that my sister would have lived if I hadn't been so bad that day."

He took her hand and squeezed but said nothing. He thought she might start crying again, but she sat up a little straighter and continued. "Mom was driving us to my swimming lesson. I was excited because we were supposed to dive off the high dive that day. I was in the back seat and my sister, Hope, was buckled into her car seat next to me. Mom told me I wouldn't be still. I unbuckled my seat belt, then I undid the buckle on Hope's car seat, even though Mom told me not to. She was half-turned to yell at me when the car went off the road and rolled. Hope was thrown from the car on impact and I was hurt badly, too. Much worse than if we had been buckled in." She shook her head. "Mom never forgave me. I'm sure she wanted to, but how could she? She drank more and more after that. She always managed to keep a job, but she would come home from work and drink until she passed out. She died of liver failure while I was still in college. So I guess you could say I killed her, too."

"You were a child," Declan said. "It was wrong of her to blame you. And wrong of you to blame yourself."

"I was a child, but I knew better," she said. "I was old enough to know better."

"Where was this?" he asked. "When?"

"A little town called Simpson, Iowa. July, more than twenty years ago."

"A long time ago, and a long way away from here." He tried to pull her close, but she leaned away.

"I understand if you want to go now," she said.

"I'm not going anywhere," he said. "I'm not going to leave you by yourself." Not when she was drowning in this old pain.

"I killed my baby sister and my mother," she said. "Why would you want to have anything to do with me?"

"It was an accident," he said. "It's not the same. And you were a child. You're a woman now, and you're not a killer. No more than I am."

"How could this not change how you think about me?" She stared at him, searching his face, as if for some indication that he was lying.

"It doesn't change things because I love you."

The truth of those words, spoken out loud, hit him with the force of an avalanche. He struggled for a second to catch his breath, aware of his heart racing and a lump in his throat.

"You don't really know me," she said, but the harshness was gone from her voice, replaced with wonder.

"I think I do." He swallowed past the lump. "I know the woman who saved my life, who volunteers to save other lives. I know someone who had the strength to push past a great tragedy to make a life for herself and do important work that will help generations to come. I know that you're smart and you're kind—and you make me feel things I didn't think I was capable of feeling."

That quirk of a smile again and that same melting feeling inside his chest. "Don't tell me you've never been in love," she said.

"I've been in lust. I've been infatuated. But I'm pretty sure some wise person once said in order to love, you have to love yourself first. You're not the only one who grew up hearing you didn't measure up."

"Your father," she said.

He nodded. "I wasn't the general's idea of a perfect son,

though I doubt such a paragon exists. I thought I'd found my place in the Marshals Service, where I did a good job and was rewarded for it. I excelled even, until I didn't." A familiar tightness in his shoulders—he fought against it. "It doesn't matter how old you are or how successful you are, there are situations where you are five or ten or fifteen, being lectured on how much you disappointed someone who was counting on you. My supervisor at the Marshals Service was saying the words, but all I heard was my dad."

"Oh, Declan." She leaned into him again, and they held each other, eyes closed, fire crackling, letting the silence be a balm for the pain.

Chapter Fourteen

All the old scripts tried to play out again in Grace's head, from the one about how selfish she was, never thinking of anyone else, to the one about her being born bad, with a nasty streak that made her impossible to love. She had had enough therapy over the years to acknowledge these were lies, but really believing they were wrong took more work on some days than others.

And here was Declan, the victim of his own parental lies. Except she was sure he had never failed as spectacularly as she had. He had never contributed to the death of an innocent baby and the destruction of a family.

But he said he loved her, anyway. What a miracle that was. It made her believe that the feelings she had for him might be real and not merely wishful thinking.

Today. Right now, at least, she wasn't going to allow doubt to tarnish the moment. She shifted against him and kissed the sharp edge of his jaw, then moved to his lips— firm and warm and exactly what she wanted. He slid one hand beneath her hair and cradled her head and returned the kiss with such fierceness she knew he needed this closeness as much as she did.

"Can you stay the night?" she asked.

"I intend to," he said.

"Then let's go into the bedroom."

Would it always be this intense for them? she wondered as they began to undress each other. As if they feared the moment might slip away if they didn't rush to capture it. Or as if they couldn't contain all the emotion behind every movement.

He lifted her sweater over her head, then paused to kiss her shoulder, his mouth hot against her skin, sending tremors through her. She arched her neck as he pressed his lips to the pulse at the base of her throat, and she imagined her heartbeat becoming a part of him.

When they were both naked, she led him to the bed. He retrieved the condom from the bedside table this time and arranged the pillows and blankets so they would both be more comfortable. As if he planned for them to stay awhile.

"What are you smiling about?" he asked.

She hadn't even realized she was smiling. "I'm just happy," she said.

"I want to make you happy." He lay back and pulled her on top of him, and she gave herself up to exploring him, the way she might examine an as-yet-undiscovered mountain valley. She shivered as she skimmed her hands across the crisp curls on his chest and felt the heat rise in her as she traced the ridges of his abdomen. When she dipped her head to the juncture of his thighs, he groaned and threaded his fingers through her hair, as if he needed that hold to weight him to the earth.

They took turns on these journeys of discovery, trading places on the bed, letting fingers and mouths reveal all the outer mysteries, now that they had shared so much of their inner secrets. When they came together at last, she had never felt closer to anyone. Was it love or merely strong passion that allowed her to lose herself so fully?

And then she stopped thinking altogether, focused only on physical sensation, tension pulling tighter and tighter until she let go, falling and falling, only to land safely in his arms.

"You were smiling again," he whispered, his mouth close to her ear.

"Mmm." She wrapped her legs more tightly around him. "Better hurry and catch up," she said, and so he did.

DECLAN RELUCTANTLY LEFT Grace the next morning. What they had between them felt too fragile to push for too much. He wanted to give Grace plenty of space, and he welcomed a little time to process things himself.

First, there was the childhood tragedy Grace had revealed and the enormous burden she had carried all these years. It was just as well her mother was no longer around—if Declan had ever met her, he didn't know if he could have stopped himself from berating her for the cruel way she had treated her daughter.

He tried to picture Grace at nine—small and thin or short and sturdy, no sign of the woman to come in her body. Had she loved her little sister or been jealous of her? But would she really have unfastened the child's car seat? Why do so? To play with her? He hadn't been around children enough to know if that was something they would do or not.

But it didn't matter. Even if Grace had unbuckled her sister and distracted her mother, she'd been a child. How could a mother not see that?

He knew he wouldn't get anywhere, running that sad story over and over in his mind, so he turned his attention to the chief reason he was in Eagle Mountain: Terrence Barclay.

He started at the sheriff's department, where he caught

Gage as the sergeant was headed out the door. "We need to talk," Declan said. "Something happened to Grace yesterday afternoon that you should know about."

Gage led the way back to his office. "Is Grace all right?" he asked.

"She was pretty shaken up, but she's all right now." Declan settled into the visitor's chair. "Do you know a guy named Tommy? Lives in a van by the river and works nights at the Ranch Motel."

"I know who you're talking about," Gage said. "What about him?"

"He followed Grace up to her cabin yesterday afternoon," Declan said. "Or almost to the cabin. He drove up to the end of the Forest Service road. Apparently, he saw her in the library and asked her out, but she turned him down."

"Did he threaten her or try to harm her?" Gage asked.

"She says no, but she called me, clearly upset by it all. He said he wanted to see where she lived. She told him to leave, and he finally did." He gripped the arms of the chair and leaned toward Gage. "What if Tommy is really Terrence Barclay and he's fixated on Grace as his next victim? He's the right age, he just moved to town and he's following Barclay's pattern of taking a temporary job while he's here."

Gage turned to his computer. "Do you have a last name?"

"Llewellyn."

"Let's see what we can find." Gage began typing. "I'll try Thomas and Tom, too." He scanned the list of names, then typed some more. "I think I've found him." He slid the chair back and angled the monitor to show a mug shot, clean-shaven with the hair a little shorter. Mug shots were notoriously unflattering, but Declan thought this was the same man he had driven to the motel two nights before.

"What does his sheet say?" Declan asked.

"Petty stuff," Gage said. "Shoplifting. Possession. He did six months in the Larimer County jail for breaking and entering." He scrolled some more. "Looks like he was released about two months ago. If this is the same guy, he's not Terrence Barclay."

"No," Declan conceded. "But what was he doing, frightening Grace?"

Gage slid his chair back. "Let's go ask him."

Declan rose also.

"You can come with me," Gage said, "but don't say anything. I'd like for you to get a good look at this guy and confirm that he isn't Barclay."

Declan didn't volunteer that he had already spent a good half hour in a car with Llewellyn and nothing about him had seemed familiar.

He rode in the passenger seat of Gage's department-issue SUV, after moving aside a file box, a leather coat, a pair of headphones and a half box of ammunition. "I was out at the shooting range yesterday afternoon," Gage said by way of explanation.

"Do you know where Llewellyn is camping?" Declan asked as Gage drove out of town.

"I've got a pretty good idea," Gage said. "There are a couple of popular places, though usually no one uses them this time of year."

"It would get awfully cold in a van at night," Declan said.

"Maybe that's why Llewellyn works the night shift at the motel—to stay warmer."

Maybe, Declan agreed. Though for someone trying to stay out of the public eye, the night shift was a good choice, too.

"I'm curious why Grace contacted you about this instead of the sheriff's department," Gage said.

"She was frightened, but Llewellyn talked to her on public land," Declan said. "He didn't lay a hand on her, and he wasn't even trespassing. I don't think most people would have called the sheriff's department."

"But she called you. I take it the two of you have stayed in touch."

"Do you have a problem with that?"

"No. I'm just nosy." Gage grinned. "And I've always been curious about Grace. There aren't many young women who would choose to live so isolated. I remember seeing her a few times in the summers, when she would come to stay with her grandfather."

"You grew up here?" Declan asked.

"Travis and I grew up on a ranch outside of town, but we spent plenty of time in town, playing baseball, going to church camp, things like that. We ran into Grace a few times."

"What was she like?"

"Quiet. I don't think she ever said a word to me, though I tried to get her attention. We all wondered about her, partly because she was from somewhere else, but mostly because she lived with a man we called the Hermit of the Hills. We made up scary stories about the old man, like he killed trespassers and buried them in his backyard, or he had a hidden stash of gold he was guarding. Silly kid stuff."

"Grace says she loved spending summers with him. She didn't want to leave, but she had to return to school."

"I've read a few articles about the work he did in that cabin," Gage said. "He was way ahead of his time, studying the climate and natural history. We've had scientists from all over the world who have traveled here to see him or to study his records. It's nice that Grace is able to carry on his work, but it's not a life everyone would choose."

Declan started to say that Grace was happy, but was she? How could she be, when she carried such deep sadness inside of her over a childhood tragedy she couldn't even remember?

Gage turned onto a narrow Forest Service road, guiding his SUV through icy ruts. After about a mile, they spotted a faded red van parked on the right side of the road. "I think this is the place," Gage said. He pulled in behind the van and sat for a moment with the engine running. "I'm going to run the plate," he said and began typing into the laptop mounted between the seats.

"It comes back registered to Bernard Gross," he said. "Gross died six months ago and the van's not listed as stolen. Maybe he was a relative?"

The door to the van opened and Llewellyn, dressed in gray sweats and house slippers, stepped out and frowned in their direction.

"Let's see what he has to say," Gage said and opened the door.

Declan followed, automatically taking up a defensive position a few steps behind and to one side, his gaze fixed on Llewellyn's hands, but the young man made no suspicious moves. "Hello, Deputy," he said and nodded to Gage.

"Tommy Llewellyn?" Gage asked.

"Yes, sir. Is there something wrong? I was told it was okay to camp here, on public land."

"We wanted to talk to you about a young woman you followed home yesterday afternoon," Gage said. "Apparently you asked her out and wouldn't take no for an answer."

"Aw, man, it wasn't like that." He held out both hands in a pleading gesture. "I mean, yeah, I asked her out. I liked her. She was nice to me."

"Just because someone is nice to you doesn't give you

permission to harass them." So much for Declan's pledge not to say anything. Gage glared at him.

"I wasn't harassing her, truly." Llewellyn looked stricken. "I just… I followed her because I had heard she lived in this cabin up in the mountains, off-grid and everything. It sounded so cool. I just wanted to see it. I just wanted to be friends." He looked from Gage to Declan, then stared hard at Declan. "Hey, you're the guy who gave me a lift to work the other night. I didn't know you were a cop."

Another hard look from Gage, which Declan ignored.

Gage turned back to Llewellyn. "Can you understand how a woman would be frightened by a man who followed her from town all the way to her home?" he asked.

"I guess so, but I didn't mean it that way. Honest!" He wiped a hand across his mouth and looked stricken. "I'm not in trouble, am I? I don't want to cause anyone trouble. You probably already know I've got a record, but I did my time and I'm staying out of trouble. I have a job and everything. I don't want to bother anybody."

"Do yourself a favor and stay away from Grace," Gage said. "And the next time you want to be friends with a woman, don't follow her around if she tells you no."

"I won't," Llewellyn said. "I promise."

Gage nodded. "You have a good day."

Declan followed Gage back to the SUV. They drove past Llewellyn, turned around and headed back to town. "You didn't tell me you knew him," Gage said.

"I don't know him," Declan said. "I gave him a ride to work after I picked him up walking on the side of the road on a freezing cold night. It was dark and I didn't get that good a look at him."

"What do you think—does he look like Barclay?"

"He didn't look familiar, but that doesn't mean a lot when

it comes to Barclay," Declan said. "Plenty of people who know him a lot better than I do have failed to recognize him."

"And they weren't hit on the head and dealing with memory loss," Gage said.

Declan didn't reply.

"My take is he really liked Grace and went about trying to be friends in the wrong way," Gage said. "There's no malice behind it."

"People thought Barclay was harmless, too," Declan said. He sighed. "But you're right. Llewellyn struck me as more pathetic than anything."

"I know you've been talking to people around town," Gage said. "Is there anyone else we need to take a closer look at?"

He appreciated Gage wasn't merely dismissing him. "Most of the businesses I've talked to haven't hired many people lately," he said. "They're waiting for the summer tourist season. One guy I found was way too short to be Barclay, and another turned out to be from here originally and had just moved back to town. I found his picture in a high school yearbook at the library, so that checked out. The only other person on my list is Mike—the guy we saw in Mo's Pub the other day."

"He said he's the son of a friend of Arnie's, who runs the natural foods store," Gage said.

"Yeah, but we only have his word for that."

"Then let's have a word with Arnie."

Ten minutes later, Gage parked in front of a simple storefront with the sign Natural Foods. "How long has this place been here?" Declan asked.

"Three or four years," Gage said. "This used to be a house."

A leather harness festooned with old-fashioned sleigh

bells jangled as they opened the door, and their footsteps echoed on the worn wooden floors. A stout man with bald spot above a rim of graying brown curls looked up from behind the counter. "Hello, Gage," he said. "What can I do for you today?"

"Hey, Arnie." Gage walked to the counter. "How's it going?"

While the two of them made small talk, Declan assessed the place. It reminded him of an old-fashioned general store, with products displayed on racks of plain wooden shelves or in deep baskets. Red-checked curtains flanked the windows, and framed photographs filled the walls. On closer inspection, these proved to be a younger version of Arnie engaged in various adventures. Declan paused in front of a photo of a quartet of men in heavy parkas gathered around a small plane in an icy landscape.

"That was taken at the Amundsen-Scott research station at the South Pole." Arnie came to stand beside Declan. "That's me in the middle." He pointed a stubby finger at the shortest of the trio, his thick mustache frosted with ice. A notation in pen in the photo's bottom margin identified the mustached man as Arnie Cowdrey.

"What were you doing at the South Pole?" Declan asked.

"Geological surveying," Arnie said. "I was there for six months right out of college. Terrific adventure." He moved over to a second picture with the same group of men, this time sprawled on sofas in a room crowded with bookshelves and cardboard boxes. Arnie wore a lumberjack checked shirt and a knit cap "There were a group of us young guys who hung out. In our off time, we played a lot of video games and watched a lot of TV," Arnie said.

"Is that where you knew Mike's dad?" Gage asked.

Arnie looked over his shoulder at Gage. "You know Mike?"

"I met him in Mo's the other day," Gage said. "He told me he was working for you."

Arnie nodded. "That's his dad right there." He stabbed his finger at the person posed next to him in the photo, a tall, thin man with thick brown hair and the beginnings of a beard. "Mickey Randolph. Terrific guy."

"That was good of you to take on his son," Gage said.

Arnie waved away the praise. "The kid came in here and said his dad told him to look me up and say hello. But it didn't take long to find out he was desperate to find work and settle down. He said he'd gotten in a little trouble back home and was trying to get his life back on track. Hey, I was young once. I know what it's like to do something foolish. I'd been thinking I could use some help here, so it worked out well all around. He's doing a great job for me."

"That's good to hear," Gage said. He met Declan's gaze over the top of Arnie's head and shook his head slightly. They weren't going to find anything here.

"It's been fun having the kid around," Arnie said. "He reminds me a lot of his old man." He tapped the photo.

Declan studied the image again. Did Mike look like the man in the photo? They both had dark hair, but beyond that, it was impossible to tell. The faces in the photo were no bigger than Declan's thumb, faded and blurred with time.

Arnie moved back to the counter. "Is that why you stopped in—to talk about Mike?"

"Actually, I need some more of that ginger lemonade you sell." Gage walked toward a cooler in the back. "Maya says it's the only thing that settles her stomach right now."

"We'll fix her up," Arnie said. "And tell her I have some ginger chews she can try, too. Some women swear by them."

Gage paid for his purchase and stowed it in the SUV. "My wife is pregnant," he said by way of explanation.

"Your first?" Declan asked.

"Her first pregnancy, but we adopted her niece. Casey is seven now. She's a great kid."

What would that be like, Declan wondered, not for the first time, to have a family who depended on you? Would it make it harder to put on a weapon and a ballistics vest and put your life on the line every day? Or would you feel the work you did was even more important?

They got back into the SUV and Gage started the engine, but he didn't drive away. "Do you still think Terrence Barclay is here in Eagle Mountain?" he asked.

"Yes."

"Because he killed Agnes Cockrell and he won't leave until he's planned and carried out the murder of another woman," Gage said.

"Yes. That's the pattern he's followed twice that we know of, but probably all three times, in three different places," he said.

"What if he's decided to break pattern?" Gage asked. "What if he dumped Agnes's car in Delta, stole another vehicle there and headed to Utah or farther west?"

"Have there been killings in those areas that might be linked to Barclay?" Declan asked. "Have you checked?"

"I've checked," Gage said. "I didn't spot anything, but maybe it hasn't shown up in any databases or made the news."

"Why would he break that pattern now?" Declan said. "I'm not an expert, but it seems from what I've read that something traumatic would need to happen to cause a break in the pattern. Killers like this seem to fixate on behaving in certain ways. It's often how they're caught—because they can't break the pattern even if they would be better off if they did."

"So if he didn't break the pattern and he is here, what happens next?" Gage asked.

"He's probably picked out his next victim and is watching her, planning to make his move," Declan said.

"That's why you freaked out when Llewellyn followed Grace."

"Yes." He swallowed down the remnants of that fear from when he had thought she might have come to Barclay's attention. "But he might not be so obvious as to follow the woman. It could be someone he works with, who he sees every day. Or someone who lives near him. She probably doesn't realize she's caught his attention."

"We could use some help trying to find him," Gage said.

"We could," Declan agreed. "But I don't know if we're going to get any. I talked to my boss. The marshals and the FBI don't think Barclay is here. They're not sending anyone to look for him."

"Then I guess it's up to us."

One disgraced US deputy marshal and a small-town sheriff's department against a man who had eluded scores of law enforcement for a number of local and federal agencies. His father had always chided him for taking on what he termed foolish risks. Why change his approach now?

Chapter Fifteen

Grace was on the phone with Declan when she received a text from Search and Rescue. "I guess you won't be coming up to see me tonight," she said after she read the text. "I need to help search for a missing skier."

"Would you call me when you get in so I know you're all right?" he asked. "It doesn't matter how late."

"I will." She realized she was smiling when she hung up the phone. Who knew having someone to worry about you would feel so good?

But she didn't have time to savor the feeling. She hurried to change clothes, fed Bear, then gathered her gear and headed to her Jeep for the trip to Search and Rescue headquarters.

"We've got a seventy-year-old man who was skiing by himself and failed to return home for dinner," Sheri told the assembled volunteers half an hour later. "Eddie Pearlman."

A murmur went through the group at the name. "Eddie is an experienced skier," Danny Irwin said. "He knows all the local trails."

"According to his wife, he planned to ski one of the trails at Alexander Basin. He left the house at 10:00 a.m. and thought he would be home by four." She checked her watch. "He's almost three hours overdue. We'll divide up in teams to search the trails. Watch for tracks, but there was heavy snow in the higher elevations around noon, so it's possible his tracks will have been covered over."

At the trailhead, Grace clicked into her skis. She was paired with Eldon Ramsey, and they headed up Sharp Shin Trail. The earlier clouds had cleared, and the night was cold and still, the Milky Way a wide ribbon of glitter overhead. Grace quickly found a rhythm and glided along, skis buoyant in the deep snow. She was comfortable on skis, having covered miles with her grandfather, checking animal dens and stands of aspen, photographing, measuring or merely sitting quietly, waiting for the animals to emerge. If you were very still and waited long enough, they would go about their normal activities, unspooked by your presence.

Her grandfather had taught her the healing power of solitude and the natural world. Nothing there would judge her or condemn her. Animals and trees didn't look at time linearly, her grandfather had explained. For them, there was only now. They collected food for the winter because instinct told them to do so now, not because they feared the future.

She wasn't certain her grandfather had been right about that, but the idea intrigued her. Not that she wanted to live never looking back on good memories or anticipating pleasant times ahead. But it would be good to let go of the terrible things in the past and to be able to face the future without fear.

"Have you skied these trails before?" Eldon asked. She didn't know the big man well, except that he was originally from Hawaii and he worked for the biggest gold mine in the area. He was acknowledged as one of the physically strongest members of the team, an accomplished climber and skier with a cheerful outlook.

"A few times," she said. "What about you?"

He shook his head. "I mostly do downhill skiing, but this is pretty interesting." He stopped and pointed to a set of small animal tracks, each toe and segment of paw clearly outlined in the snow. "I never realized you could see so much out here. What do you think they are?"

She studied the tracks. "Probably an ermine," she said. "A long-tailed weasel's tracks would be farther apart."

He grinned at her. "We don't have those in Hawaii. I'm still learning the local wildlife and plants. It's interesting stuff."

"It is," she agreed.

"You should take the lead," he said and motioned for her to move past him. "You're obviously a better skier."

She moved past him but stayed close enough to continue their conversation. "Do you know the man we're looking for?" she asked.

"I never met him, but I know about him," Eldon said. "He heads up the local historical society, leads hikes to mine ruins in the summer and gives slideshows about mine history. Some of these old guys can hike rings around me."

"My grandfather skied and hiked right up to the day before he died, when he was eighty-six," Grace said. "I've got logs that showed him skiing one hundred miles or more in a week. He never had a snowmobile while he was living here—if he needed to go somewhere, he went on skis."

"If your grandfather had gotten hurt, what would he have done?" Eldon asked.

She considered the question. "When I was a girl, he told me if I ever got hurt when I was out alone, I should stay put for at least the first twenty-four to thirty-six hours. He told me to build a fire if I could, but if I couldn't do that and it was winter, to scrape out a snow cave. Burrow in like the mink or weasel and wait for help. If help didn't show up by the second day, then I was supposed to start moving, but only if I could keep track of where I was going. He told me to travel from one known landmark to the next. He said if I didn't know where I was, I should stop and wait."

Her voice broke and she cleared her throat and faced forward to blink away sudden, stinging tears. She hadn't thought of that conversation with her grandfather in years, but remembering it now, she was struck by how much he had cared for her. "Pay attention," he had said that day. "I don't want anything bad to happen to you." How could she have forgotten that?

"That all makes a lot of sense," Eldon said. He looked around them, the beam of his headlamp illuminating dark evergreens and sparkling snow. "So let's say you're Eddie Pearlman. If he had a heart attack, he would have keeled over right on the trail and we would have found him by now. But let's say instead he fell and hurt himself—maybe he got off the trail in some deep snow." He sniffed. "I don't smell any smoke, so he probably didn't build a fire. But a snow cave—let's look for something like that."

"It would be off the trail a bit," she said, trying to picture it. "But what would it look like?"

"A mound of snow?" He looked around at the uneven terrain. "Maybe with disturbed ground around, where he had raked up the snow. It's not going to be easy to see, but it's something to watch for."

She nodded, then cupped her hands to her mouth and shouted. "Eddie! Eddie, are you okay?"

No response but her own pulse, thudding in her ears. "Come on," Eldon said. "Let's keep going. We're not going to give up yet."

Grace and Eldon continued down the trail for another mile, scanning either side. The headlamps cast a weak beam only a short distance into the woods, and starlight provided little illumination in the thick cover. They paused every few minutes to shout for Eddie and listen for a reply, but only a complaint from an aggrieved owl nearby answered. The cold had seeped through Grace's clothing until her fingers and toes ached, and she was wondering how much longer they could continue to search when her light swept across an odd shape to the right of the trail.

She stopped and focused more closely on what appeared to be a pile of evergreen branches, dusted with snow.

"Why are you stopping?" Eldon asked.

"Those branches over there." She pointed. "I remember something else my grandfather told me. He said if I was hurt or lost during the summer, I should gather branches to make a shelter. Maybe that's what Eddie did. If he couldn't dig in the snow, he could drag branches into a pile to make a kind of shelter."

"It does look out of place," Eldon said. "Let's check it out." He used his pole to click out of his skis, and she did the same. She sank almost to her knees in snow as soon as she stepped off the trail, but there were too many downed tree trunks and protruding boulders here to make navigating on skis possible.

She let Eldon break trail toward the pile of snow-covered branches. "Eddie!" he shouted. "Eddie Pearlman! Are you all right?"

"Help! Over here!"

Eldon took off running, and Grace stumbled after him. They found Eddie Pearlman lying in a tunnel of branches, one leg held awkwardly to his side. "I think I broke my leg," he said. "I figured I'd wait out the night here and try to crawl back to the trail in the morning."

"You don't have to do that now," Eldon said and pulled out his radio to contact Sheri and the others.

Within half an hour, four volunteers had arrived with a litter. Danny Irwin administered pain medication and stabilized the injured leg while Grace and Hannah placed warming packs around Eddie and blankets over him. They gave him water and an energy gel and carefully loaded him onto the litter for the trip out to the trailhead, where an ambulance waited.

Eldon helped carry the litter while Grace followed. Sheri met them at the trailhead. "Good work, you two," she said and clapped them both on the back.

"Grace deserves all the credit," Eldon said. "She's the one who thought to look for some kind of shelter, and she spotted the pile of branches Eddie was under."

"I was just remembering what my grandfather taught me," she said. "Eldon asked the right questions to make me think of it. I'm glad Eddie is okay."

"He's going to be fine," Hannah said.

Everyone took turns congratulating Grace. By the time she left headquarters, she felt as if she was floating, she was so happy.

She was also hungry. Maybe she would treat herself to pizza. No one delivered to where she lived, and anything she got to-go would be ice-cold by the time she got back to the cabin.

She remembered her promise to call Declan. "Hey," he answered. "How's it going?"

"Good. We found the skier, and he's going to be all right."

"That's great. Where are you now?"

"I'm still in town, and I'm starving. Want to meet me at Mo's and get pizza? I know it's late, but—"

"I'll be there in five minutes."

IT WAS CLOSER to ten minutes, but Declan met her in front of the pub and soon they were seated at a table by the front window, awaiting an order of a pepperoni-and-mushroom pizza. She was telling him the story of their discovery of Eddie Pearlman when she was distracted by something behind him. She stopped speaking and stared over his shoulder.

"What is it?" Declan started to turn around, but she put a hand on his arm.

"It's just the guy who works at the natural foods store," she said. "Why is he glaring at you?"

Declan turned to look, in time to see Mike moving toward the bar.

"Do you know him?" Grace asked.

"Not really." He sipped from the beer he had ordered. "He's probably angry that I was asking his boss questions about him."

"He's the son of a friend of Arnie's."

"So I heard. I just wanted to make sure that was true."

"Why wouldn't it be true?"

"Because people don't always tell the truth."

"Are you always this cynical?"

"Being a cop makes me more suspicious, I guess."

She stiffened. "Are you suspicious of me?"

He had upset her, and that was the last thing he wanted to do. "No." He took her hand in his and caressed it. "You know I'm still looking for Terrence Barclay. He's good at disguising himself, so I'm checking out everyone who could be him."

"Do you mean like Tommy?"

"Has he bothered you anymore?" he asked.

She shook her head. "No. I haven't seen or heard anything from him. But do you think—"

"No. Gage and I checked him out. He's not Barclay. And I don't think he meant you any harm. He's just clueless."

She relaxed a little. "I feel bad now, like maybe I over-reacted," she said.

"Pepperoni-and-mushroom pizza?" A server slid the pizza pan between them. "You two need anything else?"

"Thanks," Declan said. "We're good." As soon as the server was gone, he turned back to Grace. "Don't feel bad. He had no right to follow you that way. You live by yourself in a remote location. It's good that you're careful."

She slid a slice of pizza onto her plate. "I've never been afraid up there before," she said. "It was the one place where I always felt safest. I was thinking today about how nothing in nature judges you or cares about what you did in the past."

"I don't judge you or care about what you did in the past."

She met his gaze, and the sadness in her eyes made him hurt. He would do anything to remove that sadness. He turned the conversation back to that night's search and her triumph in finding Eddie Pearlman.

"It felt really good," she admitted. "It's why I joined Search and Rescue. To truly help people. All the training has been interesting and the other volunteers have really welcomed me, but tonight was the first time I really felt like part of something bigger."

They finished their pizza, and while they waited for the check, he took her hand. "Will you come back to the Alpiner with me?" he asked.

"You know my friend Hannah works and lives there, right? It's going to be awkward if she sees me going up to your room. I mean, is the rate different for two people? Do I have to register? And I can't leave Bear locked in the cabin all night."

"It's okay," he said, hiding his disappointment.

"You know I want to be with you, right?" she said. "I'm not ashamed or anything like that."

"Even if I'm a cynical cop?" He smiled to take the sting from the words.

"It's probably a good thing for a cop to be cynical," she said. "It's just, this is a small town and everyone talks about everyone else."

"And you're a private person who likes to keep things to yourself," he said.

She nodded. "Yes."

He leaned closer and spoke more softly. "Then what if I come back to the cabin with you?"

Heat sparked in her eyes. "That would be great."

He paid the check, helped her with her coat and they walked out. The plan was for him to follow her up to her place.

As he was walking to his truck, he passed Mike Randolph, standing at the entrance to the alley beside the pub, smoking a cigarette. Declan nodded in greeting, but Mike turned away. Guess he had made an enemy there. But that was nothing new. Another thing about being a cop he hadn't shared with Grace: your real friends were few and far between.

Chapter Sixteen

Grace lay awake that night, long after Declan had fallen asleep. What Declan said about being suspicious of everyone had stuck with her. He didn't trust people. He naturally thought the worst of them. He had said that didn't apply to her, but if that was his nature, how could he help himself? Maybe right now, in the first rush of emotion between them, he thought she was wonderful, but what happened later, when life wore the shine off their relationship? She had confessed to him that she had done something terrible. Something unforgivable. How could that not tarnish every aspect of her life, including his feelings for her?

Even her grandfather, who had loved her more than anyone in the world, had believed she wasn't like other people. She shuddered as she thought back to a conversation she had overheard in this very cabin, when she was thirteen or fourteen. Her mother had arrived to take her back to Iowa for the school year. She had been sent to her bedroom in the loft to gather her things, but she had returned in time to hear her mother say, "The older she gets, the harder she is for me to deal with. I've never met a more sullen child, or one so deliberately contrary."

"She doesn't behave that way for me," her grandfather had said.

"Only because you spoil her. And because you haven't been around children enough to know what's normal and what's not."

"Grace is different," her grandfather had said. "I think everything she's been through has damaged more than her memory."

Grace had hurried back to her room then, not wanting to hear more. Her grandfather thought she was damaged—broken. Unable to be repaired. Declan would learn that about her soon enough.

She rolled over and squeezed her eyes shut, trying to cry without making a sound. She didn't think she would sleep, but she must have, because when she woke, Declan's side of the bed was empty.

She found him stoking the fire in the woodstove. He looked up and smiled at her. He had showered, the ends of his hair still damp, and she caught the clean, herbal smell of the shaving cream he had borrowed.

"Good morning, sleepyhead," he said. "I made coffee."

"Thanks." She headed for the kitchen, ignoring her first instinct, which was to kiss him, to linger in his warm embrace, maybe even suggest they both head back to bed. Instead, she poured a mug of coffee and stood staring out the kitchen window at the glittering white world.

He moved in behind her and wrapped his arms around her. "What say I make some breakfast?" he asked. "You have everything here for pancakes."

"I really need to get to work." She moved out of his embrace, as far away as the small room would let her, which was only a few feet. "I think you should probably go."

Suddenly, the room was several degrees colder. She couldn't look at him, but she felt the chill and the new stiffness in his body. "What's wrong?" he asked.

She shook her head. She owed him an explanation, but how to explain? "I know you're going back to Denver soon," she said. "To your job and your old life. And my life is here. It's been great, but what we have between us, it isn't sustainable."

"What do you mean it isn't sustainable? Denver is only six hours from here. We have phones and cars. It's not like we'll never see each other."

"You don't need to feel obligated just because I pulled you out of that blizzard. Anyone would have done the same."

"I'm not with you because I feel obligated." His voice rose, real anger behind the words. "Grace, what is going on? Last night everything was fine between us. Better than fine. And this morning you're sending me away like I've done something to hurt you."

She forced herself to look him in the eye. She owed him that much. "You haven't hurt me," she said. "You've been wonderful. But you will hurt me one day. You won't be able to help it. The two of us look at the world in completely different ways, and it isn't going to work out between us. Not for the long haul. I'd rather end this now, before we're in any deeper."

"I love you," he said. "Didn't you hear me say that?"

"You think you love me. But you don't even know me."

"I know that I connect with you in a way I've never connected with anyone before. It doesn't matter that we've only known each other a couple of weeks. I know you. And you know me."

She shook her head, feeling the tears threatening. She was weakening, and that wasn't a good thing. "Please leave," she said. "Please."

He stood still for so long she began to wonder what she

would do if he simply refused to go. Would she have to leave the cabin and not come back until it was empty again?

But finally, he exited the room. She followed the sound of his footsteps as he went into the bedroom, then emerged to linger by the kitchen door for a long minute. She stared at the floor, refusing to look at him again until he left, out the door this time. He would have a long, cold walk to his truck, but that couldn't be helped. Maybe the fact that she had forced him to make that walk would anger him enough that he would stay away.

When she was sure he was gone, she sank to her knees on the kitchen floor. Bear came over to her, and she buried her face in the soft fur of his neck and cried and cried.

DECLAN SCARCELY FELT the cold on the walk back to his truck. He was too angry, hurt and confused to notice any physical sensation. What had prompted Grace's complete change of heart? He could think of nothing he had said or done to set her off this way. She had seemed enthusiastic about the prospect of him spending the night at her house last night, and their lovemaking had been as passionate and tender as ever. As he'd lain beside her before he'd drifted to sleep, he couldn't remember ever being happier.

He replayed the conversation with her over in his head. No, she wasn't angry at him. She was sad. Hurt. But not hurt by him. He had taken enough psychology courses as part of his law enforcement training to recognize that. He didn't even have to ask himself what had hurt her because she had told him herself. Her whole life had been built around the auto accident when she was nine and its aftermath: the death of her sister, her own injuries and resultant amnesia, the blame her mother placed on her for everything that happened.

Grace had said she wanted to end her relationship with him now because it would hurt less than waiting until later. She was sure he would fall out of love with her, but why?

Because she believed he would eventually blame her for what had happened to her sister? That was impossible. Or maybe she thought he would fall out of love with her because she didn't deserve love?

The idea she would think that made him want to shout with anger. It also made him feel utterly helpless. Because if that was what Grace believed, what could he do about it? He could urge her to see a therapist. He could tell her every day that she deserved love. He could try to show her.

But he couldn't fight the beliefs people had about themselves, whether he was up against a serial killer or the woman he loved.

He wasn't the type of person who could remain passive. His whole life had been spent around doing, from the tasks his father set in which Declan tried to prove himself to his job in law enforcement. As a marshal, he had work to do all day, whether it was transporting a prisoner or tracking down a fugitive. He had to use his brain as well as his body to do these things, but there were always lists of actions he could take. A lawman didn't sit behind a desk and wait for criminals to come to him.

Back at the Alpiner, Declan booted up his computer and turned to what he knew best—the task of researching and strategizing and taking action to solve a problem.

He logged into a newspaper database and was able to pull up the issue of the Simpson, Iowa, *Sentinel* for the time of Grace's car accident. He might have expected the story he was looking for to be on the front page, but he had to scroll through several pages before he found it: one car accident resulting in one fatality.

The facts were pretty much as Grace had stated. Thirty-six-year-old Jennifer Wilcox had lost control of her Chevrolet Cobalt. The car had left the road and rolled once before slamming into a tree. Wilcox's three-year-old daughter was thrown from the vehicle and died as a result. Her nine-year-old daughter suffered a serious head injury and was in critical condition. Mrs. Wilcox had suffered a broken right arm and a fractured collarbone. At the time the news article was written, the cause of the accident had not been determined.

He searched through several months of back issues of the paper but found no further mention of the accident. He took out his phone.

"Simpson Police Department," a woman's crisp voice answered his call.

"This is US Deputy Marshal Declan Owen," he said. "I'm looking into an incident in Simpson that happened more than twenty years ago. Do you have anyone who was working in the department who could answer a few questions for me?"

"What kind of incident?" the woman asked.

"A one-car accident in which a child was killed."

"Let me see what I can find. Can you hold?"

Declan was prepared to wait long minutes, but only seconds passed before a man came on the line. "Deputy Mashal Owen, this is Lieutenant Marco Carpenter. How can I help you?"

"I'm looking into one-car accident involving a woman named Jennifer Wilcox that happened twenty years ago."

"I know the case," Carpenter said. "I worked that accident. You remember the children, you know?"

"Do you know what happened? What caused the accident?" Declan held his breath, steeling himself for the answer.

"The mom was drunk, that's what happened."

All the breath went out of him, and it was a fraction of a second before he could speak. "I thought the little girl—the oldest one—distracted her while she was driving," he said.

"Maybe that's what the lady told people, but I was there. You could smell the alcohol on her breath. She had been picked up for public intoxication once before. I told the paramedics she needed a blood alcohol test, but between the woman's hysterics and the dead baby and injured girl, it got overlooked. By the time they tested her, she was below the limit."

"And the baby died when she was ejected from the car?"

"Mom hadn't buckled her into the child seat. We had ticketed her two weeks before the accident for failing to secure the baby. The little girl was old enough to buckle herself in, or she might have been killed, too, though she was pretty seriously hurt."

"What happened to the mother?"

"With no proof that she was over the legal limit, nothing happened. She moved out of town before the girl was even out of the hospital. Why are you looking into this now, after so many years?"

He started to make up a story that would make it sound like he was looking into a case, but why bother? Sometimes the truth really was better. "I know the daughter," he said. "Grace Wilcox. She had questions about what really happened, so I told her I'd do some checking."

"Not a good story to have to tell her," Carpenter said.

"No, but sometimes it's good to have things cleared up."

He thanked Carpenter for the information, then ended the call and sat back. Grace had said her mother had started drinking heavily after the accident, but apparently it wasn't a new problem. Instead of admitting her own fault in the accident, she had blamed Grace. Maybe, after so many years of repeating the story, she even came to believe it.

Grace had to hear this. Never mind her feelings about him—she needed to know this. He started to call her, then changed his mind. This was news he needed to deliver in person.

He was pulling on his coat when his phone rang again. The screen showed an unfamiliar number from Denver. "Hello?" he answered.

"Declan Owen?" a woman's crisp voice asked.

"This is he."

"This is Victoria Green from the US Marshals Service in Denver, Human Resources. I'm sending you some documents you'll need to sign so that we can request a copy of your medical report related to your recent injury," she said. "I'll be emailing those. I need you to sign the forms electronically and send them back to me ASAP."

"Why do you need my medical records?" he asked.

"You're currently on medical leave due to a traumatic brain injury with resultant amnesia," she said. "That is correct, isn't it?" she asked.

"I was hit in the head, and I can't remember the events of a few hours," he said, cold creeping up his spine.

"A traumatic brain injury with resultant amnesia," she said. "The review board needs your medical records in order to determine if you are fit to return to duty."

"I'm going to return to duty as soon as a doctor releases me," he said. He hadn't thought much about when that might be. Right now, it suited him to remain in Eagle Mountain, close to both Terrence Barclay and Grace Wilcox.

"A review board will review your records and decide whether or not you are physically and mentally capable of returning to your duties with the Marshals Service," Victoria said.

"Do I have any say in the matter?" he asked. "Do I need to secure an attorney?"

"This isn't a legal proceeding," she said. "It's an employment review."

"What happens if I don't sign the release form?" he asked.

"You won't be allowed to return to work."

He ended the call and sat, fuming. Ever since Barclay had escaped, Declan had feared for his job. He had thought by doing his best work and perhaps even by helping to recapture Barclay, he could redeem himself and once more excel at work he had loved. But as the weeks had passed, and especially since coming to Eagle Mountain, that possibility had felt more and more remote.

The general was going to come apart if he learned Declan had been kicked out of the Marshals Service. Declan would never hear the end of this, his biggest failure yet. Ironic, since law enforcement was the one thing he knew he had been good at. What was he going to do now? He could try to find a job with another agency, but that head injury was on his record now, and who was going to overlook that?

Terrence Barclay had a lot to answer for. He would probably smile when he learned he had been responsible for the death of Declan's career.

THE TEXT ALERT on her phone roused Grace from the stupor she had fallen into. She was still on the floor with Bear, who hadn't moved, other than to lean against her comfortingly, occasionally licking tears from her face. She pulled the phone from her pocket and stared at a text from Search and Rescue. Car off-road at Dixon Pass.

Almost the exact message she had received the day Declan stumbled out of that blizzard and into her life. At least the weather was better today. And this accident didn't involve Declan, she reminded herself. She untangled herself from the dog and stood. The best thing she could do right now was to leave the cabin and help someone else.

"Come on, Bear," she said. "You go outside while I change." She let the dog out, then went to dress for a trek in the snow. A search and rescue call would keep her so busy for the next few hours that she wouldn't have time to think about her mess of a life.

DECLAN LEFT THE ALPINER, intending to head to Grace's cabin. But first, he had to stop for gas. As he pulled up to the pump, Arnie was coming out of the station. He spotted Declan and headed his way.

"Hey there," Arnie said. "Good to see you again. I didn't catch your name the other day."

"It's Declan. Declan Owen."

"You're the fed who's been staying at the Alpiner, right?"

Declan winced. Maybe to some people, a "fed" was anyone who worked for the US government. "I'm with the US Marshals Service, yes. How did you know?"

Arnie laughed. "You can't keep something like that quiet in a town this size," he said. "Stay here long enough and people will know your whole history. If you're like me and your two ex-wives also live in town, they'll know things about you that even you don't know."

"How is Mike doing?" Declan asked.

A shadow passed across the older man's expression. "He's okay."

"Is something wrong?" Declan asked.

Arnie shook his head. "Not really."

Was Arnie having doubts about his friend's son? "I guess

Mickey is pretty grateful to you for taking in his son," he said. "Is he going to visit soon? I bet that'll be some re-union."

"Mickey's in Peru right now."

"I forgot. You mentioned that before. He's probably even more relieved to know he's got someone in the state to help Mike."

"I guess so."

Doubt rang loud and clear in those three words, or at least it seemed to Declan. The hair on the back of his neck stood up. Call it cop sense or old-fashioned paranoia. Something wasn't right. "When was the last time you talked to Mickey?" he asked.

Arnie folded his arms across his barrel chest. "I haven't talked to him, actually."

"Why not?"

"Mike said he's impossible to get hold of down there."

"He doesn't have a cell phone?"

"Mike said where's he's working, they don't have good coverage."

Declan considered this. "When was the last time you talked to Mickey?" he asked, his voice gentle.

Arnie studied the ground between his boots. "About thirty years ago. To tell you the truth, we'd lost touch until Mike showed up."

"Have you talked to him at all since Mike came to live with you?"

Arnie shook his head, then looked up at Declan again. "Do you think I'm being conned?"

"You said Mike hadn't asked for anything, right?"

"No. And he's been a good worker. He's just...very secre-tive. Maybe that's just young people, but I'm worried he's in some kind of trouble, maybe with drugs or something. What do you think I should do?"

Declan wanted to tell the older man to run as far as he could from "Mike"—who might very well be a serial killer named Terrence Barclay. But Declan had zero proof of that assumption. If Mike was Barclay and Arnie confronted him, he might end up as Barclay's next victim. Barclay had avoided killing men thus far, but that didn't mean he wouldn't make an exception if he felt cornered.

"If I were you, I wouldn't do anything," Declan said. "See how things play out and let him come to you if he needs help."

Arnie nodded. "You're right. I'm probably worrying for nothing. Thanks for the advice. I need to get back to the store."

He left and Declan finished filling up the truck, but before he pulled away from the pump, he pulled out his phone and dialed Gage's number. "Where are you now?" he asked.

"I'm on my way back from Delta," Gage said. "Why?"

"I just spoke with Arnie Cowdrey. He's having doubts about Mike."

"What do you mean 'doubts'?"

"It turns out Arnie hadn't spoken to his friend Mickey in three decades before Mike turned up in his store. And he hasn't talked to him since, either. Arnie is beginning to wonder if Mickey is really in Peru, and why he can't be reached, even by cellphone."

"Yeah, that story did sound a little too convenient," Gage said. "But if he isn't Mickey's son, how did he know about Arnie in the first place?"

"You saw those pictures he has in the store, all neatly labeled with the names of the people in them. It sounded to me as if Arnie is happy to tell anyone the story behind those pictures. It was one of the high points of his life. It wouldn't have been that hard for someone clever to see the names on the photographs and feel Arnie out about his friend. He could have asked him when was the last time they spoke, did Arnie know where he was now and things like that. When he has all the information he needs, he breaks out this story of being Mickey's son."

"Arnie's too smart to fall for that."

"You and I both know smart people get taken in all the time."

"I'll admit, it's suspicious," Gage said. "But you don't have proof Mike isn't exactly who he says he is."

"Maybe you could stop him for a traffic violation and run his license," Declan said.

"He doesn't drive. He lives over the store and walks everywhere he needs to go."

"That fits Barclay's pattern, too," Declan said. "When he needs a car, he steals one, then abandons it." He rubbed the tight spot in the middle of his chest. "Mike could be Barclay."

"Or he could be exactly who he says he is."

"We can't take the chance of him being Barclay and killing again."

"All we can do is keep an eye on him. You know that."

He knew. No judge was going to give them a warrant to search Mike's rooms, and they had zero reason to detain him or surveil him. A force the size of the Rayford County Sheriff's Department didn't have the personnel for that kind of operation.

"I'm going to stick close and keep an eye on him," Declan said.

"You can't watch him twenty-four hours," Gage said.

"And if he sees you, he can complain you're harassing him and I'd have to warn you off."

"He won't see me."

"He spotted you in Purgatory."

Declan grimaced. His history with Barclay was riddled with screwups like that and had serious consequences. "That won't happen again."

"Keep me posted," Gage said.

Declan ended the call and pocketed his phone. His visit to Grace would have to wait. At least until he was more certain about who Mike Randolph really was and what he was up to.

Chapter Seventeen

Though the accident had occurred near the place where Declan's car had been found, this scene was very different. When Search and Rescue arrived, two sheriff's department vehicles and a highway patrol cruiser were already on site and had closed one lane of traffic to clear the way for rescue workers.

"Witnesses saw the car go over and called 911 right away," Deputy Shane Ellis told the group of rescuers. "The car is resting upside down about halfway down the slope. When I arrived on scene, I could hear someone shouting for help. A couple of cars had stopped and one guy tried to make it down to the car, but it's so steep and there's so much snow I don't think it's possible without climbing gear."

Grace stood with the others on the edge of the drop-off and stared down at a white car, wheels up and resting in a cluster of stubby pinion trees. The foliage obscured much of the vehicle, though the side nearest them looked smashed almost flat. How had anyone survived the crash?

"Eldon, I want you as incident commander," Sheri ordered. "Ryan and I will climb down and assess the situation. We'll do what we can to stabilize the vehicle. Carrie, you and Hannah get ready to rig a long line to bring up a litter. Grace, you assist them." She assigned volunteers to a handful of other jobs that needed to be seen to, then verified that Shane had already requested an ambulance.

Though Grace's heart was pounding as she listened carefully to Sheri's instructions, no one else seemed nervous. They all knew a person's life depended on them carrying out their jobs well, but everyone moved deliberately and calmly. All those hours of training kicked in. Even though she was relatively new to the group, Grace found she had already developed the muscle memory to correctly tie knots and to safely maneuver in the rough terrain.

"We're at the car," Sheri radioed up to the others a short while later. "The driver is alert and says he's uninjured. As soon as we stabilize the vehicle, we're going to try to get him out. He's hanging upside down, caught by his seat belt."

"Amazing what airbags and seat belts can do," Eldon said. "We're ready up top when you are."

While Hannah and Danny conferred on possible injuries to look for—given that adrenaline and fear could mask a lot in the first moments after an accident—the others milled around along the roadside, waiting for further instruction. Grace looked across the canyon, and the steep walls of red, purple and gray rock laced with ice. Sun sparkled on melting frost and felt warm on her face despite the below-freezing temperatures.

"All right, we have him out!" A cheer rose up at Sheri's message. "His name is Parker Overton. Looks like he's got some minor cuts from broken glass and some bruises from getting banged around. No broken bones, no open wounds. Yeah, he looks good. I don't think Danny and Hannah need to come down. Let's get the litter so we can transport him to the road. The medical folks can check him out there."

From that point, the rescue felt more like a training exercise. They sent an empty litter down on a line, and half an hour later it began the journey back to the top. "Coming up in that litter, practically vertical and wrapped up like a mummy, would frighten me almost as much as the trip down," Grace told Carrie.

"You and me both," Carrie said. She watched, hands on hips, as the litter inched up the line. "This looks and feels routine, but it's actually really dangerous. Of course, we won't tell Mr. Overton that."

Another cheer went up when the litter arrived at the top. Carrie and Grace undid the bindings securing Overton inside, then helped him to his feet. He was white-faced beneath his beard but managed a weak smile. "I don't ever want to do that again," he said.

"Here's hoping you don't." Shane stepped forward. "Can you tell me what happened?"

Overton grimaced. "I was paying too much attention to the gorgeous scenery and not enough to the road. I hit a patch of snow on the road and the back end of the car fishtailed a little, and the next thing I knew, I was flying." He wiped a hand across his face. "I thought I was dead." He turned to look back at the litter and the busy volunteers gathering up rope and other equipment. "Thank you all so much," he said.

Hannah and Danny insisted on checking out their patient but found no injuries beyond minor cuts and bruising. Overton declined a ride in the ambulance. Instead, Shane offered to take him home and help with arranging for what was left of his car to be hauled out of the canyon.

"I wish they all ended that well," Hannah said as they gathered their gear.

"That guy was really lucky," Grace said.

"His car's still stuck in the canyon," Danny pointed out. "I wouldn't want to be the one paying to get it out."

"He probably wasn't worrying about his car when he was down there," Hannah said.

"Yeah, but I bet he is now."

Grace let the chatter wash over her as she helped clean and pack away gear. The sun was already sinking behind the mountains and there was a damp chill to the air that foretold snow. Sure enough, when she emerged from Search and Rescue headquarters at about four o'clock, light flakes began to fall.

Since Tommy had followed her home, she had fallen into the habit of watching for anyone following her. She chided herself for being silly—Tommy was harmless and he hadn't really done anything, had he?

She saw no one on the drive home, and by the time she parked her Jeep, the adrenaline of the afternoon had worn off, leaving her drained and chilled. She pulled on her helmet and started the snowmobile, anxious to take a hot shower, then sit in front of the fire with a cup of tea. She sped up the trail and stopped the snowmobile at the bottom of the cabin steps. Later she'd need to park it under the shed, but for now she only wanted to get inside and get warm.

As soon as she shut off the engine, Bear's frantic barking filled the air. He was inside the cabin, but when she turned to look, she could see him at the front window, barking and pawing at the frame. "What's wrong?" she called and mounted the stairs.

He howled, and his claws scrabbled on the wood floor as he raced to the door. As soon as she opened it, he ran out, past her and down the steps. Uneasy, Grace followed the dog to the corner of the house. He stood, back stiff, the hair at the base of his tail standing straight up, nose shoved into the snow beside a man's footprint.

Heart pounding, Grace looked around then. All was quiet,

the snow smooth and undisturbed. "Who was here, boy?" she said softly. Bear looked up at her and whined, then trotted around the side of the house, following the tracks.

The footprints led all the way around the house. They were big prints, made with waffle-soled boots. They had to be a man's, and he had stopped at both back windows. To look in? To try to break in?

Back at the front of the house, she could see now that the tracks led away, toward the snowmobile trail to the road. The trespasser had walked up from that direction and returned the same way. She had been so focused on getting home that she hadn't even noticed the tracks before.

Grace shivered, her teeth chattering. She hugged her upper arms and climbed the steps. "Come on, Bear," she said. "Come in."

The dog looked toward the trail, then turned and followed her into the cabin. She shut the door behind them and turned the dead bolt. Then she went up the stairs and retrieved her grandfather's shotgun. She checked that it was loaded, then carried it downstairs and set it beside the sofa. Bear would let her know if their visitor returned, and the shotgun would give her another layer of protection while she questioned the man. She realized she had become a cliché—the backwoods hermit who greeted visitors with a shotgun—but what else was she supposed to do? Calling the sheriff about a few footprints in the snow seemed excessive, especially since the falling snow would probably fill in the tracks before a deputy could get here.

She couldn't call Declan. Not after she had made such a big point of sending him away. She stoked up the fire, then sat, not on the sofa as she usually would, but in a chair she moved so that she was facing the front door. Then she waited. For what, she wasn't sure, but she didn't think she would be going to bed tonight. Just in case her unwanted visitor decided to return.

DECLAN, SLUMPED IN the front seat of the truck parked down the street from the natural foods store, watched as Arnie exited the store, crossed the street to a dirty white Subaru, got in and drove away. A few minutes later, Mike came out the front door. He locked the building behind him, then started walking, his steps taking him away from Declan.

Declan checked the time: 5:30. He gave Mike plenty of time to get a head start, then pulled out and followed. He was just in time to see Mike turn right on Main, so Declan went past the intersection, drove up and across one block and turned back toward Main. He parked and scanned the street and spotted Mike moving around the side of the bank.

Declan waited, but Mike didn't reappear. Had he cut across the back lot or gone into another door? Declan got out of the truck and walked quickly toward the bank. He approached cautiously, wanting to keep out of sight of his quarry. Shielded by a large lilac bush, he peered around the corner of the building and saw Mike standing in the drive-through. He passed a zippered bank bag to the teller and waited, talking. A few moments later the drawer in front of him popped open and he collected a slip of paper.

Declan turned to go back to his truck, then thought better of it. He waited until Mike walked back out on Main, then caught up with him. "Hey," Declan said.

Mike glanced at him. "Hey." He shoved both hands in his pockets and kept walking. Declan studied the side of his face. Nothing about him was familiar. "Is there something you want?" Mike asked.

"Arnie says you've been a big help to him."

Mike shrugged. "I do what I can. It's a lot, running a busy place like that by yourself."

"How did you end up in Eagle Mountain?" Declan asked.

"I like the mountains."

"And you remembered your dad had a friend here."

"I remembered after I came here. Dad said I should look him up."

"Who does he work for in Peru?"

Mike stopped and faced Declan. "What business is that of yours? Why are you asking so many questions?"

Declan took a step back, open hands at his sides, all innocence. "I'm just making conversation."

"Well, I don't feel like talking." He turned and strode down the street, back in the direction of the natural foods store.

Declan let him go. He walked back to his truck. He was getting in when a Rayford County sheriff's SUV pulled up alongside him. The window lowered. "How's it going?" Gage asked.

"About like you'd expect," Declan said. "Boring."

"So you haven't seen anything suspicious?"

"Mike just made a bank deposit. I assume that means Arnie has given him that responsibility. He'll have ready access to the money."

"Does Barclay care about that?" Gage asked. "I didn't read anything about him having stolen money in the past."

"There's nothing like that in his files," Declan said. "He doesn't even have any speeding tickets. He's as law-abiding as they come, except for murders and assaults."

"Right." Gage checked the street.

"I have a few hours I can spare you keeping an eye on him. You must have things you need to do."

He needed to see Grace. She deserved to know the truth about her accident. "You're sure?"

"Yeah." Gage held up a notebook. "I have reports to work on. I can't guarantee I won't get called for an emergency, but as long as I'm able, I'll babysit Mike for you."

"He lives above the store," Declan said. "He was walking that direction."

"I'll find him."

"Thanks." Declan turned the key in the ignition. "I should be gone only a couple of hours."

Gage drove away, and Declan pulled out. He drove toward Grace's, slowing as he reached the turn for the Forest Service road. He was just about to make the turn when a dark vehicle shot onto the highway, back end fishtailing as it made the sharp turn from the Forest Service road. Declan leaned on the horn while he waited for his breathing to return to normal. That guy had almost hit him. He looked over his shoulder, but all he could see was a pair of taillights disappearing over a hill.

He bumped the truck along the Forest Service road, knowing that if he tried to go much faster, the truck wouldn't stay in the ruts. Twenty-five minutes later, he parked beside Grace's Jeep, then turned the collar up on his parka and started the long trek up the snowmobile path.

Light glowed behind the drawn curtains on the cabin's front window, and Declan could hear Bear barking before he stepped into the clearing in front of the house. Grace's snowmobile was parked at the bottom of the front steps, her helmet on the seat. He felt the engine as he passed, but it was cold. He trudged toward the house and had his foot on the bottom step when the door eased open.

"Who's there?" Grace demanded. Or he thought it was Grace. Her voice sounded much harsher. Angrier.

He froze. "It's me, Declan," he said. When she didn't answer right away, he added, "I know you probably don't want to see me, but there's something really important I need to tell you."

The door opened wider, a triangle of golden light arcing across the porch. Then she stepped out, cradling a shotgun. "What are you doing here?" she asked, her voice more normal now. But she still hugged that gun like a lifeline.

"What's happened?" He wanted to go to her, but he didn't want to startle her. Not as nervous as she looked. "Why do you have that shotgun?"

Bear came out and sat behind her and regarded Declan with a grave expression. "Someone was here," she said and looked past him, into the darkness. "I came home and Bear was really upset, and there are footprints."

He took a few steps toward her now. "When was this?" he asked.

"I came home at about four-thirty or a quarter to five."

"You should have called me."

"I can't expect you to come running every time something spooks me."

"I'll be here for you anytime."

She moved past him, still cradling the gun. "You're here now. Look at this and tell me what you think."

He followed her as she pointed out the faint imprints from a man's boots. The snow was filling in the depressions, but there was still a faint outline visible here, a ridge of waffle sole there. The prints were clearer under the eaves, where the trespasser had walked up to look in the rear windows or maybe to test the locks. Declan crouched and took a few pictures with his cell phone, though he didn't know how well they would turn out.

"You say you saw these between four-thirty and five o'clock?" he asked. Almost two hours ago.

"Yes. They go all the way around the house, and then back into the woods alongside the snowmobile trail. I can't believe I didn't notice them when I rode in."

"I just walked that trail and I didn't see footprints," he said. Though it had been growing dark and he had been focused on staying to the narrow, packed trail.

"Maybe he walked in the woods, alongside the track," she said.

"Did you see anyone on the way in?" he asked.

"No, and the parking area was empty when I arrived."

"Just now, when I drove up, a car almost ran over me, coming from the Forest Service road onto the highway," he said. "Something big and dark-colored. Like a van."

"Bear was so upset," she said. "I think seeing him upset frightened me the most. He was frantic. You can see where he was scratching, trying to get out the door." She led the way back up the steps and into the cabin.

"Look." She pointed to fresh scratches and bite marks in the wood of the door and the frame. "He's never done that before," she said.

He pulled out his phone. "I'm going to call Gage."

"There's nothing he can do," she said.

"There might be."

Gage answered on the third ring. "Mike is in his apartment and hasn't moved," he said.

"I'm not calling about Mike," Declan said.

"What is it?" Gage was immediately all business.

"I'm at Grace's. She got home this afternoon and someone had been prowling around her cabin. I saw the footprints. She didn't see anyone or any vehicle, but when I was headed up here, a vehicle coming from this direction almost ran me off the road. I'm pretty sure it was a van. A van like the one Tommy Llewellyn drives."

"His van is broken down," Gage said.

"Maybe he had it repaired. I'm going to stay here in case he comes back. Can you put someone else on Mike Randolph and check out Llewellyn? I want to know where he was and what he was doing between four and six o'clock."

"I'll see what I can do, but we may have to leave Mike on his own for a while. He may not even be the person we're looking for."

"All right," Declan agreed. The Marshals Service should have had a full team looking into Mike and following his movements. But Declan and maybe Gage were the only people who seemed to think he could be Terrence Barclay. "I just want to know if Llewellyn is harassing Grace after we warned him off."

"I'll see what I can find out," Gage said.

"I'll be here." He ended the call and turned to Grace. She had leaned the gun beside the door and stood facing him.

"If you need to go, I'll be all right," she said.

"I'm not leaving you."

She crossed her arms over her chest. "You don't owe me anything."

"No, but we need to talk."

"There's nothing to talk about. I've already explained—"

He touched her shoulder. "Just listen to me. Please? I learned some things today that you need to know."

Chapter Eighteen

Something in Declan's voice softened Grace's resolve. He didn't sound angry or hurt, more…excited. As if what he had to tell her was something good. Something she wanted to hear.

She moved to the sofa and sat. "All right," she said. "What is it?"

He sat at the other end of the sofa, and she was reminded of the first time he had sat here, naked and bleeding and confused. He had been imposing in spite of his vulnerability. She hadn't known then how gentle he could be or how complicated he would make her life.

"I called the police department in Simpson, Iowa," he began.

She stiffened. "Why did you do that?"

"I wanted to hear what really happened the day you were injured."

He wanted to confirm that her carelessness really had led to her sister's death.

"The story they told me wasn't the one you've heard all your life," he said.

"What do you mean?" Was it worse? Was there something else her mother hadn't told her?

"You didn't have anything to do with your sister's death,"

he said. "The officer I spoke to was at the accident that day. He said he could smell alcohol on your mother's breath. She had been arrested for public intoxication before. He asked for a blood alcohol test at the hospital, but the order got overlooked until it was too late. But he's certain she was impaired and that caused the accident."

"But my sister wasn't buckled in her car seat. Mom said I unbuckled Hope and distracted her."

"You didn't. The officer said your mother had been ticketed only two weeks before for not securing the baby in her car seat. He thinks she overlooked it that day, too. You were old enough to fasten your own seat belt—that's the reason you were protected that day."

Grace tried to make sense of his words, but they wouldn't sink in, floating on top of her consciousness. "But why would my mother tell me those things if they weren't true?"

"Because she didn't want to admit the accident was all her fault. You told me she started drinking heavily after the accident, but I think she was probably already struggling with alcohol when the accident occurred."

She squeezed her eyes shut, trying to look back and see her life as it had been then. But she couldn't. "I don't remember."

Declan took her hand. His skin was so warm, his voice so gentle. "It doesn't matter if you don't remember," he said. "Lieutenant Carpenter does. I can give you his name and number if you want to talk to him yourself."

"Maybe later." She leaned toward him. "Why did you do it? Why did you get in touch with the police?"

"Because I wanted to know the truth. Not what your mother told you, but the truth. It didn't make sense to me that you would have unbuckled your sister's car seat. Why would a child do such a thing?"

She swallowed and blinked past the prick of tears. She couldn't even decide how she felt—sad, hurt, angry.

"It's a lot to process," he said. "And maybe it would help to talk to a professional therapist about it. But for now, just know that you are not a bad person. You never were. What your mother did and said to you—that's part of her own illness, not on you. Can you believe that?"

"I want to try."

She sat for a long moment, head bowed, her hand still clasped in his. After a while, he cleared his throat. "I had another interesting phone call," he said. "From the Marshals Service."

This was it. He had been called back to Denver. She tried to prepare herself for this news. "What did they want?" she asked.

"This was from the human resources department. They're going to be requesting my medical records for a review."

"They must be getting ready for you to return to work."

"I think it's more likely they're looking for a reason to let me go," he said.

She stared. He didn't look upset about this. "Why would they let you go?"

"The woman said they were concerned my head injury and subsequent amnesia would disqualify me from active duty."

"Oh no. What will you do?"

"I don't know. I know I'm good at my job and I can still do it. But it's been clear for a while that my supervisor doesn't want me around. I don't know what I'll do. Law enforcement is what I'm best at, I think."

"If they have to review your records, it sounds like you've got some time to decide."

"I do." He released her hand, his expression grim. "My dad is going to be furious."

She shifted, inching a little closer to him. "I'm not really one to give advice on relating to parents," she said, "but maybe, like my mom, he isn't seeing you as you really are."

"You mean I'm better than he thinks I am?"

"Something like that."

She moved closer, and he pulled her close and kissed her. It was the most natural thing in the world, and afterward they sat with their arms around each other, looking at the fire. Where was this going to lead? Grace didn't know, but she wouldn't waste time worrying. She had wasted too much time regretting a past that had apparently never happened. She wouldn't forfeit any chance at happiness, no matter how brief.

From his cruiser parked at the corner, Gage watched the rooms above the natural foods store. Flickering bluish light indicated the television was on, and infrequently a man's shadow moved across one window. Mike moving about. He seemed to have settled in for the night.

He pulled out his phone and hit the number for his wife. Maya answered on the second ring. "I'm going to be a little later than I thought," he said. "Something has come up."

"It's okay," she said. "Casey and I are going over to Sharon's place. Delia is coming, too, with her twins. The kids are going to play, and the moms are going to eat junk food and talk until we're hoarse."

He could hear the smile in her voice and pictured her playing with a strand of her blue-tipped hair as she talked. Everything about her was a little rounder with her pregnancy, and he was almost embarrassed to admit how much it turned him on. He would have laughed if someone had told him two years ago how much he would still be besotted with his wife.

"Sounds like an evening," he said.

She laughed. "You would hate it, but it's exactly what I need."

"Then have a good time."

"I will. And you be careful."

"Always."

With a last glance at Mike's apartment—nothing had changed—he put the SUV into gear and headed out to County Road 7. New snowfall hid the ruts in the road, and he had to slow even more to avoid being thrown about. He hit the high beams and hunched forward, watching for the turnout where Tommy Llewellyn's van had been parked. He braked as he drew alongside the place he was sure it had been, but the van wasn't there. The only indication that anyone had been there was a snow-free space the length and width of a van, and a fire ring of sooty stones. Had Tommy cleared out?

Gage drove farther, but the road began to narrow even more and he saw nowhere else with enough room to park a van. He had to go back a quarter mile before he found a place where he could turn the SUV around.

In town, he drove to the Ranch Motel. An older woman looked up as he entered, deep lines across her forehead getting deeper as she took in his uniform. "Can I help you, Deputy?" she asked.

"I'm looking for Tommy Llewellyn," Gage said. "I believe he works here."

"He gave his notice this morning," she said. "I told him he

had to work two more weeks and give me time to find someone else for his position, but he said he had to move on."

"Did he say something had happened?" Gage asked. "A family emergency or something?"

"He just said it was time for him to be going." She waved her hand in the air. "I should have known better, hiring someone who lived in a van, but he seemed like a nice guy and I wanted to give him a chance. He was a good worker while he was here, anyway. Left everything in order."

"Did he leave a forwarding address or a place to send his final check?" Gage asked.

"No. He said I could donate whatever he was owed to a good cause." She wrinkled her nose. "That right there probably explains why he's still living in a van."

"Let me know if you hear from him." Gage handed her a card.

She read the card, then tucked it into a drawer beneath the front counter. "Has he done something wrong?"

"I just want to talk to him, that's all."

He left and returned to his SUV, but he didn't leave right away. He sat for a long time, thinking about Tommy, and about Mike, and about Terrence Barclay. Rootless young men who had all ended up in Eagle Mountain. At least, they were assuming Barclay was here. Gage sensed Declan's certainty about that, but was he making a mistake, believing the marshal?

What would Travis have done if he were here? As much as Gage wanted to prove that he was capable of running the sheriff's department by himself, he wouldn't have minded having his brother here to bounce ideas off of him. But Travis was apparently living up to his promise to his wife not to check in.

Gage put the SUV in gear and drove back downtown to the sheriff's department. Time to do a little more digging into Tommy Llewellyn, Mike Randolph, Terrence Barclay and Declan Owen.

DECLAN MADE PANCAKES for dinner, and they were as delicious as he had boasted. While they ate, Grace told him about the search and rescue call she had responded to that afternoon. "I can't believe how lucky that guy was," she said. "He went off the road into that canyon, and he walked away with only a few cuts and bruises. The other volunteers have all kinds of stories about people who have been killed or seriously hurt in similar accidents."

"Does it bother you, responding to traffic accidents, given your personal history?" he asked.

"I was afraid it would, but it doesn't," she said. "I guess because I don't remember my accident. And apparently what I thought I knew was wrong, anyway." Her voice broke and she set down her fork and stared at her plate. "I'm sorry," she whispered.

"Don't be." He leaned across the table and squeezed her hand. "It's been a big shock. I imagine it will take a while to process. But don't think you have to hide your feelings from me."

She nodded. "I'm used to hiding my feelings. I can't promise that will change."

"You don't have to change for me," he said. He cut a wedge from his stack of pancakes. "It doesn't work, trying to change for someone else, anyway. I tried it with my father for years and years."

"Do you think we ever get old enough for our parents to stop having so much influence on us?" she asked.

"I don't know. But I'm going to try to stop fighting the

general so hard. I'm going to focus less on his opinion and more on what I think is right."

"That's a good idea." She picked up her fork again. She had been so preoccupied with his revelation about the real circumstances of her accident that she had almost forgotten about the stranger who had left those footprints around her cabin. "Do you think Tommy was back up here?" she asked.

Declan pushed his plate to one side and rested his elbows on the table, hands clasped. "I don't know," he said. "I didn't get a very good look at the vehicle that almost hit me at the intersection with the highway. It might not have been Tommy. And it might not have been coming from here."

"I didn't see any vehicles parked near the other trails along the road."

"Is there anywhere else he could have parked, to keep his van out of sight?"

"I don't know. Maybe. There are some private lots. Old mining claims. Someone could have pulled up in there, but it would be tough to do without getting stuck in the snow."

"Maybe he did get stuck and that's why he passed me two hours after you arrived home."

"I was wondering about that. I hate to think he was here all the time I was in the house alone, watching and waiting."

He pushed back his chair and stood. "After we do the dishes, I'll make another check outside."

Grace stood at the front door while Declan made a circuit of the outside of the house. It was snowing harder now, big flakes dancing in the beam of the flashlight he shone into the woods around the cabin. "Should I put the snowmobile in the shed?" he asked.

She regarded the machine, already dusted with snow. "Leave it out," she said. "Just in case." In case one of them had to go for help quickly. She stared toward the trail to the road. She was probably worrying over nothing. Who would be out on a night like this?

DECLAN LAY AWAKE after they went to bed, Grace breathing evenly beside him. Was that Tommy's van he had seen? Why would he come back up here? Had Gage and Declan been wrong when they deemed him harmless? And what was Mike up to? Gage would have called if he had learned anything important about either man, but not knowing made Declan uneasy.

Bear growled, low and menacing. Declan was out of bed before his mind had fully registered the origin of the noise. By the time he had pulled on jeans and a sweater and shoved his feet into boots, the dog was barking and scratching at the front door.

"Don't let him out." Grace came into the living room behind him, her robe pulled around her. "I don't want him hurt."

"Is the shotgun the only weapon you have?" Declan asked.

"Yes."

He picked up the gun from beside the door and checked the load. Bird shot. He could hurt someone with this but not stop them. "Call 911," he said. "Tell them you've got a trespasser."

"You really think someone is out there?"

"I don't think Bear is upset over nothing."

"It will take forever for anyone to get here," she said.

"Call them, anyway."

"All right." She left the room and he turned back to the window. He couldn't see anything in the darkness. Bear had stopped barking but still paced the room, agitated.

Grace returned. She had dressed and was holding her phone. "I called. They said they would send someone, but it might be a while. I think there's only one officer on duty this time of night."

"I haven't seen or heard anyone moving around," he said. "Maybe Bear's barking scared them off."

"I'll make some coffee." She started for the kitchen but took only a few steps before she froze.

"What is it?" Declan hurried to her side.

"I saw a light in the kitchen," she said, her voice low. "There shouldn't be a light."

He stared into the room, seeing nothing, then a flare of light, like the flame of a candle or a lighter or...

"I smell smoke," Grace said. She started toward the kitchen and he pulled her back as the small flare he had seen became a big one.

"The kitchen's on fire," he said. "We have to get out of here."

She grabbed Bear's collar and dragged him toward the door, where she snapped on his leash. They shrugged into their coats and stepped onto the porch.

The cold hit them like a slap, and sharp pellets of snow stung their cheeks. "Get on the snowmobile and go to your Jeep," Declan said. "You need to get out of here." He didn't think the fire was an accident, and he didn't want her around to face whoever had set the blaze.

She must have come to the same realization. "I can't leave you here with whoever this is," she said.

"I'll be fine." He took her by the shoulders and leaned close, wanting to make sure she could see his face. "I'm trained for this kind of thing," he said. "But I won't be as effective if I'm distracted by you. Go and get help."

She nodded and moved toward the snowmobile. She

called for Bear, but the dog was already trotting around the corner of the house, nose to the ground. Declan racked the shotgun and headed after him.

Chapter Nineteen

Grace floundered through the deep snow to the snowmobile. She had forgotten her boots and had trouble finding purchase in her sheepskin slippers. She grabbed the helmet and shoved it on, then straddled the seat and fumbled for the key, her hands shaking with fear and cold. She didn't want to leave Declan and Bear, but going for help did seem the best way she could help.

The snowmobile's engine turned over, then died. She tried again. "Come on, come on," she chanted under her breath.

Then she was grabbed around the shoulders and flung to the ground. She screamed and tried to fight back, but a hard knee in her back drove her into the snow. She rolled over and tried to get up, but her attacker straddled her. She stared up at Tommy Llewellyn. At least, this man wore Tommy's orange knit hat, but he looked different. Harder and meaner.

"You're not going anywhere," he said. "Never again."

She screamed, and he hit her in the face, hard enough that her head snapped back and her vision blurred.

Frantic barking drew closer, and Grace struggled up to see Bear bounding toward them. "Bear, no!" she shouted.

Tommy turned away from her and the boom of a gun

left her ears ringing. She tried to grapple with him, but he fought her off, and Bear bounded away.

"No!" The shout echoed around them. Tommy shifted his attention to somewhere behind her. She turned her head and saw the figure of a man stalking toward them through the snow. Declan was not naked this time, but the glow of the burning house patterned his body and face with patches of light and dark, like streaks of blood.

Tommy rose and dragged her up with him. "Drop the gun," he ordered.

Declan tossed the shotgun he had been carrying aside. Only then did Grace realize Tommy had the still-warm muzzle of a pistol pressed against her throat. She went very still, terrified to move, and stared at Declan, afraid of what he might or might not do.

"You're surprised to see me, aren't you?" Tommy asked. "I could tell you had no idea who I was. I heard that knock I gave you on your head did a number on your memory." He laughed, and Declan clenched his jaw to keep from roaring with outrage. He had to stay calm. To find a way to outmaneuver this killer.

"Hello, Terrence," he said. "Since I can't remember, why don't you tell me what happened that day?" He remembered the transcripts he had read of Barclay's interrogations, in which he talked about his crimes with what read like pride.

"Easy enough." Barclay shifted to tighten his hold on Grace. Declan forced himself not to look at her. He had to stay focused on Barclay. "I saw that woman on the side of the road, her arm in a sling, her tire flat," Barclay said. "I was the charming Good Samaritan, coming to her aid. I knew you were behind me. I stuck your gun—the one I took from you before—in her back and ordered her to flag you down. Then I hid behind her car while she did so. I knew you'd stop. You were crouched over her tire when I came up behind you and hit you in the head. Then I shot her. I stuffed her in your car, then stripped you and tipped you over into the canyon. The last time I saw you, you were sprawled on a ledge in the snow. I figure you'd freeze to death before you woke up, but I guess I was wrong about that. I drove the car I had stolen in Purgatory to a canyon I had passed a couple miles back, shoved it in, then walked the two miles back to where I'd left you. The weather was nasty, so nobody was around. They probably wouldn't have seen me in the snow, anyway. I took the woman's car and left. I ditched that car in some little town and found the van, parked behind a house that didn't look like anyone was in it. Then I drove back to Eagle Mountain and became Tommy Llewellyn."

"Who is Tommy Llewellyn?" Declan asked.

"A loser I met in jail the last time they picked me up. He said he was headed back home to Ohio or Michigan or wherever he was from as soon as they let him out. Easy enough to become him."

Grace made a choking noise, and Declan had to look at her. She had grown very still, but not passive. He could feel how alert she was. Waiting for a chance. The heat from the fire was intense enough that he could feel it here, fifty feet away. Grace had something in her hand. He realized it was the keys to the snowmobile, laced between her fingers.

Their eyes met. He blinked once, slowly, an acknowledgment that he knew what to do. Barclay was still going on about Tommy Llewellyn being such a loser when Declan groaned, clutched his chest and sank to his knees in the snow.

Barclay stopped talking. "What the—" He leaned toward

Declan, loosening his grip just enough that Grace brought her hand up and stabbed the key right in his eye.

Barclay howled. He clutched at his face with his free hand. Grace grabbed for the gun in his other hand and it went off, firing into the snow, then they both lost hold of the weapon and it fell, disappearing beneath the snow. She jerked away from him and ran, not away and not toward Declan, but straight to the cabin.

"Grace, no!" Declan shouted, but she gave no indication that she heard. Barclay was already struggling back to his feet. Declan found the shotgun in the snow and used it like a club to hit Barclay in the head. Barclay dropped like a felled tree, landing facedown in the snow.

Declan pulled the laces from Barclay's own boots to tie his wrists and ankles, then he pulled off the boots and hurled them as far away as he could. Satisfied that the fugitive wouldn't be going anywhere, he ran after Grace.

More than half of the cabin was fully engulfed, choking smoke filling the rooms that had not been consumed. Declan pulled his jacket over his head, then plunged into what had been the living room and spotted Grace in the corner. She was clearing the shelves of her grandfather's notebooks, piling them onto a blanket she had spread on the floor.

"You have to get out of here!" he shouted over the crackling and popping of the fire.

She gathered the corners of the blanket and thrust the resulting bundle at him. "You take these," she said. "I'll get the rest." She picked up a second bundle he hadn't noticed before. "These are the ones I haven't transcribed yet."

"We have to get out of here," he said again.

"We will. But I'm taking these with me. This research is priceless." She hefted the bundle and turned, not to the door where Declan had entered, but to the window at the end of the house farthest from the fire. She shoved it up, knocked out the screen, then pitched the blanket full of notebooks into the snow. Declan did the same, then urged her out the window. He followed and they rested for a moment, on their knees in the snow, coughing out smoke and trying to catch their breath. "Bear!" she gasped. She struggled to her feet. "Bear!" she shouted.

The dog peered around the back of the woodshed. "Oh, Bear, it's okay." She beckoned and he crept toward her, then closed the gap between them and began licking her face.

She hugged the dog, and checked him all over. "I thought Barclay shot him," she told Declan. "But I guess he just scared him away."

Declan stood and helped her to her feet. "Where is Tommy?" she asked. "Or Terrence? Or whatever his name is?"

"He's tied up out front. I need to get back to him."

"I'm going to drag these farther away from the fire, then I'll join you."

Bear began barking again as Declan rounded the corner of the burning house, then he heard the roar of engines and a parade of snowmobiles pulled into the clearing, one after another. The lead snowmobile came to rest beside Terrence Barclay's prone body.

Gage cut the engine and lifted the visor on his helmet. "I heard the 911 call come in and figured you might need some help," he said. "But maybe I was wrong." He climbed off the snowmobile and met Declan beside Barclay. "What was Tommy Llewellyn doing up here?" he asked.

"Tommy Llewellyn is probably somewhere in Ohio or Michigan or whatever he's from and has no idea what's been going on here," Declan said. "Barclay says he met him in jail and decided to assume his identity during his time in Eagle Mountain."

Gage nudged Barclay with the toe of his boot, and the bound man moaned. "I guess he looks enough like that mug shot to fool most people," he said. He bent and grabbed Barclay's arm. "Come on."

Declan and Gage pulled Barclay to his feet. "Do you want to do the honors of taking him into custody?" Gage asked.

Declan shook his head. "I'm not officially on duty. You'd better do it."

While Gage read Barclay his rights and prepared to transport him back to Eagle Mountain, Declan joined Grace and Bear at the edge of the circle of light cast by the burning cabin. "I'm sorry about your home," he said.

"I'm sorry, too," she said. "But I'm glad we saved the notebooks. They were the most important things in there."

He put his arm around her. "Are you okay physically? Barclay didn't hurt you, did he?" His voice broke on the last words, the knowledge of how close she had come to death leaving him weak in the knees.

"I'm fine." She touched her cheek, where he could see a bruise forming. "He hit me, but I think I hurt him a lot worse."

He squeezed her more tightly against him. "You were amazing."

"I knew if I didn't do something, he'd kill me, and then he'd hurt you and Bear."

Gage joined them. "I'm sending Barclay to town with a couple of deputies," he said. "We'll stay until the fire is out and to gather what evidence we can. You two should get somewhere warm as soon as you can. I can have someone take you to Eagle Mountain."

"We'll take Grace's snowmobile and Jeep," Declan said. "I still have my room at the Alpiner. We can stay there."

"I'll want your statements as soon as possible," Gage said. "Tonight, preferably."

"We'll take care of it," Declan said.

"I have my grandfather's notebooks." Grace indicated the two blanket-wrapped bundles at her feet. "They need to be put somewhere dry as soon as possible."

"We'll see to that," Gage said. He clapped Declan on the back. "Good work," he said, then left to oversee the rest of the job.

Declan drove the snowmobile to Grace's Jeep, Bear loping along beside them. By the time they reached the Jeep, he and Grace were both shaking with cold. Fortunately, she kept the Jeep keys on the ring with those of the snowmobile, and the engine soon began pumping warmth into the cab.

Hannah Richards met them at the Alpiner and gave them hot chocolate and extra blankets. "You might as well take a hot shower and get into some dry clothes before you go to the sheriff's department," she said. "Jake already texted me that everyone is still up at the cabin." She patted Grace's shoulder. "I'm sorry about your home," she said. "But you can borrow some of my clothes. We're about the same size."

Declan thought he would never forget the details of that evening. He repeated the story so many times over the next few days, beginning with his statement at the sheriff's department that evening.

"You were right about Barclay being here," Gage said. "And everyone who wouldn't listen to you was wrong. That has to be a good feeling."

"Not really," Declan said. Grace had lost her home. He had almost lost her. He doubted this was going to endear him to his colleagues at the Marshals Service. He was relieved Barclay was in custody again but couldn't help wondering if he couldn't have done more to keep things from reaching this point.

It was almost morning when he and Grace finally returned to the Alpiner and crawled into bed, having to shove Bear over to make room for both of them.

She rested her head on his shoulder and sighed. "I guess we're even now," she said.

"Even?"

"I saved your life, and now you've saved mine."

"I didn't know we were keeping score."

"We aren't. But I like symmetry."

"You're a scientist," he said. "How often does nature come out even?"

She chuckled. "Almost never."

"You're wrong, anyway," he said. "You were the one who brought Barclay to his knees. All I did was overact and fake a heart attack."

"That was what really stopped him," she said. "You might have a career in melodrama." She snuggled closer. "I guess you'll just have to stick around and try to even things up again."

He started to ask her if that meant she wanted him to stick around, but he sensed she had already fallen asleep. It was a moot question, anyway. He had no intention of going anywhere.

DECLAN AND GRACE were drinking coffee and eating a late breakfast the next morning in the sunroom of the Alpiner when Gage stopped by. From the shadows under his eyes and the wrinkles in his uniform, Declan suspected the sergeant had not yet been to bed.

"I wanted to let you know Terrence Barclay is being

transported to jail in Junction," Gage said. He moved to the buffet and helped himself to a cup of coffee, then came to sit across from Declan at the table.

"I hope you warned his escorts to never let down their guard," Declan said.

"I did. And I sent three people instead of two." He sipped his coffee and closed his eyes.

"You look exhausted," Grace said.

He opened his eyes again. "It's been a long night, but it was worth it. And your grandfather's notebooks are in the evidence vault at the station. You can have them whenever you're ready."

"Thank you," she said. "A lot of people are going to be really happy to know they're safe."

"Looks like you're getting all the loose ends tied up," Declan said. "And I guess we don't have to worry about Mike Randolph."

"His name isn't Mike Randolph," Gage said. "It's Gordon Keller. He left some time last night. After I left to check on Tommy." His eyes met Declan's. "I'm kicking myself for not doing more to find Tommy after I realized he wasn't at his campsite."

"By then he was probably already up at Grace's cabin," Declan said. "What's the story with Gordon Keller?"

"Arnie called the station this morning, pretty upset," Gage said. "Apparently the person he knew as Mike cleaned out the business bank account. About ten thousand dollars. He might have gotten away with more, except he didn't have access to Arnie's other accounts. His prints came back as a match for Keller, who has a history of pulling scams like this one. We've put out an APB, but it will take some luck to apprehend him."

"It always does," Declan said. "I'm sorry about Arnie. Keller wasn't Terrence Barclay, but he was up to no good."

"I notified the Marshals Service that we had Barclay in custody," Gage said. "And I made sure they knew you were the one who captured him. They didn't have much to say."

"I don't expect they did." Declan sipped his coffee. He had lived with this knowledge enough to feel philosophical. "They don't look very smart right now, insisting that Barclay wasn't in Eagle Mountain."

"Maybe this will help you keep your job," Gage said.

"Oh, I doubt that. I'm too much of an embarrassment." He set down his cup. "I was hoping maybe I could come work for you. I heard you need another deputy."

"We can't pay what the Marshals Service offers."

"I've got other incentives for staying here." He glanced at Grace, who smiled and looked down at her plate.

"I'll have to talk to the sheriff."

"He's your brother," Grace said. "Your recommendation ought to count for a lot."

"Provided I can come to terms with the idea of working with this guy on a regular basis." He nodded to Declan. "He does grow on you, though."

"He does," she agreed.

Gage drained his coffee, then stood. "We'll be in touch," he said. "I'm headed home to try to get some rest."

As soon as they were alone again, Grace turned to Declan. "Are you serious about staying in Eagle Mountain?"

"I am." He took her hand. "Do you think you could stand having me around?"

She turned her hand to twine her fingers with his. "Ever since that first day we met, I felt a connection to you."

"I'm amazed I didn't frighten you off, staggering out of the storm that way."

"It's not every day I invite a naked man into my cabin." She grinned. "I guess you could say I liked what I saw."

"You just love me for my body," he said.

She leaned closer. "I love you for your courage and your intelligence, and because you didn't give up on me, when I'd given up on myself," she said. "We joke about me saving your life, but you really did save mine when you went to the trouble to find out what really happened when I was a little girl. No one ever did anything like that for me before."

"Seeing you hurt made me hurt," he said. "I guess we're connected that way now."

"It's a little scary, but good, too," she said.

"It's very good," he said. "I never minded being alone before I met you."

"I thought it was the way I'd always live," she said. "Like my grandfather."

"You and your grandfather had each other," he pointed out.

"But not all the time, and not forever." She pressed her palm to the side of his face, and he caught the soft scent of floral lotion. "With you feels different."

"It feels like forever," he said. And sealed the pledge with a kiss.

* * * * *

COMING SOON!

We really hope you enjoyed reading this book. If you're looking for more romance be sure to head to the shops when new books are available on

Thursday 14th September

To see which titles are coming soon, please visit

millsandboon.co.uk/nextmonth

MILLS & BOON

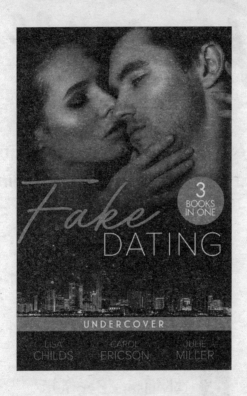

LET'S TALK

Romance

For exclusive extracts, competitions
and special offers, find us online:

f MillsandBoon

𝕏 @MillsandBoon

⧉ @MillsandBoonUK

♪ @MillsandBoonUK

Get in touch on 01413 063 232

For all the latest titles coming soon, visit
millsandboon.co.uk/nextmonth